WORLDS
ENOUGH
& TIME

Other Books by Dan Simmons

Song of Kali
Phases of Gravity
Carrion Comfort
Hyperion
The Fall of Hyperion
Prayers to Broken Stones
Summer of Night
The Hollow Man
Children of the Night
Summer Sketches
Lovedeath
Fires of Eden
Endymion
The Rise of Endymion
The Crook Factory
Darwin's Blade
Hardcase
A Winter Haunting
Hard Freeze

A Grazing Encounter Between Two Spiral Galaxies

WORLDS ENOUGH & TIME

FIVE TALES OF SPECULATIVE FICTION

DAN SIMMONS

An Imprint of HarperCollinsPublishers

"Looking for Kelly Dahl," © 1995 by Dan Simmons, first appeared in *High Fantastic*, ed. by Steve Rasnic Tem, Ocean View Books. "Orphans of the Helix," © 1999 by Dan Simmons, first appeared in *Far Horizons*, ed. by Robert Silverberg, Avon Eos. "The Ninth of Av," © 2000, by Dan Simmons, first appeared as "Le 9 av" in *Destination 3001*, ed. by Jacques Chambon and Robert Silverberg, Imagine/Flammarion (Paris). "On K2 with Kanakaredes," © 2001 by Dan Simmons, first appeared in *Redshift: Extreme Visions of Speculative Fiction*, ed. by Al Sarrantonio, Roc (New American Library). "The End of Gravity," © 2002 by Dan Simmons.

Frontispiece copyright NASA and Hubble Heritage Team (STScI)

EOS
An Imprint of HarperCollins*Publishers*
10 East 53rd Street
New York, New York 10022-5299

Copyright © 2002 by Dan Simmons
ISBN: 0-06-050604-0
www.eosbooks.com

Library of Congress Cataloging-in-Publication Data
Simmons, Dan.
    Worlds enough & time : Five tales of speculative fiction / Dan Simmons.
        p. cm.
    Contents: Looking for Kelly Dahl—Orphans of the Helix—The Ninth of Av—On K2 with Kanakaredes—The End of Gravity.
    ISBN 0-06-050604-0
    1. Science fiction, American. I. Title: Worlds enough & time. II. Title.
    PS3569.I47292 W67 2002
    813'.54—dc21   2002069224

First Eos trade paperback printing: December 2002

Eos Trademark Reg. U.S. Pat. Off. and in Other Countries,
Marca Registrada, Hecho en U.S.A.
HarperCollins® is a trademark of HarperCollins Publishers Inc.

Printed in the U.S.A.

10   9   8   7   6   5   4   3

Contents

WORLDS
ENOUGH
& TIME

Introduction

....

"Whole sight; or all the rest is desolation." This line begins and ends one of my favorite novels, John Fowles's *Daniel Martin*, and it took me four or five readings of the book to understand the full impact of the phrase—not just in relation to that novel, but as a *cri de coeur* from the very heart of the heart of art and as an imperative for all novelists, all writers, all artists. In the penultimate scene of *Daniel Martin,* the eponymous character encounters this command in the gaze of the elderly Rembrandt, the arc of uncompromised energy leaping from the aged eyes in one of the Master's final self-portraits. I've also received that sledgehammer blow of encounter with one of Rembrandt's self-portraits, and I agree with this translation as both ultimate question and ultimate answer to the creative artist's queries.

I've never really trusted introductions to stories as a means to gain a clearer view of the fiction itself. As a reader, I tend to enjoy introductions, but I'm wary of them; too many seem to have what John Keats called (in reference to bad poetry)—". . . a palpable design upon us—and if we do not agree, seems to put its hand in its breeches pocket." As a writer, I believe that fiction—like art—should stand alone and be judged alone, and not be camouflaged or apologized for in a barrage of verbiage.

And yet . . .

As both a reader and writer, I enjoy seeing the stories of some of my favorite writers set in context by introductions. My friend Harlan Ellison said in a recent *Locus* interview, "Everybody says, 'You should write your autobiography.' I say, 'I've been writing it in bits and pieces in the introductions, in every story I write.'" While I have no urge to write an autobiography, I confess that I enjoy Harlan's passionate and revelatory introductions and admit to remembering some of those intros even after I've forgotten the details in the particular stories they were introducing.

Unlike gifted performance artists who find an audience everywhere—passengers in an elevator, say, or fellow diners in a restaurant—I am a private person and fully intend to stay that way. At times, my passion for privacy in an age that seems to hold no interest in privacy and every interest in total revelation makes me seem stuffy. No, it *makes* me stuffy. "Don't tell and I won't ask" could be my policy toward much of the too-confiding world.

But as a novelist and occasional writer of short fiction, I've already voluntarily breached that wall of privacy. "Writers are exorcists of their own demons," said Mario Vargas Llosa, and the corollary to the maxim is Henry James's observation that the writer is present in ". . . every page of every book from which he sought so assiduously to eliminate himself."

So perhaps context, not clarification, is the saving grace of introductions such as those scattered through this collection. Or perhaps these intros are a simple form of good manners, such as saying "Hi" to other hikers encountered on a trail here in the Rockies where I live. Done right, it does not intrude on the scenery and solitude that are the real reasons for hiking there, or for reading these stories.

THE five long tales collected here were written over the past few years that saw dramatic but not necessarily visible changes in this particular writer. As Dante begins his *Inferno* (Mandelbaum translation)—

"When I had journeyed half our life's way,
I found myself within a shadowed forest,

for I had lost the path that does not stray.
        Ah, it is hard to speak of what it was,
that savage forest, dense and difficult,
which even in recall renews my fear:
        so bitter—death is hardly more severe!
But to retell the good discovered there,
I'll also tell the other things I saw."

This sounds a bit too melodramatic; it would seem that not many of us get a guided tour to and through the Ninth Circle of Hell—but, of course, most of us do sooner or later. And many of us—but not all—are lucky enough to crawl down (or up, since he's buried upside down in the icy Ninth Circle) the hairy shins of Satan and get out again, if not upward through the Purgatorio to Paradiso, at least back into the light of a regular workday.

I do have a recommendation here. If and when any of you suddenly find yourself in such a dark wood, at such a place where the simplest things begin to ravel (which means the same as "unravel," delightfully enough), I recommend that you scrape together enough money for a few months of therapy and then skip the therapy, but fly, instead, to the island of Maui, and then drive to the all-but-uninhabited northeast side, perhaps renting a small *hale* near the village of Hana (population 800) and, once there, eat mostly rice and vegetables, go to sleep to the sound of the surf, awake to the predawn "white rain of Hana" on the metal roof, hike much, draw some, write a little (if you can), and listen to some music if your mood allows. Near Hana, Waiana-panapa State Park and its black sand beach are a great jumping off point for coastal hikes—either south toward Hana Town or, more interestingly, north several miles toward the little Hana airport. If you walk away from Hana, be careful, for the ancient Hawaiian "paved trail" that runs along the bare, volcanic shore cliffs is neither paved nor much of a trail and is sometimes treacherous, requiring the hiker to jump over blowholes and to find one's way along high bluffs falling away to rocks and crashing surf. Even if there's a mild siren's song there, the walk is wonderful—far too perfect with its mild rains and following rainbows arching above the great green shoulder of Haleakala for you to be distracted for long.

Five days there should suffice. A week would be better.

THE long stories collected here in WORLDS ENOUGH & TIME—I suspect they're mostly novellas, or perhaps novelettes, but I always forget the word-length distinction, so I'll just call them "long stories"— have no overriding architecture, but they probably do resonate to some common themes.

When writers get into discussing themes, they tend to sound pretentious, so I'll apologize in advance if the following comments come across that way. But sooner or later, everyone has to talk about his or her craft—in terms, at least, of ambition, if not necessarily of accomplishment.

Ideally, these stories (and my longer fiction) would embody the concept of *niwa*, which, in turn, would include the elements of *fukinsei*, *kanso*, *koko*, *datsuzoku*, *seijaku*, and *shibui*, with all of these attributes being enhanced by the resonance of *wabi* and *sabi*. This doesn't happen to be the case, but more and more it appears to be my goal.

About ten years ago, I traveled with a friend to Japan and other parts of Asia, ostensibly to research a novel (although the research decided that the novel should not be written) but actually to visit Zen gardens.

The Japanese word for garden is *niwa*, but it also means "a pure place." As with appreciating any fine art, a certain amount of education is required before reviewing Zen gardens or moss gardens or any of a variety of Japanese gardens. As with fiction or visual art, a simple thing can mean much more than first encounter suggests: raked gravel for the sea, a rock for islands holding millions of souls, a simple shrub for all the forests.

In such gardens—and increasingly, I think, in my fiction—a controlling element is *fukinsei*—*the precept that the principle controlling the balance of composition should always be asymmetrical*. A little-known fact of aesthetics is that all human beings seem to be wired to prefer—whether they know it or not—in flower arrangements, the composition of smooth stones interior design, architecture, art, fiction—either symmetry or asymmetry. Most people in Western cultures gravitate to symmetry, sometimes rigid symmetry. The elements of a Japanese garden, as in so much of that aesthetic, celebrate asymmetry. Life, I think, is not so symmetrical as our local sensibilities would have it be.

The themes of my work, I've noticed after almost two decades of professional striving, seem to circle back to certain explorations of love and loss, while my craft increasingly becomes a search for *kanso* (simplicity) and its sibling but not-twin, *koko,* a quest for austerity and maturity, a return to the bare essentials and an honoring of the venerable. For style, as much as I love reading Oondatje or Nabokov-type lyrical prose, I would, as the gardener in Nara would, choose *shizen,* a naturalness, a deliberate absence of pretense. Sometimes such simplicity is obtained through finding *seijaku*—a choice of silence rather than noise, of calm rather than excitation.

Sometimes not.

Shibui, wabi, and *sabi* are complex ideas and while I have not obtained them as goals in life or fiction, neither can I escape them as recurring obsessions in my work. *Wabi* includes the underlying Zen-essence of understanding that in the bloom of time comes the first embrace of oblivion. The Zen-garden of Ryoanzi Garden is raked thrice daily, clearing the gravel of the fallen petals from the overhanging tree, but the perfection of the gravel and stone garden is found in precisely those aberrant petals—precisely in that random but inevitable encounter with the dying beauty that is being raked away, reminding us that even as we celebrate life and beauty, we're being deprived of something irreplaceable. *Sabi,* the discovery of such beauty in the patina of time, in the lichen on the stone and the weathered fallen tree, tends to remind us that time is generous to things but brutal as hell to us human beings. Perhaps we have worlds enough in our three-score-and-ten, but time denies us room to celebrate those worlds; time is the only gift that takes away everything and everyone we love if we get enough of it. The acknowledgment and perhaps celebration of *sabi*—that first embrace of oblivion even as we hold tight those people and things we love—is the touchstone for several of the stories in this collection.

Quite a few of us have encountered the word *shibui*, that all-but-untranslatable word that signifies good taste but which means, literally, the puckery, stringent quality found when biting into a green persimmon. This has been my life experience with nature—a celebration of its beauty and complexity while always resisting the urge to sentimentalize it. We are, I think, in an age not only of sentimentality, but of regressive immaturity, where we find it all but impossible to see that there is something not sweet or benevolent in nature, a restraint, an essential sour tang that makes the central purity all the sweeter in the tasting. My strange girl-prophet, Kelly Dahl, tries to teach this persimmon tartness reality of life to her former teacher, and perhaps this is part of the undelivered message carried to Earth by Kanakaredes and his crèche brothers. I know that it was the central message of Aenea, the reluctant messiah who shaped the human universe in "Orphans of the Helix."

Yugen requires a subtlety profound, demands suggestion rather than revelation. Combine that with the principle of *datsuzoku*—an unworldliness having nothing to do with eccentricity, a transcendence of the conventional in ways never imagined by conforming rebel types—and fiction achieves that element of strangeness which the critic Harold Bloom points out is the common element of enduring literature, whether encountered in Shakespeare or Jane Austen or John Fowles.

COME with me, then, into a Zen-garden. There will be fire in the form of a stone or iron lantern. There will be earth in the form of a stone. There will be water, air, plants, and animals in their true forms. There will always be water, even if just by suggestion or by the elegant parade of raindrops down a waterfall chain.

The garden path, the *roji*, is more philosophy than stone.

Every step is designed to bring the visitor and viewer further from the mirror of the passing world and into its opposite. The stepstones of the *roji* are deliberately placed in irregular cadence (in obedience to the principles of *fukinsei*) so as to make the watcher look down, to take nothing for granted, to watch his step, and to notice the vistas and views. There are larger standing-on stones for those vistas and views, and also to create pauses for mediation on what has been seen or missed.

To see a Zen-garden fully, we will need the subtle vision of *yugen*—the Zen-gardener's mastery of partly hidden views, of deliberately indistinct areas made relative to shadows, as well as an eye for the completeness glimpsed in partial reflections in water, and a full sense of the beauty of darkly revealed forms and layers of meaning. Such joy is found in moon shadows in pond reflections, in stone, in sand textures, in symbols, and in subtle shadows of bamboo on bamboo in moonlight.

Whole sight; or all the rest is desolation.

Introduction to "Looking for Kelly Dahl"

....

This is a story about love, loss, betrayal, obsession, and middle-aged angst—in other words, your basic light romantic comedy.

"Kelly Dahl" appeared on OMNI-online and was printed in High Fantastic, a hardcover anthology edited by Steve Rasnic Tem and featuring all Colorado authors of fantastic fiction, but the story was written for none of these markets. It was just written.

One reaction I've received repeatedly to the story is odd. People ask, "Is there a real Kelly Dahl?"

Well, there is, actually. Kelly Dahl is the name of a Colorado campground set along the Peak to Peak Highway south of Nederland but north of the old mining towns (now gambling towns) of Blackhawk and Central City.

I got lost in a darkling wood near Kelly Dahl some years ago. I'm fairly certain it's the only time I've ever been lost in the woods or mountains, and it was silly since I'd just gone a quarter of a mile or so from the national forest campground (I usually camp far from such places, backpacking away from people) to watch a sunset from a high ridge. Then, in taking a shortcut back to the campsite, I ended up wandering for a couple of hours through a pitch-black forest of lodgepole pine. I hate lodgepole pine woods. The trees are scruffy, pruning their branches lower down so that only the tops of the trees have living needles to catch the sunlight—which results in a forest of telephone poles

*growing so close together it's hard to squeeze through them
while the canopy above blots out the sky. Even someone with a
reliable built-in sense of direction such as me can get lost while
wiggling and waggling his way through hillsides of lodgepole
pine.*

Or so I reassure myself.

At any rate, I found a road after ninety minutes or so of push-
ing through undergrowth and lodgepole pine, but it wasn't the
Peak to Peak Highway, the only road running north and south
along the Continental Divide there. It was dark. It was very
dark, and although I wasn't really lost any longer since following
that access road uphill would, theoretically, get me back to the
Peak to Peak, I decided to stop at a farmhouse—the only home
along this road—to ask if Kelly Dahl Campground lay north or
south of the theoretical intersection with the highway.

The house was a Bumpus House. (If you've read Jean Shep-
herd, or seen some of the TV specials or the movie based on his
work, you'll know what I mean.) Weathered, no paint, yard
filled with junked vehicles, at least two outhouses out back, a
side porch that had been ripped off—probably by one of the
Bumpuses in a fit of rage—with weeds growing six feet high and
glimpses of gray animals, looking like possums only with larger
teeth, wandering through the junked cars and weeds. Your basic
Bumpus House.

Still, there was a faint light glowing from the closed front
door and through the torn shades, so I thought I'd ask directions. I almost changed my mind when I realized that the light
was green and pulsing—not the universal blue pulse of a television in a darkened room, but a sick, viscous green, and pulsing,
throbbing, not to the ADD editing speed of a flickering TV, but
pulsing, like something from a 1930s Universal horror movie. I
still kept going, climbing cinderblocks where the porch had been
and raising my hand to knock, when the most ferocious and unearthly growling I've ever heard in my life erupted . . . exploded.
Not just from inside the house but from outside—from the backyard and the side yard and the black lodgepole pine forest be-

yond. Perhaps . . . just perhaps . . . if someone in the house was raising wolf-dogs (a not unusual circumstance in rural Colorado) and had ten of them inside the house and twenty in the backyard and another twenty in the side yard and fifty staked down in the woods above, the growling might be reasonably explained.

Perhaps.

Anyway, I decided to forego directions and just keep walking—well, jogging for a bit—up the black access road in the starlight. And there, after another forty minutes of walking and guessing that I had to turn south at the Peak to Peak Highway, was Kelly Dahl Campground with its scattering of dome tents and campfires and campers along the high ridgeline. I'm not sure if any sight has been more welcome.

ALL of this has precious little to do with the story, of course.

One of the love stories imbedded in "Kelly Dahl" is about the love of teaching. Another is the love of the Colorado high country.

For a dozen years after moving to Colorado in 1974, I was able to combine these two loves in our annual "Eco-Week Experience" where we sixth-grade teachers brought kids to the mountains for three days and two nights. (The other two days of the "Eco-Week" were separate field trips to our town's water supply reservoir in the mountains, water purification plant, and then the sewage-treatment plant—a place of "great de-stinktion.")

But the heart of Eco-Week was the three days and two nights at Camp St. Malo, an aging Catholic summer camp some twenty-five or thirty miles north of Kelly Dahl Campground along the same Peak to Peak Highway. Most of the schools went in the autumn, when the aspen leaves were at their height. Some of the unluckier schools in the district had to go up in May, when there might be three feet of snow at the camp. It didn't matter too much to the sixth-graders; they—and some of us teachers—looked forward to Eco-Week year round. And we didn't just dump the kids at camp and hope they had a good time. Our sci-

ence preparation went on for many months and there were experiments to do during our stay there—testing the pH of the water and soil, doing increment bores of the trees, identifying trees by smell and touch during blind walks, compass reading and orienteering, studying the glacially formed landscape, finding squirrel kitchens and studying insect behavior with magnifying glasses, mapping the evolution from Pikes Peak granite to pebbles to soil to humus, observing animal and bird behavior . . . you get the idea.

God, I loved Eco-Week. (The year after I left teaching, the new triple-knit district superintendent, a mouth-breather from some podunk district in Wyoming, killed Eco-Week, which had been the high point for thousands of sixth-graders for sixteen years, as "too expensive"—even though it paid its own way— and then he left in the midst of a sexual scandal, the district having to buy up his contract to the tune of more than $200,000 just to get rid of him. But Eco-Week stayed dead.)

You'll find some of my love of teaching in the pages of "Looking for Kelly Dahl," even some of the love of teaching ecology, but more important than my love of teaching is the love of learning— perhaps learning science—that was quickened, if not conceived, in the hearts of some of the kids. The scene where Kelly Dahl gets the class to shut up and listen to nature occurred—in one variation or another—in every one of our Eco-Week experiences.

Overcoming the fears of administrators, parents, the students, and many of the teachers, I instigated night hikes while up there (on the night before I told the "Gronker Story" to a hundred kids by the fireplace to scare the wits out of them—no one wanted to go outside after the "Gronker Story.") During the night hikes, we walked silently through the moonlight or starlight-dappled woods, found safe but silent places to be alone, and just sat for thirty minutes. For most of our kids, who had grown up in a town of some 60,000 people, it was probably the only time they had ever been alone in the woods, in the dark, listening to the stir of small mammals and the flap of owl wings and the rustle of ponderosa-pine branches in the night breeze. They loved it.

I'm not sure it's just an accident that when I finally bought mountain property and a cabin—the 115 acres called Windwalker—it was just down the road from Camp St. Malo (now gussied up into a Catholic "Executive Conference Center"— Pope John Paul II stayed there, going hiking in Gronker territory in his white sneakers with gold laces). Nor was it necessarily an accident that some of these former Eco-Week sixth-graders chose careers in science, some in environmental sciences. One of those students should be finishing up her Ph.D. thesis this year on the reproductive strategies of alpine plants; every day she hikes to her study fields of marsh marigolds at a chilly 12,000 feet on Niwot Ridge along the Divide, above treeline, situated about mid-distance between Camp St. Malo and Kelly Dahl Campground. I know that neither Eco-Week nor I created this love of science and the out of doors in her—her parents and she herself formed that before she was a sixth-grader— but I was privileged to see her do her first eco-science in the field.

Perhaps my favorite scene in "Kelly Dahl" is set in tundra above treeline like that, where Kelly Dahl—if there is a Kelly Dahl—seems to have the narrator in her gunsights and is communicating telepathically with him and sharing her love of the sheer poetry of tundra terms—"Fellfield, meadow vole, boreal chorus frog, snowball saxifrage, solifluction terraces, avens and sedges, yellow-bellied marmots, permafrost, nivation depressions, saffron ragworts, green-leaf chiming bells, man-hater sedge . . ."

There's a chance that this "man-hater sedge" serves more than one function in that passage.

I should point out that nowhere are the wabi and sabi palettes of time acting on nature more visible than in the krummholz— the "elfin timber," gnarled and twisted little trees at treeline that might be a thousand years old—and in the glacial moraines and fallen trees and lichened rocks and runic eskers of the alpine.

❋　❋　❋

Finally, a definition of the following terms might be useful—

Chiaroscuro—*the use and distribution of light and dark in a painting.*

Pentimento—*the reemergence in a painting of an image that's been painted over.*

Palimpsest—*a parchment from which writing has been erased (at least partially) to make room for another text.*

Palinode—*a poem in which the poet retracts something said in an earlier poem.*

LOOKING FOR KELLY DAHL

I
Chiaroscuro

I awoke in camp that morning to find the highway to Boulder gone, the sky empty of contrails, and the aspen leaves a bright autumn gold despite what should have been a midsummer day, but after bouncing the Jeep across four miles of forest and rocky ridgeline to the back of the Flatirons, it was the sight of the Inland Sea that stopped me cold.

"Damn," I muttered, getting out of the Jeep and walking to the edge of the cliff.

Where the foothills and plains should have been, the great sea stretched away east to the horizon and beyond. Torpid waves lapped up against the muddy shores below. Where the stone-box towers of NCAR, the National Center for Atmospheric Research, had risen below the sandstone slabs of the Flatirons, now there were only shrub-stippled swamps and muddy inlets. Of Boulder, there was no sign—neither of its oasis of trees nor of its low buildings. Highway 36 did not cut its accustomed swath over the hillside southeast to Denver. No roads were visible. The high rises of Denver were gone. All of Denver was gone. Only the Inland Sea stretched east and north and south as far as I could see, its color the gray-blue I remembered from

Lake Michigan in my youth, its wave action desultory, its sound more the halfhearted lapping of a large lake than the surf crash of a real ocean.

"Damn," I said again and pulled the Remington from its scabbard behind the driver's seat of the Jeep. Using the twenty-power sight, I scanned the gulleys leading down between the Flatirons to the swamps and shoreline. There were no roads, no paths, not even visible animal trails. I planted my foot on a low boulder, braced my arm on my knee, and tried to keep the scope steady as I panned right to left along the long strip of dark shoreline.

Footprints in the mud: one set, leading from the gully just below where I stood on what someday would be named Flagstaff Mountain and crossing to a small rowboat pulled up on the sand just beyond the curl of waves. No one was in the rowboat. No tracks led away from it.

A bit of color and motion caught my eye a few hundred meters out from the shore and I raised the rifle, trying to steady the scope on a bobbing bit of yellow. There was a float out there, just beyond the shallows.

I lowered the Remington and took a step closer to the drop-off. There was no way that I could get the Jeep down there—at least not without spending hours or days cutting a path through the thick growth of ponderosa and lodgepole pine that grew in the gully. And even then I would have to use the winch to lower the Jeep over boulders and near-vertical patches. It would not be worth the effort to take the vehicle. But it would require an hour or more to hike down from here.

For what? I thought. The rowboat and buoy would be another red herring, another Kelly Dahl joke. *Or she's trying to lure me out there on the water so that she can get a clean shot.*

"Damn," I said for the third and final time. Then I returned the rifle to its case, pulled out the blue daypack, checked to make sure that the rations, water bottles, and .38 were in place, tugged on the pack, shifted the Ka-bar knife in its sheath along my belt so that I could get to it in one movement, set the rifle scabbard in the crook of my arm, took one last look at the Jeep and its contents, and began the long descent.

Kelly, you're sloppy, I thought as I slid down the muddy slope, using aspens as handholds. *Nothing's consistent. You've screwed this up just like you did the Triassic yesterday.*

This particular Inland Sea could be from one of several eras—the late Cretaceous for one, the late Jurassic for another—but in the former era, some seventy-five million years ago, the great interior sea would have pushed much further west than here, into Utah and beyond, and the Rocky Mountains I could see twenty miles to the west would have been in the process of being born from the remnants of Pacific islands that had dotted an ocean covering California. The slabs of Flatirons now rising above me would exist only as a layer of soft substrata. Conversely, if it were the mid-Jurassic, almost a hundred million years earlier than the Cretaceous, this would all be part of a warm, shallow sea stretching down from Canada, ending in a shore winding along northern New Mexico. There would be a huge saline lake south of there, the mudflats of southern Colorado and northern New Mexico stretching as a narrow isthmus for almost two hundred miles between the two bodies of water. This area of central Colorado would be an island, but still without mountains and Flatirons.

You got it all wrong, Kelly. I'd give this a D–. There was no answer. *Shit, this isn't even that good. An F.* Still silence.

Nor were the flora and fauna correct. Instead of the aspen and pine trees through which I now descended, this area should have been forested during the Jurassic by tall, slender, cycadlike trees, festooned with petals and cones; the undergrowth would not be the juniper bushes I was picking my way around but exotic scouring rushes displaying leaves like banana plants. The late-Cretaceous flora would have been more familiar to the eye—low, broad-leaved trees, towering conifers—but the blossoms would be profuse, tropical, and exotic—with the scent of huge, magnolialike blossoms perfuming the humid air.

The air was neither hot nor humid. It was a midautumn Colorado day. The only blossoms I saw were the faded flowers on small cacti underfoot.

The fauna were wrong. And dull. Dinosaurs existed in both the Cretaceous and Jurassic, but the only animals I had seen this fine morning were some ravens, three white-tailed deer hustling for cover a mile before I reached the cliffs, and some golden-mantled ground squirrels near the top of the Flatirons. Unless a plesiosaur raised its scrawny neck out of the water below, my guess was that the Inland Sea had been transplanted to our era. I had been mildly disappointed the last couple of times the chase had taken me through ancient eras. I would like to have seen a dinosaur, if only to see if Spielberg and his computer animators had been correct as to how the creatures moved.

Kelly, you're sloppy, I thought again. *Lazy. Or you make your choices from sentiment and a sense of aesthetics rather than from any care for accuracy.* I was not surprised that there was no answer.

Kelly had always been quirky, although I remembered little sentimentality from either of the times I had been her teacher.

I thought, *She hadn't cried the time I left the sixth-grade class to take the high school job. Most of the other girls did. Kelly Dahl was eleven then. She had not shown much emotion when I'd had her in English class when she was . . . what? . . . seventeen.*

And now she was trying to kill me. Not much sentiment there, either.

I came out of the woods at the edge of the gully and began following human footprints in the mud across the flats. Whether the Inland Sea was from the Jurassic or the Cretaceous, the person who had crossed these tidal flats before me had worn sneakers—cross-trainers from the look of the sole patterns. *Are these tidal flats? I think so . . . the Kansas Sea was large enough to respond to tides.*

There was nothing in the rowboat but two oars, shipped properly. I glanced around, took the rifle out to scope the cliffsides, saw nothing there, tossed the pack in the boat, set the Remington across my lap, shoved off through low waves, and began to row toward the yellow buoy.

I half expected a rifle shot, but suspected that I would not hear it. Despite her missed chances a few days earlier, Kelly Dahl was obviously a good shot. When she decided to kill me, if she had a shot as clear as this one must be—she could fire from any spot along the cliff face of the Flatirons—I would almost certainly be hit on her first try. My only chance was that it would not be a fatal shot and that I could still handle the Remington.

Sweating, the rifle now on the thwart behind me, my shirt soaked from the exertion despite the cool autumn air, I thought of how vulnerable I was out here on the chalky sea, how stupid this action was. I managed to grunt a laugh.

Do your worst, kid. Sunlight glinted on something behind the rocks on Flagstaff Mountain. A telescopic sight? My Jeep's windshield? I did not break the rhythm of my rowing to check it out. *Do your worst, kid. It can't be worse than what I had planned for myself.*

The yellow "buoy" was actually a plastic bleach jar. There was a line tied to it. I pulled it up. The wine bottle on the end of it was weighted with pebbles and sealed with a cork. There was a note inside.

BANG, it read. YOU'RE IT.

ON the day I decided to kill myself, I planned it, prepared it, and carried it out. Why wait?

The irony was that I had always detested suicide and the suicides themselves. Papa Hemingway and his ilk, someone who will put a Boss shotgun in his mouth and pull the trigger, leaving the remains at the bottom of the stairs for his wife to find and a ceiling full of skull splinters for the hired help to remove . . . well, I find them disgusting. And self-indulgent. I have been a failure and a drunk and a fuck-up, but I have never left my messes for others to clean up, not even in the worst depths of my drinking days.

Still, it is hard to think of a way to kill yourself without leaving a mess behind. Walking into the ocean like James Mason at the end of the 1954 *A Star Is Born* would have been nice, assuming a strong current going out or sharks to finish off the waterlogged remains, but I live in Colorado. Drowning oneself in one of the puny reservoirs around here seems pathetic at best.

All of the domestic remedies—gas, poison, hanging, an overdose of sleeping pills, the shotgun from the closet—leave someone with the Hemingway problem. Besides, I despise melodrama. The way I figure it, it's no one's business but my own how or why I go out. Of course, my ex-wife wouldn't give a shit and my only child is dead and beyond embarrassment, but there are still a few friends out there from the good days who might feel betrayed if news of my death came in the black-wrapped package of suicide. Or so I like to think.

It took me not quite three beers in the Bennigan's on Canyon Boulevard to arrive at the answer; it took even less time to make the preparations and to carry them out.

Some of the few things left me after the settlement with Maria were my Jeep and camping gear. Even while I was drinking, I would occasionally take off for the hills without notice, camping somewhere along the Peak to Peak Highway or in the National Forest up Left Hand Canyon. While not a real off-road type—I hate 4-wheel-drive assholes who pride themselves on tearing up the landscape, and all snowmobilers, and those idiots on motorcycles who befoul the wilderness with noise and fumes—I have been known to push the Jeep pretty hard to get to a campsite far enough back to where I wouldn't have to listen to anyone's radio or hear traffic or have to look at the rump end of some fat-assed Winnebago.

There are mineshafts up there. Most of them are dug horizontally into the mountains and run only a few hundred feet back before ending in cave-in or flood. But some are sinkholes, some are pits where the soil has caved in above an old shaft. Some are vertical dropshafts, long since abandoned, that fall two or three hundred feet to rocks and water and to whatever slimy things there are that like to live in such darkness.

I knew where one of these dropshafts was—a deep one, with an opening wide enough to take the Jeep and me. It was way the hell above the canyon back there behind Sugarloaf Mountain, off the trail and marked by warning signs on trees, but someone trying to turn a Jeep around in the dusk or dark might drive into it easily enough. If they were stone stupid. Or if they were a known drunk.

It was about seven on a July evening when I left Bennigan's, picked up my camping stuff at the apartment on 30th Street, and headed up north on Highway 36 along the foothills for three miles and then west up Left Hand Canyon. Even with the two or three hard miles of 4-wheel-drive road, I figured I would be at the mineshaft before eight P.M. There would be plenty of light left to do what I had to do.

Despite the three beers, I was sober. I hadn't had a real drink in almost two months. As an alcoholic, I knew that I wasn't recovering by staying just on this side of the sober line, only suffering.

But I wanted to be almost sober that night. I had been almost sober—only two beers, perhaps three—the evening that the pickup crossed the lane on Highway 287 and smashed into our Honda, killing Allan instantly and putting me into the hospital for three weeks. The driver of the pickup had survived, of course. They had tested his blood and found that he was legally drunk. He received a suspended sentence and lost his license for a year. I was so badly injured, it was so obvious that the pickup had been at fault, that no one had tested my blood-alcohol level. I'll never know if I could have responded faster if it hadn't been for those two or three beers.

This time I wanted to know exactly what I was doing as I perched the Jeep on the edge of that twenty-foot opening, shifted into 4-wheel low, and roared over the raised berm around the black circle of the pit.

And I did. I did not hesitate. I did not lose my sense of pride at the last minute and write some bullshit farewell note to anyone. I didn't think about it. I took my baseball cap off, wiped the faintest film of sweat from my forehead, set the cap on firmly, slammed the shifter into low, and roared over that mound of dirt like a pit bull going after a mailman's ass.

The sensation was almost like going over the second hill on the Wildcat 'coaster at Elitch Gardens. I had the urge to raise my arms and scream. I did not raise my arms; my hands stayed clamped to the wheel as the nose of the Jeep dropped into darkness as if I were driving into a tunnel. I had not turned the headlights on. I caught only the faintest glimpse of boulders and rotted timbers and layers of granite whipping by. I did not scream.

THE last few days I have been trying to recall everything I can about Kelly Dahl when I taught her in the sixth grade, every conversation and interaction, but much of it is indistinct. I taught for almost twenty-six years, sixteen in the elementary grades and the rest in high school. Faces and names blur. But not because I was drinking heavily then. Kelly was in my last sixth-grade class and I didn't really have a drinking problem then. Problems yes; drinking problem, no.

I remember noticing Kelly Dahl on the first day; any teacher worth his or her salt notices the troublemakers, the standouts, the teacher's pets, the class clowns, and all of the other elementary-class stereotypes on the first day. Kelly Dahl did not fit any of the stereotypes, but she was certainly a standout kid. Physically, there was nothing unusual about her—at eleven she was losing the baby fat she'd carried through childhood, her bone structure was beginning to assert itself in her face, her hair was about shoulder length, brown, and somewhat stringier than the blow-dried fussiness or careful braidedness of the other girls. Truth was, Kelly Dahl carried a slight air of neglect and impoverishment about her, a look we teachers were all too familiar with in the mid-'80s, even in affluent Boulder County. The girl's clothes were usually too small, rarely clean, and bore the telltale wrinkles of something dredged from the hamper or floor of the closet that morning. Her hair was, as I said, rarely washed and usually held in place by cheap plastic barrettes that she had probably worn since second grade. Her skin had that sallow look common to children who spent hours inside in front of the TV, although I later found that this was not the case with Kelly Dahl. She was that rarest of things—a child who had never watched TV.

Few of my assumptions were correct about Kelly Dahl.

What made Kelly stand out that first day of my last sixth-grade class were her eyes—startlingly green, shockingly intelligent, and surprisingly alert when not concealed behind her screen of boredom or hidden by her habit of looking away when called upon. I remember her eyes and the slightly mocking tone to her soft, eleven-year-old girl's voice when I called on her the few times that first day.

I recall that I read her file that evening—I made it a practice never to read the students' cumulative folders before I met the actual child—and I probably looked into this one because Kelly's careful diction and softly ironic tone contrasted so much with her appearance. According to the file, Kelly Dahl lived in the mobile home park to the west of the tracks—the trailer park that gave our school the lion's share of problems—with her mother, divorced, and a stepfather. There was a yellow Notice slip from second grade warning the teacher that Kelly's biological father had held custody until that year, and that the court had removed the girl from that home because of rumors of abuse. I checked back in the single sheet from a county social worker who had visited the home and, reading between the lines of bureaucratese, inferred that the mother hadn't wanted the child either but had given in to the court's ruling. The biological father had been more than willing to give the girl up. Evidently it had been a noncustody battle, one of those "You take her, I have a life to live" exchanges that so many of my students had endured. The mother had lost and ended up with Kelly. The yellow Notice slip was the usual warning that the girl was not to be allowed to leave the school grounds with the biological father or be allowed to speak on the phone if he called the school, and if he were observed hanging around the school grounds, the teacher or her aide were to notify the principal and/or call the police. Too many of our kids' files have yellow Notice slips with that sort of warning.

A hasty note by Kelly's fourth-grade teacher mentioned that her "real father" had died in a car accident the previous summer and that the Notice slip could be ignored. A scrawled message on the bottom of the social worker's typed page of comments let it be known that Kelly Dahl's "stepfather" was the usual live-in boyfriend and was out on parole after sticking up a convenience store in Arvada.

A fairly normal file.

But there was nothing normal about little Kelly Dahl. These past few days, as I actively try to recall our interactions during the seven months of that abbreviated school year and the eight months we spent together when she was a junior in high school, I am amazed at how strange our time together had been. Sometimes I can barely remember the faces or names of any of the other sixth-graders that year, or the sullen faces of the slouching juniors five years after that, just Kelly Dahl's ever-thinning face and startling green eyes, Kelly Dahl's soft voice—ironic at eleven, sarcastic and challenging at sixteen. Perhaps, after twenty-six years teaching, after hundreds of eleven-year-olds and sixteen-year-olds and seventeen-year-olds and eighteen-year-olds taught—suffered through, actually—Kelly Dahl had been my only real student.

And now she was stalking me. And I her.

II
Pentimento

I awoke to the warmth of flames on my face. Lurching with a sense of falling, I remembered my last moment of consciousness—driving the Jeep into the pit, the plunge into blackness. I tried to raise my arms, grab the wheel again, but my arms were pinned behind me. I was sitting on something solid, not the Jeep seat, the ground. Everything was dark except for the flicker of flames directly in front of me. *Hell?* I thought, but there was not the slightest belief in that hypothesis, even if I were dead. Besides, the flames I could see were in a large campfire; the ring of firestones was quite visible.

My head aching, my body echoing that ache and reeling from a strange vertigo, as if I were still in a plummeting Jeep, I attempted to assess the situation. I was outside, sitting on the ground, still dressed in the clothes I had worn during my suicide attempt, it was dark, and a large campfire crackled away six feet in front of me.

"Shit," I said aloud, my head and body aching as if I were hung over. *Screwed up again. I got drunk and messed up. Only imagined driving into the pit. Fuck.*

"You didn't screw up again" came a soft, high voice from somewhere in the darkness behind me. "You really did drive into that mineshaft."

I started and tried to turn to see who had spoken, but I couldn't move my head that far. I looked down and saw the ropes crossing my chest. I was tied to something—a stump, perhaps, or a boulder. I tried to remember if I had spoken those last thoughts aloud about getting drunk and screwing up. My head hurt abysmally.

"It was an interesting way to try to kill yourself" came the woman's voice again. I was sure it was a woman. And something about the voice was hauntingly familiar.

"Where are you?" I asked, hearing the raggedness in my voice. I swiveled my head as far as it would go but was rewarded with only a glimpse of movement in the shadows behind me. The woman was walking just outside the reach of firelight. I was sitting against a low boulder. Five strands of rope were looped around my chest and the rock. I could feel another rope restraining my wrists behind the boulder.

"Don't you want to ask who I am?" came the strangely familiar voice. "Get that out of the way?"

For a second I said nothing, the voice and the slight mocking tone beneath the voice so familiar that I was sure that I would remember the owner of it before I had to ask. Someone who found me drunk in the woods and tied me up. *Why tie me up?* Maria might have done that if she had been around, but she was in Guatemala with her new husband. There were past lovers who disliked me enough to tie me up and leave me in the woods—or worse—but none of them had this voice. Of course, in the past year or two there had been so many strange women I'd awakened next to . . . and who said I had to know this person? Odds were that some crazy woman in the woods found me, observed that I was drunk and potentially violent—I tend to shout and recite poetry when I am at my drunkest—and tied me up. It all made sense—except for the fact that I didn't remember getting drunk, that the aching head and body did not feel like my usual hangover, that it made no sense for even a crazy lady to tie me up, and that I *did* remember driving the fucking Jeep into the mineshaft.

"Give up, Mr. Jakes?" came the voice.

Mr. Jakes. That certain tone. A former student . . . I shook my head with the pain of trying to think. It was worse than a hangover headache, different, deeper.

"You can call me Roland," I said, my voice thick, squinting at the flames and trying to buy a moment to think.

"No, I can't, Mr. Jakes," said Kelly Dahl, coming around into the light and crouching between me and the fire. "You're Mr. Jakes. I can't call you anything else. Besides, Roland is a stupid name."

I nodded. I had recognized her at once, even though it had been six or seven years since I had seen her last. When she had been a junior, she had worn her hair frosted blonde and cut in a punk style just short of a mohawk. It was still short and cut raggedly, still a phony blonde with dark roots, but no longer punk. Her eyes had been large and luminous as a child of eleven, even larger and lit with the dull light of drugs when she was seventeen, but now they were just large. The dark shadows under her eyes that had been a constant of her appearance in high school seemed gone, although that might be a trick of the firelight. Her body was not as angular and lean as I remembered from high school, no longer the bone-and-gristle gaunt, as if the coke or crack or whatever she'd been taking had been eating her up from the inside, but still thin enough that one might have to glance again to see the breasts before being certain it was a woman. This night she was wearing jeans and work boots with a loose flannel shirt over a dark sweatshirt and there was a red bandana tied around her head. The firelight made the skin of her cheeks and forehead very pink. Her short hair stuck out over the bandana above her ears. She held a large camp knife loosely in her right hand as she squatted in front of me.

"Hi, Kelly," I said.

"Hi, Mr. Jakes."

"Want to let me loose?"

"No."

I hesitated. There had been none of the old bantering tone in her voice. We were just two adults talking, she in her early twenties, me fifty-something going on a hundred.

"Did you tie me up, Kelly?"

"Sure."

"Why?"

"You'll know in a few minutes, Mr. Jakes."

"Okay." I tried to relax, settle back against the rock as if I were accustomed to driving my Jeep into a pit and waking up to find an old student threatening me with a knife. *Is she threatening me with a knife?* It was hard to tell. She held it casually, but if she was not going to cut me loose, there was little reason for it to be there. Kelly had always been emotional, unusual, unstable. I wondered if she had gone completely insane.

"Not completely nuts, Mr. Jakes. But close to it. Or so people thought . . . back when people were around."

I blinked. "Are you reading my mind, Kelly?"

"Sure."

"How?" I asked. Perhaps I hadn't died in the suicide attempt, but was even at that second lying comatose and brain-damaged and dreaming this nonsense in a hospital room somewhere. Or at the bottom of the pit.

"*Mu*," said Kelly Dahl.

"I beg your pardon?"

"*Mu*. Come on, don't tell me you don't remember."

I remembered. I had taught the juniors . . . no, it had been the sixth-graders that year with Kelly . . . the Chinese phrase *mu*. On one level *mu* means only *yes*, but on a deeper level of Zen it was often used by the master when the acolyte asked a stupid, unanswerable, or wrongheaded question such as "Does a dog have the Buddha-nature?" The Master would answer only, *Mu*, meaning—*I say "yes" but mean "no," but the actual answer is—Unask the question.*

"Okay," I said, "then tell me why I'm tied up."

"*Mu*," said Kelly Dahl. She got to her feet and towered over me. Flames danced on the knife blade.

I shrugged, although the tight ropes left that as something less than a graceful movement. "Fine," I said. I was tired and scared and disoriented and angry. "Fuck it." *If you can read my mind, you goddamn neurotic, read this.* I pictured a raised middle finger. *And sit on it and swivel.*

Kelly Dahl laughed. I had heard her laugh very few times in sixth grade, not at all in eleventh grade, but this was the same memorable sound I had heard those few times—wild but not quite crazy, pleasant but with far too much edge to be called sweet.

Now she crouched in front of me, the long knife blade pointed at my eyes. "Are you ready to start the game, Mr. Jakes?"

"What game?" My mouth was very dry.

"I'm going to be changing some things," said Kelly Dahl. "You may not like all the changes. To stop me, you'll have to find me and stop me."

I licked my lips. The knife had not wavered during her little speech. "What do you mean, stop you?"

"Stop me. Kill me if you can. Stop me."

Oh, shit . . . the poor girl is crazy.

"Maybe," said Kelly Dahl. "But the game is going to be fun."
She leaned forward quickly and for a mad second I thought she
was going to kiss me; instead she leveraged the flat of the blade
under the ropes and tugged slightly. Buttons ripped. I felt the
steel point cold against the base of my throat as the knife slid
sideways.

"Careful . . ."

"Shhhh," whispered Kelly Dahl and did kiss me, once, lightly,
as her hand moved quickly from left to right and the ropes separated as if sliced by a scalpel.

When she stepped back I jumped to my feet . . . *tried* to jump
to my feet . . . my legs were asleep and I pitched forward, almost
tumbling into the fire, catching myself clumsily with arms and
hands that were as nerveless as the logs I could see lying in the
flames.

"Shit," I said. "Goddammit, Kelly, this isn't very . . ." I had
made it to my knees and turned toward her, away from the fire.

I saw that the campfire was in a clearing on a ridgeline, somewhere I did not recognize but obviously nowhere near where I
had driven into the mineshaft. There were a few boulders
massed in the dark and I caught a glimpse of the Milky Way
spilling above the pines. My Jeep was parked twenty feet away. I
could see no damage but it was dark. A breeze had come up and
the pine branches began swaying slightly, the needles rich in
scent and sighing softly.

Kelly Dahl was gone.

WHEN I was training to be a teacher, just out of the army and not
sure why I was becoming a teacher except for the fact that it was
the furthest thing from humping a ruck through Vietnam that I
could imagine, one of the trick questions the professors used to
ask was— "Do you want to be the sage on the stage or the guide
on the side?" The idea was that there were two kinds of teachers: the "sage" who walked around like a pitcher full of knowl-

edge occasionally pouring some into the empty receptacle that was the student, or the "guide" who led the student to knowledge via furthering the young person's own curiosity and exploration. The obvious right answer to that trick question was that the good teacher-to-be should be "the guide on the side," not imposing his or her own knowledge, but aiding the child in self-discovery.

I soon found out that the only way I could enjoy teaching was to be the sage on the stage. I poured knowledge and facts and insights and questions and doubts and everything else that I was carrying around directly from my overflowing pitcher to those twenty-five or so empty receptacles. It was most fun when I taught sixth grade because the receptacles hadn't been filled with so much social moose piss and sheer misinformation.

Luckily, there were a lot of things I was both acutely interested in, moderately knowledgeable about, and innocently eager to share with the kids: my passion for history and literature, my love of space travel and aviation, my college training in environmental science, a love of interesting architecture, my ability to draw and tell stories, a fascination with dinosaurs and geology, an enjoyment of writing, a high comfort level with computers, a hatred of war coupled with an obsession with things military, firsthand knowledge of quite a few remote places in the world, a desire to travel to see *all* of the world's remote places, a good sense of direction, a warped sense of humor, a profound fascination with the lives of world historical figures such as Lincoln and Churchill and Hitler and Kennedy and Madonna, a flair for the dramatic, a love of music that would often lead to my sixth-grade class lying in the park across the street from the school on a warm spring or autumn day, sixty feet of school extension cord tapping my mini-stereo system into the electrical outlet near the park restrooms, the sound of Vivaldi or Beethoven or Mozart or Rachmaninoff irritating the other teachers who later complained that they had to close their classroom windows so that their students would not be distracted. . . .

I had enough passions to remain a sage on the stage for twenty-six years. *Some of those years,* said the inscription on a tombstone I once saw, *were good.*

One of the incidents I remember with Kelly Dahl was from the week of environmental study the district had mandated for sixth-graders back when they had money to fund the fieldtrips. Actually, we studied environmental science for weeks before the trip, but the students always remembered the actual three-day excursion to an old lodge along the Front Range of the Rockies. The district called those three days and two nights of hiking and doing experiments in the mountains the Environmental Awareness and Appreciation Unit. The kids and teachers called it Eco-Week.

I remember the warm, late-September day when I had brought Kelly Dahl's class to the mountains. The kids had found their bunks in the drafty old lodge, we had hiked our orientation hikes, and in the hour before lunch I had brought the class to a beaver pond a quarter of a mile or so from the lodge in order to do pH tests and to begin my stint as Science Sage. I pointed out the fireweed abounding around the disturbed pond edge—*Epilobium angustifolium* I taught them, never afraid to introduce a little Latin nomenclature into the mix—and had them find some of the fireweed's cottony seeds along the bank or skimming across the still surface of the pond. I pointed out the aspen's golden leaves and explained why it shimmered—how the upper surface of the leaf did not receive enough sunlight to photosynthesize, so the leaf was attached by a stem at an angle that allowed it to quake so that both sides received the light. I explained how aspen clone from the roots, so the expansive aspen grove we were looking at was—in a real sense—a single organism. I pointed out the late asters and wild chrysanthemums in their last days before the killing winter winds finished them for another season, and had the children hunt for the red leaves of cinquefoil and strawberry and geranium.

It was at this point, when the kids were reconvened around

me in an interested circle, pointing to the fallen red leaves and gall-swollen branches they had gathered, that Kelly Dahl asked, "Why do we have to learn all this stuff?"

I remember sighing. "You mean the names of these plants?"

"Yes."

"A name is an instrument of teaching," I said, quoting the Aristotle maxim I had used many times with this class, "and of discerning natures."

Kelly Dahl had nodded slightly and looked directly at me, the startling, unique quality of her green eyes in sharp contrast to the sad commonness of her cheap K-market jacket and corduroys. "But you can't learn it all," she had said, her voice so soft that the other kids had leaned forward to hear it above the gentle breeze that had come up. It was one of those rare times when an entire class was focused on what was being said.

"You can't learn it all," I had agreed, "but one can enjoy nature more if you learn some of it."

Kelly Dahl had shaken her head, almost impatiently I'd thought at the time. "You don't understand," she said. "If you don't understand it *all,* you can't understand any of it. Nature is . . . *everything.* It's all mixed up. Even we're part of it, changing it by being here, changing it by trying to understand it . . ." She had stopped then and I only stared. It certainly had been the most I had heard this child say in one speech in the three weeks of class we had shared so far. And what she said was absolutely accurate, but—I felt—largely irrelevant.

While I paused to frame a reply that all of the kids could understand, Kelly had gone on. "What I mean is," she said, obviously more impatient with her own inability to explain than with my inability to understand, "that learning *a little* of this stuff is like tearing up that painting you were talking about on Tuesday . . . the woman . . ."

"The *Mona Lisa,*" I said.

"Yeah. It's like tearing up the *Mona Lisa* into little bits and handing around the bits so everyone would enjoy and understand the painting." She stopped again, frowning slightly, although whether at the metaphor or at speaking up at all, I did not know.

For a minute there was just the silence of the aspen grove and the beaver pond. I admit that I was stumped. Finally, I said, "What would you suggest we do instead, Kelly?"

At first I thought that she would not answer, so withdrawn into herself did she seem. But eventually she said softly, "Close our eyes."

"What?" I said, not quite hearing.

"Close our eyes," repeated Kelly Dahl. "If we're going to look at this stuff, we might as well look with something other than big words."

We all closed our eyes without further comment, the class of normally unruly sixth graders and myself. I remember to this day the richness of the next few minutes: the butterscotch-and-turpentine tang of sap from the ponderosa pine trees up the hill from us, the vaguely pineapple scent of wild camomile, the dry-leaf dusty sweetness of the aspen grove beyond the pond, the equally sweet decayed aroma of meadow mushrooms such as *lactarius* and *russula*, the pungent seaweed smell of pond scum and the underlying aromatic texture of the sun-warmed earth and the heated pine needles beneath our legs. I remember the warmth of the sun on my face and hands and denim-covered legs that long-ago September afternoon. I recall the sounds from those few minutes as vividly as I can call back anything I have ever heard: the soft lapping of water trickling over the sticks-and-mud beaver dam, the rustle of dry clematis vines and the brittle stirring of tall gentian stalks in the breeze, the distant hammering of a woodpecker in the woods toward Mt. Meeker and then, so suddenly that my breath caught, the startling crash of wings as a flight of Canada geese came in low over the pond and, without a single honk, veered south toward the highway and the larger ponds there. I think that none of us opened our eyes then, even when the geese flew low over us, so that the magic spell would not be broken. It was a new world, and Kelly Dahl was—somehow, inexplicably, unarguably—our guide.

I had forgotten that moment until yesterday.

ON the morning after she had tied me up, Kelly Dahl shot the shit out of my Jeep.

I had waited until sunrise to find my way back to Boulder. The night was too dark, the woods were too dense, and my head hurt too much to try to drive down the mountain in the dark. *Besides,* I had thought at the time with a wry smile, *I might drive into a mineshaft.*

In the morning my head still hurt and the woods were still thick—not even a sign of a Jeep trail or how Kelly had got my vehicle this far back—but at least I could see to drive. The Jeep itself had multiple abrasions and contusions, a dented fender, flaking paint, and a long gouge on the right door, but these were all old wounds; there was no sign of tumbling down a three-hundred-foot mineshaft. The keys were in the ignition. My billfold was still in my hip pocket. The camping gear was still in the back of the Jeep. Kelly Dahl might be as crazy as a loon, but she was no thief.

It had taken me about an hour to drive up to the mineshaft the previous evening; it took me almost three hours to get back to Boulder. I was way the hell beyond Sugarloaf Mountain and Gold Hill, northeast of Jamestown almost to the Peak to Peak Highway. I had no idea why Kelly Dahl would drag me that far . . . unless the entire mineshaft experience had been an hallucination and she had found me elsewhere. Which made no sense. I put the puzzle out of my mind until I could get home, take a shower, have some aspirin and three fingers of Scotch, and generally start the day.

I should have known things were screwed up long before I got to Boulder. The paved road in Left Hand Canyon, once I crept out of the woods and got onto it headed east, seemed wrong. I realize now that I was driving on patched concrete rather than asphalt. The Greenbriar Restaurant sitting at the exit of Left Hand Canyon where the road meets Highway 36 seemed weird. Looking back, I realize that the parking lot was smaller, the entrance and door painted a different color, and there was a large cottonwood where the flower garden had been for years. Small things on the short ride south to Boulder—the shoulder of Highway 36 was too narrow, the Beechcraft plant along the foothills side of the road looked spruced up and open for business despite the fact that it had been empty for a decade. Nursing my headache, mulling over Kelly Dahl and my screwed-up suicide, I noticed none of this.

There was no traffic. Not a single car or van or cyclist—unusual since those spandex fanatics on bikes are zooming along the Foothills Highway every pleasant day of the year. But nothing this morning. The strangeness of that did not really strike me until I was on North Broadway in Boulder.

No cars moving. Scores were parked by the curb, but none were moving. Nor cyclists hogging the lane. Nor pedestrians walking against the light. I was almost to the Pearl Street walking mall before I realized how empty the town was.

Jesus Christ, I remember thinking, *maybe there's been a nuclear war . . . everyone's evacuated.* Then I remembered that the Cold War was over and that the Boulder City Council had— a few years earlier and for no reason known to humankind— voted unanimously to ignore civil defense evacuation plans in case of a wartime emergency. The Boulder City Council was into that sort of thing—like declaring Boulder a Nuclear-Free Zone, which meant, I guess, that no more aircraft carriers with nuclear weapons would be tying up there again soon. It seemed probable that there hadn't been a mass evacuation even if the Rocky Flats Nuclear Weapons Plant six miles away had melted down—a core of Boulder's politically correct citizenry would protest the advancing radiation rather than evacuate.

Then where is everybody? I had the open Jeep slowed to a crawl by the time I came down the hill to Pearl Street and the walking mall there.

The walking mall was gone: no trees, no landscaped hills, no tasteful brick walkways, no flowerbeds, no panhandlers, no Freddy's hot dog stand, no skateboarders, no street musicians, no drug dealers, no benches or kiosks or phone booths . . . all gone.

The mall was gone, but Pearl Street itself remained, looking as it had before it was covered with bricks and flowerbeds and street musicians. I turned left onto it and drove slowly down the empty boulevard, noticing the drugstores and clothing stores and inexpensive restaurants lining the sidewalks where upscale boutiques, gift stores, and Haagen-Dazs parlors should have been. This looked like Pearl Street had looked when I had come to Boulder in the early '70s—just another western town's *street* with rents that real retailers could afford.

I realized that it *was* the Pearl Street of the early '70s. I drove past Fred's Steakhouse where Maria and I used to have the occasional Friday steak dinner when we'd saved enough money. Fred had thrown in the towel and surrendered to the mall boutique rental prices . . . when? . . . at least fifteen years ago. And there was the old Art Cinema, showing Bergman's *Cries and Whispers.* It hadn't been a real movie theater for a decade. I could not remember when *Cries and Whispers* had been released, but I seem to recall seeing it with Maria before we moved to Boulder after my discharge in '69.

I won't list all the rest of the anomalies—the old cars at the curb, the antiquated street signs, the antiwar graffiti on the walls and stop signs—just as I did not try to list them that day. I drove as quickly as I could to my apartment on 30th Street, barely noting as I did that Crossroads Mall at the end of Canyon Boulevard simply was there but drastically smaller than I remembered.

My apartment building was not there at all.

For a while I just stood up in my Jeep, staring at the fields and trees and old garages where my apartment complex should be, and resisting the urge to scream or shout. It was not so much that my apartment was gone, or my clothes, or my few mementos of the life I had already left behind—some snapshots of Maria that I never look at, old softball trophies, my 1984

Teacher of the Year finalist plaque—it was just that my bottles of Scotch were gone.

Then I realized how silly that response was, drove to the first liquor store I could find—an old mom-and-pop place on 28th where a new mini-mall had been the day before—walked in the open door, shouted, was not surprised when no one answered, liberated three bottles of Johnnie Walker, left a heap of bills on the counter—I might be crazy, but I was no thief—and then went out to the empty parking lot to have a drink and think things over.

I have to say that there was very little denial. Somehow things had changed. I did not seriously consider the possibility that I was dead or that this was like that "lost year" on the *Dallas* TV show some years ago and that I would wake up with Maria in the shower, Allan playing in the living room, my teaching job secure, and my life back together. No, this was real—both my shitty life and this strange . . . *place*. It was Boulder, all right, but Boulder as it had been about two and a half decades earlier. I was shocked at how small and provincial the place seemed.

And empty. Some large raptors circled over the Flatirons, but the city was dead still. Not even the sound of distant traffic or jet aircraft disturbed the summer air. I realized, in its absence, how much of an expected background that sound is for a city dweller such as myself.

I did not know if this was some half-assed sort of random confusion of the space-time continuum, some malfunction of the chronosynclasticinfidibulum, but I suspected not. I suspected that it all had something to do with Kelly Dahl. That's about as far as my speculations had gone by the time I had finished the first half of the first bottle of Johnnie Walker.

Then the phone rang.

It was an old payphone on the side of the liquor store twenty paces away. Even the goddamn phone was different—the side of the half-booth read Bell Telephone rather than U.S. West or one of its rivals and the old Bell logo was embossed in the metal there. It made me strangely nostalgic.

I let the thing ring twelve times before setting the bottle on the hood of the Jeep and walking slowly over to it. Maybe it would be God, explaining that I was dead but I'd only qualified for Limbo, that neither heaven nor hell wanted me.

"Hello?" My voice may have sounded a little funny. It did to me.

"Hi, Mr. Jakes." It was Kelly Dahl, of course. I hadn't really expected God.

"What's going on, kid?"

"Lots of neat stuff" came the soft, high voice. "You ready to play yet?"

I glanced over at the bottle and wished I'd brought it with me. "Play?"

"You're not hunting for me."

I set the receiver down, walked back to the Jeep, took a drink, and walked slowly back to the phone. "You still there, kiddo?"

"Yes."

"I don't want to play. I don't want to hunt for you or kill you or do anything else to you or with you. *Comprendé?*"

"Oui." This was another game I suddenly remembered from sixth grade with this kid. We would begin sentences in one language, shift to another, and end in a third. I never asked her where an eleven-year-old had learned the basics of half a dozen or more languages.

"Okay," I said. "I'm leaving now. You take care of yourself, kid. And stay the fuck away from me. *Ciao.*" I slammed the receiver down and watched it warily for at least two minutes. It did not ring again.

I secured the second bottle on the floorboards so it wouldn't break and drove north on 28th until I got to the Diagonal—the four-lane highway that runs northeast to Longmont and then continues on up the string of towns along the Front Range. The first thing I noticed was that the Boulder section of the Diagonal was two-lane . . . when had they widened it? The '80s sometime . . . and the second thing I noticed was that it ended only a quarter of a mile or so outside of town. To the northeast there was nothing: not just no highway, but no farm houses, no farm fields, no Celestial Seasonings plant, no IBM plant, no railroad tracks—not even the structures that had been there in the early '70s. What *was* there was a giant crack in the earth, a fissure at least twenty feet deep and thirty feet wide. It looked as if an earthquake had left this cleft separating the highway and Boulder from the high prairie of sagebrush and low grass beyond. The fissure stretched to the northwest and southeast as far as I could see and there was no question of getting the Jeep across it without hours of work.

"*Sehr gut,*" I said aloud. "Score one for the kid." I swung the Jeep around and drove back to 28th Street, noticing that the shorter route of the Foothills Highway had not yet been built, and drove south across town to take Highway 36 into Denver.

The fissure began where the highway ended. The cleft seemed to run all the way to the Flatirons to the west.

"Great," I said to the hot sky. "I get the picture. Only I don't think I want to stay. Thanks anyway."

My Jeep is old and ugly, but it's useful. A few years ago I had an electric winch installed on the front with two hundred feet of cable wrapped around its drum. I powered it up, took the drum brake off, secured the cable around a solid bridge stanchion about thirty feet from the edge of the fissure, set it again, and prepared to back the Jeep down the fifty-degree embankment. I didn't know if I could climb the opposite slope even in 4-wheel-low, but I figured I'd think of something when I got down there. If worse came to worse, I'd come back, find a bulldozer somewhere, and grade my own way out of this trap. Anything was preferable to playing Kelly Dahl's game by Kelly Dahl's rules.

I'd just gotten the rear wheels over the brink and was edging over with just the cable keeping me from falling when the first shot rang out. It shattered my windshield, sending the right-side windshield wiper flying into the air in two pieces. For a second I froze. Don't let anyone tell you that old combat reflexes last forever.

The second shot smashed the Jeep's right headlight and exited through the fender. I don't know what the third shot hit, because old reflexes finally reasserted themselves and I was out of the Jeep and scrambling for cover along the steep cliffside by then, my face in the dust, my fingers clawing for a hold. She fired seven times—I never doubted that it was Kelly Dahl—and each bullet created some mischief, taking off my rearview mirror, puncturing two tires, and even smashing the last two bottles of Johnnie Walker Red where I'd left them cushioned beneath the seat, wrapped in my shirt. I have to believe that last was a lucky shot.

I waited the better part of an hour before crawling out of the cleft, looking at the distant buildings for any sign of the crazy woman with the rifle, winching the Jeep out on its two flat tires, and cursing over the smashed bottle. I changed the right front with the spare I had and limped into town, thinking that I'd head for the tire place on Pearl—if that was there yet. Instead, I saw another Jeep parked in a lot near 28th and Arapaho and I just pulled in beside it, took one of its new, knobby tires, decided that my spare was in bad shape and the rear tires looked shitty with these new ones on front, and ended up changing all four tires. I suppose I could have just hotwired the new Jeep and have been done with it without all that sweat and cursing under the blazing July sun, but I didn't. I'm sentimental.

In the early afternoon I drove to the old Gart Brothers sporting goods store and chose the Remington with the twenty-power scope, the .38 handgun, the Ka-bar knife of the sort that had been prized in Vietnam, and enough ammunition for the two guns to fight a small war. Then I drove to the old army surplus store on Pearl and 14th and stocked up on boots, socks, a camouflaged hunting vest, backpacking rations, a new Coleman gas stove, extra binoculars, better raingear than I had in the old pack, lots of nylon line, a new sleeping bag, two compasses, a nifty hunting cap that probably made me look like a real asshole, and even more ammunition for the Remington. I did not leave any money on the counter when I left. I had the feeling that the proprietor was not coming back and doubted if I would be, either.

I drove back to the mom-and-pop liquor store on 28th, but the shelves were empty. The hundreds of bottles that had been there three hours before were simply gone. The same was true of the four other liquor stores I tried.

"You bitch," I said to the empty street.

A phone rang in an old glass booth across a parking lot. It kept ringing as I removed the .38 Police Special from its case, opened the yellow box, and slowly loaded the cylinder. It stopped ringing on my third shot when I hit the phone box dead center.

A pay phone across the street rang.

"Listen, you little bitch," I said as soon as I picked it up, "I'll play your game if you'll leave me something to drink."

This time I did expect God to be on the other end.

"You find me and stop me, and you'll have all the booze you want, Mr. Jakes" came Kelly Dahl's voice.

"Everything will be the way it was?" I was looking around as I spoke, half expecting to see her down the street in another phone booth.

"Yep," said Kelly Dahl. "You can even go back up in the hills and drive into a mineshaft, and I won't interfere the next time."

"So I actually drove into it? Did I die? Are you my punishment?"

"*Mu,*" said Kelly Dahl. "Remember the two other Eco-Week fieldtrips?"

I thought a minute. "The water filtration plant and Trail Ridge Road."

"Very good," said Kelly Dahl. "You can find me at the higher of those two."

"Do the roads continue to the west . . ." I began. I was talking to a dial tone.

III
Palimpsest

On the day I surprised Kelly Dahl near the mountain town of
Ward, she almost killed me. I had set an ambush, remembering
my training from the good old Vietnam years, waiting patiently
where the Left Hand Canyon road wound up to the Peak to
Peak Highway. There were only three ways to get up to the Continental Divide along this stretch of the Front Range, and I
knew Kelly would take the shortest.

There had been a chainsaw in the old firehouse in Ward. The
town itself was empty, of course, but even before Kelly Dahl
kidnapped me to this place there were never more than a hundred people in Ward—hippies left over from the '60s mostly.
The old mining town had been turned into a scrapheap of abandoned vehicles, half-built houses, woodpiles, junk heaps, and
geodesic outhouses. I set the ambush on the switchback above
the town, cutting down two ponderosa pines to block the road.
Then I waited in the aspen grove.

Kelly Dahl's Bronco came up the road late that afternoon.
She stopped, got out of the truck, looked at the fallen trees, and
then looked over at me as I stepped around a tree and began
walking toward her. I had left the Remington behind. The .38
was tucked in my waistband under my jacket; the Ka-bar knife
remained in its sheath.

"Kelly," I said. "Let's talk."

That was when she reached back into the Bronco, came out
with a powerful bow made of some dark composite material,
notched an arrow before I could speak again, and let fly. It was a
hunting arrow—steel-tipped, barbed for maximum damage—
and it passed under my left arm, tearing my jacket, ripping flesh
on the inside of my arm and above my ribcage, and embedding
itself in the aspen centimeters behind me.

I was pinned there for an instant, a bug pinned on a collecting
tray, and could only stare as Kelly Dahl notched another arrow. I

had no doubt that this one would find its target in my sternum. Before she could release the second arrow, I fumbled in my belt, came out with the .38, and fired blindly, wildly, seeing her duck behind the Bronco as I tore myself free from the tattered remnants of my jacket and leaped behind the fallen log.

I heard the Bronco roar a moment later but I did not look up until the truck was gone, driving over the fallen trees as it turned and accelerating through Ward and back down the canyon.

It took a trip back to Boulder—an early '80s version this time but still as empty—to find bandages and antibiotic for the slash on my ribs and inner arm. It is beginning to scar over now, but it still hurts when I walk or breathe deeply.

I carry the Remington everywhere now.

EVEN after I had been teaching drunk for two years, the central administration did not have the balls to fire me. Our Master Agreement specified that because I was tenured, malfeasance and gross incompetence had to be documented by one or more administrators, I had to be given at least three chances to redeem myself, and I was to enjoy due process every step of the way. As it turned out, the high school principal and the director of secondary education were too chickenshit to confront me with any documentation sessions, I didn't want to redeem myself, and everyone was too busy trying to figure out a way to hide me from sight or get rid of me outside of channels to worry about due process. In the end, the Superintendent ordered the Director of Elementary Instruction—a gray carbuncle of a woman named Dr. Maxine Millard—to observe me the required number of times, to give me my warnings and chances to rehabilitate myself, and then to do the necessary paperwork to get rid of me.

I knew the days that Dr. Max was going to be there so I could have called in sick or at least not shown up drunk or hungover, but I figured—Fuck it, let them do their worst. They did. My tenure was revoked and I was dismissed from the district three years and two days before I could have put in for early retirement.

I don't miss the job. I missed the kids, even the slumpy, acned, socially inept high school kids. Oddly, I remember the little kids from my earlier years in elementary even more clearly. And miss them more.

A sage without a stage is no sage, drunk or sober.

THIS morning I followed Kelly Dahl's tire tracks down Flagstaff Mountain on a narrow gravel road, came out where Chautauqua Park should be to find Boulder gone and the Inland Sea back again. Only this time, far out on the mudflats, reachable by a long causeway raised just feet above the quicksand beds, was a great island of stone with a walled city rising from its rocks, a great cathedral rising from the stone city, and Michael the Archangel standing on the summit of the tallest tower, his sword raised, his foot firmly planted on a writhing devil, a cock signifying eternal vigilance perched on his mailed foot.

"Christ, Kelly," I said to the tire tracks as I followed them across the causeway, "this is getting a little elaborate."

It was Mont-Saint-Michel, of course, complete down to its last stained glass window and wrought-iron balustrade. I only vaguely remembered showing my sixth-grade class the slides of it. The 12th Century structure had caught my fancy the summer before when I took my family there. Maria had not been impressed, but ten-year-old Allan had flipped over it. He and I bought every book on the subject that we could and seriously discussed building a model of the fortress-cathedral out of balsa wood.

Kelly Dahl's old Bronco was parked outside the gate. I took the Remington, actioned a round into the breech, and went through the gate and up the cobblestone walkway in search of her. My footfalls echoed. Occasionally I paused, looked back over the ramparts at the Flatirons gleaming in the Colorado sunshine, and listened for her footsteps above the lap of lazy waves. There were noises higher up.

The cathedral was empty, but a thin book made of heavy parchment bound in leather had been set on the central altar. I picked up the vellum and read:

Ço sent Rollánz que la mort le trespent
Desuz un pin i est alez curanz
Sur l'erbe verte si est suchiez adenz
Desuz lui met s'espree e l'olifant
Turnat sa teste vers la paiene gent.

This was Eleventh Century French verse. I knew it from my last year of college. This was the kind of thing I had devoted my life to translating in those final months before being drafted and sent around the world to kill small Asian people.

Then Roland feels that death is taking him;
Down from the head upon the heart it falls.
Beneath a pine he hastens running;
On the green grass he throws himself down;
Beneath him puts his sword and oliphant,
Turns his face toward the pagan army.

I set down the book and shouted into the gloom of the cathedral. "Is this a threat, kid?" Only echoes answered.

The next page I recognized as Thibaut, 13th Century:

Nus hom ne puet ami reconforte
Se cele non ou il a son cuer mis.
Pour ce m'estuet sovent plaindre et plourer
Que nus confors ne me vient, ce m'est vis,
De la ou j'ai tote ma remembrance.
Pour biens amer ai sovent esmaiance
      A dire voir.
Dame, merci! donez moi esperance
      De joie avoir.

This took me a moment. Finally I thought I had it.

There is no comfort to be found in pain
Save only where the heart has made its home.

Therefore I can but murmur and complain
Because no comfort to my pain has come
From where I garnered all my happiness.
From true love have I only earned distress
    The truth to say.
Grace, lady! give me comfort to possess
    A hope, one day.

"Kelly!" I shouted into the cathedral shadows. "I don't need this shit!" When there was no answer, I raised the Remington and fired a single slug into the huge stained-glass window of the Virgin opposite the altar. The echo of the shot and of falling glass was still sounding as I left.

I dropped the handmade book into the quicksand as I drove back across the causeway.

WHEN I returned home from the hospital after the accident that killed Allan, I found that Maria had emptied our eleven-year-old son's room of all his possessions, our house of all images and records of him. His clothes were gone. The posters and photographs and desk clutter and old *Star Trek* models hanging from black thread in his room—all gone. The rocking-horse quilt she had made for him the month before he was born was gone from his bed. The bed was stripped as clean as the walls and closet, as if his room and bed were in a dormitory or barracks, waiting sterilely for the next recruits to arrive.

There were no next recruits.

Maria had purged the photo albums of any image of Allan. It was as if his eleven years simply had not been. The family photo we had kept on our bedroom dresser was gone, as were the snapshots that had been held to the refrigerator door by magnets. His fifth-grade school portrait was no longer in the drawer in the study, and all of the baby pictures were gone from the shoebox. I never found out if she had given the clothes and toys and sports equipment to the Salvation Army, or burned the photographs, or buried them. She would not speak of it. She would not speak of Allan. When I forced the subject, Maria's eyes took on a stubborn, distant look. I soon learned not to force the subject.

This was the summer after I taught my last sixth-grade class. Allan would have been a year younger than Kelly Dahl, twenty-two now, out of college, finding his way in the world. It is very difficult to imagine.

I tracked her to Trail Ridge Road but left the Jeep behind at the beginning of the tundra. There was no Trail Ridge Road—no sign of human existence—only the tundra extending up beyond treeline. It was very cold out of the shelter of the trees. When I'd awakened at my high camp that morning, it had felt like late autumn. The skies were leaden, there were clouds in the valleys below, hiding the lateral moraines, wisps of cloud edge curling up against the mountainsides like tentacles of fog. The air was freezing. I cursed myself for not bringing gloves and balled my hands in the pockets of my jacket, the Remington cold and heavy against my forearms.

Passing the last of the stunted trees, I tried to remember the name for these ancient dwarfs at treeline.

Krummholz came Kelly Dahl's voice almost in my ear. *It means "elfin timber" or "crooked wood."*

I dropped to one knee on the frozen moss, the rifle coming up. There was no one within a hundred meters of open tundra. I scoped the treeline, the boulders large enough to hide a human figure. Nothing moved.

I love all the tundra terms you taught us, continued Kelly's voice in my mind. She had done this only a few times before. *Fellfield, meadow vole, boreal chorus frog, snowball saxifrage, solifluction terraces, avens and sedges, yellow-bellied marmots, permafrost, nivation depressions, saffron ragworts, green-leaf chiming bells, man-hater sedge . . .*

I looked up and out across the windswept tundra. Nothing moved. But I had been wrong about there being no sign of human existence: a well-worn trail ran across the permafrost field toward the summit of the pass. I began following it. "I thought you hated all the technical terms," I said aloud, the rifle ready in the crook of my arm. My ribs and the inside of my left arm ached from where her arrow had cut deep.

I like poetry. Her voice was in my mind, not my ear. The only real sound was the wind. But her voice was real enough.

Mr. Jakes, do you remember that Robert Frost thing you read us about poetry?

I was two hundred meters out from the last line of krummholz now. There were some house-sized boulders about three hundred meters above and to my left. She might be hiding there. I sensed that she was close.

"Which poem?" I said. If I could keep her talking, thinking, she might not notice my approach.

Not poem, the Frost introduction to one of his books. It was about the figure a poem makes.

"I don't remember," I said. I did. I had shared that with the high school juniors only weeks before Kelly Dahl had quit school and run away.

Frost said that it should be the pleasure of a poem itself to tell how it can. He said that a poem begins in delight and ends in wisdom. He said the figure is the same for love.

"Mmmm," I said, moving quickly across the permafrost field now, my breath fogging the air as I panted. The rifle was gripped in both hands, the cold forgotten. "Tell me more."

Stop a minute. Kelly Dahl's voice was flat in my mind.

I paused, panting. The boulders were less than fifty meters from me. The trail I had been following cut across the grassy area once used by the Ute and Pawnee women, old people, and youngsters to cross the Divide. This path looked newly used, as if the Utes had just disappeared over the rock saddle ahead of me.

I don't think the Indians left trails, came Kelly Dahl's soft voice in my mind. *Look down.*

Still trying to catch my breath, dizzy with the altitude and adrenaline, I looked down. A plant was growing on the cushioned terrace between two low rocks there. The wind was whipping snow past me; the temperature must have been in the twenties, if not lower.

Look more closely.

Still gasping for air, I went to one knee on the fellfield. When Kelly Dahl's voice began again, I took the opportunity to action a round into the Remington's chamber.

See those little trenches in the soil, Mr. Jakes? They look like smooth runways, little toboggan runs through the tundra. Do you remember teaching us about them?

I shook my head, all the time watching for movement out of the corner of my eye. I truly did not remember. My passion for alpine ecology had burned away with all of my other passions. Not even an ember of interest remained. "Tell me," I said aloud, as if hearing the echo of her mental voice would reveal her position to me.

They were originally burrows dug out by pocket gophers came her soft voice, sounding mildly amused. *The soil's so tough and rocky up here, that not even earthworms tunnel, but the pocket gopher digs these shallow burrows. When the gopher goes away, the smaller meadow voles claim them. See where their feet have made the earth smooth? Look closer, Mr. Jakes.*

I lay on the soft moss, laying my rifle ahead of me casually, as if just setting it out of the way. The barrel was aimed toward the boulders above. If something moved, I could be sighted in on it within two seconds. I glanced down at a collapsed gopher burrow. It did look like a dirt-smoothed toboggan run, one of hundreds that crisscrossed this section of tundra like an exposed labyrinth, like some indecipherable script left by aliens.

The vole keeps using these little highways in the winter, said Kelly Dahl. *Under the snow. Up here we would see giant drifts and an empty, sterile world. But under the snow, the vole is shuttling around, carrying out her business, collecting the grasses she harvested and stored in the autumn, chewing out the centers of cushion plants, munching on taproots. And somewhere nearby, the pocket gopher is digging away.*

Something gray did move near the boulders. I leaned closer to the collapsed vole run, closer to the rifle. The snow was suddenly thicker, whipping down the permafrost field like a curtain of gauze that now lifted, now lowered.

In the spring, continued Kelly Dahl's soft voice in my head, *the tops of all these pocket gopher tunnels appear from beneath the melting snowbanks. The ridges are called eskers and look like brown snakes looping around everywhere. You taught us that a pocket gopher up here could dig a tunnel more than a hundred feet long in a single night and move up to eight tons of topsoil per acre in a year.*

"Did I teach that?" I said. The gray shape in the snow separated itself from the gray boulders. I quit breathing and set my finger on the trigger guard.

It's fascinating, isn't it, Mr. Jakes? That there's one visible winter world up here on the tundra—cold, inhospitable, intolerable—but the most defenseless animals here just create another world right under the surface where they can continue to survive. They're even necessary to the ecology, bringing subsoil up and burying plants that will decompose quicker underground. Everything fits.

I leaned forward as if to set my face to the plant, lifted the rifle in a single motion, centered the moving gray form in the crosshairs, and fired. The gray figure fell.

"Kelly?" I said as I ran panting up the tundra, moving from solifluction terrace to solifluction terrace.

There was no answer.

I expected nothing to be there when I arrived at the boulders, but she had fallen exactly where I had last seen the movement. The arterial blood was bright, excruciatingly bright, the single bold color almost shocking on the dim and dun tundra. The bullet had taken her behind the right eye, which was still open and questioning. I guessed that the cow elk was an adult but not quite fully grown. Snowflakes settled on its gray, hairy side, still melted on the pink of its extruded tongue.

Gasping for breath, I stood straight and spun around, surveying the rocks, the tundra, the lowering sky, the clouds rising like wraiths from the cold valleys below. "Kelly?"

Only the wind responded.

I looked down. The elk's luminous but fading black eye seemed to be conveying a message.

Things can die here.

THE last time I saw Kelly Dahl in the real world, the other world, had been at a late-season basketball game. I hated basketball—I hated all of the school's inane and insanely cheered sports—but it was part of my job as low-man-on-the-totem-pole English teacher to do *something* at the damn events, so I was ticket-taker. At least that way I could leave twenty minutes or so into the game when they closed the doors.

I remember coming out of the gym into the freezing darkness—it was officially spring but Colorado rarely recognizes the end of winter until late May, if then—and seeing a familiar figure heading down Arapaho going the opposite direction. Kelly Dahl had not been in class for several days that week, and rumor was that she had moved. I jogged across the street, avoiding patches of black ice, and caught up to her under a streetlight a block east of the school.

She turned as if unsurprised to see me, almost as if she had been waiting for me to follow her. "Hey, Mr. Jakes. What's happening?" Her eyes were redder than usual, her face pinched and white. The other instructors were sure that she was using drugs and I had finally, reluctantly, come to the same conclusion. There was little trace of the eleven-year-old girl in the gaunt woman's face I stared into that night.

"You been sick, Kelly?"

She returned my stare. "No, I just haven't been going to school."

"You know Van Der Mere will call in your mother."

Kelly Dahl shrugged. Her jacket was far too thin for such a

cold night. When we spoke, our breath hung between us like a veil. "She's gone," said Kelly.

"Gone where?" I asked, knowing it was none of my business but feeling the concern for this child rise in me like faint nausea.

Again the shrug.

"You coming back to school on Monday?" I asked.

Kelly Dahl did not blink. "I'm not coming back."

I remember wishing at the time that I had not given up smoking the year before. It would have been good at that moment to light a cigarette and take a drag before speaking. Instead, I said, "Well, shit, Kelly."

The pale face nodded.

"Why don't we go somewhere and talk about it, kiddo."

She shook her head. A car roared past and slid into the school parking lot, latecomers shouting. Neither of us turned to look.

"Why don't we . . ." I began.

"No," said Kelly Dahl. "You and I had our chance, Mr. Jakes."

I frowned at her in the cold light from the streetlamp. "What do you mean?"

For a long moment I was sure she would say nothing else, that she was on the verge of turning away and disappearing into the dark. Instead, she took a deep breath and let it out slowly. "You remember the year . . . the seven months . . . I was in your sixth-grade class, Mr. Jakes?"

"Of course."

"You remember how I almost worshipped the ground you walked on . . . excuse the cliché."

It was my turn to take a breath. "Look, Kelly, a lot of kids in sixth grade, especially girls . . ."

She waved me into silence, as if we had too little time for such formalized dialogue. "I just meant I thought you were the one person who I might have talked to then, Mr. Jakes. In all the middle of what was going on . . . my mother, Carl . . . well, I thought you were the most solid, *real* thing in the universe that crazy, fucked-up winter."

"Carl . . ." I said.

"My mother's boyfriend," said Kelly in that soft voice. "My . . . *stepfather.*" I could hear the heavy irony in her voice, but I could hear something else, something infinitely more ragged and sad.

I took half a step in her direction. "Did he . . . was there . . ."

Kelly Dahl twitched a half-smile in the cold light. "Oh, yeah. He did. There was. Every day. Not just that school year, but most of the summer before." She looked away, toward the street.

I had the urge to put an arm around her then—seeing the girl there rather than the gaunt young woman—but all I could do was ball my hands into fists, tighter and tighter. "Kelly, I had no idea . . ."

She was not listening or looking at me. "I learned how to go away then. Find the other places."

"Other places . . ." I did not understand.

Kelly Dahl did not look at me. Her punk mohawk and streaked hair looked pathetic in the flat, cold light. "I got very good at going away to the other places. The things you were teaching us helped—I could see them, you taught them so clearly—and whatever I could see, I could visit."

My insides were shaking with the cold. The child needed psychiatric help. I thought of all the times I had referred children to school counselors and district psychologists and county social services, always to see little or nothing done, the child returned to whatever nightmare they had temporarily found themselves free of.

"Kelly, let's . . ."

"I almost told you," continued Kelly Dahl, her lips thin and white. "I worked up the nerve all that week in April to tell you." She made a brittle sound that I realized was a laugh. "Hell, I'd been working up nerve all that school year to tell you. I figured that you were the one person in the world who might listen . . . might believe . . . might *do something.*"

I waited for her to go on. Cheers came from the school gym a block away.

Kelly Dahl looked at me then. There was something wild in her green eyes. "Remember I asked if I could stay after school and talk to you that day?"

I frowned, finally had to shake my head. I could not remember.

She smiled again. "It was the same day you told us you were leaving. That you'd taken a job teaching at the high school, that they needed somebody because Mrs. Webb had died. You told us that there'd be a substitute teacher with us the rest of the year. I don't think you expected the class to get all upset the way it did. I remember most of the girls were crying. I wasn't."

"Kelly, I . . ."

"You didn't remember that I'd said I wanted to see you after school," she said, her voice an ironic whisper. "But that was okay, because I didn't stay anyway. I don't know if you remember, but I wasn't one of the kids who hugged you good-bye after the surprise going away party that the kids threw that next Friday."

We looked at each other for a silent moment. There were no cheers from the gym. "Where are you going, Kelly?"

She looked at me so fiercely that I felt a pang of fear that moment, but whether for her or me, I am not sure. "Away," she said. "Away."

"Come to the school on Monday to talk to me," I said, stepping closer to her. "You don't have to come to class. Just come by the home room and we'll talk. Please." I raised my hands but stopped just short of touching her.

Kelly Dahl's stare did not waver. "Good-bye, Mr. Jakes." Then she turned and crossed the street and disappeared in the dark.

I thought about following her then, but I was tired, I'd promised Allan that we would go into Denver to shop for baseball cards the next morning, and whenever I got home late from some school thing, Maria was sure that I'd been out with another woman.

I thought about following Kelly Dahl that night, but I did not.

On Monday she did not come. On Tuesday I called her home, but there was no answer. On Wednesday I told Mr. Van Der Mere about our conversation and a week later social services dropped by the trailer park. The trailer had been abandoned. Kelly's mother and the boyfriend had left about a month before the girl had quit coming to school. No one had seen Kelly Dahl since the weekend of the basketball game.

A month later, when word came that Kelly Dahl's mother had been found murdered in North Platte, Nebraska, and that Carl Reems, her boyfriend, had confessed to the crime after being caught in Omaha, most of the teachers thought that Kelly had been murdered as well, despite the chronology to the contrary. Posters of the seventeen-year-old were seen around Boulder for a month or so, but Reems denied doing anything to her right up to his conviction for the murder of Patricia Dahl. Kelly was probably considered to be just another runaway by the police, and she was too old for her face to appear on milk cartons. It seemed there were no relatives who cared to pursue the subject.

It was early that summer that the pickup came across the centerline and Allan died and I ceased to live.

I find Kelly Dahl by mistake.

It has been weeks, months, here in this place, these places. Reality is the chase, confirmation of that reality is the beard I have grown, the deer and elk I kill for fresh food, the pain in my side and arm as the arrow wound continues to scar over, the increasing fitness in my legs and lungs and body as I spend ten to fourteen hours a day outside, looking for Kelly Dahl.

And I find her by mistake.

I had been returning to the Front Range from following signs of Kelly Dahl south almost to the Eisenhower Tunnel, I had lost her for a full day, and now evening shadows found me south of Nederland along the Peak to Peak Highway. Since there might be no highway when morning came if the time/place shifted, I stopped at a forest service campground—empty of people and vehicles, of course—pitched my tent, filled my water bottles, and cooked up some venison over the fire. I was fairly sure that the last few days had been spent in that 1970-ish landscape in which I'd first found myself—roads and infrastructure in place, people not—and true autumn was coming on. Aspen leaves filled the air like golden parade confetti and the evening wind blew cold.

I find Kelly Dahl by becoming lost.

I used to brag that I have never been lost. Even in the densest lodgepole pine forest, my sense of direction has served me well. I am good in the woods, and the slightest landmark sets me on my way as if I have an internal compass that is never off by more than two or three degrees. Even on cloudy days the sunlight speaks direction to me. At night, a glimpse of stars will set me straight.

Not this evening. Walking out of the empty campground, I climb a mile or so through thick forest to watch the sun set north of the Arapahoes but south of Mt. Audubon. Twilight does not linger. There is no moon. Beyond the Front Range to the east, where the glow of Denver and its string of satellite cities should be, there is only darkness. Clouds move in to obliterate the night sky. I cut back toward the campground, dropping down from one ridge to climb another, confident that this way is shorter. Within ten minutes I am lost.

The sensation of being lost without my rifle, without a compass, with only the Ka-bar knife in its sheath on my belt, is not disturbing. At first. Ninety minutes later, deep in a lodgepole thicket, miles from anywhere, the sky above as dark as the forest below, I am beginning to be worried. I have worn only my sweater over a flannel shirt; it may snow before morning. I think of my parka and sleeping bag back at the campsite, of the firewood stacked in the circle of stones and the hot tea I was planning to have before turning in.

"Idiot," I say to myself, stumbling down a dark slope, almost plunging into a barbed wire fence. Painfully picking my way over the fence—sure that there had been no fences near the campground—I think again, *idiot,* and begin to wonder if I should hunker down for the cold wait until dawn.

At that moment I see Kelly Dahl's fire.

I never doubt it is her fire—I have been here long enough to know that she is now the only other person in our universe—

and, when I come closer, moving silently through the last twenty meters of brush to the clearing, it is indeed Kelly Dahl, sitting in the circle of light from the flames, looking at a harmonica in her hands and seemingly lost in thought.

I wait several minutes, sensing a trap. She remains engrossed in the play of firelight on the chrome surface of the instrument, her face mildly sunburned. She is still wearing the hiking boots, shorts, and thick sweatshirt I had last seen her in three days earlier, just after leaving Mont-Saint-Michel. Her hunting bow—a powerful bend of some space-age composite, several steel-edged killing arrows notched onto the frame—lies strung and ready against the log she sits on.

Perhaps I make a noise. Perhaps she simply becomes aware of my presence. Whatever the reason, she looks up—startled, I see—her head moving toward the dark trees where I hide.

I make the decision within a second. Two seconds later I am hurtling across the dark space that separates us, sure that she will have time to lift the bow, notch the arrow, and let fly toward my heart. But she does not turn toward the bow until the last second and then I am on her, leaping across the last six feet, knocking her down and sideways, the bow and the deadly arrows flying into the darkness on one side of the log, Kelly and me rolling near the fire on the other side.

I guess that I am still stronger but that she is quicker, infinitely more agile. I think that if I act quickly enough, this will not matter.

We roll twice and then I am on top of her, slapping away her hands, pulling the Ka-bar knife from its sheath. She swings a leg up but I pin it with my own, swing my other knee out, squeeze her legs together beneath me with the strength of my thighs. Her hands are raking at my sweater, nails tearing toward my face, but I use my left arm and the weight of my upper body to squeeze her arms between us as I lean forward, the knife moving to her throat.

For a second, as the tempered steel touches the pulsing flesh of her neck, there is no more movement, only my weight on hers and the memory of the moment's wild friction between us. We are both panting. The wind scatters the sparks of the fire and blows aspen leaves out of the darkness above us. Kelly Dahl's green eyes are open, appraising, surprised but unafraid, waiting. Our faces are only inches apart.

I move the knife so that the cutting edge is turned away from her throat, lean forward, and kiss her gently on the cheek. Pulling my face back so that I can focus on her eyes again, I whisper, "I'm sorry, Kelly." Then I roll off her, my right arm coming up against the log she had been sitting on.

Kelly Dahl is on me in a second, lunging sideways in a fluid manner that I have always imagined, but never seen, a panther strike. She straddles my chest, sets a solid forearm across my windpipe, and uses the other hand to slam my wrist against the log, catching the knife as it bounces free. Then the blade is against my own throat. I cannot lower my chin enough to see it, but I can feel it, the scalpel-sharp edge slicing taut skin above my windpipe. I look into her eyes.

"You found me," she says, swinging the blade down and to the side in a precise killing movement.

Expecting to feel blood rushing from my severed jugular, I feel only the slight razor burn where the edge had touched me a second before. That and cold air against the intact flesh of my throat. I swallow once.

Kelly Dahl flings the Ka-bar into the darkness near where the bow had gone, her strong hands pull my wrists above my head, and she leans her weight on her elbows on either side of me. "You did find me," she whispers, and lowers her face to mine.

What happens next is not clear. It is possible that she kisses me, possible that we kiss each other, but time ceases to be sequential at that moment so it is possible that we do not kiss at all. What *is* clear—and shall remain so until the last moment of my life—is that in this final second before seconds cease to follow one another I move my arms to take her weight off her elbows, and Kelly Dahl relaxes onto me with what may be a sigh, the warmth of her face envelops the warmth of my face, a shared warmth more intimate than any kiss, the length of her body lies full along the length of my body, and then—inexplicably—she continues descending, moving closer, skin against skin, body against body, but *more* than that, entering me as I enter her in a way that is beyond sexual. She passes into me as a ghost would pass through some solid form, slowly, sensually but without self-conscious effort, melding, melting into me, her form still tangible, still touchable, but moving through me as if our atoms were the stars in colliding galaxies, passing through each other without contact but rearranging the gravity there forever.

I do not remember us speaking. I remember only the three sighs—Kelly Dahl's, mine, and the sigh of the wind coming up to scatter the last sparks of the fire that had somehow burned down to embers while time had stopped.

IV
Palinode

I knew instantly upon awakening—alone—that everything had changed. There was a difference to the light, the air. A difference to me. I felt more attached to my senses than I had in years, as if some barrier had been lifted between me and the world.

But the world was different. I sensed it at once. More real. More permanent. I felt fuller but the world felt more empty.

My Jeep was in the campground. The tent was where I had left it. There were other tents, other vehicles. Other people. A middle-aged couple having breakfast outside their Winnebago waved in a friendly manner as I walked past. I could not manage a return wave.

The resident camp ranger ambled over as I was loading the tent in the back of the Jeep.

"Didn't see you come in last night," he said. "Don't seem to have a permit. That'll be seven dollars. Unless you want to stay another day. That'll be seven more. Three night limit here. Lots of folks this summer."

I tried to speak, could not, and found—to my mild surprise—
that my billfold still had money in it. I handed the ranger a ten
dollar bill and he counted back the change.

He was leaving when I finally called to him. "What month is it?"

He paused, smiled. "Still July, the last time I looked."

I nodded my thanks. Nothing else needed to be explained.

I showered and changed clothes in my apartment. Everything
was as I had left it the night before. There were four bottles of
Scotch in the kitchen cabinet. I lined them up on the counter
and started to pour them down the sink, realized that I did not
have to—I had no urge to take a drink—and set them back in
the cabinet.

I drove first to the elementary school where I had taught
years ago. The teachers and students were gone for the summer,
but some of the office staff were there for the summer migrant
program. The principal was new, but Mrs. Collins, the secretary,
knew me.

"Mr. Jakes," she said. "I almost didn't recognize you in that
beard. You look good in it. And you've lost weight and you're all
tanned. Have you been on vacation?"

I grinned at her. "Sort of."

The files were still there. I was afraid that they'd gone to the
district headquarters or followed the kids through junior high
and high school, but the policy was to duplicate essential material and start new files beginning with seventh grade.

All of the students from that last sixth-grade class were still
in the box in the storage closet downstairs, all of their cumulative record folders mildewing away with the individual class
photos of the students staring out—bright eyes, braces, bad
haircuts from a decade before. They were all there. Everyone
but Kelly Dahl.

"Kelly Dahl," repeated Mrs. Collins when I came up from the
basement and queried her. "Kelly Dahl. Strange, Mr. Jakes, but
I don't remember a child named Kelly Dahl. Kelly Daleson,
but that was several years before you left. And Kevin Dale . . .

but that was a few years before you were here. Was he here very long? It might have been a transfer student who transferred back out, although I usually remember . . ."

"She," I said. "It was a girl. And she was here a couple of years."

Mrs. Collins frowned as if I had insulted her powers of recall. "Kelly Dahl," she said. "I really don't think so, Mr. Jakes. I remember most of the students. It's why I suggested to Mr. Pembroke that this thing wasn't necessary . . ." She waved dismissively toward the computer on her desk. "Are you *sure* the child was in one of your sixth-grade classes . . . not someone in high school or someone you met . . . after?" She pursed her lips at the near *faux pas*.

"No," I said. "It was someone I knew before I was fired. Someone I knew here. Or so I thought."

Mrs. Collins ran fingers through her blue hair. "I may be wrong, Mr. Jakes." She said it in a tone that precluded the possibility.

The high school records agreed with her. There had been no Kelly Dahl. The manager at the trailer park did not remember the three people; in fact, his records and memory showed that the same elderly couple had been renting what I remembered as the Dahl trailer since 1975. There was no microfilm record of the murder of Patricia Dahl in *The Boulder Daily Camera* and calls to North Platte and Omaha revealed no arrest of anyone named Carl Reems at any time in the past twelve years.

I sat on my apartment terrace, watched the summer sun set behind the Flatirons, and thought. When I grew thirsty, ice water satisfied. I thought of the Jeep and camping gear down in the parking stall. There had been a Remington rifle in the back of the Jeep, a .38-caliber revolver in the blue pack. I had never owned a rifle or pistol.

"Kelly," I whispered finally. "You've really managed to go away this time."

I pulled out my billfold and looked at the only photograph of Allan that had escaped Maria's purge—my son's fifth-grade class picture, wallet-size. After a while I put away the photo and bill-fold and went in to sleep.

Weeks passed. Then two months. The Colorado summer slipped into early autumn. The days grew shorter but more pleasant. After three hard interviews, I was offered a job at a private school in Denver. I would be teaching sixth-graders. They knew my history, but evidently thought that I had changed for the better. It was Friday when I finished the final interview. They said they would call me the next day, on Saturday.

They were as good as their word. They sounded truly pleased when they offered me the job—perhaps they knew it meant a new start for me, a new life. They were surprised by my answer.

"No, thank you," I said. "I've changed my mind." I knew now that I could never teach eleven-year-olds again. They would all remind me of Allan, or of Kelly Dahl.

There was a shocked silence. "Perhaps you would like another day to think about it," said Mr. Martin, the headmaster. "This is an important decision. You could call us on Monday."

I started to say "no," began to explain that my mind was made up, but then I heard *Wait until Monday. Do not decide today.*

I paused. My own thoughts had echoed like this before since returning from Kelly Dahl. "Mr. Martin," I said at last, "that might be a good idea. If you don't mind, I'll call you Monday morning with my decision."

On Sunday morning I picked up *The New York Times* at Eads tobacco store, had a late breakfast, watched the 11 A.M. Brinkley news show on ABC, finished reading the *Times Book Review,* and went down to the Jeep about one in the afternoon. It was a beautiful fall day and the drive up Left Hand Canyon and then up the hard jeep trail took less than an hour.

The blue sky was crisscrossed with contrails through the aspen leaves when I stopped the Jeep ten feet from the entrance to the vertical mineshaft.

"Kiddo," I said aloud, tapping my fingers on the steering

wheel. "You found me once. I found you once. Do you think we can do it together this time?"

I was talking to myself and it felt silly. I said nothing else. I put the Jeep in first and floored the accelerator. The hood first rose as we bounced over the lip of the pit, I caught a glimpse of yellow aspen leaves, blue sky, white contrails, and then the black circle of the pit filled the windshield.

I hit the brake with both feet on the pedal. The Jeep slid, bucked, slewed to the left, and came to a stop with the right front tire hanging over the open pit. Shaking slightly, I backed the Jeep up a foot or two, set the brake, got out of the vehicle and leaned against it.

Not this way. Not this time. I did not know if the thought was mine alone. I hoped not.

I stepped closer to the edge, stared down into the pit, and then stepped back.

MONTHS have passed. I took the teaching job in Denver. I love it. I love being with the children. I love being alive again. I am once again the sage on the stage, but a quieter sage this time.

The bad dreams continue to bother me. Not dreams of Kelly Dahl, but Kelly Dahl's dreams. I wake from nightmares of Carl coming into my small room in the trailer, of trying to speak to my mother as she smokes a cigarette and does not listen. I fly awake from dreams of awakening to Carl's heavy hand over my mouth, of his foul breath on my face.

I feel closest to Kelly Dahl at these times. Sitting up on the bed, sweat pouring from me, my heart pounding, I can feel her presence. I like to think that these dreams are an exorcism for her, a long overdue offer of love and help for me.

It is impossible to explain the feeling that Kelly Dahl and I shared that last night in her world . . . in *our* world. Galaxies colliding, I think I said, and I have since looked up the photographic telescope images of that phenomenon: hundreds of billions of stars passing in close proximity as great spiral clusters pinwheel through one another, gravities interacting and changing each spiral forever but no stars actually colliding. This has some of the sense of what I felt that night, but does not explain the aftermath—the knowledge of being changed forever, of being filled with another human's mind and heart and memories, of solitude ceasing. It is impossible to share the knowledge of being not just two people, but four—ourselves here, and truly ourselves where we meet again on that alternate place of going away.

It is not mystical. It is not religious. There is no afterlife, only life.

I cannot explain. But on some days out on the recess grounds, on some warm Colorado winter days when the sunlight is like a solid thing and the high peaks of the Divide gleam to the west as if they were yards away rather than miles, then I close my eyes as the children play, allow myself to hear the wind above the familiar murmur of children at play, and then the echoes of that separate but equal reality are clear enough. Then all this becomes the memory, the echo.

THE Flatirons are gone, but a dirt road leads to low cliffs that look out over the Inland Sea. The Douglas fir, ponderosa pine, and lodgepole trees are gone; the narrow road winds through tropical forests of sixty-foot ferns and flowering cycads the size of small redwoods. Cedarlike conifers let down lacy branches and one unidentifiable tree holds clusters of seeds that resemble massive shaving brushes. The air is humid and almost dizzyingly thick with the smell of eucalyptus, magnolia, something similar to apple blossoms, sycamore, and a riot of more exotic scents. Insects buzz and something very large crashes through the underbrush deep in the fern forest to my right as the Jeep approaches the coast.

Where the Flatirons should be, tidal flats and lagoons reflect the sky. Everything is more textured and detailed than I remember from earlier visits. The sea stretches out to the east, its wave action strong and constant. The road leads to a causeway and the causeway leads across the tidal pools to Mont-Saint-Michel, the city-cathedral and its high walls gleaming in late afternoon light.

Once I pause on the causeway and reach back for my binoculars, scanning the city walls and parapets.

The Ford Bronco is parked outside the gate. Kelly Dahl is on the rampart of the highest wall, near the cathedral entrance high on the stone island. She is wearing a red sweatshirt and I notice that her hair has grown out a bit. The sunlight must be glinting on my field glasses, for as I watch she smiles slightly and raises one hand to wave at me even though I am still a quarter of a mile away.

I set the glasses back in their case and drive on. To my right, in one of the deep pools far out beyond the quicksand flats, a long-necked plesiosaur, perhaps of the alasmosaurian variety, lifts a flat head studded with its fish-catching basket of teeth, peers nearsightedly across the flats at the sound of my Jeep's engine, and then submerges again in the murky water. I stop a moment to watch the ripples but the head does not reappear. Behind me, where the Flatirons and Boulder once were—will someday be—something roars a challenge in the forest of cycads and ferns.

Focusing on the dot of red high on the miracle that is Mont-Saint-Michel, imagining that I can see her waving now—somehow seeing her clearly even without the field glasses—I get the Jeep in gear and drive on.

Introduction to "Orphans of the Helix"

....

This story started—as all stories do—as a vague rumination, quickened into focus during a Star Trek: Voyager *telephone pitch, was midwifed into existence by Robert Silverberg, and finally resulted in me missing the Ninth Annual Lincoln Street Water Fight. It is, I think, a decent story, but it wasn't worth missing the water fight.*

Some readers may know that I've written four novels set in the "Hyperion Universe"—Hyperion, The Fall of Hyperion, Endymion, and The Rise of Endymion. *A perceptive subset of those readers—perhaps the majority—know that this so-called epic actually consists of two long and mutually dependent tales, the two Hyperion stories combined and the two Endymion novels combined, broken into four books because of the realities of publishing. An even smaller subset of readers might know that I've vowed not to write any more novels set in this Hyperion universe for a variety of reasons, chief among them being that I don't want to dilute any existing vitality of the epic in a series of profitable but diminishing-returns-for-the-reader sequels.*

Still, I never promised not to return to my Hyperion universe via the occasional short story or even novella-length tale. Readers enjoy such universes and miss them when they're gone (or when the writer who created them is gone forever) and this nostalgia for old reading pleasures is precisely what gives rise to the kind of posthumous franchising—the sharecropping-for-profit

*of a writer's original vision—that I hate so much in today's pub-
lishing. But the occasional short work in an otherwise "com-
pleted" universe is my attempt at a compromise between
retilling tired fields and completely abandoning the landscape.*
Or something like that.

*At any rate, this idea for a future Hyperion story had not yet
become that supersaturated solution necessary before writing can
commence, when a* Star Trek *producer contacted me about sug-
gesting and writing an episode for their* Voyager *series. I had been
contacted by the* Star Trek *people before and had had to beg off
from even discussing such involvement, because of imminent
novel deadlines or a film script I was working on or whatever.*

*Now, I've been known to say unkind things in public places
about the* Star Trek *universe—calling* Star Trek: The Next
Generation *the "Neutered Generation" in one guest of honor
speech, for instance, or admitting in an interview that I saw
Gene Roddenberry's much-loved vision of the future as essentially fascist. Perhaps the producers had forgiven me for those
comments. Or much more likely, probably no one involved in
the* Star Trek *business had ever come across them. In any
event, they invited me to come to L.A. to "do a pitch" (a phrase
I adore for its appropriate inanity) for their program* Star
Trek: Voyager *and, when I said that I didn't have time for such
a trip, allowed me to do one over the telephone.*

In the meantime, they sent me about ten volumes of Star Trek
*background material—the "Bible" for the show, tech manuals,
character outlines, synopses of previous and future episodes, di-
agrams and floorplans of* Voyager—*the whole nine yards. I admit that I enjoyed skimming through all this stuff, especially the
"scientific explanation" of such fantasy gimmicks as the trans-
porter and warp drive and so forth. It's part of the appeal of* Star
Trek—*all the* Star Treks—*that there seems to be a complex universe there with rules and limitations and textures only partially
glimpsed by the viewer. That is, I think, what fuels so much of
the fannish speculation—whether the homoerotic fanzine tales*

concerning the original crew's characters or the endless varia-
tions on gaming.

So, the producer called me at the appointed date, although I
admit that I had all but forgotten about the impending pitch.

"Essentially," I said, "I'd like to script an episode in which the
Voyager crew doesn't get its umpteenth failed chance to get
home, but gets an opportunity to get outside the stupid ship."

"Uh-huh, uh-huh," said the producer. "What do you mean?"

"I mean even though the sets are getting bigger and they have
the holodeck and all, these characters are still Spam in a can," I
said. "These guys spend years—freaking years—in corridors and
turbolifts and on that boring post-modernist bridge. Their private quarters look like rooms in a Holiday Express. What if they
had the chance to leave the ship forever and get out into space?"

"Uh-huh, uh-huh, yeah," said the producer. "Go on."

"Okay," I say, getting the pitch-virus now, warming to the
wonderfulness of my own imagination, "say the Voyager has to
drop out of warp drive and visit a planetary system to replenish
its dilithium crystals or to clean the barnacles off its anti-matter
nacelles or to get fresh water or whatever the hell reason you've
always got them diverting into harm's way . . ."

"Uh-huh, uh-huh, go on."

"But instead of just a Sol-type system, this is a binary system
with a red giant and a G-type star and . . ." I went on to explain
the brilliant idea of an orbital forest filled with space-dwelling
indigenies adapted to hard vacuum, capable of extending magnetic butterfly wings hundreds of kilometers across, of capturing
the solar wind and of braving the magnetosphere shockwaves of
space like birds in a hurricane, of a giant, programmed eating
machine that came once every so many years in a huge elliptical
orbit, from the red giant to the G-star and back again, chewing
away at the space-dwelling butterflies' orbital forest. I explained
how the "problem" of the story could be the butterfly creatures'
offer to the Voyager crew—in exchange for just blasting the eating machine with one of their photon torpedoes—of using their

nano-machinery to adapt the crew members to deep space, to get them out of their spam-in-a-can existence and into the freedom of flying between the worlds like migrating doves. Some of the crew members would have *to want that freedom and Captain Whatshername would draw an Alamo-ish line-in-the-sand to decide who would stay, who would fly . . .*

"Uh-huh, uh-huh," interrupted the producer gently. "I have a question."

"Sure," I said.

"What exactly is a binary system?"

Well, shit.

In the end, their rejection of my pitch centered not so much on astronomical details, but on their anxiety about the cgi budget of that episode. When I pointed out that the astral butterflies wouldn't be that expensive—blobs against the usual planetary digital imagery, they reminded me that once these butterflies visited the ship, they'd have to be . . . well . . . alien. Star Trek's view of aliens was human actors with big brows or wrinkly noses or big-corded necks or all of the above. I wanted these huge, insectoid things.

We parted amicably.

I admit that I was relieved. I had never seen this little seed particle of an idea as a Star Trek episode. Besides, if I'd been hired to write the damned thing, I would have tried to have the vast majority of the crew desert to become butterflies, with Captain Mrs. Columbo staying behind with her hands on her hips and a few of the top regulars trekking on alone in their Spam can, while the liberated crew flew barrel rolls around the tin-and-plastic-and-carpet spaceship on its way out of the binary system.

Cut to some months later when Robert Silverberg contacted me about writing a long piece for his proposed anthology, *Far Horizons. Bob* saw the new book as a follow-up to his bestselling anthology, *Legends,* in which fantasy authors returned to their favorite fantasy universes to give us original tales. He was inviting SF authors of forest-killing mega-epics to reprise their settings and among the other writers contributing would be Ursula

K. Le Guin returning to her Ekumen universe, Joe Haldeman dealing with his Forever War again, Scott Card unearthing Ender, David Brin doing his Wonderbra thing with his Uplift Universe, Fred Pohl heecheeing us again, and so forth. I don't have many rules governing my career choices, but not turning down opportunities to insert myself in a pantheon of gods is one of them. I said yes.

Actually, the hard part was summarizing the million or so words of the "Hyperion Cantos" in the "1,000 words or fewer" demanded of the synopsis before my story. The story, of course, was "Orphans of the Helix" and returned my space butterflies, my fallen angels of hard vacuum, to just where they had started—as the mutated human Ousters of the four Hyperion books.

And the story was accepted. And it was published. And it was good. (Except for the fact that they printed my name as "David Simmons" in the author profiles at the back of the paperback edition, despite my regular whines and whimpers and milquetoast protests to the publishers—who, it turns out, are my editors and publishers at HarperCollins. Perhaps they—and Bob—are trying to tell me something.)

So that's it. That's the story of . . .

No, wait. I forgot the most important part.

How "Orphans of the Helix" made me miss the Ninth Annual Lincoln Street Water Fight.

Well, sometime after Far Horizons came out, Charles Brown of Locus called to inform me that "Orphans" had won the annual Locus Readers Award for Best Novelette. I've won more than a few of these Readers Poll Awards and I admit that they're very important to me . . . I mean, with the award comes another year's free subscription to Locus and my goal has been to receive the magazine forever and never pay for it. (A goal I would have realized up to this date, I should point out, were it not for Locus's small-minded policy of granting only one year's free subscription even if the author wins Readers Poll Awards in more than one category that year.)

So Charles informs me that I'm a winner at about the same time that I'm invited to attend the convention in Hawaii—Westercon 53 in Honolulu, July 1–4, 2000—and I accepted the invitation (a rarity for me, I attend very few SF conventions for reasons of schedules and deadlines.)

"You what?" said my wife Karen. "You're going to be gone on the Fourth?"

My daughter Jane put it more succinctly—"Dad, have you lost your mind?"

You see, we live in a neat old neighborhood in a not-terribly-large town along the Front Range of Colorado, near Boulder, and some years ago, in 1992, Jane and I had—on the spur of the moment—photocopied a cartoon invitation and invited everyone on our block of Lincoln Street to show up at high noon on Independence Day, in the middle of the street, with water balloons or squirt guns or hoses or buckets or whatever, to participate in the Lincoln Street Water Fight. "Be there or be dry!" read our invitation. About twenty-five people showed up that first year and we had a ball—throwing water balloons and dousing our friends and neighbors for at least an hour before collapsing from exhaustion.

By 2000, the Lincoln Street Water Fight had grown to include about 75 people. Neighbors canceled travel plans so as not to miss THE WATER FIGHT. Both the east side of Lincoln and the (boo-hisss) west side brought in friends and relatives as ringers to improve their chances during THE WATER FIGHT. Participants included three-year-olds and eighty-three-year-olds. At the stroke of noon on the Fourth, several thousand water balloons (yes, we build and use catapults) are launched and untold gallons of water fill the air as we unleash high-pressure hoses and throw from buckets the size of gondolas. No one wants to miss THE WATER FIGHT.

And the local event has evolved further since 1992. After the water fight, everyone dries off and wanders down to the local school yard—Central School, where I taught sixth grade for eleven years—and we have a long, fun softball game in the play-

ground, again toddlers to senior citizens participating, while a city band plays Sousa marches in Thompson Park across the street. Later in the afternoon, the neighbors and friends gather for a barbecue, rotating which backyard or front porch will host it. About nine P.M., people wander off—many of us to the nearby golf course—to watch the fireworks display in the fairgrounds just down the hill.

"You're really going to miss the water fight?" asked Karen.

I'd promised to attend the convention. And attend I did. I enjoyed being in Hawaii. I enjoyed the panels and discussions with fans and fellow pros. I enjoyed the conversations with my editors and publisher at HarperCollins who were in attendance. ("The name's Dan," I said more than a few times, "not David . . ." To no avail.) I enjoyed hanging around with Charlie and the Locus people. I enjoyed receiving the award.

But I flew back to the mainland on the Fourth, catching only the hint of a few remaining fireworks just visible over the port wing late, while flying out of San Francisco, arriving at DIA around midnight and driving home in the dark, my mood as dark as the midnight, knowing what I would find when I woke up the next morning—waterlogged yards, buckets and squirt guns still on the front porch, swimsuits and T-shirts still drying on the shower rod, soggy sneakers on the side steps, a few tiny fragments of 10,000 burst water balloons in the grass where they had been missed during the post-fight cleanup, and our Pembroke Welsh Corgi, Fergie, lying exhausted and water bloated (she tries to drink from every hose during the fight), that July Fifth grin of post-party satisfaction on her face.

I hope you like "Orphans of the Helix." I enjoyed returning to the Hyperion universe to see what had happened to some of the distant Ousters and the Amoiete Spectrum Helix people. I hope you enjoy this post-Hyperion glimpse of them. I confess that I have some other Hyperion-universe short fiction in mind for the future. But on the off chance that any win any awards that would be handed out on the Fourth of July—well, include me out.

In the summer of 2001, not long before I wrote this introduction, we had the Tenth and Best Lincoln Street Water Fight ever. Everyone was there. No one was dry. Later that afternoon, we played softball for hours—no one kept track of the score—while the band played in the park. The barbecue was fun. The fireworks were the best ever.

You see, as one gets older, one has to decide on priorities. And I have. Literature and travel and fame and accolades are important, but not worth missing the Lincoln Street Water Fight.

Not by a long shot.

ORPHANS OF THE HELIX

THE great spinship translated down from Hawking space into
the red and white double light of a close binary. While the
684,300 people of the Amoiete Spectrum Helix dreamed on in
deep cryogenic sleep, the five AI's in charge of the ship conferred. They had encountered an unusual phenomenon and
while four of the five had agreed it important enough to bring
the huge spinship out of C-plus Hawking space, there was a
lively debate—continuing for several microseconds—about
what to do next.

The spinship itself looked beautiful in the distant light of the
two stars, white and red light bathing its kilometer-long skin, the
starlight flashing on the three thousand environmental deep-
sleep pods, the groups of thirty pods on each of the one hundred
spin hubs spinning past so quickly that the swing arms were like
the blur of great, overlapping fan blades, while the three thousand pods themselves appeared to be a single, flashing gem
blazing with red and white light. The Aeneans had adapted the
ship so that the hubs of the spinwheels along the long, central
shaft of the ship were slanted—the first thirty spin arms angled
back, the second hub angling its longer thirty pod arms forward,
so that the deep-sleep pods themselves passed between each
other with only microseconds of separation, coalescing into a
solid blur that made the ship under full spin resemble exactly
what its name implied—*Helix*. An observer watching from some

hundreds of kilometers away would see what looked to be a ro-tating human double DNA helix catching the light from the paired suns.

All five of the AI's decided that it would be best to call in the spin pods. First the great hubs changed their orientation until the gleaming helix became a series of three thousand slowing carbon-carbon spin arms, each with an ovoid pod visible at its tip through the slowing blur of speed. Then the pod arms stopped and retracted against the long ship, each deep-sleep pod fitting into a concave nesting cusp in the hull like an egg be-ing set carefully into a container.

The *Helix*, no longer resembling its name so much now so as a long, slender arrow with command centers at the bulbous, tri-angular head, and the Hawking drive and larger fusion engines bulking at the stern, morphed eight layers of covering over the nested spin arms and pods. All of the AI's voted to decelerate to-ward the G8 white star under a conservative four hundred grav-ities and to extend the containment field to Class 20. There was no visible threat in either system of the binary, but the red giant in the more distant system was—as it should be—expelling vast amounts of dust and stellar debris. The AI who took the greatest pride in its navigational skills and caution warned that the entry trajectory toward the G8 star should steer very clear of the L_1 Roche lobe point because of the massive heliosphere shock waves there, and all five AI's began charting a deceleration course into the G8 system that would avoid the worst of the he-liosphere turmoil. The radiation shock waves there could be dealt with easily using even a Class 3 containment field, but with 684,300 human souls aboard and under their care, none of the AI's would take the slightest chance.

Their next decision was unanimous and inevitable. Given the reason for the deviation and deceleration into the G8 system, they would have to awaken humans. Saigyō, AI in charge of per-sonnel lists, duty rosters, psychology profiles, and who had made it its business to meet and know each of the 684,300 men, women, and children, took several seconds to review the list before deciding on the nine people to awaken.

DEM Lia awoke with none of the dull hangover feel of the old-fashioned cryogenic fugue units. She felt rested and fit as she sat up in her deep-sleep crèche, the unit arm offering her the traditional glass of orange juice.

"Emergency?" she said, her voice no more thick or dull than it would have been after a good night's sleep.

"Nothing threatening the ship or the mission," said Saigyō, the AI. "An anomaly of interest. An old radio transmission from a system which may be a possible source of resupply. There are no problems whatsoever with ship function or life support. Everyone is well. The ship is no danger."

"How far are we from the last system we checked?" said Dem Lia, finishing her orange juice and donning her shipsuit with its emerald green stripe on the left arm and turban. Her people had traditionally worn desert robes, each robe the color of the Amoiete Spectrum that the different families had chosen to honor, but robes were impractical for spinship travel where zero-g was a frequent environment.

"Six thousand three hundred light-years," said Saigyō.

Dem Lia stopped herself from blinking. "How many years since last awakening?" she said softly. "How many years total voyage ship time? How many years total voyage time debt?"

"Nine ship years and one hundred two time debt years since last awakening," said Saigyō. "Total voyage ship time, thirty-six years. Total voyage time debt relative to human space, four hundred and one years, three months, one week, five days."

Dem Lia rubbed her cheek. "How many of us are you awakening?"

"Nine"

Dem Lia nodded, quit wasting time chatting with the AI, glanced around only once at the two-hundred-some sealed sarcophagi where her family and friends continued sleeping, and took the main shipline people mover to the command deck where the other eight would be gathering.

THE Aeneans had followed the Amoiete Spectrum Helix people's request to construct the command deck like the bridge of an ancient torchship or some Old Earth, pre-Hegira seagoing vessel. The deck was oriented one direction to down and Dem Lia was pleased to notice on the ride to the command deck that the ship's containment field held at a steady one-g. The bridge itself was about twenty-five meters across and held command-nexus stations for the various specialists, as well as a central table—round, of course—where the awakened were gathering, sipping coffee and making the usual soft jokes about cryogenic deep-sleep dreams. All around the great hemisphere of the command deck, broad windows opened onto space: Dem Lia stood a minute looking at the strange arrangement of the stars, the view back along the seemingly infinite length of the *Helix* itself where heavy filters dimmed the brilliance of the fusion flame tail that now reached back eight kilometers toward their destination— and the binary system itself, one small white star and one red giant, both clearly visible. The windows were not actual windows, of course; their holo pickups could be changed and zoomed or opaqued in an instant, but for now the illusion was perfect.

Dem Lia turned her attention to the eight people at the table. She had met all of them during the two years of ship training with the Aeneans, but knew none of these individuals well. All had been in the select group of fewer than a thousand chosen for possible awakening during transit. She checked their color-band stripes as they made introductions over coffee.

Four men, five women. One of the other women was also an emerald green, which meant that Dem Lia did not know if command would fall to her or the younger woman. Of course, consensus would determine that at any rate, but since the emerald green band of the Amoiete Spectrum Helix poem and society stood for resonance with nature, ability to command, comfort with technology, and the preservation of endangered life-forms—and all 684,300 of the Amoiete refugees could be considered endangered life-forms this far from human space—it was assumed that in unusual awakenings the greens would be voted into overall command.

In addition to the other green, a young, redheaded woman named Res Sandre, there was a red-band male, Patek Georg Dem Mio, a young, white-band female named Den Soa whom Dem Lia knew from the diplomacy simulations, an ebony-band male named Jon Mikail Dem Alem, an older yellow-band woman named Oam Rai whom Dem Lia remembered as having excelled at ship system's operations, a white-haired blue-band male named Peter Delen Dem Tae whose primary training would be in psychology, an attractive female violet-band—almost surely chosen for astronomy—named Kem Loi, and an orange male—their medic whom Dem Lia had spoken to on several occasions—Samel Ria Kem Ali, known to everyone as Dr. Sam.

After introductions there was a silence. The group looked out the windows at the binary system, the G8 white star almost lost in the glare of the *Helix*'s formidable fusion tail.

Finally the red, Patek Georg, said, "All right, ship. Explain."

Saigyō's calm voice came over the omnipresent speakers. "We were nearing time to begin a search for Earthlike worlds when sensors and astronomy became interested in this system."

"A *binary* system?" said Kem Loi, the violet. "Certainly not in the red giant system?" The Amoiete Spectrum Helix people had been very specific about the world they wanted their ship to find for them—G2 sun, Earthlike world at least a 9 on the old Solmev Scale, blue oceans, pleasant temperatures—paradise in other words. They had tens of thousands of light-years and thousands of years to hunt. They fully expected to find it.

"There are no worlds left in the red giant system," agreed Saigyō the AI affably enough. "We estimate that the system was a G2 yellow-white dwarf star . . ."

"Sol," muttered Peter Delen, the blue, sitting at Dem Lia's right.

"Yes," said Saigyō. "Much like Old Earth's sun. We estimate that it became unstable on the main sequence hydrogen burning stage about three and one half standard million years ago and then expanded to its red giant phase and swallowed any planets that had been in system."

"How many AU's out does the giant extend?" asked Res Sandre, the other green.

"Approximately one point-three," said the AI.

"And no outer planets?" asked Kem Loi. Violets in the *Helix* were dedicated to complex structures, chess, the love of the more complex aspects of human relationships, and astronomy. "It would seem that there would be some gas giants or rocky worlds left if it only expanded a bit beyond what would have been Old Earth's or Hyperion's orbit."

"Maybe the outer worlds were very small planetoids driven away by the constant outgassing of heavy particles," said Patek Georg, the red-band pragmatist.

"Perhaps no worlds formed here," said Den Soa, the white-band diplomat. Her voice was sad. "At least in that case no life was destroyed when the sun went red giant."

"Saigyō," said Dem Lia, "why are we decelerating in toward this white star? May we see the specs on it, please?"

Images, trajectories, and data columns appeared over the table.

"What is that?" said the older yellow-band woman named Oam Rai.

"An Ouster forest ring," said Jon Mikail Dem Alem. "All this way. All these years. And some ancient Ouster Hegira seedship beat us to it."

"Beat us to what?" asked Res Sandre, the other green. "There are no planets in this system are there, Saigyō?"

"No, ma'am," said the AI.

"Were you thinking of restocking on their forest ring?" said Dem Lia. The plan had been to avoid any Aenean, Pax, or Ouster worlds or strongholds found along their long voyage away from human space.

"This orbital forest ring is exceptionally bountiful," said Saigyō the AI, "but our real reason for awakening you and beginning the in-system deceleration is that someone living on or near the ring is transmitting a distress signal on an early Hegemony code band. It is very weak, but we have been picking it up for two hundred and twenty-eight light-years."

This gave them all pause. The *Helix* had been launched some eighty years after the Aenean Shared Moment, that pivotal event in human history which had marked the beginning of a new era for most of the human race. Previous to the Shared Moment, the Church-manipulated Pax society had ruled human space for the past three hundred years. These Ousters would have missed all of Pax history and probably most of the thousand years of Hegemony history that preceded the Pax. Added to that, the *Helix*'s time-debt added more than four hundred years of travel. If these Ousters had been part of the original Hegira from Old Earth or from the Old Neighborhood Systems in the earliest days of the Hegemony, they may well have been out of touch with the rest of the human race for fifteen hundred standard years or more.

"Interesting," said Peter Delen Dem Tae, whose blue-band training included profound immersion in psychology and anthropology.

"Saigyō, play the distress signal, please," said Dem Lia.

There came a series of static hisses, pops, and whistles with what might have been two words electronically filtered out. The accent was early Hegemony Web English.

"What does it say?" said Dem Lia. "I can't quite make it out."

"Help us," said Saigyō. The AI's voice was tinted with an Asian accent and usually sounded slightly amused, but his tone was flat and serious now.

The nine around the table looked at one another again in silence. Their goal had been to leave human and posthuman Aenean space far behind them, allowing their people, the Amoiete Spectrum Helix culture, to pursue their own goals, to find their own destiny free of Aenean intervention. But Ousters were just another branch of human stock, attempting to determine their own evolutionary path by adapting to space, their Templar allies traveling with them, using their genetic secrets to grow orbital forest rings and even spherical startrees completely surrounding their suns.

"How many Ousters do you estimate live on the orbital forest ring?" asked Den Soa, who with her white training would probably be their diplomat if and when they made contact.

"Seven hundred million on the thirty-degree arc we can resolve on this side of the sun," said the AI. "If they have migrated to all or most of the ring, obviously we can estimate a population of several billion."

"Any sign of Akerataeli or the zeplins?" asked Patek Georg. All of the great forest rings and startreespheres had been collaborative efforts with these two alien races which had joined forces with the Ousters and Templars during the Fall of the Hegemony.

"None," said Saigyō. "But you might notice this remote view of the ring itself in the center window. We are still sixty-three AU out from the ring . . . this is amplified ten thousand times."

They all turned to look at the front window where the forest ring seemed only thousands of kilometers away, its green leaves and yellow and brown branches and braided main trunk curving away out of sight, the G8 star blazing beyond.

"It looks wrong" said Dem Lia.

"This is the anomaly that added to the urgency of the distress signal and decided us to bring you out of deep sleep," said Saigyō, his voice sounding slightly bemused again. "This orbital forest ring is not of Ouster or Templar bioconstruction."

Doctor Samel Ria Kem Ali, whistled softly. "An alien-built forest ring. But with human-descended Ousters living on it."

"And there is something else we have found since entering the system," said Saigyō. Suddenly the left window was filled with a view of a machine—a spacecraft—so huge and ungainly that it almost defied description. An image of the *Helix* was superimposed at the bottom of the screen to give scale. The *Helix* was a kilometer long. The base of this other spacecraft was at least a thousand times as long. The monster was huge and broad, bulbous and ugly, carbon black and insectoidal, bearing the worst features of both organic evolution and industrial manufacture. Centered in the front of it was what appeared to be a steel-toothed maw, a rough opening lined with a seemingly endless series of mandibles and shredding blades and razor sharp rotors.

"It looks like God's razor," said Patek Georg Dem Mio, the cool irony undercut slightly by a just-perceptible quaver in his voice.

"God's razor my ass," said Jon Mikail Dem Alem softly. As an ebony, life support was one of his specialties and he had grown up tending the huge farms on Vitus-Gray-Balianus B. "That's a threshing machine from hell."

"Where is it?" Dem Lia started to ask, but already Saigyō had thrown the plot on the holo showing their deceleration trajectory in toward the forest ring. The obscene machine-ship was coming in from above the ecliptic, was some twenty-eight AU ahead of them, was decelerating rapidly but not nearly as aggressively as the *Helix,* and was headed directly for the Ouster forest ring. The trajectory plot was clear—at its current rate of deceleration, the machine would directly intercept the ring in nine standard days.

"This may be the cause of their distress signal," the other green, Res Sandre, said dryly.

"If it were coming at me or my world, I'd scream so loudly that you'd hear me two hundred and twenty-eight light-years away without a radio," said the young white-band, Den Soa.

"If we started picking up this weak signal some two hundred twenty-eight light-years ago," said Patek Georg. "It means that either that thing has been decelerating in-system *very* slowly, or . . ."

"It's been here before," said Dem Lia. She ordered the AI to opaque the windows and to dismiss itself from their company.

"Shall we assign roles, duties, priorities, and make initial decisions?" she said softly.

The other eight around the table nodded soberly.

To a stranger, to someone outside the Spectrum Helix culture, the next five minutes would have been very hard to follow. Total consensus was reached within the first two minutes, but only a small part of the discussion was through talk. The combination of hand gestures, body language, shorthand phrases, and silent nods that had evolved through four centuries of a culture determined to make decisions through consensus worked well here. These people's parents and grandparents knew the necessity of command structure and discipline—half a million of their people had died in the short but nasty war with the Pax remnant on Vitus-Gray-Balianus B, and then another hundred thousand when the fleeing Pax vandals came looting through their system some thirty years later. But they were determined to elect command through consensus and thereafter make as many decisions as possible through the same means.

In the first two minutes, assignments were settled and the subtleties around the duties dealt with.

Dem Lia was to be in command. Her single vote could override consensus when necessary. The other green, Res Sandre, preferred to monitor propulsion and engineering, working with the reticent AI named Basho to use this time out of Hawking space to good advantage in taking stock.

The red-band male, Patek Georg, to no one's surprise accepted the position of chief security officer—both for the ship's formidable defenses and during any contact with the Ousters. Only Dem Lia could override his decisions on use of ship weaponry.

The young white-band woman, Den Soa, was to be in charge of communications and diplomacy, but she requested Peter Delen Dem Tae and he agreed to share the responsibility with her. Peter's training in psychology had included theoretical exobiopsychology.

Dr. Sam would monitor the health of everyone aboard and study the evolutionary biology of the Ousters and Templars if it came to contact.

Their ebony-band male, Jon Mikail Dem Alem, assumed command of life support—both in reviewing and controlling systems in the *Helix* along with the appropriate AI, but also arranging for necessary environments if they met with the Ousters aboard ship.

Oam Rai, the oldest of the nine and the ship's chess master, agreed to coordinate general ship systems and to be Dem Lia's principal advisor as events unfolded.

Kem Loi, the astronomer, accepted responsibility for all long-range sensing, but was obviously eager to use her spare time to study the binary system. "Did anyone notice what old friend our white star ahead resembles?" she asked.

"Tau Ceti," said Res Sandre without hesitation.

Kem Loi nodded. "And we saw the anomaly in the placing of the forest ring."

Everyone had. The Ousters preferred G2-type stars where they could grow their orbital forests at about one AU from the sun. This ring circled its star at only 0.36AU.

"Almost the same distance as Tau Ceti Center from its sun," mused Patek Georg. TC^2, as it had been known for more than a thousand years, had once been the central world and capital of the Hegemony. Then it had become a backwater world under the Pax until a Church cardinal on that world attempted a coup against the beleaguered pope during the final days of the Pax. Most of the rebuilt cities had been leveled then. When the *Helix* had left human space eighty years after that war, the Aeneans were repopulating and repopularizing the ancient capital, rebuilding beautiful, classical structures on broad estates and essentially turning the lance-lashed ruins into an Arcadia. For Aeneans.

Assignments given and accepted, the group discussed the option of awakening their immediate family members from cryogenic sleep. Since Spectrum Helix families consisted of triune marriages—either one male and two females or vice versa—and since most had children aboard, this was a complicated subject. Jon Mikail discussed the life support considerations—which were minor—but everyone agreed that it would complicate decision making with family awake only as passengers. It was agreed to leave them in deep sleep, with the one exception of Den Soa's husband and wife. The young white-band diplomat admitted that she would feel insecure without her two loved ones with her, and the group allowed this exception to their decision with the gentle suggestion that the reawakened mates would stay off the command deck unless there was compelling reason for them to be there. Den Soa agreed at once. Saigyō was summoned and immediately began the awakening of Den Soa's bond pair. They had no children.

Then the most central issue was discussed.

"Are we actually going to decelerate to this ring and involve ourselves in these Ousters' problems?" asked Patek Georg. "Assuming that their distress signal is still relevant."

"They're still broadcasting on the old bandwidths," said Den Soa, who had jacksensed into the ship's communications systems. The young woman with blond hair looked at something in her virtual vision. "And that monster machine is still headed their way."

"But we have to remember," said the red-band male, "that our goal was to avoid contact with possibly troublesome human outposts on our way out of known space."

Res Sandre, the green now in charge of engineering, smiled. "I believe that we made that general plan about avoiding Pax or Ouster or Aenean elements without considering that we would meet up with humans—or former humans—some eight thousand light-years outside the known sphere of human space."

"It could still mean trouble for everyone," said Patek Georg.

They all understood the real meaning of the red-band security chief's statement. Reds in the Spectrum Helix devoted themselves to physical courage, political convictions, and passion for art, but they also were deeply trained in compassion for other living things. The other eight understood that when he said the contact might mean trouble for "everyone," he meant not only the 684,291 sleeping souls aboard the ship, but also the Ousters and Templars themselves. These orphans of Old Earth, this band of self-evolving human stock, had been beyond history and the human pall for at least a millennium perhaps much longer. Even the briefest contact could cause problems for the Ouster culture as well.

"We're going to go in and see if we can help . . . and replenish fresh provisions at the same time if that's possible," said Dem Lia, her tone friendly but final. "Saigyō, at our greatest deceleration figure consistent with not stressing the internal containment fields, how long will it take us to a rendezvous point about five thousand klicks from the forest ring?"

"Thirty-seven hours," said the AI.

"Which gets us there seven days and a bit before that ugly machine," said Oam Rai.

"Hell," said Dr. Sam, "that machine could be something the Ousters built to ferry themselves through the heliosphere shock fields to the red giant system. A sort of ugly trolly."

"I don't think so," said young Den Soa, missing the older man's irony.

"Well, the Ousters have noticed us," said Patek Georg, who was jacksensed into his system's nexus. "Saigyō, bring up the windows again, please. Same magnification as before."

Suddenly the room was filled with starlight and sunlight and the reflected light from the braided orbital forest ring that looked like nothing so much as Jack and the Giant's beanstalk, curving out of sight around the bright white star. Only now something else had been added to the picture.

"This is real time?" whispered Dem Lia.

"Yes," said Saigyō. "The Ousters have obviously been watching our fusion tail as we've entered the system. Now they're coming out to greet us."

Thousands—tens of thousands—of fluttering bands of light

had left the forest ring and were moving like brilliant fireflies or radiant gossamers away from the braid of huge leaves, bark, and atmosphere. The thousands of motes of light were headed out-system, toward the *Helix*.

"Could you please amplify that image a bit more?" said Dem Lia.

She had been speaking to Saigyō, but it was Kem Loi, who was already wired into the ship's optic net, who acted.

Butterflies of light. Wings a hundred, two hundred, five hundred kilometers across catching the solar wind and riding the magnetic-field lines pouring out of the small, bright star. But not just tens of thousands of winged angels or demons of light, hundreds of thousands. At the very minimum, hundreds of thousands.

"Let's hope they're friendly," said Patek Georg.

"Let's hope we can still communicate with them," whispered young Den Soa. "I mean . . . they could have forced their own evolution any direction in the last fifteen hundred years."

Dem Lia set her hand softly on the table, but hard enough to be heard. "I suggest that we quit speculating and hoping for the moment and get ready for this rendezvous in . . ." She paused.

"Twenty-seven hours eight minutes if the Ousters continue sailing out-system to meet us," said Saigyō on cue.

"Res Sandre," Dem Lia said softly, "why don't you and your propulsion AI begin work now on making sure that our last bit of deceleration is mild enough that it isn't go to fry a few tens of thousands of these Ousters coming to greet us. That would be a bad overture to diplomatic contact."

"If they *are* coming out with hostile intent," said Patek Georg, "the fusion drive would be one of the most potent weapons against . . ."

Dem Lia interrupted. Her voice was soft but brooked no argument. "No discussion of war with this Ouster civilization until their motives become clear. Patek, you can review all ship defensive systems, but let us have no further group discussion of offensive action until you and I talk about it privately."

Patek Georg bowed his head.

"Are there any other questions or comments?" asked Dem Lia. There were none.

The nine people rose from the table and went about their business.

A largely sleepless twenty-four-plus hours later, Dem Lia stood alone and god-sized in the white star's sytem, the G8 blazing away only a few yards from her shoulder, the braided world tree so close that she could have reached out and touched it, wrapped her god-sized hand around it, while at the level of her chest the hundreds of thousands of shimmering wings of light converged on the *Helix*, whose deceleration fusion tail had dwindled to nothing. Dem Lia stood on nothing, her feet planted steadily on black space, the alien forest ring roughly at her beltline, the stars a huge sphere of constellations and foggy galactic scatterings far above, around, and beyond her.

Suddenly Saigyō joined her. The 10th Century monk assumed his usual virreal pose: cross-legged, floating easily just above the plane of the ecliptic a few respectful yards from Dem Lia. He was shirtless and barefoot, and his round belly added to the sense of good feeling that emanated from the round face, squinted eyes, and ruddy cheeks.

"The Ousters fly the solar winds so beautifully," muttered Dem Lia.

Saigyō nodded. "You notice though that they're really surfing the shock waves riding out along the magnetic-field lines. That gives them those astounding bursts of speed."

"I've been told that, but not seen it," said Dem Lia. "Could you . . ."

Instantly the solar system in which they stood became a maze of magnetic-field lines pouring from the G8 white star, curving at first and then becoming as straight and evenly spaced as a barrage of laser lances. The display showed this elaborate pattern of magnetic-field lines in red. Blue lines showed the uncountable paths of cosmic rays flowing into the system from all over the galaxy, aligning themselves with the magnetic-field lines and try-ing to corkscrew their way up the field lines like swirling salmon fighting their way upstream to spawn in the belly of the star. Dem Lia noticed that magnetic-field lines pouring from both the north and south poles of the sun were kinked and folded around themselves, thus deflecting even more cosmic waves that should otherwise have had an easy trip up smooth polar field lines. Dem Lia changed metaphors, thinking of sperm fighting their way toward a blazing egg, and being cast aside by vicious solar winds and surges of magnetic waves, blasted away by shock waves that whipped out along the field lines as if some-one had forcefully shaken a wire or snapped a bullwhip.

"It's stormy," said Dem Lia, seeing the flight path of so many of the Ousters now rolling and sliding and surging along these shock fronts of ions, magnetic fields, and cosmic rays, holding their positions with wings of glowing forcefield energy as the so-lar wind propagated first forward and then backward along the magnetic-field lines, and finally surfing the shock waves forward again as speedier bursts of solar winds crashed into more slug-gish waves ahead of them, creating temporary tsunami that rolled out-system and then flowed backward like a heavy surf rolling back in toward the blazing beach of the G8 sun.

The Ousters handled this confusion of geometries, red lines of magnetic field lines, yellow lines of ions, blue lines of cosmic rays, and rolling spectra of crashing shock fronts with seeming ease. Dem Lia glanced once out to where the surging helio-sphere of the red giant met the seething heliosphere of this bright G8 star and the storm of light and colors there reminded her of a multihued, phosphorescent ocean crashing against the cliffs of an equally colorful and powerful continent of broiling energy. A rough place.

"Let's return to the regular display," said Dem Lia and in-stantly the stars and forest ring and fluttering Ousters and slowing *Helix* were back—the last two items quite out of scale to show them clearly.

"Saigyō," said Dem Lia, "please invite all of the other AI's here now."

The smiling monk raised thin eyebrows. "All of them here at once?"

"Yes."

They appeared soon, but not instantly, one figure solidifying into virtual presence a second or two before the next.

First came Lady Murasaki, shorter even than the diminutive Dem Lia, the style of her three-thousand-year-old robe and kimono taking the acting commander's breath away. *What beauty Old Earth had taken for granted*, thought Dem Lia. Lady Murasaki bowed politely and slid her small hands in the sleeves of her robe. Her face was painted almost white, her lips and eyes were heavily outlined, and her long black hair was done up so elaborately that Dem Lia—who had worn short hair most of her life—could not even imagine the work of pinning, clasping, combing, braiding, shaping, and washing such a mass of hair.

Ikkyū stepped confidently across the empty space on the other side of the virtual *Helix* a second later. This AI had chosen the older persona of the long-dead Zen poet: Ikkyū looked to be about seventy, taller than most Japanese, quite bald, with wrinkles of concern on his forehead and lines of laughter around his bright eyes. Before the flight had begun, Dem Ria had used the ship's history banks to read about the 15th Century monk, poet, musician, and calligrapher: it seemed that when the historical, living Ikkyū had turned seventy, he had fallen in love with a blind singer just forty years his junior and scandalized the younger monks when he moved his love into the temple to live with him. Dem Lia liked Ikkyū.

Basho appeared next. The great *haiku* expert chose to appear as a gangly 17th Century Japanese farmer, wearing the coned hat and clog shoes of his profession. His fingernails always had some soil under them.

Ryōkan stepped gracefully into the circle. He was wearing beautiful robes of an astounding blue with gold trim. His hair was long and tied in a queue.

"I've asked you all here at once because of the complicated nature of this rendezvous with the Ousters," Dem Lia said firmly. "I understand from the log that one of you was opposed to translating down from Hawking space to respond to this distress call."

"I was," said Basho, his speech in modern post-Pax English but his voice gravel-rough and as guttural as a Samurai's grunt.

"Why?" said Dem Lia.

Basho made a gesture with his gangly hand. "The programming priorities to which we agreed did not cover this specific event. I felt it offered too great a potential for danger and too little benefit in our true goal of finding a colony world."

Dem Lia gestured toward the swarms of Ousters closing on the ship. They were only a few thousand kilometers away now. They had been broadcasting their peaceful intentions across the old radio bandwidths for more than a standard day. "Do you still feel that it's too risky?" she asked the tall AI.

"Yes," said Basho.

Dem Lia nodded, frowning slightly. It was always disturbing when the AI's disagreed on an important issue, but that it is why the Aeneans had left them Autonomous after the breakup of the TechnoCore. And that is why there were five to vote.

"The rest of you obviously saw the risk as acceptable?"

Lady Murasaki answered in her low, demure voice, almost a whisper. "We saw it as an excellent possiblity to restock new foodstuffs and water, while the cultural implications were more for you to ponder and act on than for us to decide. Of course, we had not detected the huge spacecraft in the system before we translated out of Hawking space. It might have affected our decision."

"This is a human-Ouster culture, almost certainly with a sizable Templar population, that may not have had contact with the outside human universe since the earliest Hegemony days, if then," said Ikkyū with great enthusiasm. "They may well be the farthest flung outpost of the ancient Hegira. Of all humankind. A wonderful learning opportunity."

Dem Lia nodded impatiently. "We close to rendezvous within a few hours. You've heard their radio contact—they say they wish to greet us and talk and we've been polite in return. Our dialects are not so diverse that the translator beads can't handle them in face-to-face conversations. But how can we know if they actually come in peace?"

Ryōkan cleared his throat. "It should be remembered that for more than a thousand years, the so-called Wars with the Ousters were provoked—first by the Hegemony and then by the Pax. The original Ouster deep-space settlements were peaceful places and this most-distant colony would have experienced none of the conflict."

Saigyō chucked from his comfortable perch on nothing. "It should also be remembered that during the actual Pax wars with the Ousters, to defend themselves, these peaceful, space-adapted humans learned to build and use torchships, modified Hawking drive warships, plasma weapons, and even some captured Pax Gideon drive weapons." He waved his bare arm. "We've scanned every one of these advancing Ousters, and none carry a weapon—not so much as a wooden spear."

Dem Lia nodded. "Kem Loi has shown me astronomical evidence which suggests that their moored seedship was torn away from the ring at an early date—possibly only years or months after they arrived. This system is devoid of asteroids and the Oort cloud has been scattered far beyond their reach. It is conceivable that they have neither metal nor an industrial capacity."

"Ma'am," said Basho, his countenance concerned, "how can we know that? Ousters have modified their bodies sufficiently to generate forcefield wings that can extend for hundreds of kilometers. If they approach the ship closely enough, they could theoretically use the combined plasma effect of those wings to attempt to breach the containment fields and attack the ship."

"Beaten to death by angels' wings" Dem Lia mused softly. "An ironic way to die."

The AI's said nothing.

"Who is working most directly with Patek Georg Dem Mio on defense strategies?" Dem Lia asked into the silence.

"I am," said Ryōkan.

Dem Lia had known that, but she still thought, *Thank God it's not Basho.* Patek Georg was paranoid enough for the AI-human interface team on this specialty.

"What are Patek's recommendations going to be when we humans meet in a few minutes?" Dem Lia bluntly demanded from Ryōkan.

The AI hesitated only the slightest of perceptible instants. AI's understood both discretion and loyalty to the human working with them in their specialty, but they also understood the imperatives of the elected commander's role on the ship.

"Patek Georg is going to recommend a hundred kilometer extension of the Class Twenty external containment field," said Ryōkan softly. "With all energy weapons on standby and pretargeted on the three hundred nine thousand, two hundred and five approaching Ousters."

Dem Lia's eyebrows rose a trifle. "And how long would it take our systems to lance more than three hundred thousand such targets?" she asked softly.

"Two point-six seconds," said Ryōkan.

Dem Lia shook her head. "Ryōkan, please tell Patek Georg that you and I have spoken and that I want the containment field not at a hundred klick distance, but maintained at a steady one kilometer from the ship. It may remain a Class Twenty field—the Ousters can actually see the strength of it, and that's good. But the ship's weapons' systems will not target the Ousters at this time. Presumably, they can see our targeting scans as well. Ryōkan, you and Patek Georg can run as many simulations of the combat encounter as you need to feel secure, but divert no power to the energy weapons and allow no targeting until I give the command."

Ryōkan bowed. Basho shuffled his virtual clogs but said nothing.

Lady Murasaki fluttered a fan half in front of her face. "You trust," she said softly.

Dem Lia did not smile. "Not totally. Never totally. Ryōkan, I want you and Patek Georg to work out the containment field system so that if even one Ouster attempts to breach the containment field with focused plasma from his or her solar wings, the containment field should go to Emergency Class Thirty-five and instantly expand to five hundred klicks."

Ryōkan nodded. Ikkyū smiled slightly and said, "That will be one very quick ride for a great mass of Ousters, ma'am. Their personal energy systems might not be up to containing their own life support under that much of a shock, and it's certain that they wouldn't decelerate for half an AU or more."

Dem Lia nodded. "That's their problem. I don't think it will come to that. Thank you all for talking to me."

All six human figures winked out of existence.

RENDEZVOUS was peaceful and efficient.

The first question the Ousters had radioed the *Helix* twenty hours earlier was "Are you Pax?"

This had startled Dem Lia and the others at first. Their assumption was that these people had been out of touch with human space since long before the rise of the Pax. Then the ebony, Jon Mikail Dem Alem, said, "The Shared Moment. It has to have been the Shared Moment."

The nine looked at each other in silence at this. Everyone understood that Aenea's "Shared Moment" during her torture and murder by the Pax and TechnoCore had been shared by every human being in human space—a gestalt resonance along the Void Which Binds that had transmitted the dying young woman's thoughts and memories and knowledge along those threads in the quantum fabric of the universe which existed to resonate empathy, briefly uniting everyone originating from Old Earth human stock. But out here? So many thousands of light-years away?

Dem Lia suddenly realized how silly that thought was. Aenea's Shared Moment of almost five centuries ago must have propogated everywhere in the universe along the quantum fabric of the Void Which Binds, touching alien races and cultures so distant as to be unreachable by any technology of human travel or communication while adding the first self-aware human voice to the empathic conversation that had been going on between sentient and sensitive species for almost twelve billion years. Most of those species had long since become extinct or evolved beyond their original form, the Aeneans had told Dem Lia, but their empathic memories still resonated in the Void Which Binds.

Of course the Ousters had experienced the Shared Moment five hundred years ago.

"No, we are not Pax," the *Helix* had radioed back to the three hundred some thousand approaching Ousters. "The Pax was essentially destroyed four hundred standard years ago."

"Do you have followers of Aenea aboard?" came the next Ouster message.

Dem Lia and the others had sighed. Perhaps these Ousters had been desperately waiting for an Aenean messenger, a prophet, someone to bring the sacrament of Aenea's DNA to them so that they could also become Aeneans.

"No," the *Helix* had radioed back. "No followers of Aenea." They then tried to explain the Amoiete Spectrum Helix and how the Aeneans had helped them build and adapt this ship for their long voyage.

After some silence, the Ousters had radioed, "Is there anyone aboard who has met Aenea or her beloved, Raul Endymion?"

Again the nine had looked blankly at each other. Saigyō, who had been sitting cross-legged on the floor some distance from the conference table, spoke up. "No one onboard met Aenea," he said softly. "Of the Spectrum family who hid and helped Raul Endymion when he was ill on Vitus-Gray-Balianus B, two of the marriage partners were killed in the war with the Pax there— one of the mothers, Dem Ria, and the biological father, Alem Mikail Dem Alem. Their son by that triune—a boy named Bin Ria Dem Loa Alem—was also killed in the Pax bombing. Alem Mikail's daughter by a previous triune marriage was missing and presumed dead. The surviving female of the triune, Dem Loa, took the sacrament and became an Aenean not many weeks af- ter the Shared Moment. She farcast away from Vitus-Gray- Balianus B and never returned."

Dem Lia and the others waited, knowing that the AI wouldn't have gone on at such length if there were not more to the story.

Saigyō nodded. "It turns out that the teenaged daughter, Ces Ambre, presumed killed in the Pax Base Bombasino massacre of *Spectrum Helix* civilians, had actually been shipped offworld with more than a thousand other children and young adults. They were to be raised on the final Pax stronghold world of St. Theresa as born-again Pax Christians. Ces Ambre received the cruciform and was overseen by a cadre of religious guards there for nine years before that world was liberated by the Aeneans and Dem Loa learned that her daughter was still alive."

"Did they reunite?" asked young Den Soa, the attractive diplomat. There were tears in her eyes. "Did Ces Ambre free herself of the cruciform?"

"There was a reunion," said Saigyō. "Dem Loa freecast there as soon as she learned that her daughter was alive. Ces Ambre chose to have the Aeneans remove the cruciform, but she re- ported that she did not accept Aenea's DNA sacrament from her triune stepmother to become Aenean herself. Her dossier says that she wanted to return to Vitus-Gray-Balianus B to see the remnants culture from which she had been kidnapped. She con- tinued living and working there as a teacher for almost sixty standard years. She adopted her former family's band of blue."

"She suffered the cruciform but chose not to become Aenean," muttered Kem Loi, the astronomer, as if it were impossible to believe.

Dem Lia said, "She's aboard in deep sleep."

"Yes," said Saigyō.

"How old was she when we embarked?" asked Patek Georg.

"Ninety-five standard years," said the AI. He smiled. "But as with all of us, she had the benefit of Aenean medicine in the years before departure. Her physical appearance and mental capabilities are of a woman in her early sixties."

Dem Lia rubbed her cheek. "Saigyō, please awaken Citizen Ces Ambre. Den Soa, could you be there when she awakens and explain the situation to her before the Ousters join us? They seem more interested in someone who knew Aenea's husband than in learning about the Spectrum Helix."

"Future husband at that point in time," corrected the ebony, Jon Mikail, who was a bit of a pedant. "Raul Endymion was not yet married to Aenea at the time of his short stay on Vitus-Gray-Balianus B."

"I'd feel privileged to stay with Ces Ambre until we meet the Ousters," said Den Soa with a bright smile.

WHILE the great mass of Ousters kept their distance—five hundred klicks—the three ambassadors were brought aboard. It had been worked out by radio that the three could take ¹⁄₁₀ normal gravity without discomfort, so the lovely solarium bubble just aft and above the command deck had its containment field set at that level and the proper chairs and lighting adapted. All of the Helix people thought it would be easier conversing with at least some sense of up and down. Den Soa added that the Ousters might feel at home among all the greenery there. The ship easily morphed an airlock onto the top of the great solarium bubble, and those waiting watched the slow approach of two winged Ouster and one smaller form being towed in a transparent spacesuit. The Ousters who breathed air on the ring, breathed 100% oxygen so the ship had taken care to accommodate them in the solarium. Dem Lia realized that she felt slightly euphoric as the Ouster guests entered and were shown to their specially tailored chairs, and she wondered if it was the pure O_2 or just the novelty of the circumstances.

Once settled in their chairs, the Ousters seemed to be studying their five Spectrum Helix counterparts—Dem Lia, Den Soa, Patek Georg, the psychologist Peter Delen Dem Tae, and Ces Ambre, an attractive woman with short white hair, her hands now folded neatly on her lap. The former teacher had insisted in dressing in her full robe and cowl of blue, but a few tabs of stik-tite sewn at strategic places kept the garment from billowing at each movement or ballooning up off the floor.

The Ouster delegation was an interesting assortment of types. On the left, in the most elaborately constructed low-g chair, was a true space-adapted Ouster. Introduced as Far Rider, he was almost four meters tall—making Dem Lia feel even shorter than she was, the Spectrum Helix people always having been generally short and stocky, not through centuries on high-g planets, just because of the genetics of their founders—and the space-adapted Ouster looked far from human in many other ways. Arms and legs were mere long, spidery attachments to the thin torso. The man's fingers must have be twenty centimeters long. Every square centimeter of his body—appearing almost naked under the skintight sweat-coolant, compression layer—was covered with a self-generated forcefield, actually an enhancement of the usual human body aura, which kept him alive in hard vacuum. The ridges above and beneath his shoulders were permanent arrays for extending his forcefield wings to catch the solar wind and magnetic fields. Far Rider's face had been genetically altered far from basic human stock: the eyes were black slits behind bulbous, nictitating membranes; he had no ears but a gridwork on the side of his head suggested the radio receiver; his mouth was the narrowest of slits, lipless—he communicated through radio transmitting glands in his neck.

The Spectrum Helix delegation had been aware of this Ouster adaptation and each was wearing a subtle hearplug, which in addition to picking up Far Rider's radio transmissions, allowed them to communicate with their AI's on a secure tightband.

The second Ouster was partially adapted to space, but clearly more human. Three meters tall, he was thin and spidery, but the permanent field of forcefield ectoplasmic skin was missing, his eyes and face were thin and boldly structured, he had no hair—and he spoke early Web English with very little accent. He was introduced as Chief Branchman and historian Keel Redt, and it was obvious that he was the chosen speaker for the group, if not its actual leader.

To the Chief Branchman's left was a Templar—a young woman with the hairless skull, fine bone structure, vaguely Asian features, and large eyes common to Templars everywhere—wearing the traditional brown robe and hood. She introduced herself as the True Voice of the Tree Reta Kasteen and her voice was soft and strangely musical.

When the Spectrum Helix contingent had introduced themselves, Dem Lia noticed the two Ousters and the Templar spending a few extra seconds staring at Ces Ambre, who smiled back pleasantly.

"How is it that you have come so far in such a ship?" asked Chief Branchman Keel Redt.

Dem Lia explained their decision to start a new colony of the Amoiete Spectrum Helix far from Aenean and human space. There was the inevitable question about the origins of the Amoiete Spectrum Helix culture and Dem Lia told the story as succinctly as possible.

"So if I understand you correctly," said True Voice of the Tree Reta Kesteen, the Templar, "your entire social structure is based upon an opera—a work of entertainment—that was performed only once, more than six hundred standard years ago."

"Not the *entire* social structure," Den Soa responded to her Templar counterpart. "Cultures grow and adapt themselves to changing conditions and imperatives, of course. But the basic philosophical bedrock and structure of our culture was contained in that one performance by the philosopher-composer-poet-holistic artist, Halpul Amoiete."

"And what did this . . . poet . . . think of a society being built around his single multimedia opera?" asked the Chief Branchman.

It was a delicate question, but Dem Lia just smiled and said, "We'll never know. Citizen Amoiete died in a mountain climbing accident just a month after the opera was performed. The first Spectrum Helix communities did not appear for another twenty standard years."

"Do you worship this man?" asked Chief Branchman Keel Redt.

Ces Ambre answered, "No. None of the Spectrum Helix people have ever deified Halpul Amoiete, even though we have taken his name as part of our society's. We do, however, respect and try to live up to the values and goals for human potential which he communicated in his art through that single, extraordinary Spectrum Helix performance."

The Chief Branchman nodded as if satisfied.

Saigyō's soft voice whispered in Dem Lia's ear. "They are broadcasting both visual and audio on a very tight coherant band which is being picked up by the Ousters outside and being rebroadcast to the forest ring."

Dem Lia looked at the three sitting across from her, finally resting her gaze on Far Rider, the completely space-adapted Ouster. His human eyes were essentially invisible behind the gogglelike, polarized, and nictitating membranes that made him look almost insectoid. Saigyō had tracked Dem Lia's gaze and his voice whispered in her ear again. "Yes. He is the one broadcasting."

Dem Lia steepled her fingers and touched her lips, better to conceal the subvocalizing. "You've tapped into their tightbeam?"

"Yes, of course," said Saigyō. "Very primitive. They're broadcasting just the video and audio of this meeting, no data subchannels or return broadcasts from either the Ousters near us or from the forest ring."

Dem Lia nodded ever so slightly. Since the *Helix* was also carrying out complete holocoverage of this meeting, including infrared study, magnetic resonance analysis of brain function, and a dozen other hidden but intrusive observations, she could hardly blame the Ousters for recording the meeting. Suddenly her cheeks reddened. Infrared. Tightbeam physical scans. Remote neuro-MRI. Certainly the fully space-adapted Ouster could *see* these probes—the man, if man he still was, lived in an environment where he could see the solar wind, sense the magnetic-field lines, and follow individual ions and even cosmic rays as they flowed over and under and through him in hard vacuum. Dem Lia subvocalized, "Shut down all of our solarium sensors except the holocameras."

Saigyō's silence was his assent.

Dem Lia noticed Far Rider suddenly blinking as if someone had shut off blazing lights that had been shining in his eyes. The Ouster then looked at Dem Lia and nodded slightly. The strange gap of a mouth, sealed away from the world by the layer of forcefield and clear ectodermal skin plasma, twitched in what the Spectrum woman thought might be a smile.

It was the young Templar, Reta Kasteen, who had been speaking. ". . . so you see we passed through what was becoming the Worldweb and left human space about the time the Hegemony was establishing itself. We had departed the Centauri system some time after the original Hegira had ended. Periodically, our seedship would drop into real space—the Templars joined us from God's Grove on our way out—so we had fatline news and occasional firsthand information of what the interstellar Worldweb society was becoming. We continued outbound."

"Why so far?" asked Patek Georg.

The Chief Branchman answered, "Quite simply, the ship malfunctioned. It kept us in deep cryogenic fugue for centuries while its programming ignored potential systems for an orbital worldtree. Eventually, as the ship realized its mistake—twelve hundred of us had already died in fugue crèches never designed for such a lengthy voyage—the ship panicked and began dropping

out of Hawking space at every system, finding the usual assortment of stars that could not support our Templar-grown tree ring
or that would have been deadly to Ousters. We know from the
ship's records that it almost settled us in a binary system consisting
of a black hole which was gorging on its close red giant neighbor."

"The accretion disk would have been pretty to watch," said
Den Soa with a weak smile.

The Chief Branchman showed his own thin-lipped smile.
"Yes, in the weeks or months we would have had before it killed
us. Instead, working on the last of its reasoning power, the ship
made one more jump and found the perfect solution—this double system, with the white star heliosphere we Ousters could
thrive in, and a tree ring already constructed."

"How long ago was that?" asked Dem Lia.

"Twelve hundred and thirty-some standard years," broadcast
Far Rider.

The Templar woman leaned forward and continued the story.
"The first thing we discovered was that this forest ring had nothing to do with the biogenetics we had developed on God's Grove
to build our own beautiful, secret startrees. This DNA was so
alien in its alignment and function that to tamper with it might
have killed the entire forest ring."

"You could have started your own forest ring growing in and
around the alien one," said Ces Ambre. "Or attempted a startree
sphere as other Ousters have done."

The True Voice of the Tree Reta Kasteen nodded. "We had
just begun attempting that—and diversifying the protogene
growth centers just a few hundred kilometers from where we
had parked the seedship in the leaves and branches of the alien
ring, when . . ." She paused as if searching for the right words.

"The Destroyer came," broadcast Far Rider.

"The Destroyer being the ship we observe approaching your
ring now?" asked Patek Georg.

"Same ship," broadcast Far Rider. The two syllables seemed
to have been spat out.

"Same monster from hell," added the Chief Branchman.

"It destroyed your seedship," said Dem Lia, confirming why the Ousters seemed to have no metal and why there was no Templar-grown forest ring braiding this alien one.

Far Rider shook his head. "It *devoured* the seedship, along with more than twenty-eight thousand kilometers of the tree ring itself—every leaf, fruit, oxygen pod, water tendril—even our protogene growth centers."

"There were far fewer purely space-adapted Ousters in those days," said Reta Kasteen. "The adapted ones attempted to save the others, but many thousands died on that first visit of the Destroyer . . . the Devourer . . . the Machine. We obviously have many names for it."

"Ship from hell," said the Chief Branchman, and Dem Lia realized that he was almost certainly speaking literally, as if a religion had grown up based upon hating this machine.

"How often does it come?" asked Den Soa.

"Every fifty-seven years," said the Templar. "Exactly."

"From the red giant system?" said Den Soa.

"Yes," broadcast Far Rider. "From the hell star."

"If you know its trajectory," said Dem Lia, "can't you know far ahead of time the sections of your forest ring it will . . . devastate, devour? Couldn't you just not colonize, or at the very least evacuate, those areas? After all, most of the tree ring has to be unpopulated . . . the ring's surface area has to be equal to more than half a million Old Earths or Hyperions."

Chief Branchman Keel Redt showed his thin smile again. "About now—some seven or eight standard days out—the Destroyer, for all its mass, not only completes its deceleration cycle, but carries out complicated maneuvers that will take it to some populated part of the ring. Always a populated area. A hundred and four years ago, its final trajectory took it to a massing of O_2 pods where more than twenty million of our non-fully-space-adapted Ousters had made their homes, complete with travel tubes, bridges, towers, city-sized platforms, and artificially grown life-support pods that had been under slow construction for more than six hundred standard years."

"All destroyed," said True Voice of the Tree Reta Kasteen with sorrow in her voice. "Devoured. Harvested."

"Was there much loss of life?" asked Dem Lia, her voice quiet.

Far Rider shook his head and broadcast, "Millions of fully space-adapted Ousters rallied to evacuate the oxygen-breathers. Fewer than a hundred died."

"Have you tried to communicate with the . . . machine?" asked Peter Delen Dem Tae.

"For centuries," said Reta Kasteen, her voice shaking with emotion. "We've used radio, tightbeam, maser, the few holo transmitters we still have, Far Rider's people have even used their wingfields—by the thousands—to flash messages in simple, mathematical code."

The five Amoiete Spectrum Helix people waited.

"Nothing," said the Chief Branchman in a flat voice. "It comes, it chooses its populated section of the ring, and it devours. We have never had a reply."

"We believe that it is completely automated and very ancient," said Reta Kasteen. "Perhaps millions of years old. Still operating on programming developed when the alien ring was built. It harvests these huge sections of the ring, limbs, branches, tubules with millions of gallons of tree-ring manufactured water . . . then returns to the red star system and, after a pause, returns our way again."

"We used to believe that there was a world left in that red giant system," broadcast Far Rider. "A planet which remains permanently hidden from us on the far side of that evil sun. A world which built this ring as its food source, probably before their G2 sun went giant, and which continues to harvest in spite of the misery it causes us. No longer. There is no such planet. We now believe that the Destroyer acts alone, out of ancient, blind programming, harvesting sections of the ring and destroying our settlements for no reason. Whatever or whoever lived in the red giant system has long since fled."

Dem Lia wished that Kem Loi, their astronomer was there.

She knew that she was on the command deck watching. "We saw no planets during our approach to this binary system," said the green-banded commander. "It seems highly unlikely that any world that could support life would have survived the transition of the G2 star to the red giant."

"Nonetheless, the Destroyer passes very close to that terrible red star on each of its voyages," said the Ouster Chief Branchman. "Perhaps some sort of artificial environment remains—a space habitat—hollowed-out asteroids. An environment which requires this plant ring for its inhabitants to survive. But it does not excuse the carnage."

"If they had the ability to build this machine, they could have simpy fled their system when the G2 sun went critical," mused Patek Georg. The red band looked at Far Rider. "Have you tried to destroy the machine?"

The lipless smile beneath the ectofield twitched lizard-wide on Far Rider's strange face. "Many times. Scores of thousands of true Ousters have died. The machine has an energy defense that lances us to ashe at approximately one hundred thousand klicks."

"That could be a simple meteor defense," said Dem Lia.

Far Rider's smile broadened so that it was very terrible. "If so, it suffices as a very efficient killing device. My father died in the last attack attempt."

"Have you tried traveling to the red giant system?" asked Peter Delen.

"We have no spacecraft left," answered the Templar.

"On your own solar wings then?" asked Peter, obviously doing the math in his head on the time such a round trip would take. Years—decades at solar sailing velocities—but well within an Ouster's life span.

Far Rider moved his hand with its elongated fingers in a horizontal chop. "The heliosphere turbulance is too great. Yet we have tried hundreds of times—expeditions upon which scores depart and none or only a few return. My brother died on such an attempt six of your standard years ago."

"And Far Rider himself was terribly hurt," said Reta Kasteen softly. "Sixty-eight of the best deep spacers left—two returned. It took all of what remains of our medical science to save Far Rider's life, and that meant two years in recovery pod nutrient for him."

Dem Lia cleared her throat. "What do you want us to do?"

The two Ousters and the Templar leaned forward. Chief Branchman Keel Redt spoke for all of them. "If, as you believe, as we have become convinced, that there is no inhabited world left in the red giant system, kill the destroyer now. Annihilate the harvesting machine. Save us from this mindless, obsolete, and endless scourge. We will reward you as handsomely as we can—foods, fruits, as much water as you need for your voyage, advanced genetic techniques, our knowledge of nearby systems, anything."

The Spectrum Helix people glanced at one another. Finally Dem Lia said, "If you are comfortable here, four of us would like to excuse ourselves for a short time to discuss this. Ces Ambre would be delighted to stay with you and talk if you so wish."

The Chief Branchman made a gesture with both long arms and huge hands. "We are completely comfortable. And we are more than delighted to have this chance to talk to the venerable M. Ambre—the woman who saw the husband of Aenea."

Dem Lia noticed that the young Templar, Reta Kasteen, looked visibly thrilled at the prospect.

"And then you will bring us your decision, yes?" radioed Far Rider, his waxy body, huge eyeshields, and alien physiology giving Dem Lia a slight chill. This was a creature that fed on light, tapped enough energy to deploy electromagnetic solar wings hundreds of kilometers wide, recycled his own air, waste, and water, and lived in an environment of absolute cold, heat, radiation, and hard vacuum. Humankind had come a long way from the early hominids in Africa on Old Earth.

And if we say no, thought Dem Lia, *three-hundred-thousand-some angry space-adapted Ousters just like him might descend on our spinship like the angry Hawaiians venting their wrath on*

Captain James Cook when he caught them pulling the nails from the hull of his ship. The good captain ended up not only being killed horribly, but having his body eviscerated, burned, and boiled into small chunks. As soon as she thought this, Dem Lia knew better. These Ousters would not attack the *Helix*. All of her intuition told her that. *And if they do,* she thought, *our weaponry will vaporize the lot of them in two point six seconds.* She felt guilty and slightly nauseated at her own thoughts as she made her farewells and took the lift down to the command deck with the other three.

"YOU saw him," said True Voice of the Tree Reta Kasteen a little breathlessly. "Aenea's husband?"

Ces Ambre smiled. "I was fourteen standard years old. It was a long time ago. He was traveling from world to world via farcaster and stayed a few days in my second triune parents' home because he was ill—a kidney stone—and then the Pax troopers kept him their under arrrest until they could send someone to interrogate him. My parents helped him escape. It was a very few days a very many years ago." She smiled again. "And he was not Aenea's husband at that time, remember. He had not taken the sacrament of her DNA, nor even grown aware of what her blood and teachings could do for the human race."

"But you *saw* him," pressed Chief Branchman Keel Redt.

"Yes. He was in delirium and pain much of the time and handcuffed to my parents' bed by the Pax troopers."

Reta Kasteen leaned closer. "Did he have any sort of . . . *aura* . . . about him?" she almost whispered.

"Oh, yes," said Ces Ambre with a chuckle. "Until my parents gave him a sponge bath. He had been traveling hard for many days."

The two Ousters and the Templar seemed to sit back in disappointment.

Ces Ambre leaned forward and touched the Templar woman's knee. "I apologize for being flippant—I know the important role that Raul Endymion played in all of our history—

but it was long ago, there was much confusion, and at that time on Vitus-Gray-Balianus B I was a rebellious teenager who wanted to leave my community of the Spectrum and accept the cruciform in some nearby Pax city."

The other three visibly leaned back now. The two faces that were readable registered shock. "You *wanted* to accept that . . . that . . . *parasite* into your body?"

As part of Aenea's Shared Moment, every human everywhere had seen—had known—had felt the full *gestalt*—of the reality behind the "immortality cruciform"—a parasitic mass of AI nodes creating a TechnoCore in real space, using the neurons and synapses of each host body in any way it wished, often using it in more creative ways by *killing* the human host and using the linked neuronic web when it was at its most creative—during those final seconds of neural dissolution before death. Then the Church would use TechnoCore technology to resurrect the human body with the Core cruciform parasite growing stronger and more networked at each death and resurrection.

Ces Ambre shrugged. "It represented immortality at the time. And a chance to get a way from our dusty little village and join the real world—the Pax."

The three Ouster diplomats could only stare.

Ces Ambre raised her hands to her robe and slipped it open enough to show them the base of her throat and the beginning of a scar where the cruciform had been removed by the Aeneans. "I was kidnapped to one of the remaining Pax worlds and put under the cruciform for nine years," she said so softly that her voice barely carried to the three diplomats. "And most of this time was *after* Aenea's shared moment—after the absolute revelation of the Core's plan to enslave us with those despicable things."

The True Voice of the Tree Reta Kasteen took Ces Ambre's older hand in hers. "Yet you refused to become Aenean when you were liberated. You joined what was left of your old culture."

Ces Ambre smiled. There were tears in her eyes and those eyes suddenly looked much older. "Yes. I felt I owed my people that—for deserting them at the time of crisis. Someone had to carry on the Spectrum Helix culture. We had lost so many in the wars. We lost even more when the Aeneans gave us the option of joining them. It is hard to refuse to become something like a god."

Far Rider made a grunt that sounded like heavy static. "This is our greatest fear next to the Destroyer. No one is now alive on the forest ring who experienced the Shared Moment, but the details of it—the glorious insights into empathy and the binding powers of the Void Which Binds, Aenea's knowledge that many of the Aeneans would be able to farcast—freecast—anywhere in the universe. Well, the Church of Aenea has grown here until at least a fourth of our population would give up their Ouster or Templar heritage and become Aenean in a second."

Ces Ambre rubbed her cheek and smiled again. "Then it's obvious that no Aeneans have visited this system. And you have to remember that Aenea insisted that there be no 'Church of Aenea,' no veneration or beatification or adoration. That was paramount in her thoughts during the Shared Moment."

"We know," said Reta Kasteen. "But in the absence of choice and knowledge, cultures often turn to religion. And the possibility of an Aenean being aboard with you was one reason we greeted the arrival of your great ship with such enthusiasm and trepidation."

"Aeneans do not arrive by spacecraft," Ces Ambre said softly.

The three nodded. "When and if the day ever comes," broadcast Far Rider, "it will be up to the individual conscience of each Ouster and Templar to decide. As for me, I will always ride the great waves of the solar wind."

Dem Lia and the other three returned.

"We've decided to help," she said. "But we must hurry."

THERE was no way in the universe that Dem Lia or any of the other eight humans or any of the five AI's would risk the *Helix* in a direct confrontation with the "Destroyer" or the "Harvester" or whatever the hell the Ousters wanted to call their nemesis. It was not just by engineering happenstance that the 3,000 life-support pods carrying the 684,300 Spectrum Helix pioneers in deep cryogenic sleep were egg-shaped. This culture had all their eggs in one basket—literally—and they were not about to send that basket into battle. Already Basho and several of the other AI's were brooding about the proximity to the oncoming harvesting ship. Space battles could easily be fought across 28 AU's of distance—while traditional lasers, or lances, or charged particle beam weapons would take more than a hundred and ninety-six minutes to creep that distance—Hegemony, Pax, and Ouster ships had all developed hyperkinetic missiles able to leap into and out of Hawking drive. Ships could be destroyed before radar could announce the presence of the incoming missile. Since this "harvester" crept around its appointed rounds at sublight speed, it seemed unlikely that it would carry C-plus weaponry, but "unlikely" is a word that has undone the planning and fates of warriors since time immemorial.

At the Spectrum Helix engineers' request, the Aeneans had rebuilt the *Helix* to be truly modular. When it reached its utopian planet around its perfect star, sections would free themselves to become probes and aircraft and landers and submersibles and space stations. Each of the three thousand individual life pods could land and begin a colony on its own, although the plans were to cluster the landing sites carefully after much study of the new world. By the time the *Helix* was finished deploying and landing its pods and modules and probes and shuttles and command deck and central fusion core, little would be left in orbit except the huge Hawking drive units with maintenance programs and robots to keep them in perfect condition for centuries, if not millennia.

"We'll take the system exploratory probe to investigate this Destroyer," said Dem Lia. It was one of the smaller modules, adapted more to pure vacuum than to atmospheric entry, although it was capable of some morphing, but compared to most of the *Helix*'s peaceful subcomponents, the probe was armed to the teeth.

"May we accompany you?" said Chief Branchman Keel Redt. "None of our race has come closer than a hundred thousand kilometers to the machine and lived."

"By all means," said Dem Lia. "The probe's large enough to hold thirty or forty of us, and only three are going from our ship. We will keep the internal containment field at one-tenth g and adapt the seating accordingly."

THE probe was more like one of the old combat torchships than anything else, and it accelerated out toward the advancing machine under two hundred and fifty hundred gravities, internal containment fields on infinite redundancy, external fields raised to their maximum of Class 12. Dem Lia was piloting. Den Soa was attempting to communicate with the gigantic ship via every means available, sending messages of peace on every band from primitive radio to modulated tachyon bursts. There was no response. Patek Georg Dem Mio was meshed into the defense/counterattack virtual umbilicals of his couch. The passengers sat at the rear of the probe's compact command deck and watched. Saigyō had decided to accompany them and his massive holo sat bare chested and cross-legged on a counter near the main viewport. Dem Lia made sure to keep their trajectory aimed *not* directly at the monstrosity in the probability that it had simple meteor defenses: if they kept traveling toward their current coordinates, they would miss the ship by tens of thousands of kilometers above the plane of the ecliptic.

"Its radar has begun tracking us," said Patek Georg when they were six hundred thousand klicks away and decelerating nicely. "Passive radar. No weapons acquisition. It doesn't seem to be probing us with anything except simple radar. It will have no idea if life forms are aboard our probe or not."

Dem Lia nodded. "Saigyō," she said softly, "at two hundred thousand klicks, please bring our coordinates around so that we will be on intercept course with the thing." The chubby monk nodded.

Somewhat later, the probes' thrusters and main engines changed tune, the starfield rotated, and the image of the huge machine filled the main window. The view was magnified as if they were only five hundred klicks from the spacecraft. The thing was indescribably ungainly, built only for vacuum, fronted with metal teeth and rotating blades built into mandiblelike housings, the rest looking like the wreckage of an old space habitat that had been mindlessly added onto for millennium after millennium and then covered with warts, wattles, bulbous sacs, tumors, and filaments.

"Distance, one hundred eighty-three thousand klicks and closing," said Patek Georg.

"Look how blackened it is," whispered Den Soa.

"And worn," radioed Far Rider. "None of our people have ever seen it from this close. Look at the layers of cratering through the heavy carbon deposits. It is like an ancient, black moon that has been struck again and again by tiny meteorites."

"Repaired, though," commented the Chief Branchman gruffly. "It operates."

"Distance one hundred twenty thousand klicks and closing," said Patek Georg. "Search radar has just been joined by acquisition radar."

"Defensive measures?" said Dem Lia, her voice quiet.

Saigyō answered. "Class Twelve field in place and infinitely redundant. CPB deflectors activated. Hyperkinetic countermissiles ready. Plasma shields on maximum. Countermissiles armed and under positive control." This meant simply that both Dem Lia and Patek Georg would have to give the command to launch them, or—if the human passengers were killed—Saigyō would do so.

"Distance one hundred five thousand klicks and closing," said Patek Georg. "Relative delta-v dropping to one hundred meters per second. Three more acquisition radars have locked on."

"Any other transmissions?" asked Dem Lia, her voice tight.

"Negative," said Den Soa at her virtual console. "The machine seems blind and dumb except for the primitive radar. Absolutely no signs of life aboard. Internal communications show that it has . . . intelligence . . . but not true AI. Computers more likely. Many series of physical computers."

"*Physical* computers!" said Dem Lia, shocked. "You mean silicon . . . chips . . . stone axe level technology?"

"Or just above," confirmed Den Soa at her console. "We're picking up magnetic bubble memory readings, but nothing higher."

"One hundred thousand klicks . . ." began Patek Georg and then interrupted himself. "The machine is firing on us."

The outer containment fields flashed for less than a second.

"A dozen CPB's and two crude laser lances," said Patek Georg from his virreal point of view. "Very weak. A Class One field could have countered them easily."

The containment field flickered again.

"Same combination," reported Patek. "Slightly lower energy settings."

Another flicker.

"Lower settings again," said Patek. "I think it's giving us all its got and using up its power doing it. Almost certainly just a meteor defense."

"Let's not get overconfident," said Dem Lia. "But let's see all of its defenses."

Den Soa looked shocked. "You're going to *attack* it?"

"We're going to see if we *can* attack it," said Dem Lia. "Patek, Saigyō, please target one lance on the top corner of that protuberance there . . ." She pointed her laser stylus at a blackened, cratered, fin-shaped projection that might have been a radiator two klicks high. ". . . and one hyperkinetic missile . . ."

"*Commander!*" protested Den Soa.

Dem Lia looked at the younger woman and raised her finger to her lips. "One hyperkinetic with plasma warhead removed, targeted at the front lower leading edge of the machine, right where the lip of that aperture is."

Patek Georg repeated the command to the AI. Actual target coordinates were displayed and confirmed.

The CPB struck almost instantly, vaporizing a seventy-meter hole in the radiator fin.

"It raised a Class Point-six field," reported Patek Georg. "That seeems to be its top limit of defense."

The hyperkinetic missile penetrated the containment field like a bullet through butter and struck an instant later, blasting through sixty meters of blackened metal and tearing out through the front feeding orifice of the harvesting machine. Everyone aboard watched the silent impact and the almost mesmerizing tumble of vaporized metal expanding away from the impact site and the spray of debris from the exit wound. The huge machine did not respond.

"If we had left the warhead on," murmured Dem Lia, "and aimed for its belly, we would have a thousand kilometers of exploding harvest machine right now."

Chief Branchman Keel Redt leaned forward in his couch. Despite the one-tenth g field, all of the couches had restraint systems. His was activated now.

"Please," said the Ouster, struggling slightly against the harnesses and airbags. "Kill it now. Stop it now."

Dem Lia shifted to look at the two Ousters and the Templar. "Not yet," she said. "First we have to return to the *Helix*."

"We will lose more valuable time," broadcast Far Rider, his tone unreadable.

"Yes," said Dem Lia. "But we still have more than six standard days before it begins harvesting."

The probe accelerated away from the blackened, cratered, and newly scarred monster.

"YOU will not destroy it then?" demanded the Chief Branchman as the probe hurried back to the *Helix*.

"Not now," responded Dem Lia. "It might still be serving a purpose for the race that built it."

The young Templar seemed to be close to tears. "Yet your own instruments—far more sophisticated than our telescopes— told you that there are no worlds in the red giant system."

Dem Lia nodded. "Yet you yourselves have mentioned the possibility of space habitats, can cities, hollowed out asteroids . . . our survey was neither careful nor complete. Our ship was intent upon entering your star system with maximum safety, not carrying out a careful survey of the red giant system."

"For such a small probability," said the Chief Branchman Ouster in a flat, hard voice, "you are willing to risk so many of our people?"

Saigyō's voice whispered quietly in Dem Lia's subaudio circuit. "The AI's have been analyzing scenarios of several million Ousters using their solar wings in a concentrated attack on the *Helix.*"

Dem Lia waited, still looking at the Chief Branchman.

"The ship could defeat them," finished the AI, "but there is some real probability of damage."

To the Chief Branchman, Dem Lia said, "We're going to take the *Helix* to the red giant system. The three of you are welcome to accompany us."

"How long will the round trip last?" demanded Far Rider.

Dem Lia looked to Saigyō. "Nine days under maximum fusion boost," said the AI. "And that would be a powered perihelion maneuver with no time to linger in the system to search every asteroid or debris field for life forms."

The two Ousters were shaking their heads. Reta Kasteen drew her hood lower, covering her eyes.

"There's another possibility," said Dem Lia. To Saigyō, she pointed toward the *Helix* now filling the main viewscreen. Thousands of energy-winged Ousters parted as the probe decelerated gently through the ship's containment field and aligned itself for docking.

THEY gathered in the solarium to decide. All ten of the humans—Den Soa's wife and husband had been invited to join in the vote but had decided to stay below in the crews' quarters—all five of the AI's, and the three representatives of the forest-ring people. Far Rider's tightbeam continued to carry the video and audio to the three hundred thousand nearby Ousters and the billions waiting on the great curve of tree ring beyond.

"Here is the situation," said Dem Lia. The silence in the solarium was very thick. "You know that the *Helix,* our ship, contains an Aenean-modified Hawking drive. Our faster-than-light passage does harm the fabric of the Void Which Binds, but thousands of times less than the old Hegemony or Pax ships. The Aeneans allowed us this voyage." The short woman with the green-band around her turban paused and looked at both Ousters and the Templar woman before continuing. "We could reach the red giant system in . . ."

"Four hours to spin up to relativistic velocities, then the jump," said Res Sandre. "About six hours to decelerate into the red giant system. Two days to investigate for life. Same ten-hour return time."

"Which, even with some delays, would bring the *Helix* back almost two days before the Destroyer begins its harvesting. If there is no life in the red giant system, we will use the probe to destroy the robot harvester."

"But . . ." said Chief Branchman Keel Redt with an all-too-human ironic smile. His face was grim.

"But it is too dangerous to use the Hawking drive in such a tight binary system," said Dem Lia, voice level. "Such short distance jumps are incredibly tricky anyway, but given the gas and debris the red giant is pouring out . . ."

"You are correct. It would be folly." It was Far Rider broadcasting on his radio band. "My clan has passed down the engineering from generation to generation. No commander of any Ouster seedship would make a jump in this binary system."

True Voice of the Tree Reta Kasteen was looking from face to face. "But you have these powerful fusion engines . . ."

Dem Lia nodded. "Basho, how long to survey the red giant system using maximum thrust with our fusion engines?"

"Three and one half days transit time to the other system," said the hollow-cheeked AI. "Two days to investigate. Three and one half days back."

"There is no way we could shorten that?" said Oam Rai, the yellow. "Cut safety margins? Drive the fusion engines harder?"

Saigyō answered, "The nine-day round trip is posited upon ignoring all safety margins and driving the fusion engines at one hundred twelve percent of their capacity." He sadly shook his bald head. "No, it cannot be done."

"But the Hawking drive . . ." said Dem Lia and everyone in the room appeared to cease breathing except for Far Rider, who had never been breathing in the traditional sense. The appointed Spectrum Helix commander turned to the AI's. "What are the probabilities of disaster if we try this?"

Lady Murasaki stepped forward. "Both translations—into and out of Hawking space—will be far too close to the binary system's Roche lobe. We estimate probability of total destruction of the *Helix* at two percent, of damage to some aspect of ship's systems at eight percent, and specifically damage to the pod life-support network at six percent."

Dem Lia looked at the Ousters and the Templar. "A six-percent chance of losing hundreds—thousands—of our sleeping relatives and friends. Those we have sworn to protect until arrival at our destination. A two-percent chance that our entire culture will die in the attempt."

Far Rider nodded sadly. "I do not know what wonders your Aenean friends have added to your equipment," he broadcast, "but I would find those figures understated. It is an impossible binary system for a Hawking drive jump."

Silence stretched. Finally Dem Lia said, "Our options are to destroy the harvesting machine for you without knowing if there is life—perhaps an entire species—depending upon it in the red giant system, however improbable. And we cannot do that. Our moral code prevents it."

Reta Kasteen's voice was very small. "We understand."

Dem Lia continued. "We could travel by conventional means and survey the system. This means you will have to suffer the ravages of this destroyer a final time, but if there is no life in the red giant system, we will destroy the machine when we return on fusion drive."

"Little comfort to the thousands or millions who will lose their homes during this final visit of the Destroyer," said Chief Branchman Keel Redt.

"No comfort at all," agreed Dem Lia.

Far Rider stood to his full four-meter height, floating slightly in the one-tenth gravity. "This is not your problem," he broadcast. "There is no reason for you to risk any of your people. We thank you for considering . . ."

Dem Lia raised a hand to stop him in midbroadcast. "We're going to vote now. We're voting whether to jump to the red giant system via Hawking drive and get back here before your Destroyer begins destroying. If there is an alien race over there, perhaps we can communicate in the two days we will have in-system. Perhaps they can reprogram their machine. We have all agreed that the odds against it accidentally 'eating' your seed-ship on its first pass after you landed are infinitesimal. The fact that it constantly harvests areas on which you've colonized—on a tree ring with the surface area equal to half a million Hyperions—suggests that it is programmed to do so, as if eliminating abnormal growths or pests."

The three diplomats nodded.

"When we vote," said Dem Lia, "the decision will have to be unanimous. One 'no' vote means that we will not use the Hawking drive."

Saigyō had been sitting cross-legged on the table, but now he moved next to the other four AI's who were standing. "Just for the record," said the fat little monk, "the AI's have voted five to zero against attempting a Hawking drive maneuver."

Dem Lia nodded. "Noted," she said. "But just for the record, for this sort of decision, the AI's vote does not count. Only the Amoiete Spectrum Helix people or their representatives can determine their own fate." She turned back to the other nine humans. "To use the Hawking drive or not? Yes or no? We ten will account to the thousands of others for the consequences. Ces Ambre?"

"Yes." The woman in the blue robe appeared as calm as her startlingly clear and gentle eyes.

"Jon Mikail Dem Alem?"

"Yes," said the ebony life-support specialist in a thick voice. "Yes."

"Oam Rai?"

The yellow-band woman hesitated. No one onboard knew the risks to the ship's systems better than this person. A two-percent chance of destruction must seem an obscene gamble to her. She touched her lips with her fingers. "There are two civilizations we are deciding for here," she said, obviously musing to herself. "Possibly three."

"Oam Rai?" repeated Dem Lia.

"Yes," said Oam Rai.

"Kem Loi?" said Dem Lia to the astronomer.

"Yes." The young woman's voice quavered slightly.

"Patek Georg Dem Mio?"

The red-band security specialist grinned. "Yes. As the ancient saying goes, no guts, no glory."

Dem Lia was irritated. "You're speaking for 684,288 sleeping people who might not be so devil-may-care."

Patek Georg's grin stayed in place. "My vote is yes."

"Dr. Samel Ria Kem Ali?"

The medic looked as troubled as Patek had brazen. "I must say . . . there are so many unknowns . . ." He looked around. "Yes," he said. "We must be sure."

"Peter Delen Dem Tae?" Dem Lia asked the blue-banded psychologist.

The older man had been chewing on a pencil. He looked at it, smiled, and set it on the table. "Yes."

"Res Sandre?"

For a second the other green-band woman's eyes seemed to show defiance, almost anger. Dem Lia steeled herself for the veto and the lecture that would follow.

"Yes," said Res Sandre. "I believe it's a moral imperative."

That left the youngest in the group.

"Den Soa?" said Dem Lia.

The young woman had to clear her throat before speaking. "Yes. Let's go look."

All eyes turned to the appointed commander.

"I vote yes," said Dem Lia. "Saigyō, prepare for maximum acceleration toward the translation point to Hawking drive. Kem Loi, you and Res Sandre and Oam Rai work on the optimum inbound translation point for a systemwide search for life. Chief Branchman Redt, Far Rider, True Voice of the Tree Kasteen, if you would prefer to wait behind, we will prepare the airlock now. If you three wish to come, we must leave immediately."

The Chief Branchman spoke without consulting the others. "We wish to accompany you, Citizen Dem Lia."

She nodded. "Far Rider, tell your people to clear a wide wake. We'll angle above the plane of the ecliptic outward bound, but our fusion tail is going to be fierce as a dragon's breath."

The full space-adapted Ouster broadcast, "I have already done so. Many are looking forward to the spectacle."

Dem Lia grunted softly. "Let's hope it's not more of a spectacle than we've all bargained for," she said.

THE *Helix* made the jump safely, with only minor upset to a few of the ship's subsystems. At a distance of three AU's from the surface of the red giant, they surveyed the system. They had estimated two days, but the survey was done in less than twenty-four hours.

There were no hidden planets, no planetoids, no hollowed-out asteroids, no converted comets, no artificial space habitats— no sign of life whatsoever. When the G2 star had finished its evolution into a red giant at least three million years earlier, its helium nuclei began burning its own ash in a high-temperature second round of fusion reactions at the star's core while the original hydrogen fusion continued in a thin shell far from that core, the whole process creating carbon and oxygen atoms that added to the reaction and . . . presto . . . the short-lived rebirth of the star as a red giant. It was obvious that there had been no outer planets, no gas giants, no rocky worlds beyond the new red sun's reach. Any inner planets had been swallowed whole by the expanding star. Outgassing of dust and heavy radiation had all but cleared the solar system of anything larger than nickel-iron meteorites.

"So," said Patek Georg. "That's that."

"Shall I authorize the AI's to begin full acceleration toward the return translation point?" said Res Sandre.

The Ouster diplomats had been moved to the command deck with their specialized couches. No one minded the one-tenth gravity on the bridge because each of the Amoiete Spectrum specialists—with the exception of Ces Ambre—was enmeshed in a control couch and in touch with the ship on a variety of levels. The Ouster diplomats had been silent during most of the search and they remained silent now as they turned to look at Dem Lia at her center console.

The elected commander tapped her lower lip with her knuckle. "Not quite yet." Their searches had brought them all around the red giant and now they were less than one AU from its broiling surface. "Saigyō, have you looked inside the star?"

"Just enough to sample it," came the AI's affable voice. "Typical for a red giant at this stage. Solar luminosity is about two thousand times that of its G8 companion. We sampled the core—no surprises. The helium nuclei there are obviously engaged despite their mutual electrical repulsion."

"What is its surface temperature?" asked Dem Lia.

"Approximately 3,000 degrees Kelvin" came Saigyō's voice. "About half of what the surface temperature had been when it was a G2 sun."

"Oh, my God," whispered the violet-band Kem Loi from her couch in the astronomy station nexus. "Are you thinking . . ."

"Deep radar the star, please," said Dem Lia.

The graphics holos appeared less than twenty minutes later

as the star turned and they orbited it. Saigyō said, "A single rocky world. Still in orbit. Approximately four-fifths Old Earth's size. Radar evidence of ocean bottoms and former riverbeds."

Samel—Dr. Sam—said, "It was probably Earthlike until its expanding sun boiled away its seas and evaporated its atmosphere. God help whoever or whatever lived there."

"How deep in the sun's troposphere is it?" asked Dem Lia.

"Less than a hundred and fifty thousand kilometers," said Saigyō.

Dem Lia nodded. "Raise the containment fields to maximum," she said softly. "Let's go visit them."

IT'S like swimming under the surface of a red sea, Dem Lia thought as they approached the rocky world. Above them, the outer atmosphere of the star swirled and spiraled, tornadoes of magnetic fields rose from the depths and dissipated, and the containment field was already glowing despite the thirty micromonofilament cables they had trailed out a hundred and sixty thousand klicks behind them to act as radiators.

For an hour the *Helix* stood off less than twenty thousand kilometers from what was left of what could once have been Old Earth or Hyperion. Various sensors showed the rocky world through the swirling red murk.

"A cinder," said Jon Mikail Dem Alem.

"A cinder filled with life," said Kem Loi at the primary sensing nexus. She brought up the deep radar holo. "Absolutely honeycombed. Internal oceans of water. At least three billion sentient entities. I have no idea if they're humanoid, but they have machines, transport mechanisms, and citylike hives. You can even see the docking port where their harvester puts in every fifty-seven years."

"But still no understandable contact?" asked Dem Loi. The *Helix* had been broadcasting basic mathematical overtures on every bandwidth, spectrum, and commununications technology the ship had—from radio maser to modulated tachyons. There had been a return broadcast of sorts.

"Modulated gravity waves," explained Ikkyū. "But not responding to our mathematical or geometrical overtures. They are picking up our electromagnetic signals but not understanding them, and we can't decipher their gravitonic pulses."

"How long to study the modulations until we can find a common alphabet?" demanded Dem Lia.

Ikkyū's lined face looked pained. "Weeks, at least. Months more likely. Possibly years." The AI returned the disappointed gaze of the humans, Ousters, and Templar. "I am sorry," he said, opening his hands. "Humankind has only contacted two sentient alien races before, and *they* both found ways to communicate with *us*. These . . . beings . . . are truly alien. There are too few common referents."

"We can't stay here much longer," said Res Sandre at her engineering nexus. "Powerful magnetic storms are coming up from the core. And we just can't dissipate the heat quickly enough. We have to leave."

Suddenly Ces Ambre, who had a couch but no station or duties, stood, floated a meter above the deck in the one-tenth g, moaned, and slowly floated to the deck in a dead faint.

Dr. Sam reached her a second before Dem Lia and Den Soa. "Everyone else stay at your stations," said Dem Lia.

Ces Ambre opened her startlingly blue eyes. "They are so *different*. Not human at all . . . oxygen breathers but not like the Seneschai empaths . . . modular . . . multiple minds . . . so fibrous . . ."

Dem Lia held the older woman. "Can you communicate with *them*?" she said urgently. "Send *them* images?"

Ces Ambre nodded weakly.

"Send them the image of their harvesting machine and the Ousters," said Dem Lia sternly. "Show them the damage their machine does to the Ouster city clusters. Show them that the Ousters are . . . human . . . sentient. Squatters, but not harming the forest ring."

Ces Ambre nodded again and closed her eyes. A moment later she began weeping. "They . . . are . . . so . . . *sorry*," she whispered. "The machine brings back no . . . pictures . . . only the food and air and water. It is programmed . . . as you suggested, Dem Lia . . . to eliminate infestations. They are . . . so . . . so . . . *sorry* for the loss of Ouster life. They offer the suicide of . . . of their species . . . if it would atone for the destruction."

"No, no, no," said Dem Lia, squeezing the crying woman's hands. "Tell them that won't be necessary." She took the older woman by the shoulders. "This will be difficult, Ces Ambre, but you have to ask them if the harvester can be reprogrammed. Taught to stay away from the Ouster settlements."

Ces Ambre closed her eyes for several minutes. At one point it looked as if she had stopped breathing. Then those lovely eyes opened wide. "It can. They are sending the reprogramming data."

"We are receiving modulated graviton pulses," said Saigyō. "Still no translation possible."

"We don't need a translation," said Dem Lia, breathing deeply. She lifted Ces Ambre and helped her back to her couch. "We just have to record it and repeat it to the *Destroyer* when we get back." She squeezed Ces Ambre's hand again. "Can you communicate our thanks and farewell?"

The woman smiled. "I have done so. As best I can."

"Saigyō," said Dem Lia. "Get us the hell out of here and accelerate full speed to the translation point."

THE *Helix* survived the Hawking space jump back into the G8 system with no damage. The Destroyer had already altered its trajectory toward populated regions of the forest ring, but Den Soa broadcast the modulated graviton recordings while they were still decelerating, and the giant harvester responded with an indecipherable gravitonic rumble of its own and dutifully changed course toward a remote and unpopulated section of the ring. Far Rider used his tightbeam equipment to show them a holo of the rejoicing on the ring cities, platforms, pods, branches, and towers, and then he shut down his broadcast equipment.

They had gathered in the solarium. None of the AI's were

present or listening, but the humans, Ousters, and Templar sat in a circle. All eyes were on Ces Ambre. That woman's eyes were closed.

Den Soa said very quietly, "The beings . . . on that world . . . they had to build the tree ring before their star expanded. They built the harvesting spacecraft. Why didn't they just . . . leave?"

"The planet was . . . is . . . home," whispered Ces Ambre, her eyes still shut tight. "Like children . . . not wanting to leave home . . . because it's dark out there. Very dark . . . empty. They love . . . *home*." The older woman opened her eyes and smiled wanly.

"Why didn't you tell us that you were Aenean?" Dem Lia said softly.

Ces Ambre's jaw set in resolve. "I am *not* Aenean. My mother, Dem Loa, gave me the sacrament of Aenea's blood—through her own, of course—after rescuing me from the hell of St. Theresa. But I decided *not* to use the Aenean abilities. I chose *not* to follow the others, but to remain with the Amoiete."

"But you communicated telepathically with . . ." began Patek Georg.

Ces Ambre shook her head and interrupted quickly. "It is *not* telepathy. It is . . . being connected . . . to the Void Which Binds. It is hearing the language of the dead and of the living across time and space through pure empathy. Memories not one's own." The ninety-five-year-old woman who looked middle-aged put her hand on her brow. "It is *so* tiring. I fought for so many years not to pay attention to the voices . . . to join in the memories. That is why the cryogenic deep sleep is so . . . restful."

"And the other Aenean abilities?" Dem Lia asked, her voice still very soft. "Have you freecast?"

Ces Ambre shook her head with her hand still shielding her eyes. "I did not want to *learn* the Aenean secrets," she said. Her voice sounded very tired.

"But you could if you wanted to," said Den Soa, her voice

awestruck. "You could take one step—freecast—and be back on Vitus-Gray-Balianus B or Hyperion or Tau Ceti Center or Old Earth in a second, couldn't you?"

Ces Ambre lowered her hand and looked fiercely at the young woman. "But I *won't*."

"Are you continuing with us in deep sleep to our destination?" asked the other green-band, Res Sandre. "To our final Spectrum Helix colony?"

"Yes," said Ces Ambre. The single word was a declaration and a challenge.

"How will we tell the others?" asked Jon Mikail Dem Alem. "Having an Aenean . . . a potential Aenean . . . in the colony will change . . . everything."

Dem Lia stood. "In my final moments as your consensus-elected commander, I could make this an order, Citizens. Instead, I ask for a vote. I feel that Ces Ambre and only Ces Ambre should make the decision as to whether or not to tell our fellow Spectrum Helix family about her . . . gift. At any time after we reach our destination." She looked directly at Ces Ambre. "Or never, if you so choose."

Dem Lia turned to look at each of the other eight. "And we shall never reveal the secret. Only Ces Ambre has the right to tell the others. Those in favor of this, say aye."

It was unanimous.

Dem Lia turned to the standing Ousters and Templar. "Saigyō assures me that none of this was broadcast on your tightbeam."

Far Rider nodded.

"And your recording of Ces Ambre's contact with the aliens through the Void Which Binds?"

"Destroyed," broadcast the four-meter Ouster.

Ces Ambre stepped closer to the Ousters. "But you still want some of my blood . . . some of Aenea's sacramental DNA. You still want the choice."

Chief Branchman Keel Redt's long hands were shaking. "It

would not be for us to decide to release the information or allow the sacrament to be distributed . . . the Seven Councils would have to meet in secret . . . the Church of Aenea would be consulted . . . or . . ." Obviously the Ouster was in pain at the thought of millions or billions of his fellow Ousters leaving the forest ring forever, freecasting away to human-Aenean space or elsewhere. Their universe would never be the same. "But the three of us do not have the right to reject it for everyone."

"But we hesitate to ask . . ." began the True Voice of the Tree Reta Kasteen.

Ces Ambre shook her head and motioned to Dr. Samel. The medic handed the Templar a small quantity of blood in a shock-proof vial. "We drew it just a while ago," said the doctor.

"You must decide," said Ces Ambre. "That is always the way. That is always the curse."

Chief Branchman Keel Redt stared at the vial for a long moment before he took it in his still-shaking hands and carefully set it away in a secure pouch on his Ouster forcefield armor. "It will be interesting to see what happens," said the Ouster.

Dem Lia smiled. "That's an ancient Old Earth curse, you know. Chinese. 'May you live in interesting times.' "

Saigyō morphed the airlock and the Ouster diplomats were gone, sailing back to the forest ring with the hundreds of thousands of other beings of light, tacking against the solar wind, following magnetic lines of force like vessels of light carried by swift currents.

"If you all don't mind," said Ces Ambre, smiling, "I'm going to return to my deep-sleep crèche and turn in. It's been a long couple of days."

THE originally awakened nine waited until the *Helix* had successfully translated into Hawking space before returning to deep sleep. When they were still in the G8 system, accelerating up and away from the ecliptic and the beautiful forest ring which now eclipsed the small white sun, Oam Rai pointed to the stern window and said, "Look at that."

The Ousters had turned out to say good-bye. Several billion wings of pure energy caught the sunlight.

A day into Hawking drive while conferring with the AI's was enough to establish that the ship was in perfect form, the spin arms and deep-sleep pods functioning as they should, that they had returned to course, and that all was well. One by one, they returned to their crèches—first Den Soa and her mates, then the others. Finally only Dem Lia remained awake, sitting up in her crèche in the seconds before it was to be closed.

"Saigyō," she said and it was obvious from her voice that it was a summons.

The short, fat Buddhist monk appeared.

"Did you know that Ces Ambre was Aenean, Saigyō?"

"No, Dem Lia."

"How could you not? The ship has complete genetic and med profiles on every one of us. You must have known."

"No, Dem Lia, I assure you that Citizen Ces Ambre's med profiles were within normal *Spectrum Helix* limits. There was no sign of posthumanity Aenean DNA. Nor clues in her psych profiles."

Dem Lia frowned at the hologram for a moment. Then she said, "Forged bio records then? Ces Ambre or her mother could have done that."

"Yes, Dem Lia."

Still propped on one elbow, Dem Lia said, "To your knowledge—to any of the AI's knowledge—are there other Aeneans aboard the *Helix*, Saigyō?"

"To our knowledge, no," said the plump monk, his face earnest.

Dem Lia smiled. "Aenea taught that evolution had a direction and determination," she said softly, more to herself than to the listening AI. "She spoke of a day when all the universe would be green with life. Diversity, she taught, is one of evolution's best strategies."

Saigyō nodded and said nothing.

Dem Lia lay back on her pillow. "We thought the Aeneans so generous in helping us preserve our culture—this ship—the distant colony. I bet the Aeneans have helped a thousand small cultures cast off from human space into the unknown. They want the diversity—the Ousters, the others. They want many of us to pass up their gift of godhood."

She looked at the AI, but the Buddhist monk's face showed only his usual slight smile. "Good night, Saigyō. Take good care of the ship while we sleep." She pulled the top of the crèche shut and the unit began cycling her into deep cyrogenic sleep.

"Yes, Dem Lia," said the monk to the now sleeping woman.

THE *Helix* continued its great arc through Hawking space. The spin arms and life pods wove their complex double helix against the flood of false colors and four-dimensional pulsations which had replaced the stars.

Inside the ship, the AI's had turned off the containment field gravity and the atmosphere and the lights. The ship moved on in darkness.

Then, one day, about three months after leaving the binary system, the ventilators hummed, the lights flickered on, and the containment field gravity activated. All 684,300 of the colonists slept on.

Suddenly three figures appeared in the main walkway halfway between the command center bridge and the access portals to the first ring of life pod arms. The central figure was more than three meters tall, spiked and armored, bound about with chrome razorwire. Its faceted eyes gleamed red. It remained motionless where it had suddenly appeared.

The figure on the left was a man in early middle-age, with curly graying hair, dark eyes, and pleasant features. He was very tan and wore a soft blue cotton shirt, green shorts, and sandals. He nodded at the woman and began walking toward the command center.

The woman was older, visibly old even despite Aenean medical techniques, and she wore a simple gown of flawless blue. She walked to the access portal, took the lift up the third spin arm, and followed the walkway down into the one-g environment of the life pod. Pausing by one of the crèches, she brushed ice and condensation from the clear face plate of the umbilically monitored sarcophagus.

"Ces Ambre," muttered Dem Loa, her fingers on the chilled plastic centimeters above her triune stepdaughter's lined cheek. "Sleep well, my darling. Sleep well."

On the command deck, the tall man was standing among the virtual AI's.

"Welcome, Petyr, son of Aenea and Endymion," said Saigyō with a slight bow.

"Thank you, Saigyō. How are you all?"

They told him in terms beyond language or mathematics. Petyr nodded, frowned slightly, and touched Basho's shoulder. "There are too many conflicts in you, Basho? You wished them reconciled?"

The tall man in the coned hat and muddy clogs said, "Yes, please, Petyr."

The human squeezed the AI's shoulder in a friendly embrace. Both closed their eyes for an instant.

When Petyr released him, the saturnine Basho smiled broadly. "Thank you, Petyr."

The human sat on the edge of the table and said, "Let's see where we're headed."

A holocube four meters by four meters appeared in front of them. The stars were recognizable. The *Helix's* long voyage out from human-Aenean space was traced in red. Its projected trajectory proceeded ahead in blue dashes—blue dashes extending toward the center of the galaxy.

Petyr stood, reached into the holocube, and touched a small star just to the right of the projected path of the *Helix*. Instantly that section magnified.

"This might be an interesting system to check out," said the man with a comfortable smile. "Nice G2 star. The fourth planet is about a seven point six on the old Solmev Scale. It would be higher, but it has evolved some very nasty viruses and some very fierce animals. Very fierce."

"Six hundred eighty-five light-years," noted Saigyō. "Plus forty-three light-years course correction. Soon."

Petyr nodded.

Lady Murasaki moved her fan in front of her painted face. Her smile was provocative. "And when we arrive, Petyr-san, will the nasty viruses somehow be gone?"

The tall man shrugged. "Most of them, my Lady. Most of them." He grinned. "But the fierce animals will still be there." He shook hands with each of the AI's. "Stay safe, my friends. And keep our friends safe."

Petyr trotted back to the nine-meter chrome-and-bladed nightmare in the main walkway just as Dem Loa's soft gown swished across the carpeted deckplates to join him.

"All set?" asked Petyr.

Dem Loa nodded.

The son of Aenea and Raul Endymion set his hand against the monster standing between them, laying his palm flat next to a fifteen-centimeter curved thorn. The three disappeared without a sound.

The *Helix* shut off its containment field gravity, stored its air, turned off its interior lights, and continued on in silence, making the tiniest of course corrections as it did so.

Introduction to "The Ninth of Av"

....

In the fall of 1999, I was a guest at the Festivaletteratura in Mantua, Italy, and in the process of being interviewed by Italian SF writer Valerio Evangelisti in the courtyard of a 14th Century compound with several hundred people in attendance, when two aliens—serious aliens, with huge heads, space helmets, silver-lamé spacesuits, and only two oversized fingers on each hand— appeared and began walking—lurching, really—toward us behind the raised dais on which Evangelisti and I were carrying out the interview. The audience laughed. Valerio and I turned. The aliens had tricorder-type devices that made small, electronic beeps and the creatures lurched along to the beeps. Since the hour for the interview and discussion was about up anyway, Evangelisti and I jumped down off the platform to greet the aliens, who had an odd bump and grind, hip bounce, and two-fingered high five way of saying hello.

Good fun. But the conversation the Italian writer and I had been having before the aliens' arrival had been interesting. Evangelisti was talking about the frustration of so many Italian and French and other European writers in seeing their SF and fantasy and horror bestseller lists dominated by American and British writers translated from English (often translated by the very European novelists who were the local competition), while those same European writers were never—never—translated into English for American readers. The New York publishing scene makes almost no allowance for bringing gifted European and Asian genre writers to the attention of the American reading public and the monolingual status of most of us Americans will keep us ignorant of the existence of these writers. It's a real problem and a maddening frustration to many gifted writers and I admire both the restraint and generosity of the various European authors who have been so gracious to me and other visiting Americans while acting as interpreters and interviewers and guides in such circumstances as the Salon du Livre in Paris or the Mantua Festival or the Danish Book Fair or whatever.

So when my good friend and the frequent editor of French editions of my work, Jacques Chambon, got in touch with me to let me know that they were bringing out an anthology of stories by both American and European SF writers, to be released simultaneously in Europe and the United States, I thought it was a great idea and immediately agreed to write something for it. Robert Silverberg was the U.S.-based editor on the project. In addition to rounding up some of the usual American suspects— Scott Card, Greg Benford, Nancy Kress, Joe Haldeman, Bob Silverberg himself—the anthology, christened Destination 3001, also boasted the fiction of many other writers I admire, including Philippe Curval, Sylvie Denis, Jean-Claude Dunyach, Franco Riciardiello, Serge Lehman, Andreas Eschbach, and my fellow Close Encounters survivor, Valerio Evangelisti. As it turned out, Destination 3001 appeared in France from Flammarion in the winter of 2000, but no American publisher was ever found. Too bad for us American readers.

But in the spring of 2000, my attention was focused on finding an original story idea. The binding premise of the anthology—presumably because of the millennial fever that was still raging when the book was proposed—was that the tales should be set around the year 3001. As any writer of speculative fiction can tell you, a thousand years is a staggering span of time to write anything other than space opera. Imagine, if you will, a writer in the year 1000 A.D. writing a simple short story set in the year 2001. What would the common elements be from that *millennium to the projected one? Imagine a contemporary Tom Wolfe-ish story including the themes of race relations, corporate backstabbing, and sexual hanky-panky set in Manhattan.*

Race relations? Meaningless to the author in 1000 A.D. The concept of race, as we are enslaved by it today, didn't exist then.

Corporate intrigue? The intrigue part would be immediately understandable to a European from the year 1000, but the very idea of private corporations and modern capitalism had yet to be invented. For the next 500 years, the entire concept of loaning money for interest fell under the heading of mortal sin—usury—and had to be restricted to non-Christians (Jews) who were going to hell (or Limbo) anyway.

Sexual hanky-panky? Well, yes, that would have been perfectly understood in 1000 A.D. (or 1000 B.C. for that matter) but the leering, smirking, modern fictional obsession with it might not have been.

Manhattan? An undreamt of city on an undiscovered continent.

So, I had to ask myself, what common element will bind 2001 and 3001? What eternal human verity—other than sex and intrigue—will survive the erosive winds of a full millennium?

The answer, when it arrived, hit me with the full nausea of certainty.

The one constant thread between today and a thousand years from now will be that someone, somewhere, will be planning to kill the Jews.

CUT to the summer of 2000 A.D. Just after returning from a convention in Hawaii—and missing the Fourth of July waterfight!—I was off to New Hampshire for a week as visiting instructor in Jeanne Cavelos's Odyssey Writers' Workshop. Odyssey is an interesting workshop and the adults who attend— at least in that summer of 2000—were interesting people: an astrophysicist, a computer programmer, two lawyers seeking to go straight, people fluent in Russian and German and music, a couple of recent college graduates—mostly serious adult human beings, successful in their respective fields, brought together by a common desire to write publishable SF and fantasy. For a week I would teach in the mornings and join in the critique of the sixteen participants' fiction through the long, hot afternoons.

I don't sit in critique circles without offering work of my own for criticism, so I brought along "The Ninth of Av." It was critiqued late in the week and the effect was not so dissimilar from tossing a grenade into a sewing circle.

The Odysseans were nothing if not earnest in their analysis. They did Web searches on the background of the Voynich Manuscript (a topic probably more interesting than my story); they deeply researched Scott's doomed Antarctic expedition in search of hidden meaning; they sought out the meaning of the name "Moira" and one Odyssean did a comprehensive analysis of the significance of the number 9,114 from the Bible through prime numbers (he found no real significance); others criticized the story's "vagueness" and "murkiness" and questionable technologies. Most disliked the story. Some were actively irritated. A few defended it.

No one, I think, understood the thing. No one, for instance, really paid attention to the title—"The Ninth of Av"—or to the Jewish observance of it as Tisha B'Av.

Titles are important. Sometimes, as in "The Ninth of Av" they carry almost as much freight as the text of the tale. I think of stories like Hemingway's "Hills Like White Elephants" or "A Clean, Well-lighted Place" and wonder that titles are so easily tossed off and then ignored these days. In this case, when the French edition of Destination 3001 containing this story was about to come out in the autumn of 2000, I learned that my good friend (and editor) Jacques Chambon and good friend (and translator) Jean-Daniel Breque had changed the title of my story to "Le Dernier Fax" ("The Final Fax") and I hit the roof, threatening—not idly—to pull the story completely rather than to lose the original title. I understood that the title "meant nothing" in French and, worse, that it would sound like "The Ninth of April" since the French word for April is "Avril," usually shortened to "Av." I understood when both my editor friend and my translator friend explained that the average French reader did not know Jewish holidays and would not understand the importance of the Ninth of Av.

It didn't matter. To change the title to "The Final Fax" emasculated the story. I would rather burn down my city, burn the rubble, plow it up, and salt the earth so nothing ever grows there again than agree to this kind of benign vandalism of something so central. (This, I confess, is a common reaction of mine to many editorial "improvements.")

Jacques and Jean-Daniel changed the title back.

Titles are important.

The Odysseans were good people, smart, successful in their respective professions, and earnest in their commitment to reading well and eventually writing well. But they missed it. For better or worse, my fault or theirs (theirs!), they missed it.

Itbah al-Yahud!

ALWAYS enjoying any excuse for a party, I was still leery of the millennial madness in the waning years, months and hours of the 1990s, and not just because I was one of those stuffy purists who thought that the new millennium began on Jan. 1, 2001. (It's moot now.) (And I do understand the odometer attraction of all those zeroes. I remember my family driving our 1948 Buick around and around the block until those digits clicked over to all zeroes.)

There is a scene in the thoughtful movie Sunshine (in which Ralph Fiennes plays three generations of men in a upper-middle-class Jewish Hungarian family in Budapest) where the family celebrates the beginning of the 20th Century—the film did not say whether it was New Year's Eve of 1899 or 1900 (probably 1900, since they understood simple calendar-keeping better then)—and they kiss and toast "to the coming century of compassion and justice and human progress."

Well, no.

It is a powerfully sad moment. As viewers, we want to rush

into the scene and warn them that Europe's future in the 20th Century is a pit of oppression, chaos, injustice and slaughter and that as Jews, they will bear the brunt of it. But these characters were products of the last half of their century, which had seen the Austro-Hungarian Empire create a liberal bulwark—if not of true social justice, then at least of social sanity in which even Jews could rise in wealth and status and legal equity—and they were celebrating decades of European peace during which the very idea of war receded further and further. It's hard for us now, in the surfy shallows of the 21st Century, even to conceive of decades of real peace.

One wants to rush into the scene and cry, "Nazis! Auschwitz! World Wars so frequent you'll have to number them like movie sequels! Death camps! Communism! Gulags! Hiroshima! Pogroms and pestilence, bombs and starvation and genocide rampant!"

I enjoyed New Year's Eve, 1999, e-mailing my friends in Moscow and Paris and Berlin at midnight their time, calling our closest friends in England as midnight passed them by, asking if all was well and hearing their voices coming from the new century. But as the world went ga-ga that night—as we all celebrated in the first true worldwide event, a planetary party, as the wave of 2000 swept around the globe like a curtain of fireworks—I could not help but wonder what now-meaningless nouns and all-too-meaningful verbs a time traveler from the year 2100 would shout at us in warning if they could. It's best, I know, that we don't know, but I suspect that the irony of our celebration now is even greater—and sadder—than the irony of the Austro-Hungarian Jewish family's celebration of the bright dawning of the 20th Century with all of its compassion, and justice, and human progress.

Itbah al-Yahud!

As I write this introduction on an early September afternoon in 2001, the NPR station playing classical music takes its brief hourly news break and the lead story is an optimistic, even *hopeful take on the first United Nations international conference on racism "scrambling to be a success in its final hours." Well, NPR may be upbeat and hopeful, but not this writer. The UN gathering, its reality as clumsy and pretentious and confused as its formal title—*World Conference Against Racism, Racial Discrimination, Xenophobia, and Related Intolerance—*featured leadership from such bastions of 20th Century human freedom as Fidel Castro, Yasser Arafat, and Jesse Jackson and immediately descended into a spittle-flying attack on Israel.*

From Ecclesiastes, 1:4–5, 1:11, 1:14–15—

One generation passeth away, and another generation cometh: but the earth abideth for ever.
The sun also ariseth. . . .
The thing that hath been, it is that which shall be; and that which is done is that which shall be done: and there is no new thing under the sun. . . .
There is no remembrance of former things; neither shall there be any remembrance of things that are to come with those that shall come later.

From the First United Nations World Conference Against Racism, Racial Discrimination, Xenophobia, and Related Intolerance—

Itbah al-Yahud! Kill the Jews!

THE NINTH OF AV

THIRTY days before the final fax, the posthumans threw a going-away party in the New York City Archipelago. Many of the 9,114 old-styles attended. The majority simply faxed in, but some arrived via glowing, transparent bio-zeppelins that tied up at the Empire State Building's mooring tower, some came by oversized squidsubs, an unimaginative five hundred-some arrived on the refitted *QE2*, and a handful flew or floated in via personally fitted sonies.

Pinchas and Petra faxed in on the second evening of the five-day fete. They had hoped that Savi would be there but no prox-net beacon blinked and a physical search of the archipelago proved fruitless. She remained absent and invisible. Pinchas and Petra were disappointed, but they spent a few hours at the party anyway.

The archipelago was ablaze with light. Besides the glowing Empire State Building and other lighted historical towers rising out of the dark waters, clusters of candleglobes floated among the swamp conifers and above the fern forest canals, festive bulbs burned in and above the *QE2* where it was moored to the Chrylser Building, the luminescent, jellyfish glow of the zeppelins above and submersibles below lighted the scene, and sky-rockets exploded in an almost constant barrage of color and noise. Far above the fireworks, both the e-ring and p-ring shifted through every color in the spectrum—and some beyond the human reach of vision—in honor of the first of a thousand pre-final-fax bashes.

"Quite a wake," said Pinchas.

Petra squeezed his upper arm. "Stop that. You promised."

Pinchas nodded and cadged a cold drink from a passing servitor. He and Petra moved around the small square of the Empire State Building's expanded observation deck, stepping aside to let parties of zeppeliners descend the wrought-iron spiral staircase from the mooring platform. Everyone seemed quite merry except for the occasional and inevitable voynix standing here or there like a sightless scarab forged in rusted iron and smoked leather.

Pinchas poured some of his drink over the carapace of one.

"Are you drunk?" asked Petra.

"I wish I were." Pinchas made a fist and clubbed the hollow-sounding voynix ovoid half a meter above him. "I wish the goddamn things had eyes."

"Why?"

"I'd stick my thumb in one." He flicked his middle finger against the chitinous ebony ovoid. It echoed dully.

The voynix did what voynix do. It ignored him.

A posthuman in the iteration known to Petra and Pinchas as Moira floated over to them through the crowd. She was wearing a formal gold gown and her gray hair was cut close to her delicate skull.

"My dears," she said, "are you having an absolutely marvelous time?"

"Absolutely," said Petra.

"Marvelous," said Pinchas. He looked at Moira and wondered, not for the first time in his two centuries and more, why all of the posts were female.

Moira laughed easily. "Good. Good. Later on, the illusionist Dahoni is going to entertain us. I understand that he plans to make the *QE2* disappear. Yet again." She laughed a second time.

Petra smiled and sipped her iced wine. "We were looking for our friend—Savi."

Moira hesitated an instant and Pinchas wondered if she remembered who they were. They had met a score of times over the centuries—or Pinchas assumed they had, based on the theory that it was the same post choosing the Moira iteration—but she had called them "My dears," thus fueling the old-style paranoia that all old-style humans looked alike to the posts.

"Savi, the cultural historian?" said Moira, exploding that theory. "She was invited, of course, but we received no confirmation from her. I remember that she was a special friend of yours, Petra, and of you as well, Pinchas. When she arrives, I will be sure to tell her that you are here."

Pinchas nodded and sipped the rest of his drink. He had forgotten for an instant just how readable his handsome but unrefined homosap face was to these constructs. Who needed telepathy?

"Who indeed?" agreed Moira and laughed again. She touched his arm, patted Petra's cheek, waved over a servitor carrying a tray of warmed handbites, and floated away among the revelers.

"She's not here," said Pinchas.

Petra nodded and looked at her palm. "No beacon, no compoint, no fax trail, no messages for us on far or prox. I know she does these solitude things, but I'm beginning to get worried."

"Maybe she final faxed early," said Pinchas.

Petra gave him a look.

"All right," said Pinchas, raising his empty hand in apology. "Not funny."

"Agreed," said Petra. She took his drink and set the glass on the observation deck's railing. Someone was standing on that railing a few yards away, ready to bungee jump toward the black waters thirty stories below. Petra turned her back on the crowd counting down to the jumper's leap. "Let's go find her," she said.

Pinchas nodded and took her hand. They faxed out.

❖   ❖   ❖

SAVI was dreaming of manhauling yet again.

Turning and tossing in her blue-lighted ice cavern, pinpoint heaters and a thick fell of thermoblank keeping her far from freezing, she dreamt of cold glaciers, naked cliffs, pemmican hoosh, and of smudge-faced, canvas-and-wool-garbed men leaning steep into leather harnesses as they man-hauled impossibly heavy sledges across the high Antarctic plateau.

Savi dreamed of Wilson's sketchbook and of windcut sastrugi. Tossing and turning in her blue-iced cavern, she dreamed of camping at the site of the Norwegians' frayed, black-bunting flag and of seeing their wind-softened ski tracks heading south the few remaining miles to the pole. She dreamed of Oates and Evans and Bowers and of Scott, a small man, half hidden by blowing snow and sunglare on the ice. She suspected that she was dreaming these things from Edward Wilson's point of view. At least she never saw Wilson's face or form, although the pages of his diary and sketchbooks often appeared to haunt her.

Savi woke and remained very still. She felt her heart pounding and listened to silence unbroken except for some creaking as her ice floe shifted in the northbound current.

She had flown out from her home a week earlier, but only after poring over orbital infrared photos for some weeks, finally choosing this iceberg for its size and solidity and for its path, already broken free of the milling icepack endlessly circling in the Barrier slush of the south Ross Sea. The berg was some hundred yards long by a third that height above the dark sea and it was stable; its bulk ran deep. The upper surface had smooth spots where she successfully landed her sonie in the dark and stored the machines and provisions she had ordered fabricated from the p-ring or had foraged herself from the old McMurdo dump.

What she had anticipated the toughest chore—using the big-bore burner to carve out her caverns and ladders and tunnels— had actually proved the easiest. And certainly the most fun. Twenty yards down into the iceberg, making sure to dip low and then up to create cold air traps, using handheld slashers for the steps and rungs and railings, she had found a natural and mean-dering fault in the ice which she had followed down another fifty yards, finally cutting away from it when it narrowed to a fissure.

Savi lighted the caverns with glowglobes and self-powered halogen sticks. There was no daylight so deep in the belly of the Antarctic winter. The heavy work came in hauling down her supplies and furniture to her living caverns, somewhere under sea level and burned into the heart of the heart of the iceberg. Using the pinpoint heaters, she managed to warm the air and space around her without melting her home. She slept on foam and thermoblank and fur and played with her old machines and documents.

As was Savi's custom when on sabbaticals from the world, she blanked all of the com and fax connections she was capable of blanking. But this time, with fewer and fewer days remaining before the final fax, she had added incentive to think. She pored over hard disks and vellum files. When claustrophobia threat-ened, she went up and out into the frigid night—visiting her hoar-frosted sonie, running the heater high, and tapping into farnet babble without taking part. More and more in recent days, when restlessness claimed her, Savi merely burned an-other tunnel, adding to her blue-glow ice maze.

The dreams bothered her some. They had started before her sabbatical. Considering her profession and passions, the dreams were reasonable enough. But the urgency of them bothered her. She knew the ending of this particular expedition and seemed to be approaching it night by night for each of their days. Not much time was left.

PETRA and Pinchas had imaged faxing directly into Savi's foyer—every old-style with a home or apartment had a fax foyer—but they were surprised to find upon arrival that the fax-system failsafe had directed Pinchas's formal robes and Petra's party gown to add a molecular thermsuit layer, complete with hoods, visors, headlamps, and heated air veins.

It was a good thing. The foyer was a deepfreeze, black and cold.

"What the hell?" said Pinchas. He had not visited Savi's Mt. Erebus home before, despite the fact that he and she had been lovers for several years before she moved here, but he knew that she would never abandon her home to the elements just to go on vacation.

Petra nodded at the door to Savi's home. It was open.

Feeling like a trespasser, Pinchas led the way in. Savi's place was filled with furniture and scavenged goods, some of the stacks reaching almost to the low ceiling, but it was long and multistoried—she had built the house out of ancient apartment modules and even more ancient dwellings dug up from what was left of the Antarctic Republic's capital of McMurdo—and it took twenty minutes or more for Petra and Pinchas to wander through it.

Petra found a light switch, but the recessed lamps stayed off. Savi must have taken the house off the grid. But why?

Pinchas found some halogen sticks and their bright light added to their headlamp beams as the two went from room to room. Long, triple-glazed windows must have had an amazing view in the Antarctic summer—the house was high on the slopes of the volcano and the view would be to the north—but now only night pressed against the frost-limned glass. Savi's living quarters looked comfortable and less cluttered than the rest of the place and Petra said that she thought that some pieces of furniture were missing—she had spent time here with Savi a few times when the two of *them* had been lovers—but she was not certain.

The long, narrow workshops, libraries, and storage cubbies seemed surreal in the headlamps: ice particles floating in the air, surfaces covered with hoarfrost and spindrift, everything cold to the touch even through the molecular thermsuit gloves.

Pinchas touched some trilobite-sized, smooth, black lumps on a desk. "What are these?"

"DNA computers," said Petra. "Early 21st Century, I think. Savi dug them out of McMurdo dumps."

Pinchas had to grin despite the eerie surroundings. "Computers used to have shells? They were physical things?"

"Yes," said Petra. "Look." They had come back to Savi's central living module. Petra had lifted some old readers and bound books and was holding up a sheet of modern vellum. "This is Savi's handwriting."

Pinchas was impressed. "You can read?"

"No," said Petra. "But I recognize her handwriting. I know it would be adding trespass to trespass if we actually read this, but . . ."

"But it might be a note to us . . . well, to you," said Pinchas. He set his palm over the vellum, ready to activate a reading function and to let the golden words flow up his arm.

Petra seized his wrist. "No! Don't."

Pinchas was surprised and puzzled, but he lowered his hand.

Petra looked embarrassed behind her visor. "I just think . . . I mean, if you invoke a reading function, it has to go through one of the rings. I mean . . ." She trailed off.

Pinchas frowned at her. "Getting a little paranoid, are we?"

"I guess," said Petra. "But I'd rather find an old-style who can read and have them translate it for us."

"You know someone who can read?"

Petra stared at the vellum and nodded. "A scholar named Graf. And he knew Savi pretty well when the two worked on the Paris excavation. We can get in touch with him. Bring this with us." She folded the vellum and pressed it through the thermsuit membrane into her pocket.

"I think we should wait before reading it," said Pinchas. "We still have thirty days left. Let's give Savi time to reappear before before we start reading her private notes."

"Agreed," said Petra. "We won't bring this to Graf for a couple of weeks. But if Savi doesn't show up, perhaps this can tell us why."

The two stood in the cold desert of Savi's living room for an extra moment.

"Do you think that something's happened to her?" Pinchas said at last.

Petra forced a smile. "What could happen? Any serious accident and there would have been the record of a reconstruction transcription. When we asked farnet, they just said that she was all right."

"I wish they'd just tell us where she is," said Pinchas.

"Privacy," said Petra.

They both had to smile at that. Petra took a last look around and the two faxed north.

OATES died first. Everyone knows about this. Or at least everyone *did* know, back when history was of any relevance to anyone. So Savi thought with fifteen days until final fax. She had given up sleeping some days earlier.

Oates left Scott's tent on the night of March 15, 1912, saying, "I am just going outside and may be some time." Scott, Bowers, and Wilson all knew that the failing Oates was going out into the blizzard to his death. They did not stop him. Fourteen days later, on March 29, the other three would die in their tent only eleven miles short of One Ton Depot and their salvation.

Scott spent his last hours of strength scribbling notes and letters. He defended the expedition. He extolled the courage and manliness of his comrades. His last entry read—"For God's sake, look after our people." He wrote a short farewell letter to his dear friend, Sir J. M. Barrie—the author of *Peter Pan.* It turned out that it was Scott and his party who were The Lost Boys.

Savi's dreams had turned malignant and cold. She decided not to dream any longer. Sitting in the carpeted ice cavern in the heart of her iceberg, she popped stayawakes and drank mug after mug of black coffee. She pored over her notes and ancient computer records, checking her information, attacking but then confirming her conclusions. Things looked bad.

But she had a secret weapon. Literally. The pistol was black and ugly in the way that only mass-tooled artifacts of the post-industrial century could be ugly, but it worked. She had fired it on the shoulder of Mt. Erebus and she fired it again on the night-dark surface of her iceberg. The weapon roared when fired, and the first time she had squeezed the trigger, Savi had dropped the thing and not fired it again for some weeks. But now she rather enjoyed carrying the black weight of the pistol. It was reassuring. And she had boxes of extra cartridges.

With two weeks and one day left before final fax, she decided that it was time to bring her friends—especially Pinchas and Petra—into her plans. Leaving her caverns heated and lighted, thinking that this might be a good place for her cadre to fly to for their secret conferences, she went up into the howling dark and followed the guide cables to her sonie. The sonie was gone.

Savi tasted bile and fear, but fought both back. Her mistake. She had formatted the vehicle for three weeks' use, not thinking that she would be gone that long, and it had simply flown itself back for recycle at one of the supply stations at the end of that time.

Savi went back down into the blue-glow ice to think. Despite her newfound aversion to faxing, she decided that she did not have the patience to wait for a new sonie to be fabricated and flown here. She activated her fax function and imaged Mantua.

Nothing happened.

For a full moment, Savi could not even think. Then, in a panic unprecedented in her two centuries of life, she tried to access farnet and prox. No response. Silence.

Shaking badly, holding the black pistol on her lap, she sat on her beautiful Persian carpet and tried to think.

A shadow moved in one of the ice corridors behind her. Hobnailed boots crunched on ice.

Sari whirled. "Oates?" she called. And again, "Oates?"

DESPITE the summer heat and humidity—Mantua was surrounded by lakes and canals—some of the old-styles liked the city and gathered there now and then. With fourteen days until final fax, Pinchas and Petra and four of their friends were dining in the warm open air of the Piazza Erbe. The white tablecloth was spread with *agnoli, tortelli di zucca, insalata di cappone, risotto,* and *costoletta d'agnello al timo,* Everyone had enjoyed their frog soup and was drinking freely from the bottles of fresh, bubbly lambrusco. It was about eleven P.M. and the day's heat had all but dissipated from the cobblestones. A cooling breeze stirred the linen canopies above them. A half moon rose high, frequently eclipsed by the p-ring. Doves cooed in the nearby towers.

Graf leaned over the page of vellum. He was a dark man with a well-groomed beard—one of the few old-style men to sport facial hair—and when he frowned as he was doing now, he could have been mistaken for one of the long-dead Gonzagas whose frescoed images still graced the walls of the nearby Ducal Palace.

"Can you read it?" asked Penta.

"Of course I can read it," said Graf. "It's understanding it that may pose a problem."

"We were pretty sure that it was in pre-rubicon English," said Pinchas.

Graf stroked his beard and nodded. "Most of it is."

"For heaven's sake," said Hannah, Graf's current partner. "Read it out loud."

Graf shrugged, said, "It's more of a list than a note," and read it aloud.

1) Voynix = Voynich Ms.?
2) P's don't fax. 20th C. fax machines worked from origs.
3) Moira? Atlantis?
4) Jews. Rubicon. Tel Aviv.
5) We're fucking eloi.
6) Kaddosh. Haram esh-Sharif.
7) Itbah al-Yahud.

"I give up," said Stephen, who had faxed in from Helsinki with his partner Frome. "I was never worth a damn at riddles. What does it all mean?"

Graf shrugged.

" 'We're fucking eloi,' " quoted Hannah. "Is 'fucking' a verb or adjective in that sentence?"

"More to the point," said Pinchas, "what are eloi?"

Graf knew the answer to that. He told them about H. G. Wells's time travel tale.

"Great," said Frome. "Either way it translates, Savi's sentence isn't very flattering to the rest of us. Maybe it just means that Savi's lovers have been too passive."

Pinchas and Petra exchanged glances. Even Graf blinked and looked up from the vellum.

Not aware of the reactions, Frome continued, "And if we're all *eloi*, who are the Morlocks? The posts?"

Petra had to smile. "I haven't noticed the posts eating any of us over the past couple of centuries."

"Besides," said Graf, "the posts are vegetarians."

"What does 'Voynich Ms.' mean?" asked Pinchas.

Everyone was silent for a minute. Finally Graf said, "I'll check it." He raised his palm but Petra put her small fingers around his wrist, stopping him.

"I think we shouldn't call up any functions related to Savi's note unless we have to," she said softly, glancing to make sure that none of the servitors or voynix were close enough to hear. "Is there another way to research that phrase?"

"I have a physical library back in Berlin," said Graf. "I'll check there later tonight."

"Wasn't 'Ms.' an honorific for females back in pre-rubicon days?" asked Frome. "Some sort of honorary degree for not getting married or something?"

"Something like that," said Graf. "But it could also stand for 'manuscript.' "

"Anyone have any idea why Savi might have been writing about the post named Moira or about Atlantis?" asked Pinchas.

The other five sipped their lambrusco or nibbled at food. No one ventured a thought. Finally Hannah said, "I've never been to Atlantis."

It turned out that none of them had. It was not a place that old-style humans were likely to visit.

"I would guess that 'P's don't fax' means that posts don't fax," said Petra, "but why would she write that down? We all know that."

"But the part that follows is interesting," said Pinchas. "What was it exactly, Graf?"

"*20th C. fax machines worked from origs,*" read the scholar.

"Origs?" said Stephen.

"I think it's short for 'originals,'" said Pinchas. "I've heard about fax machines. They were a way to send written documents digitally before the first internet existed. Way before the first successful quantum faxing borrowed the language."

"I think they still used them after the internet evolved," said Graf. "But the original mechanical fax devices just copied from an original, physical-on-paper written source. After the fax duplicate was sent electronically, the original document still existed. But so what?"

"Maybe Savi's saying that the posts keep an original of all of us somewhere," said Petra. "Bodies frozen like Popsicles, thawed out and lobotomized for their pleasure. Maybe they use the original us as slave labor up there or something. Sex slaves."

There was uneasy laughter around the table.

"Good," said Hannah, "that makes me feel better about the final fax. I was afraid that I'd stay a neutrino forever. They say that they'll take us out of transmission mode in ten thousand years or so, when they've got the Earth fixed the way they want it, but who knows? This way, if the neutrino stream is lost out there, they can just defrost the original me. I wouldn't mind being a sex slave . . . except that all of the posts are female and I don't lean that way."

Rather than laughter, this brought on a silence. Finally Pinchas said, "I thought that I was reasonably fluent in pre-rubicon English, but I didn't recognize lines six and seven in Savi's note."

Graf nodded. "Part of it is in Hebrew," he said softly. "'*Kad-*

dosh'—I think it would translate here as 'holy.' Maybe. '*Haram esh-Sharif*' and '*Itbah al-Yahud*' are Arabic. *Haram esh-Sharif* is a site in Jerusalem. The Temple Mount. Where the Dome of the Rock used to stand."

"Wasn't the Dome of the Rock blown up during the dementia?" said Frome.

Graf nodded. "Before that, the First and Second Temples stood on that site. In fact, we're approaching the date called Tisha B'Av when the Jews traditionally lamented those events. A lot of sad things happened on that date."

Petra took the vellum from the scholar and frowned at the writing she could not understand. "Perhaps that's why Savi wrote this about—what was it? '*Jews. Rubicon. Tel Aviv*'?"

"Yes," said Graf. "I think the first cases of rubicon were reported on or around the date of Tisha B'Av. In fact, a lot of people believed that the virus first escaped from . . ."

"Oh, Jesus," interrupted Hannah. "That old blood libel. Even I've heard the myth about the rubicon virus escaping from some biowar lab in Tel Aviv. That lie was a product of the dementia years."

Graf shrugged. "How do we know that? We weren't alive then and the posthumans sure as hell don't talk about it. And it *is* true that all of us—all nine thousand some—are descended from Jews."

"We're all sterile, too," said Hannah bitterly. "So what? A few of the Jews had the rare gene that offered protection from rubicon, but the by-product was that their descendents are all mules. Even the transcription doohickies can't fix that. And we're all descended from some African hominid as well, even the posts, but that doesn't mean that we remember anything about African tribal culture. The Jews were just that . . . a tribe. A primitive culture. A forgotten tribe."

"Not completely forgotten," said Graf, staring at Hannah. The couple carried some weight of anger separate from the burden of the current argument.

"Perhaps the Jew-connection could be a motive," said Pinchas. "A reason, I mean."

Everyone looked at him. The linen strips above them rustled in a rising wind. Clouds had covered the moon and rings.

"A motive for what?" asked Petra, ignoring his softer word choice. "Mass murder? Is the final fax a new, improved version of Auschwitz?" Everyone at the table understood the allusion. Even in the post-rubicon, post-historical, post-literate world, certain words held their power.

"Sure, sure," said Frome with an attempt at a laugh, "the six or seven hundred million posts are all—what was the name of the Jews' enemy?"

"Their enemies were legion," Graf said softly.

"Arabs," said Frome as if he had not heard. "All the posts are Arabs. Or maybe your whatchamacallems, Petra—Nazis. All the posts have swastikas and flatscans of Hitler up there in their millions of orbital bunkers."

Hannah did not smile. "Who knows? No old-style has ever been up there. They could have anything in the rings."

Petra was shaking her head. "None of this makes any sense. Even if Savi was clinically paranoid, she must have known that the posts could have eliminated us any time in the last three centuries. We're completely at their mercy every time we fax. If they wanted to . . . to kill us . . . they didn't have to give us a date for the final fax."

"Unless they wanted to torture us as well," said Hannah.

The five others nodded at this and quit talking while servitors cleared their dishes and brought coffee, *gelato*, and *tartufo*.

Pinchas cleared his throat. "That last part—'Itbah al-Yahud'—you say that it's also in Arabic?"

"Yes," said Graf. "It means 'Kill the Jews.'"

IT was impossible, but the lights and heaters were failing in Savi's iceberg grottoes.

They did not fail at once, but one by one the glowglobes and halogen sticks faded and died and on every day that passed, the pinpoint heaters put out less and less heat. Not everything failed. She still had enough light to see by and enough heat to survive, but while struggling to stay awake and alert, Savi had to deal with encroaching darkness and deepening cold. She wondered if the grid was down and the world was ending out there in the world.

Savi slept in short, treacherous catnaps. Usually she still dreamed of manhauling, but more frequently now she dreamt of being in the tent with Bowers and Scott. Oates was gone. When she startled awake, the cold was still around her as in the dream, but she could also still hear the wind howl, smell the smoke and blubber, and share the absolute exhaustion of the defeated explorers. When she was fully awake, the wind still howled down her caverns and corridors. And she was still exhausted.

And there was someone in the iceberg with her.

At first she was sure that it was hallucinations, but the footsteps were more audible now, the corner-of-the-eye glimpses of movement more frequent. Savi would have thought that voynix were visiting except for the fact that voynix neither moved nor made sound. She often wondered about the voynix, those intruders that the posts referred to only as "chronosynthetic artifacts" or "temporal incongruities," but these half-glimpsed figures—always lurking in the shadows, disappearing around the curve of the next ice corridor—were short and canvas-wrapped rather than tall and blind and carapaced.

But there was definitely something frozen in the ice. Savi found it with thirteen days left until final fax. Something dark but solid, visible about two yards beneath the ice wall in the corridor she had carved down the natural fissure. She could see the shape of it in her flashlight beam.

Savi was burning new tunnels daily now—the big-bore burner still worked well—but she hesitated before burning in to the dark object. It was roughly pyramidal and roughly half the size of her lost sonie. But the shape was rumpled, almost random. It disturbed her.

On November 12, 1912, at the approach of the next Antarctic high summer, a search party sent out to determine the fate of Scott's polar party found their tent. Apsley Cherry-Garrard, a veteran polar explorer who had almost accompanied Scott to the pole, was with Atkinson and Dimitri when they found the Scott death tent, a "mere mound" with three feet of bamboo center-pole sticking up from the snow. They burrowed down.

"Bowers and Wilson were sleeping in their bags," wrote Cherry-Garrard in his diary. Savi had a copy of this diary with her. "Scott had thrown back the flaps of his bag at the end. His left hand was stretched over Wilson, his lifelong friend. Beneath the head of his bag, between the bag and floor-cloth, was the green wallet in which he carried his diary. The brown books of diary were inside; and on the floor-cloth were some letters."

And later:

"We never moved them. We took the bamboos of the tent away, and the tent itself covered them. And over them we built the cairn."

The tent had been almost two hundred miles south from the Barrier Edge separating iceshelf from sea in 1912. But the ice had been moving out toward McMurdo Sound and the Ross Sea every minute since the day Atkinson and Cherry-Garrard had collapsed the tent on the three bodies.

Savi laughed aloud at what she was thinking. It was absurd. Even without access to a math function, she knew that the tent must have reached the Barrier Edge many centuries earlier. However deep it had been buried by accumulating ice and snow, it was long gone—carried north through the South Polar Sea and then to oblivion. She laughed again.

Somewhere deep in the ice tunnels, a man laughed as if in answer.

PINCHAS and Petra had other things than Savi's whereabouts to ponder. The two weeks before final fax blurred into a gauntlet of farewell parties to avoid, friends to see, real farewells to tender, places to visit before the end, and emotions to sort. They did not quit waiting for Savi to reappear—nor did they give up their amateur sleuthing over Savi's cryptic notes—but they had little luck on either front. "Curiosity," as Petra said only half ironically, "doesn't seem to be an eloi trait." Perhaps it had been the "fucking eloi" line that had hurt Pinchas and her and made them less eager to find their former lover.

Graf called them the day after the Mantua dinner. His physical library turned up nothing on "Voynich ms" and so—he confessed to them—he had turned to farnet archives. There was nothing there either. But no jackbooted posts had shown up at his door demanding to know why he was interested in these terms. The only reaction, Graf said, had been a sincere apology from the librarian construct for not finding his reference.

With seven days until final fax, Pinchas took Petra on one last sonie flight across the North American Preserve. They picnicked in the Adirondaks, snapped photos of dinosaurs in the Midwest swamplands, put down to swim in a predator-free area of the Central Inland Sea, and had dinner near the Three Heads.

The days were very long so they had time to climb Harney Peak from its base. Both were in excellent physical condition, but both were panting a bit as they reached the rocky summit of the mountain. The view was very nice. The sun was close to the horizon far to the west. The three surviving heads of Mt. Rushmore were visible just a few miles to the northeast. Farther to the east, the Badlands burned white, deep black shadows lengthened between the ridges, and the dark green sea gleamed beyond it all.

Pinchas removed bottles of water and some oranges from his pack. Knowing that twilight would linger long after sunset this time of the summer, not worried about the descent, they took their time enjoying the oranges and watching the light deepen to a general golden glow.

"You know why I wanted to come here?" said Pinchas.

Petra nodded. "Center of the universe. Black Elk spoke. Savi brought you here before. Me too."

Pinchas looked up at the rings moving majestically south and east above the deep blue South Dakota sky. "Yes," he said. "Of course, Black Elk said that wherever you go to find a true vision can be the center of the universe."

Petra licked her sticky fingers and set the orange rinds back in the outside pocket of their pack. Her brown eyes seemed very deep when she looked at Pinchas. "Have you found a true vision?"

"Yes," he said, and kissed her.

WITH three days before final fax, several hundred of the old-styles met on the Barrier Reef for a farewell barbecue on the beach. After the meal, they drifted off to dunes and spurs and private peninsulas to drink beer and watch the moon rise. Pinchas and Petra found themselves in a group of about ten old friends.

"Any regrets?" said a thoughtful man named Abe.

"For us personally or for the species about to go extinct?" replied a dark-haired beauty named Barbara. Her voice was light, mocking.

"Let's start with species," Abe said in serious tones.

There was a silence broken only by the wind and crash of white-topped waves. Then laughter came from a group a few hundred yards down the beach who were skinny-dipping in the surf while servitors hovered protectively over the water, watching for sharks. Finally a bronze-skinned man name Kile said, "I'm sorry that we never went out in space. You know, found life or anything."

"Maybe the posts did and didn't tell us about it," said Pinchas.

Kile shook his head. "I don't think so. They're not interested. I keep looking in the archives, but . . . nothing. And now we'll never know."

A woman named Sarah held up her beer and lightened the conversation. "Maybe the voynix are really aliens," she said. "Extraterrestrials."

"No, no, no," said a short, bearded man named Caleb. "They're temporal incongruities and chronosynthetic artifacts."

Everyone laughed and the tension lifted a bit.

"If the posts are telling the truth," she said, "and they bring us back from fax in ten thousand years, what do you think will be different?"

"Damned near everything," said a famous athlete named William. "Their goal is to eliminate all of the dementia-year experiments and get back to original plants and animals. I think they're even going to shift the climate back the way it was . . . well, whenever. Before all the shit hit the fan."

"There go the cycad forests, primitive conifers like *araucarius*, soda lakes, podocarps, tree ferns, turtles . . ." began Caleb.

"No," said Abe. "The turtles were here before rubicon."

". . . not to mention the *tenontosauruses, microvenatars, camptosauruses, T-rexes, haplocanthosauruses,*" continued Caleb.

"Bloody good riddance," said a ruddy-faced man named Pol. "Never liked the damned dinosaurs. Almost got eaten twice. Here's to their quick demise." He raised his beer and the others raised theirs.

"Any other regrets?" asked Abe.

"Species or personal?" said Sarah.

"Personal this time," said Abe.

There was a silence. Finally Petra stood. "If we're going to get into that, we'll need a lot more beer. I'll be right back."

ON the day before the final fax, Pinchas and Petra faxed to the former coast of Israel. Pinchas had ordered a large, 4-wheel drive vehicle and they picked it up at a supply station in the ruins of the old coastal city of Caesarea and drove through a gap in the tumbled-down Coast Wall and then on down into the Mediterranean Basin.

"I wonder if the posts are going to get rid of the Dam and all of this reclaimed land," said Petra at one point.

"I would think so," said Pinchas.

It was a mostly silent drive. In the rougher basin slopes they zigzagged past boulders, fissures, and frequent shipwrecks rising from the rocky soil. Lower down, dirt roads ran through the endless servitor-tended fields and wild cycad forests, but the whole basin had a dementia-era feel to it that gave both of them the creeps. Atlantis was no better. Driving through the wide streets—empty except for the inevitable voynix—Petra suggested that the abandoned posthuman city reminded her of a three-dimensional version of a circuit board.

"What's a circuit board?" asked Pinchas.

"Something that Savi showed me years ago," said Petra and dropped the subject.

There were several egg-shaped shuttles parked near the city nexus. Pinchas looked at the nearest shuttle and wondered idly what would happen if he and Petra somehow managed to get into one and ordered it to return to the e-ring with them. Nothing, he was sure. They had all learned that old-style humans and posthuman technology did not mix well.

The main nexus rose in a thousand short, irregular slabs, some topped with violet energy or shifting from phase state to phase state and place to place like the oversized electrons they were. It was an impressive sight, but not pretty to Pinchas or Petra. *Alien.*

Moira met them on the irregularly spaced front steps of the structure. "It was nice of you to come, my dears," said the post. A few other posts were visible moving in the nexus shadows and walking atop the airborne bronze conduits beyond it.

"Your message said that you knew something about Savi's whereabouts," said Petra.

Moira nodded. "Would you like a drink first? Lunch?"

Petra shook her head and waited.

"Your friend was found in a hollowed-out iceberg south of the Falklands," said Moira. "She had brought some life-support equipment there but the iceberg was breaking up—calving—literally falling apart around her, so it was lucky that we searched for her when we did."

Pinchas frowned. "What do you mean? Why didn't she just fax out? Is Savi all right?"

Moira nodded and wiped sweat from her brow. Her gray hair

was only an inch or so long but it shined silver in the heavy Mediterranean light. "Physically she is well enough," said Moira, "but she appears to have suffered what used to be called a nervous breakdown. A neurological persona wavefront collapse."

"What are you talking about?" snapped Petra. "That sort of thing doesn't happen to us."

"Of course it does, my dear," said Moira. "All of the old-styles are prone to neurological and psychological problems. It comes from the extended life span. Stress, tension, and worries can trigger them and do, more frequently than you know. My dears, you were not designed for such long lives."

"Where is she?" said Pinchas. "Where is Savi now?"

Moira raised her finger. "In the fax matrix, of course. Undergoing transcription repair. I assure you that she will be well and happy upon her return."

Petra took a breath. "Do you keep . . . originals?"

"Original what, my dear?"

"You know, bodies," said Petra. "Original old-styles. Savi. Pinchas. Me."

Moira laughed easily. "No, no, my dear. The only originals we keep are the original quantum state patterns in fax memory. Surely you must understand that. And even those aren't 'original' as you put it, since updated memories and persona wavefronts are never the same from microsecond to microsecond, much less from fax to fax. No, my dear, there are no hidden originals."

"When will Savi be back?" said Pinchas. "Can we see her today?"

"I'm afraid not," said Moira. "The transcription repair will not be complete for two or three days."

"I understood that quantum state alterations were instantaneous," said Petra, suspicion in her voice.

Moira's smile was gentle. "They are, my dear, to all intents and purposes. But the organic reconstruction does take time. Your friend will join you in a few days."

"But we'll be *gone* in a few days," said Petra. She had not intended it, but her tone came perilously close to a whine.

Moira shook her head. "Not gone, Petra my dear. Merely in modulated quantum state, perfectly safe, actually, in the mobius loop of the neutrino stream. Savi will be there as well. Certainly you understand that there will be no sense of time passing. It will be less than a blink of an eye for all of you— even if it entails a rather tiresome ten thousand years for the rest of us."

"So you say," said Pinchas.

"Yes," said Moira. She smiled at them.

Pinchas and Petra crawled back into their vehicle and drove back to the Israeli highlands.

ON the morning of the final fax, Petra and Pinchas went scuba diving in the Red Sea, down along the great wall. On their dive belts were palm-sized dissuaders in case the hammerheads or other sharks in the sun-shafted waters took interest in them, but the only attention they received was from sea fans and softer things waving slightly in the tricky currents.

They made love later, on the soft sand, and then made love again. Lying there afterward, as was their private habit, Pinchas's head on Petra's left breast, her fingers gently kneading his relaxed penis and scrotum, they spoke in whispers.

"Did you believe the post . . . about Savi, I mean," said Petra. Her fingers knew him perfectly.

With his eyes closed, smelling the distant iodine of seaweed and the much closer scent of Petra's skin and sweet perspiration, Pinchas said, "I don't know. I don't really give a damn."

"Well," said Petra, kissing the top of his head, "we'll know tomorrow."

Pinchas kissed her nipple. "Yes. We'll know tomorrow."

"If there is a tomorrow," whispered Petra.

"Yes," said Pinchas and moved his cheek across her breast. His penis stirred and stiffened in her hand.

"Good heavens," said Petra, grasping him tighter and kissing him as his face came up to hers.

"Yes," breathed Pinchas in her ear.

❋   ❋   ❋

The final fax was scheduled for just after sunset in the Mid-East. All of the old-styles on Earth would be faxed away at the same instant, of course. Many of them planned final parties for the event, but a majority chose to meet the event in solitude or—like Petra and Pinchas—alone with someone they loved.

The two faxed to Jerusalem for dinner. Pinchas had been there before, but Petra had not. The city was empty except for servitors who prepared them an excellent meal in the King David Hotel west of the walls of the Old City. A city empty except for servitors and voynix. There seemed to be a lot of voynix around.

The vegetables were fresh and well-prepared, the mutton very good, and the wine was excellent, but neither of them took much notice. They held hands from time to time.

After dinner, with the sun red and low above the trees to the west along Gaza Road, they strolled hand in hand through the Jaffa Gate and into the Old City. Avoiding David Street and the other main thoroughfares, Pinchas and Petra made their way through the souk-vaulted maze of the Former Christian Quarter and the Former Muslim Quarter. The souks were mostly in deep shadow, but near the Church of the Holy Sepulchre they came out of that shadow and crossed an ancient bridge in a rush of rose-colored light.

"Moving in glory, across a bridge of gossamer," Petra said very softly.

"What is that?"

"Just some prophecy that Savi told me about decades and decades ago," said Petra. "Some entering Jerusalem at the End of Days myth. I can't remember if it was Christian or Muslim or Jewish. It doesn't matter." She took his hand and they continued walking toward the Haram esh-Sharif.

"We'd better hurry," said Pinchas, glancing up anxiously between steep stone walls at the rings meshing in the cloudless sky. The orbital cities were brightening in the long rays of the setting sun.

There were, really, an amazing number of voynix in the otherwise empty city. Pinchas and Petra had to dodge around their motionless, rusted bulks as they hurried toward the Western Wall. It was five minutes until final fax.

Emerging on the raised area just above the plaza in front of the Kotel, both of them stopped their jogging and froze in place, still holding hands.

The plaza lights had come on, even though the twilight was still bright. Below them, filling almost all of the space between them and the Wall, stood hundreds or thousands of voynix, all of them oriented toward the Kotel—the Wall itself.

"Come on," said Pinchas, a strange, thick urgency filling his chest and throat. He took her hand and started to lead her down the steps into the silent, inhuman throng.

A floating servitor blocked their way. The thing's cartoonlike arms and hands tugged insistently at Pinchas's sleeve. Pinchas understood. He took a paper kippa from the servitor and placed it on his head. The servitor slid aside and let them pass.

Pinchas stopped again. "Look," he said, pointing. His voice trembled. It was one minute until final fax.

"I know," whispered Petra. "So many of them. I've never seen so many. . . ."

"No," said Pinchas. He pointed again.

The empty Temple Mount was no longer empty. The last time he had visited Jerusalem, there had been only the rubble of the Dome of the Rock and the Al-Aksa Mosque on the raised area. Now a heavy structure of gleaming white Jerusalem stone was in the process of being erected atop the Mount. Voynix were visible everywhere on the rising walls and readied stones.

"Oh, damn," whispered Pinchas. "They're rebuilding the Temple."

"Who?" said Petra, totally confused.

Before Pinchas could answer, every voynix in sight—those thousands in the Kotel plaza, those hundreds more huddled at the base of the Wall, the many more spaced along the new Temple works—turned toward the two old-style humans.

The sound, when it came, was not an actual noise—certainly

not speech or sound as Pinchas or Petra had ever encountered it—but more a modulated rumble that moved through their bodies and echoed in their skulls via some terrible bone conduction. It was loud enough to be the voice of God, but it was clearly not the voice of God.

Thirty seconds until final fax and the noise struck Petra and Pinchas to their knees, their hands covering their ears in a useless attempt to block out the roaring words, on their knees and screaming in pain in front of the countless blind but staring voynix as the bone-conducted rumble grew louder and louder in them and around them.

"Itbah al-Yahud!"

SAVI, still in her iceberg a few minutes before final fax, reading the time on the luminous dial of her watch, decided that it was time to act.

She used the big-bore burner to cut her way from the fissure-tunnel to the buried tent, but carefully, carefully.

It *was* the tent, of course. It had been collapsed, but the lateral pressure from the ice had forced it up almost into its original pyramidal shape and it seemed to expand as Savi finished melting the ice around it. She drove an ice piton into the roof of her new ice cave and clipped a carabiner onto the apex of the ancient tent canvas, using the piton to lift it as the bamboo centerpole once had.

Only one halogen stick worked now, but she kept it with her as she dragged her thermoblank and diary into the black mouth of the tent with her. The pistol lay forgotten in one of the abandoned caves. There were two minutes left until final fax.

Bowers, Wilson, and Scott were exactly as Cherry-Garrard had described them. Savi knew that this was impossible after all this time, but she did not have time to worry about that. Making room between Bowers's body and Wilson's, Savi squeezed in and opened her diary to the last page. In such tight quarters, she subconsciously expected to be warmer, but the frozen corpses seemed to steal her warmth. The small space, briefly warmed by the big-bore burner but now cooling rapidly, smelled like a supply station meat locker Savi had visited long, long ago. Savi was still historian enough to note that—just as Cherry-Garrard had said—the rock-hard flesh of Scott, Wilson, and Bowers showed no signs of the men having taken morphine from Wilson's medical chest at the end. There were no dark circles under the dead, sunken, closed eyes.

Savi's hand was shaking with the cold but she managed to steady her stylus long enough to write—*"We were all The Lost Boys. It was never the posthumans. It was always a case of . . ."*

She stopped and laughed out loud. Setting her stylus back in her thermsuit pocket, tucking her frozen hands in her armpits, Savi continued laughing. Who was she kidding? The only old-style she knew who could read her last note without invoking a function was a scholar named Graf, and he would be gone in . . . thirty-six seconds.

Savi's laughter echoed in the lightless ice caverns. Suddenly, with thirty seconds until final fax, the laughter stopped.

The last halogen stick was fading away in Savi's lap, but it still shed a sick and dying circle of light in the tent. Enough for her to see by.

Wilson, Scott, and Bowers had opened their eyes.

Savi did the only thing that an old-style human being could do under the circumstances. "Fuck it," she said. "Fuck it all." And she laughed again.

Introduction to "On K2 with Kanakaredes"

....

One of the few pieces of conventional wisdom that I've come to believe is the statement that people tend to be attracted to either the mountains or the ocean. I'm a mountain person. My wife's an ocean person.

This isn't to say that I don't love being near the sea, I do, or that my wife doesn't love the mountains . . . well, she doesn't actually, she's lived in Colorado for twenty-seven years now and while she appreciates the aesthetics of the high peaks, she certainly hasn't grown to love them . . . but I do enjoy the ocean. It's just that in most cases one has to choose to live near mountains or ocean (if one has the luxury of even that choice), and since 1974 I've chosen mountains—the Colorado Rockies, to be exact.

Both high mountains and ocean, according to Freud, tend to give rise to what he called an "oceanic" feeling—the sense that one is confronted with something vaster than comprehension, not bound by human scale, and quite possibly alive, if not sentient. The sea certainly seems more alive than the high peaks; its most salient feature to me, when I am living by the shore, is its constant susurration, its night-whispers and morning declarations, that constant low conversation that can shift into a scream of wind and surf with almost no notice. The ocean has the potential to calm or terrify the human spirit, shifting both its mood and ours in a blink of the eye. In that sense, living near the sea is like living with another human being.

But mountains also speak to us. Windwalker *is the name of my 115 acres of isolated property situated near Allenspark, Colorado, at 8,400 feet altitude along the base of the Continental Divide. The name of the place is appropriate, since the wind— often swooping from the jet stream and being channeled down and off the east side of the Divide through the glacial valley funnel of Wild Basin directly onto my hillside—walks through the trees and grasses and rock ledges there. At night, especially in winter, the Douglas fir and lodgepole and ponderosa pines whisper and shake and sigh, even on the leeward side of the hill where my cabin rocks to the gusts some three hundred feet above the valley floor. The tall grasses on the south-facing hillside, grasses returning from their cheatgrass and grazed state to the more-graceful native species in the eight years or so that I've been steward there, also stir and hiss to the movement of the mountain wind, as do the taller, greener, softer grasses of the wetlands on the east side of the big pond in the valley below. Sometimes those cattails and marsh grasses ripple to the breezes like a cat's hair being stroked and the sound of the wind's passing is as soothing as the roll of surf.*

Watching the ocean change is a lifelong vocation, but so is living in sight of serious mountains. The high peaks are never the same from hour to hour, much less from day to day. From the windows of my full-time home and office in a small town on the high prairie some ten miles from the foothills, I watch the moods of the mountains. The sunlight is different here in Colorado, richer, harsher, since even at just my hometown's altitude of 5,300 feet, we are above almost half of the Earth's atmosphere, and often the light plays pointtillist tricks with the snowfields and trailing vegetation and gray granite visible above treeline to the west. The forests of pine and fir below treeline glow lichen-green one second and glower brooding-black the next. Clouds pile thirty thousand feet high along the line of peaks as they try to carry their weight of moisture from the west side of the Divide to the dryer east. That cloud-dam accumulates high and white, curling even higher upon itself in its daylong attempt to spill over the Divide. There's a certain pleasant tension in waiting for this cloud-tsunami to spill over onto the high plains, and on summer days it does so almost every afternoon, sending storms dragging along the prairie or simply releasing herds of puffy cumulus parading eastward like so many sheep against the blue. The Continental Divide is our weather-maker here in the same way that Lake Erie was when I lived in Buffalo, New York, responsible for everything from rare, rainy upslope conditions that leave us entombed in fog and rain for days, to the snow-eating Chinook winds in the winter that blow down from the northwest to raise temperatures forty degrees in an hour.

Look once and the high peaks twenty-five miles west are crystal clear, stone-sharp, knife-edge bold—from my office window I can see from the Mummy Range in Wyoming sixty miles to the north to Pikes Peak a hundred and twenty miles to the south— but look again a few hours later and the peaks and foothills are layers of shade, patterns of subtlety, as muted and soft as any Japanese watercolor.

I've written a bit about mountains. In my science fiction novel The Rise of Endymion *I have a world where the lower atmosphere is poisonous and acidic, and the human colonists must live on the hundreds of high peaks and ridgelines and pinnacles rising above the deadly soup. The world is called T'ien Shan— the Mountains of Heaven—and at one point my narrator-character, Raul Endymion, lists many of those mountain realms, all named after sacred peaks on Earth or legends of high peaks and their divine or monstrous inhabitants. The list was fun for me to share—Harney Peak (Black Elk's "center of the universe"), Nanda Devi where the Yellow Goddess of Bliss is said to dwell; Muztagh Alta where thousands of Islam's faithful guard the tombs of Ali and the other saints of Islam; Chomo Lori, "Queen of the Snow"; Helgafell—the Mead Hall of the Dead— shrouded in white glaciers; Demchog, the Buddhist peak, meaning "One of Supreme Bliss"—and so on. It was so much fun to list these sacred high places that I was sure that my editor would round on it, ready to cut it, appalled at its redundancy. She was and did. I didn't. What's the value of being a novelist if one can't indulge in such asides from time to time?*

The truth is that most real mountains on Earth are sacred to someone—often to many peoples at once—but those tribes and villagers and holy men who hold the high peaks sacred never climb the damned things. Too holy. Too far away. Too deadly. Besides, something climbed and "conquered" loses its aura of sacred power (except to those who have climbed it.)

The oceans of the world are deadly—we have to feed our seas to earn the right to sail on them or live near them—but one can weave metaphors of a mother's warm embrace during a burial at sea; death in the mountains is invariably cold and lonely.

My real reasons for writing "On K2 with Kanakaredes" are— as with all works of fiction—varied and probably neither fully understood nor worth the effort of pursuing, but my motive for writing the story was simple enough. During my teaching stint at the Odyssey Writers' Workshop in the summer of 2000, I ran across several adult students who could really write. One of them, a former lawyer named Laura Whitton, had an almost-realized story that I found so compelling I recommended it to editor Al Sarrantonio, who had recently contacted me about contributing to a major anthology called Redshift. *I hadn't planned to write a short piece for Al's anthology—as much as I love short fiction, I write little of it because of the deadlines and demands of my novels, screenplays, and other longer projects— but when he accepted Ms. Whitton's story, "Froggie Dreams," it seemed only polite that I should write a story for him.*

K2 has always been known as an especially deadly mountain and I've always wanted to trek in to the base of it. But the closest I've gotten to the Himalayas or the Karakoram was a nightmare few days and nights in Calcutta more than twenty years ago, so I had to resort to research and the memories of climbers' tales. I set aside a week (well, it was the week before Al's deadline) to write this story, and the first thing I did was to decide on the route up K2 and the mountaineering techniques my characters would use to climb the peak. The route chosen for the story is common enough, the techniques less reliant on technology than a lot of Himalayan climbs are today. (This is the nice paradox about truly advanced technology—it allows outdoors people to get back to basics.)

The characters use an "alpine-style ascent," which is coming more and more into vogue with the exceptionally bold and fit climbers in the Himalayas and Karakoram at the beginning of the 21st Century. An alpine ascent is the classic go-for-it climb used on lower peaks—demanding very little in the way of logistics or materiel or time—as opposed to the more traditional pyramid-style attempt on an 8,000-meter peak, starting with dozens or even hundreds of load-bearers and climbers, moving up and down the ascent route repeatedly on fixed ropes, establishing camp above camp while moving materiel ever higher, and finally sending only a few climbers from the highest camp on a dash for the summit. With alpine-style ascents, everyone goes for the top. It's all or nothing and a few days of storm—being pinned down on a ridge near 24,000 feet—means death for everyone. Such alpine ascents offer less time to acclimate but also demand less time spent in the Death Zone. Any mountain rising to 8,000 meters or more (you'll notice that I mix both metric units and English units in the story, as do many veteran American and English climbers I've known) demands the mountaineers risk the Death Zone, a hostile, alien region filled not only with terrible winds, lunar cold, and the worst objective dangers a mountain can offer, but also with the inevitability of oxygen-starvation, severely reduced mental capacity, and the probability of embolisms and blood clots in the lungs. One element common to climbers' tales at that altitude is the sense that there are other, nonworldly climbers on the rope, ghosts climbing with you even on a solo ascent. Climber after climber—from Mallory's day to the present—have come down to lower camps only to report long conversations with climbers who were not there, or who had died days or decades before. Human beings did not evolve to work and function at such altitude and—as it turns out—neither did the "mantispid" alien in our tale.

I've rarely used nonhumanoid aliens in my fiction, so it was fun designing both Kanakaredes and his home world. Somewhere in my stacks and piles of documents here, I have a drawing—a diagram, really—of Kanakaredes and his ilk, and if I can find it, I'll end this introduction with it. (If I can't find the sketch, you'll just have to go on imagining Kanakaredes, which—I suspect—is better anyway.)

The Bugs, for their purposes in this story, might just as well have sent their emissary to join three human friends who were planning to sail around the world in a small boat. The risks would have been as great. The test, if test it is, would be as real. I wish I could start this story over, or write its twin, with just that premise, and revel in the research and aesthetics of sailing the open ocean as I did with the dangers of K2.

As Wordsworth wrote—

Two voices are there: one is of the sea,
One of the mountains; each a mighty voice.

On K2 with Kanakaredes

The South Col of Everest, 26,200 feet

IF we hadn't decided to acclimate ourselves for the K2 attempt by secretly climbing to the 8,000-meter mark on Everest, a stupid mountain that no self-respecting climber would go near anymore, they wouldn't have caught us and we wouldn't have been forced to make the real climb with an alien and the rest of it might not have happened. But we did and we were and it did.

What else is new? It's as old as Chaos theory. The best-laid plans of mice and men and so forth and so on. As if you have to tell *that* to a climber.

Instead of heading directly for our Concordia Base Camp at the foot of K2, the three of us had used Gary's nifty little stealth CMG to fly northeast into the Himalaya, straight to the *bergeschrund* of the Khumbu Glacier at 23,000 feet. Well, fly *almost* straight to the glacier; we had to zig and zag to stay under HK Syndicate radar and to avoid seeing or being seen by that stinking prefab pile of Japanese shit called the Everest Base Camp Hotel (rooms U.S. $4,500 a night, not counting Himalayan access fee and CMG limo fare.)

We landed without being detected (or so we thought), made sure the vehicle was safely tucked away from the icefalls, seracs, and avalanche paths, left the CMG set in conceal mode, and

started our Alpine-style conditioning climb to the South Col.
The weather was brilliant. The conditions were perfect. We
climbed brilliantly. It was the stupidest thing the three of us had
ever done.

By late on the third afternoon we had reached the South Col,
that narrow, miserable, windswept notch of ice and boulders
wedged high between the shoulders of Lhotse and Everest. We
activated our little smart tents, merged them, anchored them
hard to ice-spumed rock, and keyed them white to keep them
safe from prying eyes.

Even on a beautiful late-summer Himalayan evening such as
the one we enjoyed that day, weather on the South Col sucks.
Wind velocities average higher than those encountered near the
summit of Everest. Any high-climber knows that when you see a
stretch of relatively flat rock free of snow, it means hurricane
winds. These arrived on schedule just about sunset of that third
day. We hunkered down in the communal tent and made soup.
Our plan was to spend two nights on the South Col and acclimate ourselves to the lower edge of the Death Zone before
heading down and flying on to Concordia for our legal K2 climb.
We had no intention of climbing higher than the South Col on
Everest. Who would?

At least the view was less tawdry since the Syndicate cleaned
up Everest and the South Col, flying off more than a century's
worth of expedition detritus—ancient fixed ropes, countless tent
tatters, tons of frozen human excrement, about a million abandoned oxygen bottles, and a few hundred frozen corpses. Everest in the 20th Century had become the equivalent of the old
Oregon Trail—everything that could be abandoned had been,
including climbers' dead friends.

Actually, the view that evening was rather good. The Col
drops off to the east for about 4,000 feet into what used to be Ti-
bet and falls even more sharply—about 7,000 feet—to the
Western Cwm. That evening, the high ridges of Lhotse and the
entire visible west side of Everest caught the rich, golden sunset

for long minutes after the Col moved into shadow and then the temperature at our campsite dropped about a hundred degrees. There was not, as we outdoors people like to say, a cloud in the sky. The high peaks glowed in all of their 8,000-meter glory, snowfields burning orange in the light. Gary and Paul lay in the open door of the tent, still wearing their thermskin uppers, and watched the stars emerge and shake to the hurricane-wind as I fiddled and fussed with the stove to make soup. Life was good.

Suddenly an incredibly amplified voice bellowed, "You there in the tent!"

I almost pissed my thermskins. I *did* spill the soup, slopping it all over Paul's sleeping bag.

"Fuck," I said.

"Goddamn it," said Gary, watching the black CMG—its UN markings glowing and powerful searchlights stabbing—settle gently onto small boulders not twenty feet from the tent.

"Busted," said Paul.

Hillary Room, Top of the World, 29,035 feet

Two years in an HK floating prison wouldn't have been as degrading as being made to enter that revolving restaurant on the top of Everest. All three of us protested, Gary the loudest since he was the oldest and richest, but the four UN security guys in the CMG just cradled their standard-issue Uzis and said nothing until the vehicle had docked in the restaurant airlock-garage and the pressure had been equalized. We stepped out reluctantly and followed other security guards deeper into the closed and darkened restaurant even more reluctantly. Our ears were going crazy. One minute we'd been camping at 26,000 feet and a few minutes later the pressure was the standard airline equivalent of 5,000 feet. It was painful, despite the UN CMG's attempt to match pressures while it circled the dark hulk of Everest for ten minutes.

By the time we were led into the Hillary Room to the only lighted table in the place, we were angry *and* in pain.

"Sit down," said Secretary of State Betty Willard Bright Moon. We sat. There was no mistaking the tall, sharp-featured Blackfoot woman in the gray suit. Every pundit agreed that she was the single toughest and most interesting personality in the Cohen administration, and the four U.S. Marines in combat garb standing in the shadows behind her only added to her already imposing sense of authority. The three of us sat, Gary closest to the dark window wall across from Secretary Bright Moon, Paul next to him, and me farthest away from the action. It was our usual climbing pattern.

On the expensive teak table in front of Secretary Bright Moon were three blue dossiers. I couldn't read the tabs on them, but I had little doubt about their contents: Dossier #1, Gary Sheridan, 49, semiretired, former CEO of SherPath International, multiple addresses around the world, made his first millions at age seventeen during the long lost and rarely lamented dot-com gold rush of yore, divorced (four times), a man of many passions, the greatest of which was mountain climbing; Dossier #2, Paul Ando Hiraga, 28, ski bum, professional guide, one of the world's best rock-and-ice climbers, unmarried; Dossier #3, Jake Richard Pettigrew, 36, Boulder, Colorado, married, three children, high school math teacher, a good-to-average climber with only two 8,000-meter peaks bagged, both thanks to Gary and Paul, who invited him to join them on international climbs for the six previous years. Mr. Pettigrew still cannot believe his good luck at having a friend and patron bankroll his climbs, especially when both Gary and Paul were far better climbers with much more experience. But perhaps the dossiers told of how Jake, Paul, and Gary had become close friends as well as climbing partners over the past few years, friends who trusted each other to the point of trespassing on the Himalaya Preserve just to get acclimated for the climb of their lives.

Or perhaps the blue folders were just some State Department busywork that had nothing to do with us.

"What's the idea of hauling us up here?" asked Gary, his voice controlled but tight. Very tight. "If the Hong Kong Syndicate wants to throw us in the slammer, fine, but you and the UN can't just drag us somewhere against our will. We're still U.S. citizens . . ."

"U.S. citizens who have broken HK Syndicate Preserve rules and UN World Historical Site laws," snapped Secretary Bright Moon.

"We have a valid permit . . ." began Gary again. His forehead looked very red just below the line of his cropped, white hair.

"To climb K2, commencing three days from now," said the Secretary of State. "Your climbing team won the HK lottery. We know. But that permit does not allow you to enter or overfly the Himalaya Preserve, nor to trespass on Mt. Everest."

Paul glanced at me. I shook my head. I had no idea what was going on. We could have *stolen* Mt. Everest and it wouldn't have brought Secretary Betty Willard Bright Moon flying around the world to sit in this darkened revolving restaurant just to slap our wrists.

Gary shrugged and sat back. "So what do you want?"

Secretary Bright Moon opened the closest blue dossier and slid a photo across the polished teak toward us. We huddled to look at it.

"A bug?" said Gary.

"They prefer 'Listener,'" said the Secretary of State. "But mantispid will do."

"What do the bugs have to do with us?" said Gary.

"This particular bug wants to climb K2 with you in three days," said Secretary Bright Moon. "And the government of the United States of America in cooperation with the Listener Liaison and Cooperation Council of the United Nations fully intend to have him . . . or her . . . do so."

Paul's jaw dropped. Gary clasped his hands behind his head and laughed. I just stared. Somehow I found my voice first.

"That's impossible," I said.

Secretary Betty Willard Bright Moon turned her flat, dark-eyed gaze on me. "Why?"

Normally the combination of that woman's personality, her position, and those eyes would have stopped me cold, but this was too absurd to ignore. I just held out my hands, palms upward. Some things are too obvious to explain. "The bugs have six legs," I said at last. "They look like they can hardly walk. We're climbing the *second tallest mountain* on Earth. And the most savage."

Secretary Bright Moon did not blink. "The bu . . . the mantispids seem to get around their freehold in Antarctica quite well," she said flatly. "And sometimes they walk on two legs."

Paul snorted. Gary kept his hands clasped behind his head, his shoulders back, posture relaxed, but his eyes were flint. "I presume that if this bug climbed with us, that you'd hold us responsible for his safety and well-being," he said.

The Secretary's head turned as smoothly as an owl's. "You presume correctly," she said. "That would be our first concern. The safety of the Listeners is always our first concern."

Gary lowered his hands and shook his head. "Impossible. Above eight thousand meters, no one can help anyone."

"That's why they call that altitude the Death Zone," said Paul. He sounded angry.

Bright Moon ignored Paul and kept her gaze locked with Gary's. She had spent too many decades steeped in power, negotiation, and political in-fighting not to know who our leader was. "We can make the climb safer," she said. "Phones, CMG's on immediate call, uplinks . . ."

Gary was shaking his head again. "We do this climb without phones and medevac capability from the mountain."

"That's absurd . . ." began the Secretary of State.

Gary cut her off. "That's the way it is," he said. "That's what real mountaineers *do* in this day and age. And what we don't do is come to this fucking obscenity of a restaurant." He gestured toward the darkened Hillary Room to our right, the gesture including all of the revolving Top of the World. One of the Marines blinked at Gary's obscenity.

Secretary Bright Moon did not blink. "All right, Mr. Sheridan. The phones and CMG medevacs are not negotiable. I presume everything else is."

Gary said nothing for a minute. Finally, "I presume that if we say no, that you're going to make our lives a living hell."

The Secretary of State smiled ever so slightly. "I think that all of you will find that there will be no more visas for foreign climbs," she said. "Ever. And all of you may encounter difficulties with your taxes soon. Especially you, Mr. Sheridan, since your corporate accounts are so . . . complicated."

Gary returned her smile. For an instant it seemed as if he were actually enjoying this. "And if we say yes," he said slowly, almost drawling, "what's in it for us?"

Bright Moon nodded and one of the lackeys to her left opened another dossier and slid a slick color photograph across the table toward us. Again all three of us leaned forward to look. Paul frowned. It took me a minute to figure out what it was—some sort of reddish shield volcano. Hawaii?

"Mars," Gary said softly. "Olympus Mons."

Secretary Bright Moon said, "It is more than twice as tall as Mt. Everest."

Gary laughed easily. "Twice as tall? Shit, woman, Olympus Mons is more than three times the height of Everest—more than eighty-eight thousand feet high, three hundred and thirty-five miles in diameter. The caldera is fifty-three miles wide. Christ, the outward facing cliff ringing the bottom of the thing is taller than Everest—thirty-two thousand eight hundred feet, vertical with an overhang."

Bright Moon had finally blinked at the "Shit, woman"—I wondered wildly when the last time had been that someone had spoken to this Secretary of State like that—but now she smiled.

Gary said, "So what? The Mars program is dead. We chickened out, just like with the Apollo Program seventy-five years ago. Don't tell me that you're offering to send us there, because we don't even have the technology to go back."

"The bugs do," said Secretary Bright Moon. "And if you agree to let the son of the mantispid speaker climb K2 with you, the Listeners guarantee that they will transport you to Mars within twelve months—evidently the transit time will be only two weeks each direction—and they'll outfit a mountain climbing expedition up Olympus Mons for you. Pressure suits, re-breathers, the whole nine yards."

The three of us exchanged glances. We did not have to discuss this. We looked back at the photograph. Finally Gary looked up at Bright Moon. "What do we have to do other than climb with him?"

"Keep him alive if you can," she said.

Gary shook his head. "You heard Paul. Above eight thousand meters, we can't guarantee even keeping ourselves alive."

The Secretary nodded, but said softly, "Still, if we added a simple emergency calling device to one of your palmlogs—a dis-tress beacon, as it were—this would allow us to come quickly to evacuate the mantispid if there were a problem or illness or in-jury to him, without interfering with the . . . integrity . . . of the rest of your climb."

"A red panic button," said Gary but the three of us ex-changed glances. This idea was distasteful but reasonable in its way. Besides, once the bug was taken off the hill, for whatever reason, the three of us could get on with the climb and maybe still get a crack at Olympus Mons. "What else?" Gary asked the woman.

Secretary Bright Moon folded her hands and lowered her gaze a moment. When she looked up again, her gaze appeared to be candid. "You gentlemen know how little the mantispids have talked to us . . . how little technology they have shared with us . . ."

"They gave us CMG," interrupted Gary.

"Yes," said Bright Moon, "CMG in exchange for their Antarctic freehold. But we've only had hints of the other wonders they could share with us—generation starflight technology, a cure for cancer, free energy. The Listeners just . . . well, *listen*. This is the first overture they've made."

The three of us waited.

"We want you to record everything this son of the Speaker says during the climb," said Secretary Bright Moon. "Ask questions. Listen to the answers. Make friends with him if you can. That's all."

Gary shook his head. "We don't want to wear a wire." Before Bright Moon could object, he went on, "We have to wear thermskins—molecular heat membranes. We're not going to wear wires under or over them."

The Secretary looked as if she was ready to order the Marines to shoot Gary and probably throw Paul and me out the window, not that the window could be opened. The whole damned restaurant was pressurized.

"I'll do it," I said.

Gary and Paul looked at me in surprise. I admit that I was also surprised at the offer. I shrugged. "Why not? My folks died of cancer. I wouldn't mind finding a cure. You guys can weave a recording wire into my overparka. Or I can use the recorder in my palmlog. I'll record the bug when I can, but I'll summarize the other conversations on my palmlog. You know, keep a record of things."

Secretary Betty Willard Bright Moon looked as if she was swallowing gall, but she nodded, first to us and then at the Marine guards. The Marines came around the table to escort us back to the UN CMG.

"Wait," said Gary before we were led away. "Does this bug have a name?"

"Kanakaredes," said the Secretary of State, not even looking up at us.

"Sounds Greek," said Paul.

"I seriously doubt it," said Secretary Bright Moon.

K2 Base Camp, 16,500 feet

I guess I expected a little flying saucer—a smaller version of the shuttle craft the bugs had first landed near the UN nine years earlier—but they all arrived in an oversized, bright red Daimler Chrysler CMG. I saw them first and shouted. Gary and Paul came out of the supply tent where they had been triple-checking our provisions.

Secretary Bright Moon wasn't there to see us off, of course—we hadn't spoken to her since the night at the Top of the World three days earlier—but the Listener Liaison guy, William Grimes, and two of his aides got out of the CMG, as did two bugs, one slightly larger than the other. The smaller mantispid had some sort of clear, bubbly backpack along his dorsal ridge, nestled in the "V" where its main body section joined the prothorax.

The three of us crossed the boulder field until we were facing the five of them. It was the first time I had ever seen the aliens in person—I mean, who ever sees a bug *in person*?—and I admit that I was nervous. Behind us, above us, spindrift and cloud whirled from the ridges and summit of K2. If the mantispids smelled weird, I couldn't pick it up since the breeze was blowing from behind the three of us.

"Mr. Sheridan, Mr. Hiraga, Mr. Pettigrew," said the bureaucrat Grimes, "may I introduce Listener Speaker Aduradake and his . . . son . . . Kanakaredes."

The taller of the two bugs unfolded that weird arm or foreleg, swiveled the short forearm thing up like a praying mantis unlimbering, and offered Gary its three-fingered hand. Gary shook it. Paul shook it. I shook it. It felt boneless.

The shorter bug watched, its two primary eyes black and unreadable, its smaller side-eyes lidded and sleepy-looking. It—Kanakaredes—did not offer to shake hands.

"My people thank you for agreeing to allow Kanakaredes to accompany you on this expedition," said Speaker Aduradake. I don't know if they used implanted voice synthesizers to speak to us—I think not—but the English came out as a carefully modulated series of clicks and sighs. Quite understandable, but strange, very strange.

"No problem," said Gary.

It looked as if the UN bureaucrats wanted to say more—make some speeches, perhaps—but Speaker Aduradake swiveled on his four rear legs and picked his way across the boulders to the CMG's ramp. The humans scurried to catch up. Half a minute later and the vehicle was nothing more than a red speck in the blue southern sky.

The four of us stood there silent for a second, listening to the wind howl around the remaining seracs of the Godwin-Austen Glacier and through niches in the wind-carved boulders. Finally Gary said, "You bring all the shit we e-mailed you about?"

"Yes," said Kanakaredes. His forearms swiveled in their high sockets, the long mantis femur moved up and back, and the third segment swiveled downward so that the soft, three-fingered hands could pat the clear pack on his back. "Brought all the shit, just as you e-mailed." His clicks and sighs sounded just like the other bug's.

"Compatible North Face smart tent?" said Gary.

The bug nodded—or at least I took that movement of the broad, beaked head as a nod. Gary must also have. "Rations for two weeks?" he asked.

"Yes," said Kanakaredes.

"We have the climbing gear for you," said Gary. "Grimes said that you've practiced with it all—crampons, ropes, knots, weblines, ice axe, jumars—that you've been on a mountain before."

"Mt. Erebus," said Kanakaredes. "I have practiced there for some months."

Gary sighed. "K2 is a little different from Mt. Erebus."

We were all silent again for a bit. The wind howled and blew my long hair forward around my face. Finally Paul pointed up the glacier where it curved near Base Camp and rose toward the east side of K2 and beneath the back side of Broad Peak. I could just see the icefall where the glacier met the Abruzzi Ridge on K2. That ridge, path of the first attempt on the mountain and line of the first successful summit assault, was our fallback route if our attempt on the North-East Ridge and East Face fell behind schedule.

"You see, we could fly over the glacier and start the climb from the base of the Abruzzi at 18,000 feet," said Paul, "miss all the crevasse danger that way, but it's part of the climb to start from here."

Kanakaredes said nothing. His two primary eyes had clear membranes but the eyes never blinked. They stared blackly at Paul. The other two eyes were looking God knows where.

I felt that I should say something. Anything. I cleared my throat.

"Fuck it," said Gary. "We're burning daylight. Let's load 'em up and move 'em out."

Camp One, North-East Ridge, about 18,300 feet

They call K2 "the savage mountain" and a hundred other names—all respectful. It's a killer mountain; more men and women have died on it in terms of percentage of those attempting to climb it than on any other peak in the Himalayas or the Karakoram. It is not malevolent. It is simply the Zen-essence of *mountain*—hard, tall, pyramidal when seen from the south in the perfect child's-drawing iconic model of the Matterhorn, jagged, steep, knife-ridged, wracked by frequent avalanche and unearthly storms, its essentially airless summit almost continuously blasted by the Jet Stream. No contortion of sentiment or personification can suggest that this mountain gives the slightest shit about human hopes or human life. In a way that is impossible to articulate and politically incorrect even to suggest, K2 is profoundly masculine. It is eternally indifferent and absolutely unforgiving. Climbers have loved it and triumphed on it and died on it for more than a century.

Now it was our turn to see which way this particular prayer wheel turned.

Have you ever watched a mantispid bug walk? I mean, we've all seen them on HDTV or VirP—there's an entire satellite channel dedicated to them, for Christ's sake—but usually that's just quick cuts, long-lens images, or static shots of the bug Speaker and some political bigshots standing around somewhere. Have you ever watched them *walk* for any length of time?

In crossing the upper reaches of the Godwin-Austen Glacier under the eleven-thousand-foot vertical wall that is the East Face of K2, you have two choices. You can stay near the edges of the glacier, where there are almost no crevasses, and risk serious avalanche danger, or you can stick to the center of the glacier and never know when the snow and ice underfoot are suddenly going to collapse into a hidden crevasse. Any climber worth his or her salt will choose the crevasse-route if there's even a hint of avalanche risk. Skill and experience can help you avoid crevasses; there's not a goddamn thing in the world you can do except pray when an avalanche comes your way.

To climb the glacier, we had to rope up. Gary, Paul, and I had discussed this—whether or not to rope with the bug—but when we reached the part of the glacier where crevasses would be most probable, inevitable actually, we really didn't have a choice. It would have been murder to let Kanakaredes proceed unroped.

One of the first things all of us thought when the bugs landed almost ten years ago was "Are they wearing clothes?" We know now that they weren't—that their weird combination of chitinous exoskeleton on their main body section and layers of different membranes on the softer parts serve well in lieu of clothing—but that doesn't mean that they go around with their sexual parts showing. Theoretically, mantispids are sexual creatures—male or female—but I've never heard of a human being who's *seen* a bug's genitals, and I can testify that Gary, Paul, and I didn't want to be the first.

Still, the aliens rig themselves with toolbelts or harnesses or whatever when necessary—just as Kanakaredes had shown up with that weird bubblepack on his back with all of his climbing gear in it—and as soon as we started the ascent, he removed a harness from that pack and rigged it around that chunky, almost armored upper section of himself where his arm and midleg sockets were. He also used a regulation-sized metal ice axe, gripping the curved metal top in those three boneless fingers. It seemed strange to see something as prosaic as a red nylon climbing harness and carabiners and an ice axe on a bug, but that's what he had.

When it came time to rope up, we clipped the spidersilk line onto our 'biners, passing the line back in our usual climbing order, except that this time—instead of Paul's ass slowly slogging up the glacier in front of me—I got to watch Kanakaredes plod along ten paces ahead of me for hour after hour.

"Plod along" really doesn't do bug locomotion justice. We've all seen the bugs balance and walk on their midlegs, standing more upright on those balancing legs, their back straightening, their head coming up until they're tall enough to stare a short human male in the eye, their forelegs suddenly looking more like real arms than praying mantis appendages—but I suspect now that they do that just for that reason—to appear more human in their rare public appearances. So far, Kanakaredes had stood on just two legs only during the formal meeting back at Base Camp. As soon as we started hiking up the glacier, his head came down and forward, that "V" between his main body section and prothorax widened, those mantis-arms stretched straight ahead like a human extending two poles ahead of him, and he fell into a seemingly effortless four-legged motion.

But, Jesus Christ, what a weird motion. All of a bug's legs have three joints, of course, but I realized after only a few minutes of following this particular bug up the Godwin-Austen Glacier that those joints never seem to bend the same way at the same time. One of those praying mantis forelegs would be bent double and down so that Kanakaredes could plant his ice axe in the slope, while the other bent forward and then back so that he could scratch that weird beak of a snout. At the same time, the midlegs would be bending rather like a horse's, only instead of a hoof, the lower, shortest section ended in those chitinous but somehow dainty, divided . . . hell, I don't know, hoof-feet. And the hind legs, the ones socketed at the base of the soft prothorax . . . those are the ones that made me dizzy as I watched the bug climbing through soft snow in front of me. Sometimes the alien's knees—those first joints about two-thirds of the way down the legs—would be higher than his back. At other times one knee would be bending forward, the other one back, while the lower joints were doing even stranger things.

After a while, I gave up trying to figure out the engineering of the creature, and just began admiring the easy way it moved up the steep snow and ice. The three of us had worried about the small surface area of a bug's feet on snow—the V-shaped hoof-things aren't even as large as an unshod human foot—and wondered if we'd be tugging the mantispid out of every drift on our way up the mountain, but Kanakaredes managed quite well, thank you. I guess it was due to the fact that I guessed at that time that he probably only weighed about a hundred and fifty pounds, and that weight was spread out over four—and sometimes six, when he tucked the ice axe in his harness and scrambled—walking surfaces. To tell the truth, the bug had to help me slog clear of deep snow two or three times on the upper reaches of the glacier.

During the afternoon, with the sun blazing on the reflective bowl of ice that was the glacier, it got damned hot. The three of us humans damped our thermskin controls way down and shed our parka outer layers to cool off. The bug seemed comfortable enough, although he rested without complaint while we rested, drank water from his water bottle when we paused to drink, and chewed on something that looked like a shingle made of compressed dog poop while we munched our nutrient bars (which, I realize now, also looked a lot like a shingle made of compressed dog poop). If Kanakaredes suffered from overheating or chill that first long day on the glacier, he didn't show it.

Long before sunset, the mountain shadow had moved across us and three of the four of us were raising our thermskin thresholds and tugging on the parka shells again. It had begun snowing. Suddenly a huge avalanche calved off the East Face of K2 and swept down the slope behind us, boiling and rolling over a part of the glacier we had been climbing just an hour earlier.

We all froze in our tracks until the rumbling stopped. Our tracks in the shadowed snow—rising in a more-or-less straight line for a thousand-foot elevation gain over the last mile or so—looked like they had been rubbed out by a giant eraser for a swath of several hundred yards.

"Holy shit," I said.

Gary nodded, breathing a little hard since he had been breaking trail for most of the afternoon, turned, took a step, and disappeared.

For the last hours, whoever had been in the lead had probed ahead with his ice axe to make sure that the footing ahead was real and not just a skim of snow over a deep crevasse. Gary had taken two steps without doing this. And the crevasse got him.

One instant he was there, red parka glowing against the shadowed ice and the white snow on the ridge now so close ahead of us, and the next instant he was gone.

And then Paul disappeared as well.

No one screamed or reacted poorly. Kanakaredes instantly braced himself in full-belay posture, slammed his ice axe deep into the ice beneath him, and wrapped the line around it twice before the thirty feet or so of slack between him and Paul had played out. I did the same, digging crampons in as hard as I could, fully expecting the crevasse to pull the bug in and then me.

It didn't.

The line snapped taut but did not snap—genetically tailored spidersilk climbing rope almost never breaks—Kanakaredes's ice axe stayed firm, as did the bug holding it in the glacier ice, and the two of us held them. We waited a full minute in our rigid postures, making sure that we weren't also standing on a thin crust over a crevasse, but when it was obvious where the crevasse rim was, I gasped, "Keep them tight," unclipped, and crawled forward to peer down the black gap.

I have no idea how deep the crevasse was—a hundred feet? A thousand? But both Paul and Gary were dangling there—Paul a mere fifteen feet or so down, still in the light, looking fairly comfortable as he braced his back against the blue-green ice wall and rigged his climbing jumars. That clamp and cam device, infinitely lighter and stronger but otherwise no different than the jumars our grandfathers might have used, would get him back up on his own as long as the rope held and as soon as he could get the footloops attached.

Gary did not look so comfortable. Almost forty feet down, hanging headfirst under an icy overhang so that only his crampons and butt caught the light, he looked as if he might be in trouble. If he had hit his head on the ice on the way down . . .

Then I heard him cursing—the incredible epithets and shouts almost muffled in the crevasse, but still echoing deep as he cursed straight into the underbelly of the glacier—and I knew that he was all right.

It took only a minute or so for Paul to jumar up and over the lip, but getting Gary rightside up and then lifted up over the overhang so he could attach his own jumars, took a bit longer and involved some manhauling.

That's when I discovered how goddamned strong this bug was. I think that Kanakaredes could have hauled all three of us out of that crevasse if we'd been unconscious, almost six hundred pounds of deadweight. And I think he could have done it using only one of those skinny, almost muscleless-looking praying mantis forearms of his.

When Gary was out and untangled from his lines, harness, and jumars, we moved carefully around the crevasse, me in the lead and probing with my axe like a blind man in a vale of razor blades, and when we'd reached a good site for Camp One just at the base of the ridge, offering only a short climb in the morning to the crest of the northeast ridge that would eventually take us up onto the shoulder of K2 itself, we found a spot on the last patch of sun, unhooked the rope from our carabiners, dumped our 75-pound packs, and just gasped for a while before setting up camp.

"Fucking good beginning to the goddamned motherfucking expedition," said Gary between slugs on his water bottle. "Absolutely bastardly motherfucking brilliant—I walk into goddamned sonofabitching whoremongering crevasse like some pissant whoreson fucking day tripper."

I looked over at Kanakaredes. Who could read a bug's expression? That endless mouth with all of its jack-o'-lantern bumps and ridges, wrapped two-thirds around its head from its beaky proboscis almost to the beginning of its bumpy skullcrest, *always* seemed to be smiling. Was it smiling more now? Hard to tell and I was in no mood to ask.

One thing was clear. The mantispid had a small, clear device out—something very similar to our credit card palmlogs—and was entering data with a flurry of its three fingers. *A lexicon,* I thought. Either translating or recording Gary's outburst which was, I admit, a magnificent flow of invective. He was still weaving a brilliant tapestry of obscenity that showed no sign of abating and which would probably hang over the Godwin-Austen Glacier like a blue cloud for years to come.

Good luck using this vocabulary during one of your UN cocktail parties, I thought at Kanakaredes as he finished his data entry and repacked his palmlog.

When Gary finally trailed off, I exchanged grins with Paul—who had said nothing since dropping into the crevasse—and we got busy breaking out the smart tents, the sleeping bags, and the stoves before darkness dropped Camp One into deep lunar cold.

Camp Two, between a cornice and an avalanche slope, about 20,000 feet

I'm keeping these recordings for the State Department intelligence people and all the rest who want to learn everything about the bugs—about the mantispids' technology, about their reasons for coming to Earth, about their culture and religions—all the things they've somehow neglected to tell us in the past nine and a half years.

Well, here's the sum total of my recording of human-mantispid conversation from last night at Camp One—

Gary: *Uh . . . Kan . . . Kanakaredes? We were thinking of merging our three tents and cooking up some soup and hitting the sack early. You have any problem keeping your tent separate tonight? There's room on this snow slab for both tent parts.*

Kanakaredes: *I have no problem with that.*

So much for interrogating our bug.

WE should be higher tonight. We had a long, strong day of climbing today, but we're still on the low part of the North-East Ridge and we have to do better if we're going to get up this hill and down safely in the two weeks alotted to us.

All this "Camp One" and "Camp Two" stuff I'm putting in this palmlog diary are old terms from the last century when attempts at 8,000-meter peaks literally demanded armies of men and women—more than two hundred people hauling supplies for the first American Everest expedition in 1963. Some of the peaks were pyramid-shaped but *all* of the logistics were. By that I mean that scores of porters hauled in uncounted tons of supplies—Sherpa porters and high-climbers in the Himalayas, primarily Balti porters here in the Karakoram—and teams of men and women man-hauled these tons up the mountains, working in relays to establish camps to last the duration of the climb, breaking and marking trail, establishing fixed ropes up literally miles of slope, and moving teams of climbers up higher and higher until, after weeks, sometimes months of effort, a very few of the best and luckiest climbers—say six or four or two or even one from the scores who started—were in a position to make an attempt on the summit from a high camp—usually Camp Six, but sometimes Camp Seven or higher—starting somewhere in the Death Zone above 8,000 meters. "Assault" on a mountain was a good word then, since it took an army to mount the assault.

Gary, Paul, the bug and I are climbing alpine style. This means that we carry everything we need—starting heavy and getting lighter and lighter as we climb—essentially making a direct bid on the summit, hoping to climb it in a week or less. No series of permanent camps, just temporary slabs cut out of the snow and ice for our smart tents—at least up until whatever camp we designate as our summit-attempt jumping-off point. Then we'll leave the tents and most of the gear there and go for it, hoping and praying to whatever gods we have—and who knows what gods Kanakaredes prays to, if any—praying that the weather won't turn bad while we're up there in the Death Zone, that we won't get lost coming down to our high camp in the dark, that nothing serious happens to any us of during that final attempt since we really can't help each other at that altitude— essentially just praying our asses off that we don't fuck up.

But that is *if* we can keep moving steadily up this hill. Today wasn't so steady.

We started early, breaking down Camp One in a few minutes, loading efficiently, and climbing well—me in the lead, then Paul, then the bug, then Gary. There's a bitch of a steep, razor-edge traverse starting at about the 23,300-foot level—the hardest pitch on the North-East Ridge part of our route—and we wanted to settle into a secure camp at the beginning of that scary traverse by nightfall tonight. No such luck.

I'm sure I have some of Kanakaredes comments recorded from today, but they're mostly monosyllables and they don't reveal any great bug secrets. They're more along the lines of— "Kana . . . Kanaka . . . hey K, did you pack the extra stove?" "Yes" "Want to take a lunch break?" "That would be fine." and

Gary's "Shit, it's starting to snow." Come to think of it, I don't believe the mantispid initiated any conversation. All the clicks and sighs on the palmlog chip are K replying to our questions. All of the cursing was ours.

It started to snow heavily about noon.

Until then things had been going well. I was still in the lead—burning calories at a ferocious rate as I broke trail and kicked steps in the steep slope for the others to follow. We were climbing independently, not roped. If one of us slipped or caught his crampons on a rock rather than ice, it was up to that person to stop his slide by self-arrest with his ice axe. Otherwise one had just bought a really great amusement-park ride of a screaming slide on ice for a thousand feet or so and then a launch out over the edge to open space, dropping three or four thousand feet to the glacier below.

The best idea is not to think about that, just keep points attached to the snowslope at all times and make damned sure that no matter how tired you were, that you paid attention to where you kicked your crampons into the ice. I have no idea if Kanakaredes had a fear of heights—I made a fatigued mental note to ask him—but his climbing style showed caution and care. His "crampons" were customized—a series of sharp, plastic-looking spikes lashed to those weird arrow-shaped feet of his—but he took care in their placement and used his ice axe well. He was climbing two-legged this day, his rear legs folded into his elevated prothorax so that you wouldn't know they were there unless you knew where to look.

By 10:30 or 11:00 A.M., we'd gained enough altitude that we could clearly see Staircase Peak—its eastern ridge looks like a stairway for some Hindu giant—on the northeast side of K2. The mountain is also called Skyang Kangri and it was beautiful, dazzling in the sunlight against the still-blue eastern sky. Far below, we could see the Godwin-Austen Glacier crawling along the base of Skyang Kangri to the 19,000-foot pass of Windy Gap. We could easily see over Windy Pass now, scores of miles to the browning hills of what used to be China and now was the mythical country of Sinkiang, fought over even as we climbed by troops from the HK and various Chinese warlords.

More pertinent to our cause right now was the view up and westward toward the beautiful but almost laughable bulk of K2, with its wild knife-edge ridge that we hoped to reach by nightfall. At this rate, I thought just before looking up at it again, it shouldn't be any problem . . .

That was precisely the moment when Gary called up, "Shit! It's starting to snow!"

The clouds had roiled in from the south and west when we weren't watching and within ten minutes we were enveloped by them. The wind came up. Snow blew everywhere. We had to cluster up on the increasingly steep slope just to keep track of one another. Naturally, at precisely this point in the day's climb, our steep but relatively easy snow slope turned into a forbidding wall of ice with a band of brittle rock visible above for the few minutes before the clouds shut off all of our view for the rest of the day.

"Fuck me," said Paul as we gathered at the foot of the ice slope.

Kanakaredes's bulky, beaked head turned slowly in Paul's direction, his black eyes attentive, as if he was curious as to whether such a biological improbability was possible. K asked no questions and Paul volunteered no answers.

Paul, the best ice climber among us, took the lead for the next half-hour or so, planting his axe into the near-vertical ice wall, then kicking hard with the two spike points on the front of his boot, then pulling himself up with the strength of his right arm, kicking one foot in again, pulling the axe out, slamming it in again.

This is basic ice-climbing technique, not difficult, but exhausting at almost 20,000 feet—twice the altitude where CMG's and commercial airlines are required to go to pressurized O_2— and it took time, especially since we'd roped up now and were belaying Paul as he kick-climbed.

Paul was about seventy feet above us now and was moving cautiously out onto the rockband. Suddenly a slew of small rocks came loose and hurtled down toward us.

There was no place for us to go. Each of us had hacked out a tiny platform in the ice on which we could stand, so all we could do was press ourselves against the ice wall, cover up, and wait. The rocks missed me. Gary had a fist-sized rock bounce off his pack and go hurtling out into space. Kanakaredes was hit twice by serious-sized rocks—once in his upper left leg, arm, whatever it is, and again on his bumpy dorsal ridge. I heard both rocks strike; they made a sound like stone hitting slate.

"Fuck me," K said clearly as more rocks bounced around him.

When the fusillade was over, after Paul had finished shouting down apologies and Gary had finished hurling up insults, I kick-stepped the ten or so paces to where K still huddled against the ice wall, his right mantis forearm raised, the ice axe and his toe points still dug in tight.

"You hurt?" I said. I was worried that we'd have to use the red button to evacuate the bug and that our climb would be ruined.

Kanakaredes slowly shook his head—not so much to say "no" but to check things out. It was almost painful to watch—his bulky head and smiling beak rotating almost 270 degrees in each direction. His free forearm unlimbered, bent impossibly, and those long, unjointed fingers carefully patted and probed his dorsal ridge.

Click. Sigh. Click—"I'm all right."

"Paul will be more careful on the rest of the rock band."

"That would be good."

Paul *was* more careful, but the rock was rotten and there were a few more landslides, but no more direct hits. Ten minutes and sixty or seventy feet later, he had reached the crest of the ridge, found a good belay stance, and called us up. Gary, who was still pissed—he liked few things less than being pelted by rocks set loose by someone else—started up next. I had Kanakaredes follow thirty feet behind Gary. The bug's ice technique was by the book—not flashy but serviceable. I came up last, trying to stay close enough that I could see and dodge any loosened boulders when we all reached the rock band.

By the time we were all on the North-East Ridge and climbing it, the visibility was close to zero, the temperature had dropped about fifty degrees, the snow was thick and mushy and treacherous, and we could hear but not see avalanches roaring down both the East Face of K2 and this very slope somewhere both ahead of us and behind us in the fog. We stayed roped up.

"Welcome to K2," Gary shouted back from where he had taken the lead. His parka and hood and goggles and bare chin were a scary, icicled mass mostly obscured by horizontally blowing snow.

"Thank you," click-hissed K in what I heard as a more formal tone. "It is a great pleasure to be here."

Camp Three—under a serac on the crest of the ridge at the beginning of the knife-edge traverse, 23,200 feet

Stuck here three full days and nights, fourth night approaching. Hunkered here useless in our tents, eating nutrient bars and cooking soup that can't be replaced, using up the heating charge in the stove to melt snow into water, each of us getting weaker and crankier due to the altitude and lack of exercise. The wind has been howling and the storm raging for three full days—four days if you count our climb from Camp Two. Yesterday Gary and Paul—with Paul in the lead on the incredibly steep ridge—tried to force the way across the steep climbing traverse in the storm, planning to lay down fixed rope even if we had to make the summit bid with only whatever string remained in our pockets. They failed on the traverse attempt, turning back after three hours in the howling weather and returning ice-crusted and near frostbitten. It took more than four hours for Paul to quit shaking, even with the thermskins and regulated smart clothing raising his body temperature. If we don't get across this traverse soon—storm or no storm—we won't have to worry about what gear and supplies will be left for the summit bid. There won't be any summit bid.

I'm not even sure now how we managed the climb two days ago from Camp Two to this narrow patch of chopped out ridge-crest. Our bug was obviously at the edge of his skill envelope, even with his extra legs and greater strength, and we decided to rope together for the last few hours of climbing, just in case K peeled loose. It wouldn't do much good to push the red panic button on the palmlog just to tell the arriving UN CMG guys that Kanakaredes had taken a header five thousand feet straight down to the Godwin-Austen Glacier.

"Mr. Alien Speaker, sir, we sort of lost your kid. But maybe you can scrape him up off the glacier ice and clone him or something." No, we didn't want that.

As it was, we ended up working after dark, headlamps glowing, ropes 'binered to our harnesses and attached to the slope via ice screws just to keep us from being blown into black space, using our ice axes to hack a platform big enough for the tent—there was only room for a merged cluster of the smart tents, wedged ten feet from a vertical drop, forty feet from an avalanche path, and tucked directly beneath an overhanging serac the size of a three-story building—a serac that could give way any time and take us and the tent with it. Not the best spot to spend ten minutes in, much less three days and nights during a high-altitude hurricane. But we had no choice; everything else here was knife-ridge or avalanche slope.

As much as I would have preferred it otherwise, we finally had time for some conversation. Our tents were joined in the form of a squished cross, with a tiny central area, not much more than two feet or so across, for cooking and conversation and just enough room for each of us to pull back into our small nacelles when we curled up to sleep. The platform we'd hacked out of the slope under the overhanging serac wasn't big enough or flat enough to serve all of us, and I ended up in one of the downhill segments, my head higher than my feet. The angle was flat enough to allow me to doze off but still steep enough to send me frequently lurching up from sleep, fingers clawing for my ice axe to stop my slide. But my ice axe was outside with the others, sunk in the deepening snow and rock-hard ice, with about a hundred feet of spidersilk climbing rope lashed around it and over the tent and back again. I think we also used twelve ice screws to secure us to the tiny ice shelf.

Not that any of this will do us a damned bit of good if the serac decides to go or the slope shifts or the winds just make up their minds to blow the whole mass of rope, ice axes, screws, tent, humans, and bug right off the mountain.

We've slept a lot, of course. Paul had brought a softbook loaded with a dozen or so novels and a bunch of magazines, so we handed that around occasionally—even K took his turn reading—and for the first day we didn't talk much because of the effort it took to speak up over the wind howl and the noise of snow and hail pelting the tent. But eventually we grew bored even of sleeping and tried some conversation. That first day it was mostly climbing and technical talk—reviewing the route, listing points for and against the direct attempt once we got past this traverse and up over the snow dome at the base of the summit pyramid—Gary arguing for the Direct Finish no matter what, Paul urging caution and a possible traverse to the more frequently climbed Abruzzi Ridge, Kanakaredes and me listening. But by the second and third days, we were asking the bug personal questions.

"So you guys came from Aldebaran," said Paul on the second afternoon of the storm. "How long did it take you?"

"Five hundred years," said our bug. To fit in his section of the tent, he'd had to fold every appendage he had at least twice. I couldn't help but think it was uncomfortable for him.

Gary whistled. He'd never paid much attention to all the me-dia coverage of the mantispids. "Are you that old, K? Five hundred years?"

Kanakaredes let out a soft whistle that I was beginning to suspect was some equivalent to a laugh. "I am only twenty-three of your years old, Gary," he said. "I was born on the ship, as were my parents and their parents and so on far back. Our life span is roughly equivalent to yours. It was a . . . generation-ship, I believe is your term for it." He paused as the howling wind rose to ridiculous volume and velocity. When it died a bit, he went on, "I knew no other home than the ship until we reached Earth."

Paul and I exchanged glances. It was time for me to interrogate our captive bug for country, family, and Secretary Bright Moon. "So why did you . . . the Listeners . . . travel all the way to Earth?" I asked. The bugs had answered this publicly on more than one occasion, but the answer was always the same and never made much sense.

"Because you were there," said the bug. It was the same old answer. It was flattering, I guess, since we humans have always considered ourselves the center of the universe, but it still made little sense.

"But why spend centuries traveling to meet us?" asked Paul.

"To help you learn to listen," said K.

"Listen to what?" I said. "You? The mantispids? We're interested in listening. Interested in learning. We'll listen to you."

Kanakaredes slowly shook his heavy head. I realized, viewing the mantispid from this close, that his head was more saurian—dinosaur/birdlike—than buggy. "Not listen to us," *click, hiss*. "To the song of your own world."

"To the song of our world?" asked Gary almost brusquely. "You mean, just appreciate life more? Slow down and smell the roses? Stuff like that?" Gary's second wife had been into transcendental meditation. I think it was the reason he divorced her.

"No," said K. "I mean listen to the sound of your world. You have fed your seas. You have consecrated your world. But you do not listen."

It was my turn to muddle things even further. "Fed our seas

and consecrated our world," I said. The entire tent thrummed as a gust hit it and then subsided. "How did we do that?"

"By dying, Jake," said the bug. It was the first time he'd used my name. "By becoming part of the seas, of the world."

"Does dying have something to do with hearing the song?" asked Paul.

Kanakaredes's eyes were perfectly round and absolutely black, but they did not seem threatening as he looked at us in the glow of one of the flashlights. "You cannot hear the song when you are dead," he whistle-clicked. "But you cannot have the song unless your species has recycled its atoms and molecules through your world for millions of years."

"Can *you* hear the song here?" I asked. "On Earth, I mean."

"No," said the bug.

I decided to try a more promising tack. "You gave us CMG technology," I said, "and that's certainly brought wonderful changes." *Bullshit,* I thought. I'd liked things better before cars could fly. At least the traffic jams along the Front Range where I lived in Colorado had been two-dimensional then. "But we're sort of . . . well . . . curious about when the Listeners are going to share other secrets with us."

"We have no secrets," said Kanakaredes. "Secrecy was not even a concept to us before we arrived here on Earth."

"Not secrets then," I said hurriedly, "but more new technologies, inventions, discoveries . . ."

"What kind of discoveries?" said K.

I took a breath. "A cure to cancer would be good," I said.

Kanakaredes made a clicking sound. "Yes, that would be good," he breathed at last. "But this is a disease of your species. Why have you not cured it?"

"We've tried," said Gary. "It's a tough nut to crack."

"Yes," said Kanakaredes, "it is a tough nut to crack."

I decided not to be subtle. "Our species need to learn from one another," I said, my voice perhaps a shade louder than necessary to be heard over the storm. "But your people are so reticent. When are we really going to start talking to each other?"

"When your species learns to listen," said K.

"Is that why you came on this climb with us?" asked Paul.

"I hope that is not the result," said the bug, "but it is, along with the need to understand, the reason I came."

I looked at Gary. Lying on his stomach, his head only inches from the low tent roof, he shrugged slightly.

"You have mountains on your home world?" asked Paul.

"I was taught that we did not."

"So your home world was sort of like the South Pole where you guys have your freehold?"

"Not that cold," said Kanakaredes, "and never that dark in the winter. But the atmospheric pressure is similar."

"So you're acclimated to about—what?—seven or eight thousand feet altitude?"

"Yes," said the mantispid.

"And the cold doesn't bother you?" asked Gary.

"It is uncomfortable at times," said the bug. "But our species has evolved a subcutaneous layer which serves much as your thermskins in regulating temperature."

It was my turn to ask a question. "If your world didn't have mountains," I said, "why do you want to climb K2 with us?"

"Why do *you* wish to climb it?" asked Kanakaredes, his head swiveling smoothly to look at each of us.

There was silence for a minute. Well, not really silence since the wind and pelting snow made it sound as if we were camped behind a jet exhaust, but at least none of us humans spoke.

Kanakaredes folded and unfolded his six legs. It was disturbing to watch. "I believe that I will try to sleep now," he said and closed the flap that separated his niche from ours.

The three of us put our heads together and whispered. "He sounds like a goddamned missionary," hissed Gary. "All this 'listen to the song' doubletalk."

"Just our luck," said Paul. "Our first contact with an extraterrestrial civilization, and they're freaking Jehovah's Witnesses."

"He hasn't handed us any tracts yet," I said.

"Just wait," whispered Gary. "The four of us are going to stagger onto the summit of this hill someday if this fucking storm ever lets up, exhausted, gasping for air that isn't there, frostbitten to shit and back, and this bug's going to haul out copies of the Mantispid *Watchtower.*"

"Shhh," said Paul. "K'll hear us."

Just then the wind hit the tent so hard that we all tried digging our fingernails through the hyper-polymer floor to keep the tent from sliding off its precarious perch and down the mountain. If worse came to worse, we'd shout "Open!" at the top of our lungs, the smart tent fabric would fold away, and we'd roll out onto the slope in our thermskins and grab for our ice axes to self-arrest the slide. That was the theory. In fact, if the platform shifted or the spidersilk snapped, we'd almost certainly be airborne before we knew what hit us.

When we could hear again over the wind roar, Gary shouted, "If we unpeel from this platform, I'm going to cuss a fucking blue streak all the way down to impact on the glacier."

"Maybe that's the song that K's been talking about," said Paul, and sealed his flap.

Last note to the day: Mantispids snore.

ON the afternoon of day three, Kanakaredes suddenly said, "My crèche brother is also listening to a storm near your South Pole at this very moment. But his surroundings are . . . more comfortable and secure than our tent."

I looked at the other two and we all showed raised eyebrows.

"I didn't know you brought a phone with you on this climb, K," I said.

"I did not."

"Radio?" said Paul.

"No."

"Subcutaneous intergalactic *Star Trek* communicator?" said Gary. His sarcasm, much as his habit of chewing the nutrient bars too slowly, was beginning to get on my nerves after three days in this tent. I thought that perhaps the next time he was sarcastic or chewed slowly, I might just kill him.

K whistled ever so slightly. "No," he said. "I understood your climbers' tradition of bringing no communication devices on this expedition."

"Then how do you know that your . . . what was it, crèche brother? . . . is in a storm down there?" asked Paul.

"Because he is my crèche brother," said K. "We were born in the same hour. We are, essentially, the same genetic material."

"Twins," I said.

"So you have telepathy?" said Paul.

Kanakaredes shook his head, his proboscis almost brushing the flapping tent fabric. "Our scientists think that there is no such thing as telepathy. For any species."

"Then how . . ." I began.

"My crèche brother and I often resonate on the same frequencies to the song of the world and universe," said K in one of the longest sentences we'd heard from him. "Much as your identical twins do. We often share the same dreams."

Bugs dream. I made a mental note to record this factoid later.

"And does your crèche brother know what you're feeling right now?" said Paul.

"I believe so."

"And what's that?" asked Gary, chewing far too slowly on an n-bar.

"Right now," said Kanakaredes, "it is fear."

Knife-edge ridge beyond Camp Three—about 23,700 feet

The fourth day dawned perfectly clear, perfectly calm.

We were packed and climbing across the traverse before the first rays of sunlight struck the ridgeline. It was cold as a witch's tit.

I mentioned that this part of the route was perhaps the most technically challenging of the climb—at least until we reached the actual summit pyramid—but it was also the most beautiful and exhilarating. You would have to see photos to appreciate the almost absurd steepness of this section of the ridge and even then it wouldn't allow you to *feel* the exposure. The North-East Ridge just kept climbing in a series of swooping, knife-edged snow cornices, each side dropping away almost vertically.

As soon as we had moved onto the ridge, we looked back at the gigantic serac hanging above the trampled area of our Camp Three perched on the edge of the ridge—the snow serac larger and more deformed and obviously unstable than ever after the heavy snows and howling winds of the last four days of storm— and we didn't have to say a word to one another to acknowledge how lucky we had been. Even Kanakaredes seemed grateful to get out of there.

Two hundred feet into the traverse and we went up and over the blade of the knife. The snowy ridgeline was so narrow here that we could—and did—straddle it for a minute as if swinging our legs over a very, very steep roofline.

Some roof. One side dropped down thousands of feet into what used to be China. Our left legs—three of Kanakaredes's— hung over what used to be Pakistan. Right around this point, climbers in the 20th Century used to joke about needing pass- ports but seeing no border guards. In this CMG-era, a Sianking HK gunship or Indian hop-fighter could float up here anytime, hover fifty yards out, and blow us right off the ridge. None of us were worried about this. Kanakaredes's presence was insurance against that.

This was the hardest climbing yet and our bug friend was working hard to keep up. Gary and Paul and I had discussed this the night before, whispering again while K was asleep, and we decided that this section was too steep for all of us to be roped together. We'd travel in two pairs. Paul was the obvious man to rope with K, although if either of them came off on this traverse, odds were overwhelming that the other would go all the way to the bottom with him. The same was true of Gary and me, climbing ahead of them. Still, it gave a very slight measure of insurance.

The sunlight moved down the slope, warming us, as we moved from one side of the knife-edge to the other, following the best line, trying to stay off the sections so steep that snow would not stick—avoiding it not just because of the pitch there, but because the rock was almost always loose and rotten—and hoping to get as far as we could before the warming sun loosened the snow enough to make our crampons less effective.

I loved the litany of the tools we were using: deadmen, pitons, pickets, ice screws, carabiners, jumar ascenders. I loved the precision of our movements, even with the labored breathing and dull minds that were a component of any exertion at almost 8,000 meters. Gary would kick-step his way out onto the wall of ice and snow and occasional rock, one cramponed boot at a time, secure on three points before dislodging his ice axe and slamming it in a few feet further on. I stood on a tiny platform I'd hacked out of the snow, belaying Gary until he'd moved out to the end of our two-hundred foot section of line. Then he'd anchor his end of the line with a deadman, piton, picket, or ice screw, go on belay himself, and I would move off—kicking the crampon points into the snow-wall rising almost vertically to blue sky just fifty or sixty feet above me.

A hundred yards or so behind us, Paul and Kanakaredes were doing the same—Paul in the lead and K on belay, then K climbing and Paul belaying and resting until the bug caught up.

We might as well have been on different planets. There was no conversation. We used every ounce of breath to take our next gasping step, to concentrate on precise placement of our feet and ice axes.

A 20th Century climbing team might have taken days to make this traverse, establishing fixed lines, retreating to their tents at Camp Three to eat and sleep, allowing other teams to break trail beyond the fixed ropes the next day. We did not have that luxury. We had to make this traverse in one try and keep moving up the ridge while the perfect weather lasted or we were screwed.

I loved it.

About five hours into the traverse, I realized that butterflies were fluttering all around me. I looked up toward Gary on belay two hundred feet ahead and above me. He was also watching butterflies—small motes of color dancing and weaving twenty-three thousand feet above sea level. What the hell would Kanakaredes make of this? Would he think this was an everyday occurrence at this altitude? Well, perhaps it was. We humans weren't up here enough to know. I shook my head and continued shuffling my boots and slamming my ice axe up the impossible ridge.

The rays of the sun were horizontal in late afternoon when all four of us came off the knife-edge at the upper end of the traverse. The ridge was still heart-stoppingly steep there, but it had widened out so that we could stand on it as we looked back at our footprints on the snowy blade of the knife-edge. Even after all these years of climbing, I still found it hard to believe that we had been able to make those tracks.

"Hey!" shouted Gary. "I'm a fucking giant!" He was flapping his arms and staring toward Sinkiang and the Godwin-Austen Glacier miles below us.

Altitude's got him, I thought. *We'll have to sedate him, tie him in his sleeping bag, and drag him down the way we came like so much laundry.*

"Come on!" Gary shouted to me in the high, cold air. "Be a giant, Jake." He continued flapping his arms. I turned to look behind me and Paul and Karakaredes were also hopping up and down, carefully so as not to fall off the foot-wide ridgeline, shouting and flapping their arms. It was quite a sight to see K moving his mantisy forearms six ways at once, joints swiveling, boneless fingers waving like big grubs.

They've all lost it, I thought. *Oxygen deprivation lunacy.* Then I looked down and east.

Our shadows leaped out miles across the glacier and the neighboring mountains. I raised my arms. Lowered them. My shadow atop the dark line of ridge shadow raised and lowered shadow-arms that must have been ten miles tall.

We kept this up—jumping shouting, waving—until the sun set behind Broad Peak to the west and our giant selves disappeared forever.

Camp Six—narrow bench on snow dome below summit pyramid, 26,200 feet

No conversation or talk of listening to songs now. No jumping or shouting or waving. Not enough oxygen here to breathe or think, much less fuck around.

Almost no conversation the last three days or nights as we climbed the last of the broadening North-East Ridge to where it ended at the huge snow dome, then climbed the snow dome itself. The weather stayed calm and clear—incredible for this late in the season. The snow was deep because of the storm that had pinned us down at Camp Three, but we took turns breaking trail—an exhausting job at 10,000 feet, literally mind-numbing above 25,000 feet.

At night, we didn't even bother merging our tents—just using our own segments like bivvy bags. We only heated one warm meal a day—super-nutrient soup on the single stove (we'd left the other behind just beyond the knife-edge traverse, along with everything else we didn't think we'd need in the last three or four days of climbing)—and chewed on cold n-bars at night before drifting off into a half-doze for a few cold, restless hours before stirring at three or four A.M. to begin climbing again by lamplight.

All of us humans had miserable headaches and high-altitude stupidity. Paul was in the worst shape—perhaps because of the frostbite scare way down during his first attempt at the traverse—and he was coughing heavily and moving sluggishly. Even K had slowed down, climbing mostly two-legged on this high stretch, and sometimes taking a minute or more before planting his feet.

Most Himalayan mountains have ridges that go all the way to

the summit. Not K2. Not this North-East Ridge. It ended at a bulging snow dome some 2,000 feet below the summit.

We climbed the snow dome—slowly, stupidly, sluggishly, separately. No ropes or belays here. If anyone fell to his death, it was going to be a solitary fall. We did not care. At and above the legendary 8,000 meter line, you move into yourself and then— often—lose even yourself.

We had not brought oxygen, not even the light osmosis booster-mask perfected in the last decade. We had one of those masks—in case any of us became critically ill from pulmonary edema or worse—but we'd left the mask cached with the stove, most of the rope, and other extra supplies above Camp Four. It had seemed like a good idea at the time.

Now all I could think about was breathing. Every move— every step—took more breath than I had, more oxygen than my system owned. Paul seemed in even worse shape, although somehow he kept up. Gary was moving steadily, but sometimes he betrayed his headaches and confusion by movement or pause. He had vomited twice this morning before we moved out from Camp Six. At night, we startled awake after only a minute or two of half-sleep—gasping for air, clawing at our own chests, feeling as if something heavy was lying on us and someone was actively trying to suffocate us.

Something *was* trying to kill us here. Everything was. We were high in the Death Zone and K2 did not care one way or the other if we lived or died.

The good weather had held, but high wind and storms were overdue. It was the end of August. Any day or night now we could be pinned down up here for weeks of unrelenting storm— unable to climb, unable to retreat. We could starve to death up here. I thought of the red panic button on the palmlog.

We had told Kanakaredes about the panic button while we heated soup at Camp Five. The mantispid had asked to see the extra palmlog with the emergency beacon. Then he had thrown the palmlog out the tent entrance, into the night, over the edge.

Gary had looked at our bug for a long minute and then

grinned, extending his hand. K's foreleg had unfolded, the mantis part swiveling, and those three fingers had encircled Gary's hand and shaken it.

I had thought this was rather cool and heroic at the time. Now I just wished we had the goddamned panic button back.

We stirred, got dressed, and started heating water for our last meal shortly after 1:30 A.M. None of us could sleep anyway and every extra hour we spent up here in the Death Zone meant more chance to die, more chance to fail. But we were moving so slowly that tugging our boots on seemed to take hours, adjusting our crampons took forever. We moved away from the tents sometime after three A.M. We left the tents behind at Camp Six. If we survived the summit attempt, we'd be back.

It was unbelievably cold. Even the thermskins and smart outer parkas failed to make up the difference. If there had been a wind, we could not have continued.

We were now on what we called Direct Finish—the top or bust—although our original fallback plan had been to traverse across the face of K2 to the oldest route up the northwest Abruzzi Ridge if Direct Finish proved unfeasible. I think that all three of us had suspected we'd end up on the Abruzzi—most of our predecessors climbing the North-East Ridge had ended up doing so, even the legendary Reinhold Messner, perhaps the greatest climber of the 20th Century, had been forced to change his route to the easier Abruzzi Ridge rather than suffer failure on the Direct Finish.

Well, by early afternoon of what was supposed to have been our summit day, Direct Finish now seems impossible and so does the traverse to the Abruzzi. The snow on the face of K2 is so deep that there is no hope of traversing through it to the Abruzzi Ridge. Avalanches hurtle down the face several times an hour. And above us—even deeper snow. We're fucked.

The day had started well. Above the almost vertical snowdome on which we'd hacked out a wide enough bench to lodge Camp Six, rose a huge snowfield that snaked up and up toward the black, star-filled sky until it became a wall. We climbed slowly, agonizingly, up the snowfield, leaving separate tracks, thinking separate thoughts. It was getting light by the time we reached the end of the snow ramp.

Where the snowfield ended a vertical ice cliff began and rose at least a hundred and fifty feet straight up. Literally fucking vertical. The four of us stood there in the morning light, three of us rubbing our goggles, looking stupidly at the cliff. We'd known it was there. We'd had no idea what a bitch it was going to be.

"I'll do the lead," gasped Paul. He could barely walk.

He free-climbed the fucker in less than an hour, slamming in pitons and screws and tying on the last of our rope. When the three of us climbed slowly, stupidly up to join him, me bringing up the rear just behind K, Paul was only semiconscious.

Above the ice cliff rose a steep rock band. It was so steep that snow couldn't cling there. The rock looked rotten—treacherous—the kind of fragile crap that any sane climber would traverse half a day to avoid.

There would be no traverse today. Any attempt to shift laterally on the face here would almost certainly trigger an avalanche in the soft slabs of snow overlaying old ice.

"I'll lead," said Gary, still looking up at the rock band. He was holding his head with both hands. I knew that Gary always suffered the worst of the Death Zone headaches that afflicted all three of us. For four or five days and nights now, I knew, every word and breath had been punctuated by slivers of steel pain behind the eyes for Gary.

I nodded and helped Paul to his feet. Gary began to climb the lower strata of crumbling rock.

We reached the end of the rock by midafternoon. The wind is rising. A spume of spindrift blows off the near-vertical snow and ice above us. We cannot see the summit. Above a narrow coloir that rises like a chimney to frigid hell, the summit-pyramid snowfield begins. We're somewhere above 27,000 feet.

K2 is 28,250 feet high.

That last twelve hundred feet might as well be measured in light-years.

"I'll break trail up the coloir," I hear myself say. The others don't even nod, merely wait for me to begin. Kanakaredes is leaning on his ice axe in a posture I've not seen before.

My first step up the coloir sends me into snow above my knees. This is impossible. I would weep now, except that the tears would freeze to the inside of my goggles and blind me. It is impossible to take another step up this steep fucking gully. I can't even breathe. My head pounds so terribly that my vision dances and blurs and no amount of wiping my goggles will clear it.

I lift my ice axe, slam it three feet higher, and lift my right leg. Again. Again.

Summit pyramid snowfield above the coloir, somewhere around 27,800 feet

Late afternoon. It will be almost dark when we reach the summit. *If* we reach the summit.

Everything depends upon the snow that rises above us toward the impossibly dark blue sky. If the snow is firm—nowhere as mushy and deep as the thigh-high soup I broke trail through all the way up the coloir—then we have a chance, although we'll be descending in the dark.

But if it's deep snow . . .

"I'll lead," said Gary, shifting his small summit-pack on his back and slogging slowly up to replace me in the lead. There is a rockband here at the top of the narrow coloir and he will be stepping off it either into or onto the snow. If the surface is firm, we'll move *onto* it, using our crampons to kick-step our way up the last couple of hours of climb to the summit—although we still cannot see the summit from here.

I try to look around me. Literally beneath my feet is a drop to the impossibly distant knife-edge, far below that the ridge where we put Camp Two, miles and miles lower the curving, rippled river of Godwin-Austen and a dim memory of Base Camp and of living things—lichen, crows, a clump of grass where the glacier was melting. On either side stretches the Karakoram, white peaks thrusting up like fangs, distant summits merging into the Himalayan peaks, and one lone peak—I'm too stupid to even guess which one—standing high and solitary against the sky. The red hills of China burn in the thick haze of breathable atmosphere a hundred miles to the north.

"Okay," says Gary, stepping off the rock onto the snowfield.

He plunges in soft snow up to his waist.

Somehow Gary finds enough breath to hurl curses at the snow, at any and all gods who would put such deep snow here. He lunges another step up and forward.

The snow is even deeper. Gary founders almost up to his armpits. He slashes at the snowfield with his ice axe, batters it with his overmittens. The snowfield and K2 ignore him.

I go to both knees on the pitched rock band and lean on my ice axe, not caring if my sobs can be heard by the others or if my tears will freeze my eyelids open. The expedition is over.

Kanakaredes slowly pulls his segmented body up the last ten feet of the coloir, past Paul where Paul is retching against a boulder, past me where I am kneeling, onto the last of the solid surface before Gary's sliding snowpit.

"I will lead for a while," says Kanakaredes. He sets his ice axe into his harness. His prothorax shifts lower. His hind legs come down and out. His arms—forelegs—rotate down and forward.

Kanakaredes thrusts himself into the steep snowfield like an Olympic swimmer diving off the starting block. He passes Gary where Gary lies armpit-deep in the soft snow.

The bug—*our* bug—flails and batters the snow with his forearms, parts it with his cupped fingers, smashes it down with his armored upper body segment, swims through the snow with all six legs paddling.

He can't possibly keep this up. It's impossible. Nothing living has that much energy and will. It is seven or eight hundred near-vertical feet to the summit.

K swims-kicks-fights his way fifteen feet up the slope. Twenty-five. Thirty.

Getting to my feet, feeling my temples pounding in agony, sensing invisible climbers around me, ghosts hovering in the Death Zone fog of pain and confusion, I step past Gary and start postholing upward, following K's lead, struggling and swimming up and through the now-broken barrier of snow.

Summit of K2, 28,250 feet

We step onto the summit together, arm in arm. All four of us. The final summit ridge is just wide enough to allow this.

Many 8,000-meter-peak summits have overhanging cornices. After all this effort, the climber sometimes takes his or her final step to triumph and falls for a mile or so. We don't know if K2 is corniced. Like many of these other climbers, we're too exhausted to care. Kanakaredes can no longer stand or walk after breaking trail through the snowfield for more than six hundred feet. Gary and I carry him, the last hundred feet or so, our arms under his mantis arms. I am shocked to discover that he weighs almost nothing. All that energy, all that spirit, and K probably weighs no more than a hundred pounds.

The summit is not corniced. We do not fall.

The weather has held, although the sun is setting. Its last rays warm us through our parkas and thermskins. The sky is a blue deeper than cerulean, much deeper than topaz, incomparably deeper than aquamarine. Perhaps this shade of blue has no word to describe it.

We can see to the curve of the earth and beyond. Two peaks are visible above that curving horizon, their summit icefields glowing orange in the sunset, a great distance to the northeast, probably somewhere in Chinese Turkestan. To the south lies the entire tumble of overlapping peaks and winding glaciers that is the Karakoram. I make out the perfect peak that is Nanga Parbat—Gary, Paul, and I climbed that six years ago—and closer, the Gasherbrums. At our feet, literally at our feet, Broad Peak. Who would have thought that its summit looked so wide and flat from above?

The four of us are all sprawled on the narrow summit, two feet from the sheer dropoff on the north. My arms are still around Kanakaredes, ostensibly propping him up but actually propping both of us up.

The mantispid clicks, hisses, and squeeks. He shakes his beak and tries again. "I am . . . sorry," he gasps, the air audibly hissing in and out of his beak nostrils. "I ask . . . traditionally, what do we do now? Is there a ceremony for this moment? A ritual required?"

I look at Paul, who seems to be recovering from his earlier inertia. We both look at Gary.

"Try not to fuck up and die," says Gary between breaths. "More climbers die during the descent than on the way up."

Karakaredes seems to be considering this. After a minute he says, "Yes, but here on the summit, there must be some ritual . . ."

"Hero photos," gasps Paul. "Gotta . . . have . . . hero photos."

Our alien nods. "Did . . . anyone . . . bring an imaging device? A camera? I did not."

Gary, Paul, and I look at each other, pat our parka pockets, and then start laughing. At this altitude, our laughter sounds like three sick seals coughing.

"Well, no hero photos," says Gary. "Then we have to haul the flags out. Always bring a flag to the summit, that's our human motto." This extended speech makes Gary so light-headed that he has to put his head between his raised knees for a minute.

"I have no flag," says Kanakaredes. "The Listeners have never had a flag." The sun is setting in earnest now, the last rays shining between a line of peaks to the west, but the reddish-orange light glows brightly on our stupid, smiling faces and mittens and goggles and ice-crusted parkas.

"We didn't bring a flag either," I say.

"This is good," says K. "So there is nothing else we need to do?"

"Just get down alive," says Paul.

We rise together, weaving a bit, propping one another up, retrieve our ice axes from where we had thrust them into the glowing summit snow, and begin retracing our steps down the long snowfield into shadow.

Godwin-Austen Glacier, about 17,300 feet

It took us only four and a half days to get down, and that included a day of rest at our old Camp Three on the low side of the knife-edge traverse.

The weather held the whole time. We did not get back to our high camp—Camp Six below the ice wall—until after three A.M., after our successful summit day, but the lack of wind had kept our tracks clear even in lamplight and no one slipped or fell or suffered frostbite.

We moved quickly after that, leaving just after dawn the next day to get to Camp Four on the upper end of the knife-edge before nightfall . . . and before the gods of K2 changed their minds and blew up a storm to trap us in the Death Zone.

The only incident on the lower slopes of the mountain happened—oddly enough—on a relatively easy stretch of snow-slope below Camp Two. The four of us were picking our way down the slope, unroped, lost in our own thoughts and in the not-unpleasant haze of exhaustion so common near the end of a climb, when K just came loose—perhaps he tripped over one of his own hindlegs, although he denied that later—and ended up on his stomach—or at least the bottom of his upper shell, all six legs spraddled, ice axe flying free, starting a slide that would have been harmless enough for the first hundred yards or so if it had not been for the drop-off that fell away to the glacier still a thousand feet directly below.

Luckily, Gary was about a hundred feet ahead of the rest of us and he dug in his axe, looped a line once around himself and twice around the axe, timed K's slide perfectly, and then threw himself on his belly out onto the ice slope, his reaching hand grabbing Kanakaredes's three fingers as slick as a pair of aerial trapeze partners. The rope snapped taut, the axe held its place, man and mantispid swung two and a half times like the working end of a pendulum, and that was the end of that drama. K had to make it the rest of the way to the glacier without an ice axe the next day, but he managed all right. And we now know how a bug shows embarrassment—his occipital ridges blush a dark orange.

Off the ridge at last, we roped up for the glacier but voted unanimously to descend it by staying close to the East Face of K2. The earlier snowstorm had hidden all the crevasses and we had heard or seen no avalanches in the past seventy-two hours. There were far fewer crevasses near the face but an avalanche could catch us anywhere on the glacier. Staying near the face carried its own risks, but it would also get us down the ice and out of avalanche danger in half the time it would take to probe for crevasses down the center of the glacier.

We were two-thirds of the way down—the bright red tents of Base Camp clearly in sight out on the rock beyond the ice—when Gary said, "Maybe we should talk about this Olympus Mons deal, K."

"Yes," click-hissed our bug, "I have been looking forward to discussing this plan and I hope that perhaps . . ."

We heard it then before we saw it. Several freight trains seemed to be bearing down on us from above, from the face of K2.

All of us froze, trying to see the snowplume trail of the avalanche, hoping against hope that it would come out onto the glacier far behind us. It came off the face and across the *bergeschrund* a quarter of a mile directly above us and picked up speed, coming directly at us. It looked like a white tsunami. The roar was deafening.

"Run!" shouted Gary and we all took off downhill, not worrying if there were bottomless crevasses directly in front of us, not caring at that point, just trying against all logic to outrun a wall of snow and ice and boulders roiling toward us at sixty miles per hour.

I remember now that we were roped with the last of our spidersilk—sixty-foot intervals—the lines clipped to our climbing harnesses. It made no difference to Gary, Paul, and me since we were running flat out and in the same direction and at about the same speed, but I have seen mantispids move at full speed since that day—using all six legs, their hands forming into an extra pair of flat feet—and I know now that K could have shifted into high gear and run four times as fast as the rest of us. Perhaps he could have beaten the avalanche since just the south edge of its wave caught us. Perhaps.

He did not try. He did not cut the rope. He ran with us.

The south edge of the avalanche caught us and lifted us and pulled us under and snapped the unbreakable spidersilk climbing rope and tossed us up and then submerged us again and swept us all down into the crevasse field at the bottom of the glacier and separated us forever.

Washington, D.C.

Sitting here in the Secretary of State's waiting room three months after that day, I've had time to think about it.

All of us—everyone on the planet, even the bugs—have been preoccupied in the past couple of months as the Song has begun and increased in complexity and beauty. Oddly enough, it's not that distracting, the Song. We go about our business. We work and talk and eat and watch HDTV and make love and sleep, but always there now—always in the background whenever one wants to listen—is the Song.

It's unbelievable that we've never heard it before this.

No one calls them bugs or mantispids or the Listeners any more. Everyone, in every language, calls them the Bringers of the Song.

Meanwhile, the Bringers keep reminding us that they did not *bring* the Song, only taught us how to listen to it.

I don't know how or why I survived when none of the others did. The theory is that one can swim along the surface of a snow avalanche, but the reality was that none of us had the slightest chance to try. That half-mile-wide wall of snow and rock just washed over us and pulled us down and spat out only me, for reasons known, perhaps, only to K2 and most probably not even to it.

They found me naked and battered more than three-quarters of a mile from where we had started running from the avalanche. They never found Gary, Paul, or Kanakaredes.

The emergency CMG's were there within three minutes—they must have been poised to intervene all that time—but after twenty hours of deep-probing and sonar searching, just when the Marines and the bureaucrats were ready to lase away the whole lower third of the glacier if necessary to recover my friends' bodies, it was Speaker Aduradake—Kanakaredes's father *and* mother, it turned out—who forbade it.

"Leave them wherever they are," he instructed the fluttering UN bureaucrats and frowning Marine colonels. "They died together on your world and should remain together within the embrace of your world. Their part of the Song is joined now."

And the Song began—or at least was first heard—about one week later.

A male aide to the Secretary comes out, apologizes profusely for my having to wait—Secretary Bright Moon was with the President—and shows me into the Secretary of State's office. The aide and I stand there waiting.

I've seen football games played in smaller areas than this office.

The Secretary comes in through a different door a minute later and leads me over to two couches facing each other rather than to the uncomfortable chair near her huge desk. She seats me across from her, makes sure that I don't want any coffee or other refreshment, nods away her aide, commiserates with me again on the death of my dear friends (she had been there at the Memorial Service at which the President had spoken), chats with me for another minute about how amazing life is now with the Song connecting all of us, and then questions me for a few minutes, sensitively, solicitously, about my physical recovery (complete), my state of mind (shaken but improving), my generous stipend from the government (already invested), and my plans for the future.

"That's the reason I asked for this meeting," I say. "There was that promise of climbing Olympus Mons."

She stares at me.

"On Mars," I add needlessly.

Secretary Betty Willard Bright Moon nods and sits back in the cushions. She brushes some invisible lint from her navy blue skirt. "Ah, yes," she says, her voice still pleasant but holding some hint of that flintiness I remember so well from our Top of the World meeting. "The Bringers have confirmed that they intend to honor that promise."

I wait.

"Have you decided who your next climbing partners will be?" she asked, taking out an obscenely expensive and micron-thin platinum palmlog as if she is going to take notes herself to help facilitate this whim of mine.

"Yeah," I said.

Now it was the Secretary's turn to wait.

"I want Kanakaredes's brother," I say. "His . . . crèche brother."

Betty Willard Bright Moon's jaw almost drops open. I doubt very much if she's reacted this visibly to a statement in her last thirty years of professional negotiating, first as a take-no-prisoners Harvard academic and most recently as Secretary of State. "You're serious," she says.

"Yes."

"Anyone else other than this particular bu . . . Bringer?"

"No one else."

"And you're sure he even exists?"

"I'm sure."

"How do you know if he wants to risk his life on a Martian volcano?" she asks, her poker face back in place. "Olympus Mons is taller than K2, you know. And it's probably more dangerous."

I almost, not quite, smile at this newsflash. "He'll go," I say.

Secretary Bright Moon makes a quick note in her palmlog and then hesitates. Even though her expression is perfectly neutral now, I know that she is trying to decide whether to ask a question that she might not get the chance to ask later.

Hell, knowing that question was coming and trying to decide how to answer it is the reason I didn't come to visit her a month ago, when I decided to do this thing. But then I remembered Kanakaredes's answer when we asked him why the bugs had come all this way to visit us. He had read his Mallory and he had understood Gary, Paul, and me—and something about the human race—that this woman never would.

She makes up her mind to ask her question.

"Why . . ." she begins. "Why do you want to climb it?"

Despite everything that's happened, despite knowing that she'll never understand, despite knowing what an asshole she'll always consider me after this moment, I have to smile.

"Because it's there."

Introduction to "The End of Gravity"

....

The final story in this collection is not exactly a story, or rather it is not just a story. The subheading for "The End of Gravity" is "a story for the screen" and it was written for this purpose—to serve as a literary equivalent to a film treatment. (If you know the format for a formal film treatment you know that some of the protocols are followed here—the use of present tense, for instance—while others, such as the capitalization of characters' names the first time they appear—are not used. You'll have to trust me that this was out of choice, not ignorance, on my part.)

Most novelists have a love-hate relationship with Hollywood and the movies. That is, they love feeling that literature is superior to movies; they hate being ignored by Hollywood; they love it when they get a shot at writing for the silver screen; they usually hate the experience (or love it and lose themselves in it so that they're frequently ruined as literary writers); they love to bitch about it.

I suppose that my experiences and reactions fall into some or all of the love-hate categories listed above, but the truth is that I love movies. I met my wife while shooting films in inner city Philadelphia in the winter of 1969. I got into teaching through filmmaking and earned my master's degree in education while doing research on the effect of television and films on children's learning and perception. When I finish a long day and evening of writing, I prefer to watch a movie on DVD before reading again at bedtime.

Unlike most readers I know, much less most writers, I have a list of films that I think are superior (or at least equal) to the books upon which they're based. (Jaws is a good example. The book, a first effort by Peter Benchley, has its characters having sex in motels half the time. Benchley helped write the screenplay, but by then, Spielberg and others had convinced him that the story was about a big, scary fish so lose the adultery. The English Patient *is a more complicated example of a beautifully written, lyrical piece of writing that fails on several levels as a novel—contorted plot, lumpy expositions, unbelievable coincidences, too many authorial games going on—but which was turned into a fine (and logical!) equivalent movie. To Kill a Mockingbird is a brilliant novel, but the film—even with events and subplots missing—is a brilliant work in its own right, brought to life by the performances of Gregory Peck, young Mary Badham, and a fine supporting cast. And I'll stop here before I get carried away with my list.*

Many of my novels and stories have been optioned for film, but as of this writing none have been produced. I've adapted two of my own short stories as teleplays that were produced for the old, ultra-low-budget Monsters *syndicated TV series, and however modest the results, the process was enjoyable. As I write this, I've recently received word that a recent novel of mine—Darwin's Blade—has been "greenlighted" as an episodic TV series on TV for the fall 2002 season. (I'll believe it when I see it.) I once was hired to adapt my thousand-page horror novel* Carrion Comfort *into a treatment for a two-hour feature film and that was an education. (Unlike most novelists, who try to keep the bulk of their novel in a screenplay whether it works for the movie or not, I kept trying to throw out the bulk of the plot, subplots, and characters to whittle the story down to feature-film size, while the producers kept insisting on keeping the novel's huge scale and complexity. It didn't work. As a mini-series, yes. As a feature, never.)*

More recently, I've spent the last three years—between novels and other projects—doing five drafts of a screenplay adaptation of my 1992 novel Children of the Night. *This wasn't for Hollywood, but for a German film production company new to the feature film business. Twice, the project came close to beginning principal photography in both the United States and Romania, but each time the project collapsed because of the inability of the European producers to get their act together . . . to get their ducks in a row . . . to get their shit together. This was a more common movie experience for a novelist—a three-year roller coaster ride of high hopes and thwarted compromises resulting in . . . nothing. In the end, the company owns a very fine screenplay which will never be worth a cent to them because—finally disgusted by their ineptitude—I will never option or sell the novel rights to them.*

But, again, the process of writing the screenplay was not painful. I loved deconstructing the novel—not just truncating or altering it, but truly deconstructing it in the literal sense, finding the core of it and shaping the new entity of the film around that core. In many places, the film script is superior to the novel— tighter, more focused, more exciting. And as a real bonus in this three-year effort, I became good friends with the young German film director, Robert Sigl, whose dream of making Children of the Night *started the whole project. It wasn't Robert's fault that the production finally tore its hull out on the coral reef of funding and production mismanagement and—knowing Robert's determination and my own Irish stubbornness—I suspect that* Children of the Night: The Movie *may yet get made some day.*

All of which has nothing to do with the following story, "The End of Gravity," except to illustrate why I was extremely skeptical about one year ago when European film producer Andrei Ujica (born in Romania, living in Berlin, often working in Russia) contacted me and asked me to write a movie that was to be shot, in part, aboard the International Space Station.

"Aboard the space station, huh?" was my response on the phone. "Uh-huh. Yeah. Right."

But I soon learned that Andrei Ujica had already shot one documentary film in space—Out of the Present, filmed by his cosmonaut friends aboard Mir in the early 1990s. Now Andrei wanted to do a nondocumentary film, a feature, filmed in Russia and aboard the station, which would include homages to 2001: A Space Odyssey and Solaris while dealing with deep psychological and philosophical issues surrounding mankind's evolutionary leap into the cosmos.

"Uh-huh," I said suspiciously. "Why me?"

Again, serendipity, for good or ill, had stepped in. A few years ago, the Fondation Cartier (a foundation for modern art) in Paris had asked me to do some catalog copy for a display of millennial art they were putting on, including an essay on a collection of toy robots and another essay about SF thoughts about the future and the art that's inspired. I looked at the photographs of the toy robot collection and the amazing art gathered for the show—it was a huge show with wonderful art—and wrote the essays, but because of one thing and another, my wife and I were unable to be their guests at the month-long show and their international receptions. I'll always regret missing that. As for my "catalog copy"—well, I half-imagined the catalog as a loose-leafed or stapled-together thing, but it turns out that both essays (translated into French, of course, as well as in the original English) were released in beautiful, expensive hardcover books that would grace any coffee table.

The SF-sees-the-future essay was in a book that included an interview with filmmaker Andrei Ujica. I couldn't read the interview with Andrei because my French is essentially nonexistent, but Andrei read my essays, thought that I might be the one to write his movie, went on to read several of my novels. . . . voilà!

For some months, Andrei and I communicated only via e-mail and occasional telephone calls. His interests and ideas for the film—The End of Gravity is his suggested title despite the fact that I once wrote a novel called Phases of Gravity—were philosophical and complex, ranging from thoughts on human evolution to theories of Heidegger and Wittgenstein. To these suggestions, *during these satellite phone calls, I would make comments such as—"Yeah, yeah, Heidegger is good . . . but what we really need is some sex. A love interest. And maybe an explosion or two."*

Andrei was very patient with me. In the end, he paid me to go off and write whatever I damned well pleased. So I did.

Andrei loves the treatment-story and my next step, scheduled for next month as I write this introduction, is to turn it into the final screenplay. He wants Dustin Hoffman as "Norman Roth."

We'll see. As I tend to say to friends or interviewers who ask about Simmons's prose appearing on the screen—"I'll believe it when I'm eating popcorn in the theater and watching the final credit crawl."

A digression here.

A few years ago Karen and I were hanging out with Stephen and Tabby King at their rented house in nearby Boulder when a funny little thing happened. King was doing his ABC mini-series remake of The Shining *that spring, shooting at the Stanley Hotel in Estes Park only a few miles from my cabin, and he and Tabby had leased a home in Boulder for several months and they'd invited us over to watch some video dailies—including a wonderful scene, edited out of the final cut, where Steve, in white tie and tails as the dead and rotting ghostly bandleader, has his rotted face literally fly apart, but not fast enough for the makeup man, whose fingers reach in on camera and begin clawing at the makeup, sending great gouts of blood and tissue everywhere.*

In the middle of this—while we all chomped on popcorn and laughed—Steve and I exchanged big grins (his more maniacal than mine, I confess).

"Damn," I said, "don't we have the greatest job in the world?"

"And they let us get away with it," said King.

Exactly.

We knew exactly what the other meant. We weren't talking about writing for film or TV at that moment, but just about being writers. About making a living as a writer. About being paid to create this stuff and have other people read it, much less have carpenters build sets and actors learn lines and makeup people do their gory best to realize the images that had hatched in our imaginations, our dreams, our fears. We both knew that we had taken the thing we most loved from childhood—exploring our fears and interests by telling stories, by playing games, by getting the other kids to play in the woods with our war games and story lines and characters as a guide as they ran and shot and fell and died and rose again—and now we got paid for doing exactly what we loved to do as kids. It's the greatest job in the world.

I suspect that William Shakespeare—a serious and ambitious man, by all accounts, although a hardy-party sort, if Ben Jonson is to be believed—had times when he just had to grin to himself that they (Queen Elizabeth, James I, the patrons, the groundlings, the actors) allowed him to get away with it.

Yale professor and critic Harold Bloom has been my literary mentor in recent years, my Virgil to guide me through not just the glorious maze of Shakespeare and the Western Canon, but also through the concentric circles of confusion that this Age of Resentment—in politics and academic ideologies—has insisted on turning into either hell or an intellectual wasteland. This too shall pass—this age of semiotic deconstructive assaults on both the tale and the teller, this age of immature feminist fury and new-historicist contempt and post-Marxist vandalism aimed at any excellence that piques their political resentment.

Back through the lonely voice of Harold Bloom to sound Romantic criticism of Harold Goddard and A. C. Bradley, then back further to that always-enjoyed voice of William Hazlitt, and we realize that even Shakespeare had his pets. Shakespeare—that master of what John Keats called "Negative Capability"—will never let us know his own thoughts on politics, or religion, or royalty, or madness, or love, or despair—but his characters encompass the most brazen and subtle facets of all those human emotions (I agree with Bloom's Bardolotous prem-

ise that Shakespeare, in a very real sense, invented *the modern human concept of personality*)—*and some of his characters must represent the creative singularity that was William Shakespeare more than others.*

Falstaff does not embody vitality; he is vitality. Hamlet does not reflect depths of personality; he redefines human personality. Iago does not play at being a villain; he out-Satans Satan in villainous creativity. Rosalind does not just exercise her wit; she extends new frontiers of joyous wit. King Lear does not encounter nihilism; he falls into a black hole of it and pulls us in with him.

I plan to spend however many decades or years that are left me rereading and rediscovering Shakespeare (along with a very finite number of my other favorite authors), but I already know the sad truth. As one scientist described quantum physics and another scientist described the workings of ecology—*"It is not more complicated than we think; it is more complicated than we can think."*

We don't really know diddly-squat about the man who was William Shakespeare and we never will if we search for him through his characters. Was he as self-conscious as Hamlet? As ambitious as MacBeth? As wise as Rosalind? As anti-Semitic as his portrayal of Shylock would have us believe? As contemptuous of the idea of redemptive love as so many of his plays would have us believe? Or as in awe of the destructive power of unleashed love as so many of his plays would have us believe? Or as bisexual as the Sonnets would have us think?

Why am I talking about Shakespeare? Or about Stephen King?

While I'm not trying to hobnob with either man, I share the same union card with them. While our abilities are light-years apart, we three have the same concerns. And sooner or later— *sooner for us, later for those who read us after we're dead (so few of us are read after we're dead!)*—*those who look for us will have to look in the tidepools of energy we leave behind in our characters.*

As I write these words in the early hours and months of the 21st Century, the great, grinding, resentful machinery of academic criticism is being run by the dead hands of a few French midgets with names like Michel Foucault and Jacques Derrida. France—a nation that most probably has given us no great writers or great literature in all of the 20th Century—nonetheless controls the discussion of literature at the beginning of the 21st Century by the simple sophistry of denying the centrality of writers or the reality of characters or of the transcendent power of language and literature itself. As Tom Wolfe put it in a recent essay—"They [Foucault and Derrida and their lycanthropic legions since] began with the hyperdilation of a pronouncement of Nietzsche's to the effect that there can be no absolute truth, merely many 'truths,' which are the tools of various groups, classes, or forces. From this, the deconstructionists proceeded to the doctrine that language is the most insidious tool of all. The philosopher's duty was to deconstruct the language, expose its hidden agendas, and help save the victims of the American 'establishment': women, the poor, nonwhites, homosexuals, and hardwood trees."

Shakespeare seems to have left behind no opinion on hardwood trees (although his favorite larks, such as As You Like It *and* A Midsummer Night's Dream *were set in lovely forests, dark and deep). What Shakespeare did leave behind was a sense of his unique consciousness, as well as his own intellectual preoccupations and human appetites—preserved in the time capsule of his plays like a multifaceted mirror that gives us (and gave him) our glimpses of human potential named Hamlet and Iago and Falstaff and Cleopatra and Rosalind and Lear.*

My own characters, dear to me only, may be—must be— wildly lesser in degree and kind, but they are still made central to me by the very similarity of their varied distortions, and that cracked mirror of my own invention shows me people—(all right, characters, not people, but never just words or the spent social energies Foucault would have us substitute for humanity)— shows me characters with the names of Richard Baedecker and

Melanie Fuller and Joe Lucas and Jeremy Bremen and Duane McBride and Cordie Cooke and Paul Duré and Raul Endymion and Aenea and Dale Stewart and Robert C. Luczak.

And now Norman Roth.

Samuel Johnson once gave a simple recipe for clear thinking that serves just as well for clear seeing—"First, clear your mind of can't."

What Norman Roth sees in "The End of Gravity"—what he tries to see, what he fails to see and yet intuits as truth through his own failure to see—may not be a compelling vision in any sense of that word "compelling," but it is an attempt, by a dying man at the end of one short human era, at clear sight, at Rembrandt's fierce gaze across worlds and time, at whole sight.

Whole sight; or all the rest is desolation.

The End of Gravity

A Story for the Screen

THIRTY-EIGHT thousand feet above the northern polar ice, Norman Roth dreams about floating.

He is four, perhaps five years old, and his father is teaching him how to swim in the ocean near their summer rental cottage on Long Island. Roth lies on his back in the salty water and forces himself to relax in the firm cradle of his father's arms. The waves break against the shore and the boy forces his nervous breathing to match the cadence of the surf. "Relax," says his father. "Just float. Let the ocean do the work. I'm going to let go."

His father releases him, keeping his arms ready to support the child if he goes under. He does not go under. The small boy floats, rising and dropping on the long waves, eyes fiercely closed, skinny arms firmly extended, skinny legs wide on the water. Eyes still closed, the child smiles in terror and joy. The noise of the surf is very loud.

Roth opens his eyes. The sound of the surf becomes the sound of the air moving through the ventilator in the darkened first-class cabin of the 747 and Norman Roth is no longer a child, but a tired, middle-aged man. He rubs his eyes, adjusts the ventilator above him, and closes his eyes again.

A darkened hospital room. Roth, apparently the same age as on the plane, is sitting next to his father's deathbed in the darkest hours of the night. The old man has been in a coma for days now. Exhausted, alone in the dark, Roth listens to his father's labored breathing—not so different from the sound of the surf sliding onto the long-forgotten Long Island beach. Roth glances at his watch in the dim light.

Suddenly his father sits straight up in bed. The old man's eyes are open and staring at something beyond the foot of the bed. His gaze is not frightened, but interested—very, very interested.

Startled, Roth leans closer and puts his arm around the older man's cancer-sharpened shoulders. "Dad?"

His father ignores him and continues to stare. Slowly, his father's right arm comes up and he points at something beyond the foot of the bed.

Roth looks. There is nothing there. The sound of the surf is very loud.

ROTH is met at Moscow's Sheremetyevo Airport by an attractive woman who identifies herself as Dr. Vasilisa Ivanova, his liaison and interpreter during his stay. In the middle of shaking hands, she sees his expression freeze. "Is there something wrong, Mr. Roth?"

"No, no . . . nothing. It's just that you remind me of someone." Roth has never said that to a woman.

Vasilisa smiles dubiously.

"You remind me strongly of someone but I can't think of who," continues Roth with a rueful smile. "Jet lag, perhaps. Or just age."

"Perhaps," says Vasilisa. "At any rate, it is an honor to have such an esteemed author to visit and write about our program. The winner of the American Pulitzer Prize and someone who came close to winning the Nobel Prize in Literature. We are honored."

"Close only counts in horseshoes and hand grenades," Roth says tiredly.

"Pardon me?"

"A stupid American idiom," says Roth. "Your English is excellent. Are you from Energia or the Russian Space Agency's public relations?"

It is Vasilisa's turn to smile without humor. "Actually, I was a flight surgeon at TsUP. After *Mir* was brought down the number of surgeons was reduced in the Russian Space Agency and I moved to administration rather than be forced to leave the program. I volunteered for this chance to show you around."

"Soup?" says Roth.

"TsUP," she says, explaining the acronym for the Russian Space Agency's mission control center.

They come out into the blowing snow where a Mercedes and driver wait for them.

"You have been to Russia before, Mr. Roth?"

"Call me Norman. Yes, once. In the early eighties. For a literary conference."

"It has changed to your eye?" asks Vasilisa as the car carries them out into traffic.

Roth looks at the traffic—so much more traffic than during his first visit almost twenty years ago, Mercedeses and other foreign luxury cars cutting each other off in the high-speed lanes—and then looks beyond the highway at the Stalinist apartment buildings and frozen fields and abandoned construction beyond. "Changed? Yes and no," he says.

"We will go to the Hotel National and get you—how do you say it?—settled into your suite," says Vasilisa as they approach the city. "You are tired? You would like to sleep?"

"I am tired, but I will not be able to sleep. It's morning here. I'll wait for tonight to try to get on a regular schedule."

"Then perhaps you would like to see TsUP?"

"By all means," says Roth. "Let's see soup."

ROTH in the brightly lighted office of his editor at *The New York Times Magazine*.

"Norman, we're excited about you doing this piece for the magazine, but I feel bad about asking you to spend your Christmas vacation in Moscow."

Roth shrugs. "What do I know about Christmas vacations?"

"If it's any consolation," says feature editor Barney Koeppe, "you end the week with a big-deal New Year's Eve party at one of the cosmonaut's dachas. Everybody you need to talk to is going to be there. They say that Gorbachev is on the guest list."

"Whoopee," says Roth. "I'd like to know why you thought of me for this piece, Barney. I don't give the slightest shit about the space program and I know even less. You're sending a humanist and a Jew and an anti-business liberal and a technological illiterate into this den of post-marxist hyper-capitalist possibly anti-Semitic techno-weenies. Why?"

"Remember Mailer's book about the moon landing—*Of a Fire on the Moon*?"

"Vaguely. That was thirty years ago."

"Well, Mailer didn't know a thing about the space program either, but he was a brilliant writer and the book was a brilliant piece of reportage."

"Yeah," says Roth, "but people *cared* about the moon landing. No one gives a damn about the International Space Station or the Russian Space Agency."

"That's why this piece is important, Norman. It's time to see this space-exploration thing from a different angle—or give it up altogether. NASA's funding is getting cut again and it's reviewing everything, including Russia's part in this space station project. Plus the Russians are sulkier than ever after they had to dump *Mir* into the ocean last year. Everybody's pissed at everybody and now the Russian Space Agency is planning to send another paying space tourist up and NASA administrators have their panties in a bunch about it."

"I can't even remember the name of the first tourist the Russians sent up," admits Roth.

"Denis Tito," says the editor. "He paid twenty million bucks. One of your jobs is to find out how much this new guy is paying."

"He's also American?"

"Yeah. Some Wall Street wünderkind with a background in mathematics. The word is that he's a few fries short of a Happy Meal—certifiably crazy. He wants to watch cloud tops the whole time he's up there."

Roth shrugs again. "Sounds like a good plan to me. It's better than torturing fruit flies or whatever the hell the astronauts do up there."

The editor puts his arm around Roth. "Are you all right, Norman?"

"Sure I'm all right. What do you mean?"

"I mean—first that long siege with your dad dying last month. And your bypass operation in August. I know from John that you haven't been sleeping well for a long time, even before the heart surgery. I mean, this damned story isn't worth killing yourself for."

"I'm not volunteering to fly to the goddamned space station, Barney. I'm just getting paid to go to Russia to talk to the idiots who do."

THE Russian Space Agency headquarters is a hulking mausoleum of a building in a northern suburb of Moscow. The Mercedes carrying Roth and Vasilisa bounces over deep potholes and has to skirt stretches of real chasms where roadwork has been started and then abandoned on the dreary sidestreet leading to the center.

The interior of TsUP is drafty, dank, labrynthine, echoing, and dark. Vasilisa explains that most of the lights are kept off to save money. The few technicians and administrators they pass in the wide hallways wear heavy sweaters or overcoats. As they enter the Mission Control room itself, two cats rush by Roth's legs.

"You allow cats in here?"

"How else to control the mice?" says Vasilisa.

Roth is introduced to flight directors, deputy flight directors, flight surgeons, ground controllers, cosmonauts, former cosmonauts, Energia executives, TsUP administrators, several chain-smoking engineers, and a janitor. No one, not even the janitor, spares Roth more than a few seconds for a cursory handshake before turning back to their conversations or cigarettes. No one seems to be working. On the largest screen against the far wall, a ground track shows the space station's slow progress around the Earth. It is over the South Pacific. There is a large model of the late, lamented *Mir* station atop one of the consoles. There is no model of the ISS.

"The American team is currently controlling the station from Houston's Mission Control," says Vasilisa. "TsUP was in charge of the first mission when there was only one module. Since the second and later modules were added, most of the space station operation is handled from Houston."

"What exactly do the Russian ground controllers do then?" asks Roth.

Vasilisa makes a graceful gesture with her hands. "Provide comm support. Plan for the next *Soyuz* launch and Progress robot resupply mission. Communicate with the Russian cosmonaut onboard. Oversee some of the science experiments."

Roth looks at her and waits.

"We miss *Mir*," Vasilisa says at last.

As dawn approaches, Norman Roth lies in his chilly Moscow hotel room and dreams about *Mir*.

He sees it as if from a deep-diving submersible approaching a sunken wreck, the *Titanic* perhaps. The water is black and the submersible's spotlights throw only thin beams through the cold currents, illuminating seaweed, schools of ugly fish, shifting silt. The only sound is the microphone-rasp of Roth's breathing. Suddenly there is *Mir* looming out of the darkness. Transparent sea creatures float in front of the wreck's airlocks, its docking ports, its darkened solar panels.

Roth moves his submersible closer to the hulk, floating in past the damaged *Spektr* science module, drifting past the *Kvant* module, pausing close to the core module where the cosmonauts and astronauts had lived and slept and eaten. There is a round porthole there and the submersible's beams illuminate it and stab into the darkness within.

A white face stares out. A young girl's face. The sound of Roth's breathing halts in shock. The girl opens her eyes. Suddenly there is a second face in the porthole, eyes staring but not at Roth—at something beyond. It is Roth's father.

Roth gasps awake in his hotel room, holding his chest.

THE flight south to Baikonur takes a little more than two hours in the Tupolev Tu-134 jet and there are only three passengers besides Dr. Vasilisa Ivanova and Norman Roth. He is surprised to learn that Russia's launch center is not in Russia, but in the nation of Kazakhstan, perched on the edge of the dying Aral Sea. His guide and interpreter explains that after the fall of the Soviet Union, Boris Yeltsin had been lucky to negotiate a lease for the isolated military base and adjacent city that had been the top-secret launch center and site of the USSR's space glories for more than three decades.

At first Vasilisa is reticent to talk about herself, but Roth draws her out. Her parents were academics: her mother a mathematician, her father a philosopher. She had earned her medical degree and then a doctorate in orbital mechanics at a very young age and been selected for the space program by one of the leading members of the Science Academy.

"You wanted to be a flight surgeon," says Roth.

"Ah, no, no," says Vasilisa. "From the time I am a child, I want to be a cosmonaut. But although I have my degree in space medicine, enter training, learn to pilot high-performance aircraft, achieve mastery at parachute school, it is not possible for me to fly in space. It is true that we Russians have sent only four doctors into space in forty years of flight, but still I might have had chance to fly to *Mir* or International Space Station except for one fact. This is that I cannot urinate—is this the right word, Mr. Roth?—I cannot urinate on wheel of bus."

Roth looks at her, trying to divine the joke.

Vasilisa makes the graceful shrugging gesture with her hands again. "This is true. It is a metaphor, but true. You see, when cosmonauts fly in space, to *Mir*, in *Soyuz*, on any mission, there is a big send-off—is this the right word? Yes? A big send-off outside the hangar where they get into their space suits. A general makes speeches. Technicians and reporters cheer. Then the astronauts board the transfer bus for the ride to the launch pad."

"Yes," says Roth, "I think it works pretty much the same at Cape Canaveral, minus the general's speeches."

Vasilisa nods. "Well, after the big ceremony, the reporters and VIPs jump into one bus and drive to launch pad to have more celebration when cosmonauts arrive, but the cosmonauts' transfer bus, it stops halfway and all cosmonauts step out and piss—this is correct vulgar slang for urinate, yes? They all fumble in space suits and then piss on right rear tire of bus."

"Why?" asks Roth. The Tu-134 is banking over the Aral Sea and beginning its descent toward Baikonur. "Some sort of superstition?"

"Yes, precisely," says Vasilisa. "Our annointed saint of space, Yuri Gagarin, did this back in 1961 before world's first orbital flight, and all cosmonauts must do same before launch."

"But there have been female cosmonauts."

Vasilisa makes that graceful gesture with her hands. "Yes. There have been three Russian women in space—Valentina Tereshkova in 1963, Svetlana Savitskaya who flew twice to the *Salyut* station in the 1980s, Elena Kondakova who was flight engineer on *Mir* in 1994 and who flew later on your shuttle."

"Three women in more than forty years," says Roth. "I wonder how many women we Americans have launched . . ."

"Thirty-two," Vasilisa says quickly. "Including Eileen Collins, who commanded the shuttle. No Russian woman has ever been command pilot on mission. Tereshkova, the first, was sent up in space so that she could be . . . bred, I think is right word . . . with male cosmonaut so Soviet space officials could see the effects of cosmic radiation on offspring. She could not even fly an airplane, much less a spacecraft. She was just biological payload."

"But the other two Russian women must have played a more active role," says Roth, smiling despite himself.

Vasilisa smiles sadly. "Have you, perhaps, read Valentin Lebedev's book, *Diary of a Cosmonaut*? Lebedev was commander of

1982 mission to *Salyut* space station where Svetlana Savitskaya was flight engineer."

"Ah, no," says Roth, still smiling. "That book is on my night-stand, but I haven't got to it yet."

Vasilisa nods, missing Roth's mild attempt at irony. "Commander Lebedev wrote—'After a communication session we invited Flight Engineer Savitskaya to the heavily laden table. We gave Sveta a blue floral print apron and told her, " 'Look, Sveta, even though you are a pilot and cosmonaut, you are still a woman first. Would you please do us the honor of being our hostess tonight?' "

"Ouch," says Roth.

"What does this mean," says Vasilisa. " 'Ouch'?"

"It means something is painful."

She nods. "Perhaps I am sounding too much like American feminist. What would American female astronaut do if American male astronaut gave her a floral print apron in space shuttle or space station?"

"Punch him in the nose," says Roth.

"In zero-gravity, this punch would be . . . an interesting problem in Newtonian action-reaction ballistics," says Vasilisa. "But yes, this is a difference between American and Russian women. We Russian women do not like feminism so much here. But then we Russian women also do not fly so much in space here."

"What about this last woman cosmonaut you mentioned—Kondakova? You say she went to *Mir.*"

"Yes," says Vasilisa. "After she was Flight Director Valery Rumin's secretary and then his wife."

"Ouch."

"This ouch, it is a very useful word," notes Vasilisa.

Roth nods and rubs his tired eyes. The Tu-134 pilot is announcing in laconic Russian that tray tables and seatbacks should be in a full, upright position. Or so Roth guesses. For all he knows, the pilot might be announcing that both wings have just fallen off. To Vasilisa he says, "You're saying that there's a sexist Old Boy Network here that made it impossible for you to become a cosmonaut."

"Yes," says Vasilisa, pulling her hair back over her right ear in a gesture that Roth is beginning to grow familiar with. "I am saying that about Old Boy Network. All cosmonauts are old boys. And I am also saying that I wish I could urinate on tire of bus while wearing space suit."

BAIKONUR Space City and launch center—Vasilisa explains that the worker's city adjoining the missile base is still called Leninsk by most Russians despite its official renaming and that the actual Baikonur was a farming village more than a hundred and fifty kilometers northeast, a typical Cold War ruse by Khrushchev, Vasilisa explains further, to tell the world that the USSR was building a rocket base on the outskirts of Baikonur and then go nowhere near Baikonur. Pre-spy-satellite strategy of misdirection from 1955.

Roth's first impression is that whatever their names are, both base and city are cold, desolate places, unsheltered by trees or hills from the wind that blows across a thousand kilometers of steppe. The city itself seems strangely empty, its apartment buildings dark, its streets largely devoid of traffic. When Roth comments on the brownish-red powder that is blowing across vacant lots with the spindrift, Vasilisa explains that this is dust blown from the frozen shores of the Aral Sea, dust rife with the pesticide that has killed the sea and its life.

"The inhabitants and workers of Leninsk think that the dust is killing them and their children," she says.

"Is it?" asks Roth.

"I think, yes."

The launch center itself strikes Roth as much more of a military base than had been his impression of the Kennedy Space Center during his one visit there years before. Actually, the Cape Canaveral complex had made Roth think more of Disney World—a tourist attraction complete with audio-animatronic mannequins standing in for long-departed flight controllers in some of the rebuilt blockhouses—than of a serious spaceport. Baikonur is no-nonsense and real enough, but it is also depressing in a frozen, ninth-circle-of-hell sort of way.

Guards escort them from the well-guarded gate to a Russian major's office. The major shakes Roth's hand, speaks rapidly to Vasilisa in Russian—Roth discovers that the officer speaks no English—and then conducts them down to an unheated sedan and they take a whirlwind tour of the complex. An enlisted man drives. The major sits up front and continues a running narrative which Roth—sitting in the back with Vasilisa—hears only fragments of in translation. There are many statistics and at first Roth attempts to make notes in his little notebook, but he can't keep up—the major does not pause for questions—and eventually Roth puts away the notebook and watches the progession of hangars, administrative buildings, grim barracks, and aging launch pads with cracking concrete and rusted metal gantries. Roth is surprised to see piles of junk—space junk—piled here and there in empty lots between the buildings and alongside the streets: old fuel tanks, payload shrouds, and large rocket sections that Vasilisa explains were stages of the old *N-1* moon rockets. Even the rail lines that run to the cracked-concrete launch aprons are coated with a thick layer of rust.

They pull up to a building which Vasilisa tells him is the Hotel Cosmonaut where the *Mir* and *Salyut* crews used to stay immediately before a flight. The car parks, the enlisted man holds the door, and they walk into the building behind the major in his forest-green military greatcoat. Cold wind whistles through the cracks around the windows in the empty lounge on the first floor. The major shows them a medical center that reminds Roth of the little infirmary he'd spent a week recovering from diphtheria in at Harvard too many decades ago. Finally they reach a second-floor lounge that seems to be their destination. The walls are covered with photographs of serious men with five-o'clock shadow—cosmonauts all, Vasilisa explains—but it is not the photographs that the major has brought them here to see.

Both sides of the door, from floor to ceiling, are covered with signatures in felt-tip pen. Roth stares at the Cyrillic scrawls and tries to look interested. The major speaks in reverent tones. Vasilisa translates some of the cosmonaut names. Roth has never heard of any of them, but he dutifully lifts his little digital camera, snaps a few pictures, and nods. The major also nods, they return to the car, drive to the administration building, and the tour is over.

The enlisted man is driving them to the gate when Vasilisa says, "Would you like to see anything else? As a TsUP administrator I am allowed to show you a few things on the base. What do you need to see, Mr. Roth? Norman?"

"A philosopher, I think," says Roth.

Vasilisa looks at him quizzically. "A philosopher?"

"I'm trying to understand the reasons behind all this," says Roth, sweeping his hand toward the complex of pads, hangars, engineering centers, railroads, runways, snowy fields, and dormitories. "Not the space-race reasons. Not the national reasons. Not even the cosmonauts' reasons—but the *human* reasons. I think I'll need a philosopher even to come close to understanding."

"A philosopher," repeats Vasilisa. Then she smiles.

THE old man is in his seventies, Roth thinks, and he lives in a single supply room in the basement of a bunker under the shattered concrete of an abandoned launch pad.

The room is windowless and heated by a jury-rigged kerosene heater that also serves as the old man's stove. There are hundreds of books lining the walls. A section of fuel tank has been hammered into a table; the chairs are modified cosmonaut couches from old *Soyuz* capsules; a radio cobbled together from spare electronic parts sits on a metal workbench and plays classical music.

The old man's face and arms have been badly burned, one ear is shapeless and he has no hair except for the gray stubble on his scarred cheeks, but the scar tissue is old and integrated into the wrinkles and lines of age. He is missing more teeth than he has kept, but he smiles repeatedly during introductions and while pouring vodka for his guests.

The old man's name is Viktor but Vasilisa—whom he refers to as his "Firebird princess" while patting her cheeks—explains that for decades he has been known as *Nichevo*. Roth is surprised by the nickname because he remembers this word from his visit to the Soviet Union almost twenty years earlier; meaning, literally, "nothing," *nichevo* summed up a national attitude then that suggested "never mind" and "there's nothing to be done" and "leave me alone." The day that Roth had shown up at the airport years ago to fly home he'd found that there were no flights leaving that afternoon. The ticket agency and airline and the Writers' Union had issued him a ticket for the wrong day. "*Nichevo*" had been the only comment from the airline people.

Now this elderly Nichevo pours vodka for all three of them. Roth has been ordered by his heart surgeon to avoid all alcohol, but he knows that seemingly every social interaction in Russia is lubricated by vodka, so he drinks two glasses before the conversation can start.

The old man's voice is thick, fluid, gentle, and Vasilisa's soft, simultaneous translation becomes part of the warm glow from the kerosene heater and the vodka:

"You wonder perhaps about these scars," says Nichevo, holding up his welted hands to touch his face and neck and melted ear. "I received these a few hundred meters from here in October of 1960. I was thirty-two years old and working for the glory of the *rodina* under the leadership of Premiere Khrushchev and under the command of Marshal Mitrofan Nedelin and through the brilliance of Chief Designer Korolev.

"Today I am a janitor . . . no, less than a janitor, a scavenger and scrapmonger for Energia . . . but then I was a sergeant in the Rocket Forces and a technician. It *was* a glorious time . . . no, do not smile, my darling Vasilisa . . . it was a *glorious* time. Does your American writer friend know our phrase *Nasha lusche*? 'Ours is the best.' Well, ours was the best then, it is true. We were the first to launch an Earth satellite in 1957. The first to send a probe around the moon and to photograph the mysterious back side, yes? The first to orbit a dog. The first to orbit a man. The first to orbit a woman. The first to land on Mars. The first to land on Venus. The first to walk in space. The first to put up a space station—the old *Salyut* stations, before *Mir,* my darling—and the first to keep a manned presence in space for months, for *years*!

"But the scars. Yes, I promised to tell of the scars.

"It was October, 1960, and the Chief Designer had produced a huge rocket—a monster of a rocket—that was designed to go to Mars, to take a payload to Mars, to send a piece of the USSR to Mars, even before a man had ever flown in Earth orbit. Liquid fuel. Many stages. Huge motors. The VIPs arrived from the Politburo and from the Red Army. The countdown was exciting, as all countdowns are . . . seven, six, five, four, three, two, one . . . and then . . . nothing.

"The rocket did not ignite. The Chief Designer conferred with the engineers. The engineers conferred with the technicians. The technicians conferred with God. It was decided by the generals that the rocket was safe but that it must be defueled and broken down and the problem fixed and prepared later for launch.

"The conscripts and the technicians refused to return to the pad. I did not refuse, but my peers refused. They thought the rocket would blow up during the tricky defueling. I thought they were cowards. So did the Chief Designer and the generals. To show that it was safe, Marshal Nedelin ordered that folding chairs be set up on the launch pad itself, in the shadow of the Mars rocket. The Marshal himself, along with his fellow generals and rocket engineers and administrators—all but the Chief Designer who was too busy—went and sat in the folding chairs by the fins of the tall rocket. It was my job to ferry the van back and forth from the blockhouse, bringing these dozens of important people to the pad so that the technicians and workers would see that there was no danger and return to their job.

Which they did. The ground crew returned to their pumps and to their stations and to their work, defueling the gigantic rocket, pumping the nitrous oxide and hypergolic fuels into holding tanks.

"It exploded, of course. If you Americans had had the spy satellites above us then that you have today, you would have thought an atomic bomb had gone off. Marshal Nedelin and the generals and 160 others died instantly, vaporized, reduced to something less than ashes, lifted into the atmosphere like fire, like plasma, like smoke, like a vapor of souls.

"I was less than half a kilometer away, driving a van, driving toward the rocket, carrying the last gaggle of VIPs to their folding chairs, to their death chairs at the pad. The explosion drove the glass of the windshield into my face and then melted the glass and blew the bus off the access road into a holding pond and then vaporized much of the water of the pond into steam and melted the tires and killed most of the people on my bus."

Nichevo smiles, showing his few remaining teeth, and pours more vodka for them all. They drink. He continues:

"But six months later, my darling Vasilisa, in April of 1961, we launched Comrade Gagarin into space from a pad still burned by that blast and we have never looked back—we have had human beings in space, or waiting to go into space, ever since that April day.

"Now, darling Vasilisa, your American friend looks like *un maladietz*—'a good boy.'"

Roth smiles at being called a boy.

"Tell him that we may now talk *dusha-dushe*," adds Nichevo.

Because Vasilisa has not interpreted the phrase, Roth asks her to clarify it.

She tucks her hair behind her ear in that gesture Roth has grown to love. "*Dusha-dushe*," she says, "means heart to heart. We also sometimes say *po-dusham*—soul to soul."

Nichevo nods and smiles and pours them each another glass of vodka.

٭ ٭ ٭

ROTH is calmly drunk on the flight back to Moscow. He looks at Vasilisa illuminated by moonlight through the aircraft window and he thinks about what the old man had said.

His question to Nichevo had been: "Why do humans go up there? What's waiting for us in space? Other than greed, glory, adventure and nationalism, why go?"

Vasilisa had interpreted slowly, carefully, obviously taking care in transferring the meaning of Roth's question.

Nichevo had nodded and poured more vodka.

"All the reasons we go are not the reason we must go," said the old man. "Things are ending here. We must go."

"What is ending here?" asked Roth, worried that the old man would give him some nonsense about the Earth's environment being used up, of humans having to find a new planet. Bullshit like that.

Nichevo had shrugged with his hands in a motion not dissimilar from Vasilisa's.

"We came from the sea to the land but have been stranded on land for too long. We dream of the sea. We have memories of our new sea, of floating, of true freedom, of who we were before we were exiled to dust. We are ready to return to the sea."

"To the sea?" repeated Roth, wondering if the old man was more drunk than he looked. Or senile.

Nichevo raised a hand palm up toward the roof of his bunker. "The greater sea. The true ocean of the cosmos. The childhood of man is ended here . . . the small nations, the small wars, the small hatreds, the small dictators, the small freedoms . . . all ended."

Nichevo smiled. "There will be nations and wars and hatreds and dictators and freedoms there . . . up there . . . but larger. Much larger. Everything will be greater when our species enters this new sea, never to return."

"What do you mean 'we have memories'?" asked Roth. "How can we have memories of a place most of us have never been? Will never be?"

"The cosmos, the universe of no gravity beyond our slim, heavy shoal of stone, is the true *rodina*," said Nichevo, not smiling now. "The real Motherland. The USSR is a sad memory, but our *rodina* lives within us. Just as the memory of the *rodina* of the cosmos persists—we dream of floating in the womb, of our mother's heartbeat surrounding us, of the freedom before birth and perhaps after death. Our species waits to swim in this new sea."

Nichevo gestured upward again.

"It is all there, this new sea, the ocean cosmos. A few have crossed the beach of flame and terror and swum in it . . . a few have drowned on the way to it or upon the return from it . . . but most have returned safely. Safe but mute. We have sent no poets. No artists. No philosophers." He smiled again. "No . . . scrapmongers." The smile faded. "But we must feed our seas."

"Feed our seas?" asked Vasilisa, translating her question for Roth.

"Feed our seas," repeated the old man. "When the first man and woman of our race is buried in this new sea of the cosmos, then we can say that we have come home, home to our new *rodina*."

They had thanked him, Vasilisa had hugged him, and they moved to the corridor of the bunker, late for their flight home. Roth himself thanked the old man repeatedly, using the little Russian he knew.

"It is nothing," said the old man, waving good-bye with his burned and scarred fingers. *"Nichevo."*

"I know who you remind me of now," Roth tells Vasilisa the next morning at breakfast.

That night his chest had pained him from the travel and vodka and tension and he had awakened from a dream, gasping and reaching for his nitroglycerine tablets, wondering if this was the hour when his heart would stop forever. It had not. But in the shock of his awakening, he had remembered his dream, his dream-memory, and in the morning he tells it to Vasilisa.

* * *

WHEN Norman Roth is eleven years old, his family rents—as they had rented every summer since his birth—a small cottage on the quiet side of Long Island. It is a middle-class Jewish summer community and the boy has always played alone there in the surf, but this year the neighboring cottage had been rented by a new family—the Klugmans—and they have a twelve-year-old girl.

Normally young Norman would ignore a girl, but none of the other guys are around here on the island and he is lonely, so he spends his days with her—with Sarah—at first grudgingly and then with the anticipation of real friendship.

Boy and girl, just on the cusp of puberty for her, a few years away for him, playing together in faded swimsuits and shorts, swimming together, bicycling together, hunting shells together, sailing together on the small *Sunbird* boat Norman's father lets them use, going to movies at the small village theater together, drawing in empty boathouses together on rainy days, lying in the dunes and watching the stars together on the nights the sky is clear. The swimming raft twenty meters out from the beach is their meeting place and their clubhouse and their summer home together.

By the middle of August, with the school year looming like a dark cloud just rising above the horizon, Norman and Sarah are inseparable.

On the beach that last night before both families head back to their respective cities, their disparate neighborhoods, their different and separate schools, Sarah takes Norman's hands in hers and they kneel together on the cool sand. The moon is full above the lighthouse. The surf makes soft lapping noises. The cowbells on small boats and the deeper bells on channel buoys ring and clank to the shifting of the waves.

She kisses him. He is so surprised that he can only stare. She takes his face in her wave-cool hands and kisses him again.

Serious, not laughing, she stands and wiggles out of her sun-faded swimsuit. She turns—the twin stripes of white skin across her shoulder blades and backside glowing palely in the moonlight—and wades into the water and swims out toward the raft.

The boy hesitates only a second before standing and pulling off his swimsuit. The moon paints the uninterrupted smoothness of his skin. He swims to the raft.

Aboard the gently bobbing raft, they lie on their backs, feet in opposite directions, the crowns of their wet heads touching. As if floating above, the man, in memory, can see the nude boy and girl—he more child than she—her breast buds pale swellings in the moonlight, the glaring absence of her groin dusted with dark stipple.

The two do not talk for some time. Then the girl raises both arms, bends back her hands blindly, like a ballerina gesturing. The boy raises his arms over his own head, his eyes on the moon, and his fingers find hers and interlock.

"Next summer," she says, her voice barely audible above the surf.

"Next summer," he promises.

"MR. Roth," says Vasilisa at breakfast. "You are a romantic."

"If you have read my novels, or heard about my three ex-wives," says Roth, "you would know that I am not."

"I have read your novels," says Vasilisa. She smiles slightly. "And I have heard stories of your three ex-wives." After a moment she says, "If this childhood story were Russian, it would not have a happy ending."

"It does not," promises Roth.

He tells her about the boy's winter—the children have not exchanged addresses, have not promised to write, have decided to keep their friendship for the summer and the beach and the water—and he tells her about the months of waiting, the literally painful expectation that built to near insanity in the weeks and then days before the families were both scheduled to return to their summer cottages on the island.

The boy races to the Klugman cottage the minute he is released from the family station wagon. He pounds on the screen door. A strange woman comes to the door—not Sarah's mother.

"Ah, the Klugmans," says the woman. "They gave us their summer lease for this place. They had a tragedy this winter and will not be coming back to the cottage. Their daughter died of pneumonia."

"Very Russian," says Vasilisa. "But why do I remind you of this girl? Do I look like her?"

"Not at all," says Roth.

"Do I speak like her?"

"No."

"Is it that you imagine that Sarah would have become a doctor if she had lived? Or would have wanted to be a cosmonaut?"

"No. I don't know." Roth raises his hands in what he realizes is a clumsy imitation of Vasilisa's graceful shrug gesture.

When he sets his hand back on the breakfast table, Vasilisa reaches across and sets her hand on top of his.

"Then I understand," she says.

ON the day before the big New Year's Eve party, two days before Roth's scheduled departure, they are driven an hour northeast of Moscow to the TsPK—the Gagarin Cosmonaut Training Center, home of the cosmonaut corps—which everyone at TsUP and NASA calls Star City.

"Norman," says Vasilisa as they leave the main highway and drive through a thick forest of pine and birch on an empty two-lane road, "I have read your books. They are very dark. One of our reviewers called your last book 'a Kabballa about death.' Perhaps that darkness is why your fiction has always been popular in Russia."

Roth laughs softly. "Maybe they like the books because they're the life-statement of an atheist, Dr. Ivanova. I'm a Jew, but I'm an atheist. The novels are a scream at the heart of an insensate universe, nothing more."

Vasilisa shakes her head. "The Soviet regime might have allowed them to be published because of the atheist sentiment, but they are more popular now than ever and Russia stinks of incense these days."

Roth laughs again. "You're not accusing me of being a closet sentimentalist, are you, Vasilisa? Or of harboring a hidden spirituality?"

"Sentimentalist, no. Spirituality, I think, yes."

Roth only shakes his head and looks past the driver as they approach the main gate of Star City.

PAST the guards and through the tall, silver gate, the forest continues and then opens onto a city square watched over by a large statue of Gagarin. Beyond the square, there rises a cluster of curiously American-looking townhouses—Vasilisa says that the American-looking townhouses are, indeed, American, built to house the astronauts who trained here for *Mir*—and then they pass a humpbacked building holding the world's largest centrifuge, glimpse the Avenue of Heroes (a strangely modest greenway, white with snow today, with no statues) and pull up to the Cosmonaut Museum.

Vasilisa points out parked cars with government plates with numbers from 1 to 125, indicating both the official numbers of their cosmonaut owners and the order in which that cosmonaut flew into space.

The driver holds the door while Roth and Vasilisa move quickly through the snow and into the dim museum, where they check their coats, glance up at a large mural of Yuri Gagarin, and climb a flight of stairs to the main Gagarin exhibit where a bust of the dead cosmonaut seems to stand guard over well-dusted cases of memorabilia. Vasilisa translates the various placards and captions, explaining that the last series of items had been taken from the wreckage of his aircraft on the day he had died, during a routine training mission, in March of 1968, seven years after his 108-minute orbital flight. Roth can see a burned photograph of Chief Designer Korolev, Gagarin's burned wallet that had carried the photo, the cosmonaut's singed driver's license, even a vial of dirt and ashes from the wreckage.

"Don't you think this is all a bit ghoulish?" asks Roth.

"I do not know this word, Norman—what is 'ghoulish'?"

"Never mind."

They move down the hall to a case holding the jumpsuits and photographs of the first three cosmonauts to live aboard the first Soviet space station—*Salyut*—in 1971.

"*Salyut* means 'salute,' doesn't it?" asks Roth.

"Precisely."

"Who or what was the *Salyut* station saluting?"

"Yuri Gagarin, of course."

Vasilisa reads the inscription next to the men's photographs. Cosmonauts Georgi Dobrovolskiy's, Vladislav Volkov's, and Viktor Patsayev's mission to *Salyut* had been wildly successful, their zero-gravity exploits and good humor broadcast to the Russian people every night via television. Their reentry into the atmosphere seemed uneventful, their landing on the Russian steppe according to plan except for an unexplained failure in radio communication. But when the recovery crews opened their capsule, all three cosmonauts were dead. A valve had broken during reentry, their air had rushed into space, and all three men had asphyxiated in their couches.

"We have fed our seas," says Vasilisa.

Roth shakes his head. "I think Nichevo meant that we must leave our dead there, in space, before the new sea is truly fed."

"Perhaps."

Beyond this exhibit is what appears to be an ordinary office but is actually a precise replica of Yuri Gagarin's office, just as he left it on the morning of his fateful flight on March 27, 1968. The hands of the clock are stopped at 10:31, the moment of impact. His day calendar lies open on his desk. Letters and memos lie unfinished.

Vasilisa points to the desk. "Each cosmonaut or crew of cosmonauts signs his name in that large brown book on the day of their flight into space," she says softly, whispering in this hallowed space. "Even our cosmonauts who fly to the International Space Station."

Roth glances at her. Vasilisa's eyes are brimming as she looks at the book. She catches him looking at her. "You think that I am sentimental, yes?"

"No," says Roth. "Spiritual."

ROTH dreams that he is aboard the International Space Station, floating in dim light. Another astronaut, a man, is sleeping, rigged in some sort of thin sleeping bag contraption that holds him seemingly upright, arms protruding and floating in front of him, wrists bent, fingers moving like seaweed in a current.

Roth is surprised how loud the ventilator fan is, how stark and functional and sharp-edged the interior of this module of the station is. The air smells vaguely of ozone and sweat and machine oil. He finds that he can move silently by kicking off some solid object and he floats head-first without even raising his arms, moving through a hatch into an adjoining module. There is a porthole here and Roth floats over to it and looks out. The Earth hangs above him, beyond the dark exclamation mark of a solar panel.

The station is approaching the sunrise terminator. The limb of the planet sharpens in a crescent of brilliant sunlight. For a second, Roth can see the thin line of atmosphere itself illuminated like a backlighted, inverted miniscus, then the sun clears the curve of the world and ignites thousands of cloud tops above a dark sea.

Suddenly Roth realizes that he is having trouble breathing. The air is too thin. Whirling in microgravity, he realizes that he can hear a constant and ominous hissing, rising in pitch but descending in volume as the air thins further. The air is rushing out of the station module.

Gasping, Roth spins in space but he has pushed away from the bulkhead, is too far from anything solid, and he can only pinwheel his arms and legs without effect, tumbling in the thinning air and unable to swim his way to safety.

✿   ✿   ✿

ROTH awakes at the touch of a cool hand on his bare chest. He blinks away the after-images of the dream and looks around the hotel room. It is dark except for slivers of moonlight coming between the heavy curtains. Vasilisa, dressed only in Roth's extra pair of blue pajamas, sits on the edge of the bed, a stethoscope around her neck, her hand on Roth's chest.

"What?" He tries to sit up but she pushes him back with her surprisingly strong fingers.

The stethoscope is cold against his chest. Vasilisa sets the instrument on the nightstand but touches his chest again, running two fingers along the large cross-shaped scar on his bare chest, then reaching down to feel the long scar on his left leg where they had taken a vein during his last surgery.

"Do you remember dinner?" she says very softly. The clock says 3:28.

"No," whispers Roth, but then he does. They had been having a late dinner in the National dining room when the chest pains started. He had fumbled for his nitroglycerine tablet, held it under his tongue, but the usual instant relief had not come. Roth dimly remembers her helping him out of the cavernous dining room, holding him upright in the elevator, opening the door to his room for him, and then . . . confused images . . . the cool prick of a needle, a dim recollection of her slipping between the sheets next to him. "Ah, Christ," says Roth. "This isn't the way I would have chosen for us to go to bed together."

Vasilisa smiles and buttons his pajama shirt. "Nor I, Norman. I had considered transporting you to hospital, but I am sure this was just a severe episode of angina, not another heart attack. Your heart sounds good, your blood pressure stabilized, your pulse has been strong." She lifts the sheets and blanket and slips in next to him again. "I think you woke because you were having a nightmare."

He turns to look at her in the moonlight. "Just a dream." Then he remembers the terrible hiss of the oxygen rushing out of the space station. "A nightmare," he acknowledges. He looks at the glowing clock face again.

"It is New Year's Eve," whispers Vasilisa. "You know, I think, how important the holiday is in Russia—a combination of your Christmas and New Year's and other holidays as well."

"Yes."

"You remember I said that my parents were academics—a philosopher and a research mathematician?"

"Yes."

"But like most Russians, they were superstitious. My mother taught me the old custom of putting three slips of paper under my pillow on New Year's Eve. One would read—Good Year. One would read—Bad Year. The last would read—Medium Year. After midnight, I would reach under the pillow and draw one."

Roth smiles at this. He reaches across her to pick up the small notebook on the nightstand and his silver pen. The last filled page of the notebook is covered with notes about Gagarin's office. He takes an empty page, tears it into three strips, and writes on the first scrap—Year with Vasilisa; on the second strip—Year without Vasilisa; the third he leaves blank.

"You tempt fate, Norman."

Roth folds the three scraps and puts them under the pillow they now share. "You are superstitious, Dr. Ivanova." He kisses her very slowly.

When the kiss is finished, she pulls her head back just far enough to be able to focus on his face. "No," she whispers. "Spiritual. *And* sentimental."

THE New Year's Eve party is at cosmonaut Viktor Afanasiev's dacha outside of Moscow. Vasilisa explains that Afanasiev was the last commander of a regular *Mir* crew and that he had been the man who literally switched off the station's lights on August 28, 1999.

"Viktor is a friend of mine," she says. "He tells me that he has had strange dreams since *Mir* deorbited."

"What kind of dreams?" asks Roth.

Vasilisa opens her hands. "Dreams of encountering the *Mir* station underwater, as if it was the *Titanic* or some other sunken ship from the past. Sometimes, Viktor says, he dreams that he sees the faces of dead people he has known looking out from *Mir.*"

Roth, who has never told her of his own dream, can only turn and stare at her as they drive down the narrow road through the trees and the snow.

Roth and Vasilisa arrive early, five P.M., but it is already dark and dozens of people are already there. Even though tables inside the spacious, beautifully decorated dacha are groaning with food—kielbasa, cheeses, vegetables and dip, slivers of fish, heaps of caviar, various *zakuski*—hors d'oeuvres that leave no need for entrees—soups, salads, and strips of beef, all surrounded by countless bottles of vodka and champagne—Roth and Vasilisa find the cosmonaut host and friends outside by the barbecue, ignoring the temperature that Roth estimates to be at least ten degrees below zero Fahrenheit, grilling *shashlyk*—mutton shish kebabs—telling jokes, laughing in the cold air and drinking vodka.

In the next few hours, Roth will be introduced to more than a hundred people and he makes the typical American mistake of trying to remember first names rather than the first name plus patronymic that would have made some sense out of the avalanche of names and faces. Still, Roth sorts some of the people out—there is the cosmonaut Sergei and his wife Yelena; Tamara, the attractive Moscow psychic who had predicted the near-catastrophic problems on Vasily Tsibliyev's *Mir* mission (being specific to foretelling the day of the collision between *Mir* and its supply rocket, according to Vasilisa); Viktor, the chain-smoking deputy flight director with white hair; flight engineer Pavel ("Pasha,") cosmonaut Aleksandr ("Sasha") and his wife Ludmilla and daughters Natasha and Yevgena; flight director Vladimir; TsUP psychologist Rotislav whom Vasilisa and others call "Steve"; the cosmonaut team of Yuri and Yuri; cosmonaut Vasily ("Vasya") and his wife Larissa; and so on and so forth.

In addition to the cosmonauts and their families and the TsUP flight controllers and directors, there are famous faces at the party—important Russian politicians, an American congressman whom Roth knows to be a complete asshole, several NASA people, two astronauts and a former astronaut (none with their wives but one with a Russian girlfriend), some Russian poets and writers (all of whom are blind drunk by the time Roth is introduced to them), a second psychic—not nearly as attractive as Tamara, the first psychic Roth had met—an American film director lobbying for a flight to the ISS, a Russian film producer who glowers a lot, a German film director who seems to know everyone at the party, a Russian actress who is staggeringly beautiful and amazingly stupid, and a dog with the most sympathetic eyes Roth has ever seen on a living creature.

A large plasma TV screen has been set up in the living room and images come in through the evening of preparations in Red Square for the New Year's celebration as well as CNN updates on revelry in China's Tiananmen Square and elsewhere.

Occasionally touching his aching chest—when Vasilisa is elsewhere or not looking—Roth wanders through the house and evening, carrying the same unconsummated glass of vodka, shaking hands, chatting with those people who speak English, listening to Vasilisa's whispered translation of songs and conversations.

The night grows darker and the party louder as the clocks crawl toward midnight.

THREE cosmonauts are on the glassed-in porch, arguing earnestly in Russian about the experience of launch and entering low-earth-orbit. Roth remembers Vasilisa's whispered capsule history of each of the men:

Anatoli Arstebarski had flown in space only once, a successful flight, before pursuing a more lucrative profession; Sergei Krikalev was perhaps the most successful cosmonaut now working, having flown on *Mir*, the International Space Station, and on the shuttle; Viktor Afanasiev, their host this evening and the last *Mir* commander, is the man with the occasional bad dreams, the man whom Roth thinks of as the captain of the space *Titanic*. Roth holds his glass of vodka and listens to the deep male voices punctuated by Vasilisa's soft whisper as she rushes to interpret.

Anatoli: "It is like birth. There is the long wait, the claustrophobia, the darkness, the distantly heard noises—the gurgle of glycol pumps, the hum and tick of power units, the whisper of half-heard voices from the world without—and then the trauma, the pain of g-forces, the terrible vibration and sudden noise, followed by the entry into light and the cosmos."

Sergei: "Nonsense. It is like sex. There is the long anticipation—sometimes so much more exciting than the real event. The foreplay—the endless, frustrating simulations. Then the preparation on the pad. The lying down on the form-fitting couches. The tease of the countdown. The pulse accelerating, the senses finely tuned. Then the explosion of release. An ejaculation of energy . . . thrust, thrust my friends. It is all about thrust. After the release and the straining and the cries aloud— oh, God . . . Go! Go! . . . there is the silence and the cool embrace of space. And then, as soon as it is finished, one wants it to start all over again."

Viktor: "What total bullshit. Launch is like dying. Ignition is the casting free from the body, the separation of spirit from matter. We claw toward the fringes of atmosphere like a drowning man fighting his way to the surface of the sea, like a soul flying free from its burden of flesh. But once to this surface, we find only vacuum. Everything and everyone we know and have known or ever could know is left behind. All of life is abandoned for the cold, silent sterility of the cosmos beyond. When the engines shut down, the ordeal and pain over, the barrier between life and death has been breached, the spirit is become one with the cosmos, but lonely . . . oh, so lonely."

The three cosmonauts are silent for a minute and then start laughing together. Viktor pours more vodka for everyone.

ROTH, standing alone in the suddenly vacated enclosed porch, sees an old man crossing the dacha's snowy lawn in the moonlight. Seen through the rim of frost on the glass panes, the old man is more apparition than reality—white clothes, white hair, white stubble, and white face glowing—arms raised like some iconic Christ. The figure shuffles through the snow, palms and face raised toward the night sky.

Roth sets his drink down on a table, ready to go out and fetch the old man—or at least see if the vision is real—when Viktor Afanasiev, Sergei Krikalev, and Vasilisa come out to the porch.

"Ah, it is Old Dmitry Dmitriovitch, Viktor's neighbor," says Sergei, whose English is excellent. The cosmonaut has trained in Houston, flown on the shuttle, and spent months on the ISS. "He lives in the caretaker's house at the neighboring dacha and wanders over here regularly. It is not a problem in the summer, but Viktor worries that the old man will freeze to death on such nights as this."

"What is he saying to the sky?" asks Vasilisa. "Is he senile?"

"Perhaps," says Viktor, pulling on a goosedown jacket and fur hat that he keeps on a peg near the back door. "He cries to the sky because his son is a cosmonaut who has not returned from space."

Roth looks surprised. "Someone who is up there now? Or someone who died?"

Viktor grins. "Old Dmitry's son is a businessman in Omsk. The old man dreams and walks in his dreams. Please excuse me." He goes outside and through the haloed glass, Roth, Sergei, and Vasilisa watch as Viktor leads the old man back across the lawn and out of sight through the bare trees.

A cassette recorder is playing loud martial music and thirty or forty Russians in the overheated main room are singing the words to the song. Vasilisa crosses the room to stand next to Roth. "It is the unofficial cosmonaut anthem," she whispers and then interprets softly as the Russians sing.

The Earth can be seen through the window
Like the son misses his mother
We miss the Earth, there is only one

However, the stars
Get closer, but they are still cold
And like in dark times
The mother waits for her son, the Earth waits for its sons.

We do not dream about the roar of the cosmodrome
Nor about this icy blue
We dream about grass, grass near the house
Green, green grass.

The Russians applaud themselves when the song is done.

AN hour before midnight, Roth meets an American million-aire—Tom Esterhazy—who is scheduled to be the next paying "tourist" that the Russians will send to the international station. Esterhazy, who is drinking only bottled water, explains that he was a research mathematician at Los Alamos and at the Santa Fe Complexity Institute before he made his millions by applying new theorems in chaos mathematics to the stock market.

"The market is just another complex system constantly tee-tering on the edge of chaos," says Esterhazy, speaking softly but close to Roth's ear to be heard over the rising noise of the crowd. "Like the moon Hyperion. Like the ripple dynamics of a flag in the wind or the rising curl of cigarette smoke." The younger man gestures toward the cloud of smoke that hangs in the room like a smog bank.

"Only you can't make hundreds of millions of dollars analyz-ing flag ripples or cigarette smoke," says Roth, who has heard of the man.

Esterhazy shrugs. "If you're smart enough you could."

Roth decides to play reporter. "So how much are you paying Energia and the Russian Space Agency to get this ride?"

The young millionaire shrugs again. "About what Denis Tito paid, I guess. It doesn't matter."

It must be nice, thinks Roth, *to be able to think that twenty million dollars doesn't matter.* He says instead, "What are you going to do during your four days up there?"

"Look at clouds."

Roth starts to laugh—his *New York Times* editor had made some joke about this guy looking at cloud tops—but stops when he realizes that the millionaire is serious. "You're paying all that money just to look at clouds?"

Esterhazy nods, still serious, and leans closer to talk. "My expertise is in fractal analyses of the edges of destabilizing complex systems. Clouds are the ultimate example of that. When I was a researcher in New Mexico, I used to set up trips to conferences just so I could look down on clouds from the planes. I never went to the conferences themselves, I just wanted the plane ride. When the Los Alamos lab found out, they turned down my conference requests. Later, when I made the money on Wall Street, I bought a Learjet just so we could fly above the clouds."

Roth nods, thinking, *This man is certifiable. No wonder the Russians are contemptuous of us.* He says, "Will it be that much better to look down at clouds from the space station rather than from a jet?"

Esterhazy looks at him as if it is Roth who is crazy. "Of *course.* I'll be able to look at cloud patterns covering tens of thousands of square miles. I'll be able to see cirrus and stratocirrus across huge swaths of the South Pacific, watch cumulus build twenty kilometers high across the Urals. Of *course* it will be better. It'll be unique."

Roth nods dubiously.

Esterhazy takes his arm in a tight grip. "I'm serious. Imagine being a mathematician trying to understand the universe through the study of waves—regular waves, ocean waves—but your only chance of seeing the waves was from five hundred feet *under* water. Nuts, right? But that's what fractal complexity studies of cloud patterns is like from inside the atmosphere, from the surface. We live at the bottom of a well."

"But you have weather satellites . . ." begins Roth.

Esterhazy shakes his head. "No, no, no. All mathematics, much less complexity/chaos math, is about seventy percent intuitive. It wasn't some sort of plodding, successive approximation that allowed me to understand the wavefront dynamic of the stock market. I was there on the floor with a broker friend one day, just gawking, looking at the computer displays and the big board and the numbers crawling and the scribbles of the guys in the pit, when I got the fractal repetition function I needed. Now to understand the fractal dynamics of clouds that way, to be able to predict the chaos at their fringes, I have to *see* the clouds. All of them. Get a gestalt view. *Feel* the dynamic of it all. Just *look.* Four days won't be enough, but it'll be a start."

"You have to become God for a while," says Roth.

"Yeah," says Esterhazy. "That won't be enough, but it'll be a start."

IT is a few minutes before midnight when Roth goes alone to the cold sunroom porch to fetch his glass of vodka and sees the old man wandering on the snowy lawn again.

Roth goes to the door to call Vasilisa or his host, but hesitates; the guests are gathered around Viktor in the crowded main room, singing together in the last minutes before the New Year, and Vasilisa is nowhere in sight.

Roth goes to the double door—it works like a glass airlock against the lunar cold outside—pulls on the fur hat Viktor has left hanging there, and walks out into the frigid night air.

Moonlight sparkles blue on the broad hillside that leads down to a frozen lake. The clouds and snow flurries are gone, leaving a sky so moonfilled and star-broken that Roth looks up for a long minute before searching for Old Dmitry again.

There he is, twenty meters downhill from the house, a white figure near the edge of the birch forest. The snow fractures and cracks under Roth's city shoes.

He opens his mouth to shout the old man's name but the air is so cold that it cuts into his chest like vacuum rushing in. Roth gasps and holds his chest. He concentrates on breathing as he crosses the last blue-glowed space to where the old man stands, back turned toward Roth, staring up through the birch branches at the night sky. Old Dmitry had been wearing baggy pants and a sweater earlier in the evening, but now he wears long white robes that remind Roth of a shroud.

Roth pauses an arm's length from the old man and looks skyward himself. Something—a satellite perhaps or a high-flying military plane or perhaps the space station itself, Roth does not know if one can see it from Moscow—cuts across the starfield like a thrown diamond.

Roth looks down again just as the old man turns toward him. It is Roth's father.

Roth lifts a hand to his own chest. As if in response, his father lifts a hand—at first Roth is sure that his father is going to touch him, touch his face, touch his son's aching heart—but the arm and hand continue rising until the long finger is pointing at something in the sky behind and above the writer.

Roth starts to turn to look when the great roar and brightness fills the air around him, surrounding him and entering him like fire. He clenches his eyes tightly shut and clasps his hands over his ears, but the flare of light and roar of noise break through and overwhelm him.

Flames. The flames of hypergolic fuels mixing, of solid-fuel boosters lighting off, of the shuttle's main engines firing and the Soyuz's tripartate boosters exploding in energy.

Sound. The roar of millions upon millions of ergs and jules and footpounds of energy exploding into the night in a second, in a millionth of a second. A Saturn V roar, five engines bellowing flame at once. An Energia roar, Mars-rocket explosion roar, controlled N-1 moon rocket three-stage bellow-roar.

He has fallen but does not fall. Roth floats sideways in the air, a meter and a half above the ground. His father holds him, cradling him.

"Relax," says his father, holding him under the shoulders and legs. "Just float. Let the ocean do the work. I'm going to let go."

His father releases him gently.

The roar and flame and vibration surround him again. Roth clutches his left arm with his right hand, feeling the roar as constriction, the flame as pain, but then he obeys his father's command and relaxes, opening his arms wide, lying back, feeling gravity relent.

Roth lets the engine roar carry him skyward, seeing Baikonur fall far below like a snowy chessboard, watching Florida fall below like a trailing finger and seeing the green of the coastal waters give way to the ultramarine blue depths of the deeper sea.

He rises with the roar and on the roar, flashing through high wisps of clouds, feeling the pressure of air and gravity lessen as the sky darkens to black and the stars burn without twinkling.

"Norman. Norman!"

He hears the voice through the roar and knows it is Vasilisa, distantly feels her knee under his head and her hands ripping open his collar buttons but then the voice is gone, lost in the roar and the glow.

The solid rocket boosters fall away.

The first stage separates, falls away, a black and white metal ring rich in solid sunlight, tumbling back toward the blue and scattered white curve of Earth below.

The limb of his world becomes curved, a scimitar of blue and yellow beneath the black cosmos. Roth hears distant voices like whispered commands or entreaties through poorly tuned earphones and knows that he must keep his eyes closed if he is to see all this, but just as he is about to open his eyes anyway, the second stage fires, the flame returns and he is pressed back by g-forces again as he continues to climb into the blackness.

"Bring my bag from the car. Hurry!"

Roth hears this in Russian but understands it perfectly. How strange it was when languages were like walls, separating understanding. Now that he is this high, he can look over any wall.

The noise and flame and compression end as suddenly as they began.

Roth is floating now, arms out, legs extended. He twists his upper body and rotates freely in space, looking down at where he has been. Where he has always been.

He flies toward sunrise. The white clouds move in procession far below him like a sheep moving across a blue meadow. A peninsula of land extends toward the sunrise like a god's finger parting the green sea. On the night side of the terminator, stratocumulus twenty kilometers high pulse with their own internal lightning.

"Stand back . . . the needle . . . into the heart."

Roth fumbles away the invisible earphones, tired of the insect buzz of the distant voices. Let TsUP and Houston give their commands. He does not have to listen. Silence rushes around him like water flooding into a compartment.

The sun fills the curve of the world, fires rays across the thin sheen of atmosphere like a stiletto fissure of gold flame, and breaks free of Earth, rising into black space like the broiling thermonuclear explosion it is. Space, he discovers, is not silent. Stars hiss and crackle; Roth has heard this before through recordings from radio telescopes, but they also sing—a chorus of perfect voices singing in a language not unlike Latin. Roth strains to hear what they are saying, this lovely chorus of unearthly voices, but the meaning slides away just beyond the cusp of his understanding. But now Roth rises into the rush and roar of the surf of the blazing sun itself, feels individual photons as they strike his bare skin and sees the curl and wave-crash of the solar wind as it dashes against the pulsing, breathing folds of the Earth's magnetosphere. Space, he realizes, is not empty at all; it is filled with tidal waves of gravity, great shock waves of light, the braided, living and constantly moving lines of magnetic force, all set against the visible and audible chorus of the stars.

Somewhere, very, very distantly, there is a countdown again—five, four, three, two, one . . . in Russian and English . . .

now people are singing and crying and laughing. Roth hears music. It is the New Year.

He opens his arms and is almost ready to let the solar wind carry him farther away, higher, deeper into the singing cosmos, forever beyond the gravity of Earth, but he has something he has to do.

"Breathe, Norman. Norman!"

He shakes the voice out of his ears again, but reaches back, under his pillow. The three folded slips of paper are still there. He chooses one. He raises his clenched fist, opens his fingers.

To read it, he has to open his eyes. He weeps, eyes clenched shut, at the thought of no longer seeing this glory of the receding Earth, of feeling the fatherly embrace of the rising sun, of touching the cool orb of moon, of hearing and understanding the chorus of the blazing stars singing in their X-ray frequencies.

But he has to know which future he has chosen.

Norman Roth opens his eyes.